DEMONIC SECT ELDER AND THE SEALED REALM

DEMONIC SECT ELDER AND THE SEALED REALM

Kalzara

Podium

ISBN: 978-1-0394-7152-8

Published in 2025 by Podium Publishing
www.podiumentertainment.com

DEMONIC SECT ELDER AND THE SEALED REALM

CHAPTER ONE

Slifer lay down in his bed, sighing as he realized he couldn't remember the last time he had gotten a good night's sleep. As a Foundation Establishment cultivator, his body still needed rest.

His mind wandered as he thought about the recent events. He, a middle-aged man living in his parents' basement, had choked to death on a pie, only to be isekai'd to this xianxia world. But not as the usual young, handsome, secretly talented protagonist. No, he was reincarnated as an old demonic elder on his last breath. By all rights, he should have died then. Yet miraculously, he had survived thanks to the mysterious System. In time, he had even managed to establish himself as the respected supreme elder of the Black Rose Sect.

While Slifer still grappled with impostor syndrome, he took some satisfaction in knowing he had done a better job teaching his disciples than the original Slifer ever could. Though, he wished he could have guided them more before they entered the Sealed Realm.

Not that the impostor syndrome will ever fully fade, he mused. Slifer was an interloper piloting another man's body, after all. No amount of achievement could change that cold fact.

At least the Black Death Sect's plot to assassinate the supreme elders and commandeer the tournament had failed. Their forces were either imprisoned or dead, and Vowron himself was sealed away in Slifer's cauldron. As for the other supreme elders, they had returned to their sects.

Tomorrow, Slifer would focus on interrogating the prisoners and uncovering

Vowron's true motives. The Immortal Realm was somehow involved; of this Slifer was certain. But many pieces still remained obscured in the shadows. Those matters could wait until morning.

For now, this supreme elder needed sleep.

The next day, Slifer sat cross-legged in his quarters devouring a mountainous breakfast. He paused mid-bite when Morvran's voice entered his mind.

"Master, the prisoners are ready for interrogation."

Slifer quickly transmitted back, "I'll be there shortly."

Wiping his mouth, he tidied his appearance before heading to the dungeon. Unlike his disciple Amelia, Slifer held no love for the place.

The stench of blood and fear permeated the air as he walked in. At the end of the hall stood a heavy oak door banded with black iron. The two guards stationed there snapped to attention as they noticed Slifer.

"Supreme Elder," one greeted respectfully before pushing the door open to allow Slifer entry.

He stepped inside, eyes scanning the larger chamber. The perimeter of the room was lined with occupied cells showing recent signs of use: blood splatters, discarded tools, wheezing prisoners.

In the center, ten figures knelt with hands chained behind their backs. They wore the black and red robes that marked them as members of the Black Death Sect. Their condition was as expected—broken fingers, deep burns, flayed skin. These injuries were the least of the prisoners' worries. Interrogation under Morvran was not for the faint of heart.

"Forgive me, Master. These dogs refuse to talk despite my efforts," Morvran said with a sigh.

"Don't apologize, my friend," Slifer reassured him. "If they withstood your talents, I doubt anything could make them speak."

Luckily for us, I have just the technique in mind for this type of situation. I just wish I didn't have to use it . . .

Stats!

Name: Slifer
Race: Human
Alignment: Demonic
Spiritual Cultivation: Peak Foundation Establishment
Body Cultivation: Peak Foundation Establishment
Lifespan Remaining: 100 years
Karmic Credits: 78,970

Skills: Insight (Intermediate), Nascent Soul Armor (Level 2), Phase Ability (Level 1), Void Being Aura (Level 1)
Items: Reversal Card, Peak Slifer Card, Caelum Card, Hughie Card, Critical Block x6, Reflection Barrier Card x3, Thunderblast Card x2, Critical Heal x3, Time Reversal Card, One Minute Rewind Card x2, Mimicry Card x3, Teleportation Marker x3
Affinities: Light (25%), Fire (15%), Space (20%), Lightning (10%)
Abilities: Firebreath, Mirror Mastery (Level 2)
Techniques: Sunrise Slash (Level 3,) Stellar Nova Strike (Level 2), Dimensional Slide (Level 2), Nascent Soul Armor (Level 1), Void Piercer (Level 1)
Weapon Mastery: Sword (20%)
Perks: Dual Cultivator Perk

Good to know that credits won't be an issue.

Opening up the Shop interface, Slifer started sorting through various spiritual arts looking for a soul-searching technique. A useful technique even if it was demonic.

Having to resort to the soul-searching technique left a bitter taste in his mouth. He knew that he no longer had the luxury to avoid the more ruthless aspects of the cultivation world. Not to mention, since arriving in this world, he had killed many times already, both directly and indirectly. But . . . some things were worse than death.

If I don't do everything in my power to find the truth, it will be me who is on the wrong end of a soul search . . . or worse. I just don't want to be like those hypocrite protagonists, pretending that I'm the good guy in all of this. I guess I'm more of an antihero . . .

Not knowing how to feel about that, Slifer turned his attention back to finding a Heaven Rank soul-searching technique that would meet his needs. Once he found one, he purchased the manual, ignoring the System's warning about Karmic Credit deductions. Some things were more valuable than losing a few points.

Ding!
Purchase successful
You have gained the technique Soul Search
10,000 Karmic Credits deducted

"Give me a few moments alone with them," Slifer instructed Morvran. No need for his follower to witness the inevitable failures to come.

Morvran obediently departed, shutting the door firmly behind him. Now they were alone, captives and captor. Two were human, the rest various demonic races: horned imps, furred beastmen, and scaled reptilians. They glared at him with pure hatred through eyes sunken with pain and exhaustion.

Slifer began to pace slowly around the kneeling figures. He said nothing at first, building tension as their eyes tracked his movements. Fear and confusion lurked beneath their defiant exteriors. They had heard about the reputation of the supreme elder and his sadistic disciples; they did not know what fate awaited them now.

"I imagine you are wondering why you're still alive," Slifer finally remarked conversationally. He stopped his circling and regarded the leader of the group—a powerfully built demon with curling ram's horns atop his head. "Fanatics like you rarely leave this place alive," Slifer continued. "And your kind are known for abandoning failures like yourselves . . ."

The horned demon bared pointed teeth in a mocking sneer. "Is this where you try to break us, human? Do your worst—you'll get nothing from us but screams."

The other prisoners muttered their agreement. Such bravado was expected.

Slifer's expression remained mild, giving no hint of his intentions. "Bold words. But I think you'll find my methods are not designed to inflict pain . . . They don't actually require your cooperation at all."

Steeling himself, his gaze moved from one prisoner to another as he contemplated where to begin. He finally settled on one of the two human cultivators: a slender man with brown hair obscuring his eyes. Humans tended to have weaker souls than demons, making them ideal initial test subjects.

"I think I'll begin with you," Slifer said. He reached out towards the prisoner's head.

"Get your filthy paws off me!" the man spat, trying to jerk away. The chains binding his wrists prevented him from moving far.

Ignoring the outburst, Slifer placed his palm directly on top of the man's hair and activated the Soul Search technique. Violet tendrils of qi were released out of Slifer's hand and made their way into the cultivator's mind. The man's back arched, a scream torn from his throat. The other prisoners watched anxiously.

"Come on, resist him!" one demon growled. "Don't let this scum plunder your mind!"

"Fight it, brother!" the other human prisoner yelled. "We must endure!"

Inside the man's psyche, Slifer sifted through memories and experiences. A small village . . . Parents killed . . . Leaving the village to join the Death Sect . . .

"Let's see what secrets you hide," Slifer muttered, ignoring the useless information as he probed deeper. The human soul wavered under the assault but held firm for now.

More images appeared: A candle-lit initiation ritual . . . The stark barracks . . . A punishing training regime . . . First kills and assignments carried out with increasing zealotry . . . Finally getting his revenge . . .

Slifer frowned, disappointed at the lack of substantial intel so far. He would have to risk plunging even deeper into the man's core.

But as the violet tendrils penetrated further, the prisoner's soul defenses suddenly collapsed. His body spasmed violently, froth bubbling from his lips as his mind fragmented from the strain.

With a gasp, Slifer withdrew the technique hastily, but it was too late—the damage was done. The man's head slumped forward, eyes staring vacantly ahead as drool dripped from his slack mouth. His soul had been utterly devastated by the search.

> *Ding!*
> You have gained 50 Karmic Credits for killing a demonic Core Formation cultivator.
> *Ding!*
> You have lost 50 Karmic Credits for using a demonic soul technique.

"No, brother!"

"Damn you, devil!" one demon snarled at Slifer, fangs bared.

Slifer sighed, ignoring the outburst as he stepped back. So much for his first attempt—while the weakness of human souls made them better test subjects, they lacked the fortitude to withstand a full invasion. Soul searching was a delicate procedure, requiring surgical precision rather than brute force. He would have to refine his control before trying again.

Looks like I have a lot of practicing to look forward to . . . Actually, maybe practicing on them isn't a good idea. If I accidentally shattered all their minds before learning anything useful, then any chance of uncovering Vowron's plans would be lost.

Clearly he needed to upgrade the Soul Search technique before attempting it again.

"What are you plotting, snake?" the horned demon leader growled.

Slifer glanced at him. "You'll see soon enough."

Opening his interface, Slifer navigated to the technique, then hesitated when he saw the upgrade cost.

One thousand Karmic Credits to upgrade to level one? Fine.

> *Ding!*
> Soul Search upgraded to level 1.
> -1000 Karmic Credits

The violet tendrils glowed brighter.

Slifer turned to the prisoners but before he tried again, he paused.

Better to be cautious and upgrade to level two . . .

> *Ding!*
> Soul Search upgraded to level 2.
> -2000 Karmic Credits

Ready to try again, Slifer's gaze settled on one of the lesser demons, a gray-skinned brute with heavy ridges protruding from his bald skull.

"Let's see what you know," Slifer remarked, reaching out.

The demon thrashed against his chains. "Get out of my head!"

Undeterred, Slifer initiated the Soul Search, tendrils spearing deep into the captive's mind. He screamed as Slifer rifled through his memories. A hell-like world . . . Hiding from larger demons . . . His first kill . . .

He rapidly skipped past the demon's early years and focused only on recent events. Finally, he uncovered memories of Vowron addressing this strike team.

Slifer listened closely to Vowron's instructions, seeking some hint about the Immortal Realm's involvement. But there was nothing beyond orders to infiltrate the tournament—no explanations given. This demon was merely a grunt acting on commands from above.

With a frustrated sigh, Slifer withdrew from his mind. The creature slumped forward.

> *Ding!*
> You have lost 50 Karmic Credits for using a demonic soul technique.

Due to Slifer's improved control and the naturally resistant soul of a demon, the captive was still alive.

Slifer turned to consider the horned leader, who was still defiantly meeting his gaze. This one surely possessed more extensive knowledge. But prudence suggested saving him for last.

"You"—Slifer gestured to another random demon—"you're next . . ."

CHAPTER TWO

Slifer let the demon leader's limp body slump to the floor, the prisoner's ram horns scraping against the stone tiles. The supreme elder sighed in frustration and stepped back, shaking his head.

The soul-searching technique had been a dead end. Slifer had plunged into the minds of all the demons, seeking some insight into Vowron's mysterious goals. But even prying into their deepest secrets had revealed little of use. Only vague glimpses and passing references to something hidden within the Sealed Realm that Vowron wanted. Unfortunately, the demons were merely grunts acting on orders. The specifics of the demonic sect master's plans remained obscured.

Slifer stroked his beard as he mentally sorted through the usual treasures and legacies often coveted in xianxia tales, searching for one that fit the hazy clues he extracted.

Could it be heavenly materials to craft rare pills or elixirs? Those had obvious value and power. Though, merely stealing ingredients seemed too minor a goal for Vowron to partner up with an Immortal. There had to be more to it.

Perhaps an ancient manual inscribed with long-lost powerful cultivation techniques and skills? That would align with Vowron's ambitions. But the tattered memories suggested something other than just some written knowledge.

A powerful artifact, then? Some super weapon like a god-slaying sword or doomsday cauldron? Entirely possible given that artifacts could level mountains and boil oceans when unleashed at full power. Yet the demons did not seem interested in pure destructive potential based on the faint remnants Slifer sensed.

What else could it be? Some demon ancestor who had been sealed away and was summoning its descendants to free it?

Slifer sighed again, frustrated. None of those guesses felt exactly right. The clues were simply too vague and fragmented. It was impossible to know for sure. And with the treasures and secrets hidden in places like the Sealed Realm being near infinite, anything was possible.

I need more information.

As Slifer turned to leave the prison chamber, a System notification popped up.

Ding!
New Task: Eliminate the demon prisoners.
Reward: 100 Karmic Credits per prisoner

Slifer paused and looked back at the prisoners. They were useless to him now. He could either let Morvran torture them to death or just end them quickly himself. Death would be a mercy compared to what Morvran had planned for them; not to mention that one could never have too many Karmic Credits . . .

"Like I told you before, I can't allow any of you to leave this place," Slifer stated calmly. He loosened his sword in its scabbard.

The demon leader, who seemed to have recovered from having his soul plundered, bared his teeth and snarled. "We won't beg for our lives, human scum! Finish it and see where it gets you." The other demons growled in agreement.

Slifer's expression remained neutral. In a blur, he drew his blade and unleashed a perfectly executed Sunrise Slash strike. The prisoners had just a brief moment of shock before their heads slid from their shoulders and thumped wetly to the floor. Their headless bodies spasmed before slumping over, gushing blood across the tiles.

Slifer flicked the blood from his sword and sheathed it in a smooth motion. He waited patiently as ten notification chimes rang out.

Ding!
Task Complete
You have gained 900 Karmic Credits.
Ding!

You have gained 50 Karmic Credits for killing a demonic Core Formation cultivator.

Stepping around the pool of blood, Slifer exited the dungeon. The way forward was clear now in his mind. The Black Death Sect still had one prisoner remaining. It was time to have a chat with Vowron himself.

But before Slifer peeked inside the cauldron, he needed to prepare. Vowron was no fool, and as a Half-Step Immortal, he certainly had contingencies in place. An opponent like that required careful planning.

The icy wind howled as Zack stepped out of the portal and into the snowy wastes of the Northern Region. He winced as the gate snapped shut behind him, sealing him alone inside the Sealed Realm.

Glancing around, he saw nothing but an endless ocean of snow sitting beneath slate-gray skies. No sign of the other participants who had entered with him. Finding them anytime soon would be impossible in this place.

"I'm guessing this is the Northern Region. Not a bad starting point . . . if it weren't freezing."

His Peak Foundation Establishment cultivation protected him from the worst of the cold. Still, the frigid temperature was an annoyance he would have to deal with.

Reaching into his storage ring, Zack retrieved a map given to him by the Main Body. He assumed the other sect disciples had similar maps from their elders. The maps were updated every century as new areas of the Sealed Realm were explored and recorded by survivors.

Checking his location, Zack muttered, "Yep, it really is the Northern Region . . ."

Typically in xianxia stories, the Central Region held the greatest treasures—and risks. The Northern Region would be good enough for now. His priority was making a breakthrough to the Core Formation Realm. Only then would he feel confident enough to wander around.

Zack suppressed his qi as he cautiously scanned the landscape. He needed to find a suitable secluded spot before attempting his breakthrough. The fluctuations in his cultivation base would act like a beacon otherwise.

I can't afford to attract any attention. Better to avoid flying for now.

The Northern Region was probably the safest region according to Slifer's briefings. Primarily icy tundra, glaciers, and some mountain ranges. Treacherous terrain, but scarce population. Most of the realm's more vicious inhabitants and enviable treasures could be found in the Central or Southern Regions.

Still, isolated threats lived even here: Ambitious loose cultivators making pilgrimages between more promising areas. Packs of Yeti or Ice Spiders hunting prey. Ancient beasts slumbering in cave lairs. Zack remained alert.

But despite all of that, his biggest concern was running into the region's inhabitants. It was well known that they didn't tend to get along well with the "outside" people . . .

Hopefully, I don't have to worry about them for now.

After some time trudging through the snow, Zack discovered a hidden cave tucked away in a snowy hillside. Perfect. He slipped inside and began laying down formations and talismans he had received from the Main Body to conceal his presence during the breakthrough.

The soul suppression talisman prevented detection from spiritual senses. The sound insulation talisman would mask any noises. And the Qi Confusion Formation obscured his energy fluctuations.

Settling down cross-legged on the chilly stone floor, Zack reflected on the events leading up to now. Before departing for the Sealed Realm, Leontius— the Legacy Disciple representing the Black Rose Sect—had tried to rope Zack and the other Black Rose disciples into some scheme.

Apparently, Leontius wanted them to help distract and entrap the other Legacy Disciples once inside the Realm. But Zack was no fool, unlike some of the young geniuses, who seemed far more I than you'd expect for twenty-year-old men. He had no intention of becoming cannon fodder for someone else's petty plots and power plays. Not when he had his own goals to achieve.

Breaking through to the Core Formation stage was essential not just for power, but for survival. Here in the Sealed Realm, there would be no deadly Heavenly Tribulations to face. But that also meant no chance to gain enlightenment or abilities from enduring those stormy trials.

Zack shook his head. "Without the Main Body's support, I'd rather play it safe anyways."

Facing the Grade 4 tribulation intended for someone of Zack's talent would be incredibly dangerous without outside help. Attempting it alone could easily prove fatal.

"At least I don't have to worry about getting struck by lightning here," Zack muttered. "Though, it is too bad that I can't upgrade my body cultivation at the same time."

To advance his body cultivation further would require a powerful external energy source to temper and transform his body. Unfortunately, that was not an option available in this strange place. He couldn't afford to delay his breakthrough; he would have to make do with a sole spiritual breakthrough for now.

But he was certain the Main Body would break through in both realms simultaneously by enduring Heavenly Tribulation.

"Lucky him."

Zack's thoughts turned to the different core types in the Core Formation Realm. The weakest were mixed cores, amalgamations of various elements and impurities. Then there were mid-grade cores, defined by their color—green, purple, red, and so on—based on one's primary cultivation method.

With my lightning cultivation method, if I were to somehow mess up and form a mid-grade core, then it would be a blue core. But being average in a world like this isn't good enough.

For those who cultivated an impeccable base and practiced a Heaven Rank method, they could form the legendary Golden Core, representing "limitless" potential. In xianxia stories, only the gifted and fortuitous accomplished this.

The purer a core's color and the more robust its structure, the greater the cultivator's qi capacity and the higher quality qi they could generate. Everything else being equal, a Golden Core practitioner would always overwhelm the same level opponent with a weaker variant core.

Unfortunately for most cultivators, the quality of one's core depended largely on either innate talent or cultivation resources.

Luckily for me, I have both in spades.

The original Slifer had formed a Golden Core; therefore, both the Main Body and Zack expected no less for themselves.

Rumors spoke of even more exotic cores like Frozen Cores, Crimson Cores, and Cores of Chaos. But Zack's orders from the Main Body were clear: focus only on forming a standard Golden Core for now.

Reaching too high would be reckless without the Main Body's support. Zack could ask for pills or treasures to be deposited into his ring, but they might not arrive in time if he was in a precarious situation.

I might not even get a chance to ask for help before I cripple myself.

"Right, let's stick to a basic Golden Core for my first go," Zack muttered.

Nodding with satisfaction, Zack pulled out a Qi Cleansing Pill. It was designed to cleanse impurities from the cultivator's cultivation base. The Main Body's advancement so far had been unassisted by pills, so he expected little corruption in his foundation.

Zack swallowed the medicinal pill and began circulating his internal energy.

Moments later, he spat out a glob of black mucus the size of a coin. As expected, his foundation was already relatively pure.

It's time . . .

Closing his eyes, Zack sank his spiritual sense into his dantian. There floated nine shimmering pillars of qi—the foundation the Main Body had built.

Taking a deep breath, Zack extended his hands and made a pulling motion. The nine pillars fractured into glittering motes of qi, which flowed together in the center of his dantian, then coalesced into a mass of swirling colors.

Brow furrowed in concentration, Zack began compacting the qi, cycling his energy through it again and again. He had to be cautious—forcing the process too quickly could damage his foundation and set him back years. But neither could he afford to delay here indefinitely.

As time passed, the ball shrank and became denser as its colors blended into a molten golden hue. Signs were promising so far.

Droplets of sweat beaded on Zack's face from the exertion as he continued compressing the qi mass. *Tighter . . . tighter . . .* He was nearing the critical point. *Just a final burst of qi to trigger the metamorphosis . . .*

Zack's eyes snapped open, a fierce grin on his face. There within his dantian floated a dazzling golden orb the size of a fist—a Golden Core!

"Core Formation—I did it!" Zack exclaimed.

He had actually formed a real Golden Core on his first try! And it felt incredibly solid and stable. The number of cultivators who could claim that, not counting his disciples, couldn't be high—even the original Slifer took three tries!

After basking in his accomplishment for a moment, Zack rose to his feet and stretched, feeling the qi circulating through his body, far purer and stronger than before. Already he could tell his spiritual sense had expanded and his qi regeneration increased. The breakthrough had been taxing but unfathomably rewarding.

A thunderous roar suddenly shook the cavern, dislodging chunks of ice from the ceiling. Zack's body tensed as an oppressive aura slammed down on him.

Someone or something extremely powerful was right outside!

Before he could react, the cave wall exploded inwards and a scaly blue claw the size of a carriage smashed through, grasping for him.

Shit!

CHAPTER THREE

Zack leapt out of the crumbling cave, and blue lightning wings burst from his back as he took to the air.

Twisting in midair, he narrowly dodged another swipe from the monstrous limb. After putting some distance between himself and his attacker, Zack finally got a good look at the beast.

It was an enormous blue dragon, easily the size of a mountain and covered in snow and ice.

Zack's eyes widened in realization. This entire time he thought he had taken shelter inside a snowy hillside. But it had actually been the sleeping dragon! No wonder his concealment talisman hadn't worked as well as he had expected.

The dragon must have been slumbering there for ages for a full ecosystem of caves and wildlife to develop on its body. Just how long had it been asleep?

The dragon lunged again, jaws wide-open. Zack quickly veered to the left, the rush of air from the snap of its jaws buffeting his robes.

He studied the beast with a critical eye as he evaded its attacks. Judging by the dragon's size and the overwhelming pressure of its Nascent Soul Realm aura, it had likely reached the late stage.

Comparing this wild dragon to Val, Zack assumed that it must be of a much lower bloodline purity. Despite possessing intelligence seemingly on par with an adult human, this dragon clearly lacked the capacity for speech that Val had. Not only that, but Val was only a baby at the Nascent Soul Realm whilst this dragon seemed fully matured.

That makes sense considering the System rewarded me for simply locating Val, Zack thought. *Higher purity bloodlines are exceptionally rare.*

Just because its bloodline was diluted didn't make the dragon any less dangerous. A late-stage Nascent Soul dragon was bad news for a new Core Formation cultivator like himself. But Zack was confident in slaying it, especially with the treasures the Main Body provided as insurance.

However, he wasn't ready to rely on those just yet. Not until he was certain the situation was truly dire. Until then, he would have to handle this with his own strength, which meant he needed a new plan, fast. Running wasn't an option with the dragon's mobility and flight range. He'd have to play matador, dancing around the strikes and waiting for an opportunity to deliver a decisive counter blow.

The dragon reared its head back as an icy glow built in its throat—definitely not good! Zack zipped behind the dragon in a flash of golden light just before it unleashed its frozen breath attack, the torrent of icy wind blasting the spot where he had just been.

Capitalizing on the opening, Zack unsheathed his sword and stabbed at the dragon's neck with all his might. But the scales were like divine metal, and his sword point barely sank an inch into the thick hide.

Zack clicked his tongue in annoyance as the dragon twisted its neck furiously. He released his lodged sword and flashed away right before the beast's massive spiked tail pulverized the spot.

Okay, new plan. His attacks were basically useless, so he would irritate the beast with tricks instead. He would wait for it to overcommit and leave an exploitable gap in its defenses, then finish it off in one decisive strike using the treasures in his ring.

Putting on a burst of speed, Zack shot through the air, zigzagging unpredictably to throw off the dragon's aim. It stomped after him, each thunderous footfall setting off localized avalanches. Zack kept just outside its attack range, letting it waste stamina on clumsy grabs and chomps.

When it reared back for a concentrated breath attack, Zack stuck his finger up in a taunting gesture, further enraging the beast. As expected, it abandoned the breath weapon in favor of a direct physical strike and overextended itself. Zack rolled smoothly under the swipe from the oversized claw.

The dragon thrashed violently, its huge frame becoming a liability as it struggled to line up a clean hit on the annoying gnat flitting around it. Zack utilized the terrain to weave through stone arches and duck into narrow ravines where the dragon couldn't fully maneuver.

After almost an hour of this exhausting dance, the dragon was frothing at the mouth in mindless fury. Now was his chance! Just as Zack readied himself to bring out one of his trump cards, he sensed two powerful qi signatures closing in fast.

Crap, no choice but to play the helpless disciple!

Changing plans in a split second, Zack put on a panicked expression, doing his best to appear like a terrified young disciple in over his head, just as an overwhelming pressure slammed down. The dragon froze mid-strike, actually seeming unnerved.

An instant later, a blurred sword flash parted the beast's head from its shoulders in one clean strike. The severed dragon head tumbled down the snowy slope, initiating a small avalanche. Its body spasmed briefly before collapsing with a ground-shaking thud.

Zack looked upwards, his face arranged in an expression of gratitude and relief. "Thank you for saving me, Senior!"

Hovering in the air above was a middle-aged man garbed in fine purple robes. His stern face and sharp eyes marked him as a seasoned cultivator who had seen countless battles. Despite appearing only forty years old at most, a dense aura swirled around him—the unmistakable pressure of Peak-stage Nascent Soul Realm.

The man simply nodded in response to Zack's thanks, his gaze studying the young cultivator curiously. But before he could speak, another figure arrived, winging through the air on top of a flying sword.

It was a young girl who looked about sixteen years old, also dressed in purple robes. Her fair face was twisted in a scowl as she pulled up next to the middle-aged man.

"Master! Why did you rush off and leave me behind?" she complained in a shrill voice. "I nearly got lost tracking your aura through this blizzard!"

The man's severe expression softened as he regarded his complaining disciple. "Apologies, Mia," he said gently. "When I sensed a fellow cultivator in grave danger, I couldn't delay."

The girl huffed as she followed her master's gaze to focus on Zack. Her scowl returned even fiercer than before.

"Hmph! It's just another talentless insect trying to curry favor with you! Look at him—he probably lured that dragon here on purpose knowing you would come and rescue him!"

Zack smiled wryly at the girl's wild accusation, holding back a laugh. He shook his head. "While I admire Senior's heroism, this was just an unfortunate ambush, nothing more." He clasped his hands together in a respectful gesture towards the man. "I'm grateful you arrived when you did, Senior. Without your help, I fear I would have ended up as dinner for sure."

The purple-robed cultivator waved a hand in dismissal. "No need for such courtesy. Helping fellow cultivators in times of trouble is only expected." He stroked his chin thoughtfully as he studied Zack. "Still, you appear quite young to be roaming the Northern Wastes alone. And your sect robes seem unfamiliar to me. You aren't from around here, are you?"

Zack hesitated briefly. These two had a strange accent he couldn't quite place. He had known that the moment he opened his mouth to speak, they would know he was an outsider. He had considered feigning muteness but decided openness might serve him better here. After all, if things went badly, he was confident, with the treasures in his arsenal, that he could deal with even a Peak Nascent Soul opponent if absolutely necessary. Though, he would rather avoid such conflict since he still needed information on this place.

Still, their friendly demeanor surprised him. Weren't they known for hating outsiders like himself? Zack plastered on his most disarming "innocent disciple" smile.

"You have a sharp eye, Senior. I'm not from the Northern Region. I left my sect on a journey to see the world." There, nice and vague.

The cultivator nodded thoughtfully. "An admirable goal for one so young. My name is Hallibur, and this is my disciple, Mia. Tell me, what is your name?"

Before Zack could respond, the girl interrupted. "Hmph, he's probably just some talentless loser who got banished here by his sect. I bet they were glad to be rid of him!" Despite her harsh words, Zack noticed a glint of curiosity in the girl's eyes as she ogled his handsomeness. Just another junior with a crush. He was used to that sort of thing after his experiences at the Black Rose Sect.

Suppressing a chuckle at the thought, Zack replied earnestly, "I promise you, I am neither talentless nor a loser seeking to take advantage of your master." He then turned back to the man. "I am Alfie."

"Alfie . . . Would you care to join us?" the man asked. "These lands can be treacherous to navigate alone."

Before Zack could respond, Mia interjected once again. "Master, we barely know this person! What if he's secretly evil?"

Hallibur gently chided his disciple. "Now, Mia, let us not judge others too hastily. As cultivators, it is our duty to aid fellow wanderers in need."

Mia sighed and shot one last petty glare Zack's way before schooling her face.

Zack smiled gratefully at the two. "Thank you for your kindness. I would be happy to join you."

* * *

Back at the Black Rose Sect headquarters, Slifer strolled casually down the hallway lost in thought. Suddenly, a notification chimed, snapping him out of his thoughts.

Ding!
Congratulations!
Your avatar, Zack, has broken through to the Core Formation Realm.
You have gained 500 Karmic Credits.

"Excellent," Slifer muttered under his breath, pleased Zack's breakthrough had proceeded smoothly. The extra Karmic Credits were welcome too. He would need all the karma he could accumulate for when his own breakthrough attempt came. That Heavenly Tribulation would not be kind.

But pushing his own advancement aside, Slifer refocused his thoughts on the task at hand: interrogating Vowron. He needed to uncover what the demonic sect master was after in the mysterious Sealed Realm. Only then could he act decisively against whatever scheme was brewing.

Before Slifer could delve back into planning, a weight suddenly dropped onto his head, followed by a cheerful chirp. "Master! Found you!"

Slifer glanced up to see Val perched on top of his head like a hat, scaly tail swishing excitedly. He couldn't help but grin at the young dragon's antics. "What are you up to now, you goofy lizard?"

Val huffed at the teasing nickname. "I was playing with Leah earlier but got bored. Wanted to find you!"

At the mention of Leah, Slifer winced internally. In the chaos of everything happening, he'd totally forgotten to check in on the girl's progress. Some righteous mentor he was turning out to be.

Just add it to the pile of things I need to deal with eventually . . .

Pushing those thoughts aside for now, Slifer refocused on Val, who wanted to know what he was up to. "Well, I'm headed to have a talk with our bad friend Vowron."

Val's eyes lit up at the prospect of action. She bared her tiny claws. "Ooh! Can I help, Master? I wanna scare the bad man!" To emphasize her scariness, Val made her most ferocious face—which looked about as intimidating as an angry kitten.

Slifer chuckled at the display. "I appreciate the offer, but don't worry. I'll call you if I need dragon backup."

Val pouted but didn't argue further as Slifer shooed her off so he could prepare. Soon he was seated comfortably in his quarters, browsing the System

Shop. He needed options to restrain Vowron in case the cauldron's sealing power proved inadequate. An ambush was guaranteed once he opened the lid.

Let's see . . . Too expensive, too situational . . . Aha—perfect!

After browsing for a minute, he purchased three cards: Heavenly Chain of Light, Vampiric Mist, and Paralysis Charm. The first would conjure golden chains of pure sun essence that could temporarily bind a demonic cultivator. The second produced an inky mist that weakened liches and vampiric creatures. And the Paralysis Charm would freeze Vowron in place for a few crucial seconds when applied.

The cards cost a total of 9,000 Karmic Credits, making Slifer wince. Credits were so easy to burn through, yet so hard to earn. But it was a necessary expense.

Shaking his head at the expenditure, Slifer steeled himself. "Right, time to find out the truth."

He retrieved the jade cauldron containing Vowron from his spirit ring, the vessel thumping heavily as it landed. Muffled swearing came from within—Vowron was clearly still lively and eager to talk.

"Let's get this chat over with so I can move on to more important things—like getting stronger," Slifer muttered. With a wave of his hand, the heavy lid flew off to reveal a withered lich head glaring murderously up at him.

"Damn you, Slife—" Vowron's curse was cut short as Slifer slapped the Paralysis Charm onto his forehead. The demonic sect master froze in place, limbs locked in an awkward position.

Slifer wasted no time triggering the Vampiric Mist and Heavenly Chain of Light cards in quick succession. The inky mist flowed over Vowron, drawing out his strength, while golden chains formed of streaming sunlight wrapped tightly around his body.

"Y-you're an Immortal!" Vowron's eyes were wide with shock.

After all, only an Immortal could manhandle him like this.

CHAPTER FOUR

Slifer smiled at Vowron; he couldn't help but act a little arrogant. "You should bow to your superiors." With that, he released his Void Realm aura, the aura of a higher being, and forced Vowron's head down.

"W-what the hell are you?" Vowron spluttered, eyes wide.

"Someone way above your pay grade," Slifer replied smugly. He placed his palm on Vowron's forehead before the Black Death Sect Master could react.

"Soul Search!"

Slifer plunged his consciousness into Vowron's soulscape, looking through the demon's memories. Images and memories flashed through Slifer's mind as he sifted through the chaos that was Vowron's life. He saw a young Vowron, no more than five or six, walk in on his father going berserk and brutally murdering his mother. The boy watched, paralyzed, as his mother's blood painted the walls.

Another vision showed a teenage Vowron joining the Black Death Sect, seduced by promises of power. Slifer watched as Vowron rose through the demonic sect's ranks, killing and backstabbing along the way. One memory showed Vowron slaying his own father under his master's instructions, his eyes cold and vacant.

Even patricide meant nothing on the path of demonic cultivation.

Slifer shook his head. Vowron was just throwing useless memories at him, hoping to obscure the truth. But Slifer would not be deterred so easily. He pressed deeper, sifting through the lich wannabe's millennia of memories.

Buried beneath the superficial recollections, Slifer found distorted images. *Is this it?*

He focused and made out a massive tree silhouetted against a crimson sky. No, not just a tree—some ancient demonic tree, but he couldn't get a good look at it. Slifer reached for it, trying to understand. But the instant he touched the memory, Slifer felt a force shove him violently from Vowron's soul. Slifer's eyes snapped open just as Vowron's lich-like form collapsed into dust before him.

Ding!
You have killed a Half-Step Immortal demonic cultivator.
You have gained 3000 Karmic Credits.

"A fail-safe on his soul," Slifer muttered. Vowron had prepared well by imprinting a self-destruct mechanism deep within his spirit.

Slifer wiped sweat from his brow. The people behind Vowron were clearly formidable, perhaps even at the Greater Immortal Realm, to implant such a potent fail-safe in a Half-Step Immortal . . . Slifer felt like he was getting in way over his head.

He stared down at the pile of ashes that minutes before had been the Black Death Sect Master. Now what to do? Destroy the remains? Use them for some creepy demonic ritual?

As he pondered, he suddenly thought of an idea. Slifer waved a hand, then gathered up Vowron's ashes into a small glass vial he produced from a ring on his finger. The vial disappeared back into his storage ring. He had little skill in alchemy, but these ashes may prove useful one day. They were the remains of a Half-Step Immortal, after all. They must count for something, right?

For now, he had more pressing concerns. Slifer needed to meet with the elders on how to deal with the Black Death Sect in Vowron's absence. And he needed to advance his own strength before things escalated further.

Something was going down; he could feel it.

Slifer sat waiting in the Disciplinary Hall, browsing idly through the Shop. He was pleased to see the Disciplinary Hall's karma farming was continuing smoothly without him having to lift a finger.

Maybe I should just hole up here indefinitely until I reach Immortal Ascension or something?

Slifer recalled reading stories where the protagonist secluded himself for centuries before emerging unstoppably powerful.

But no, hiding indefinitely wasn't an option, as tempting as it sounded. He couldn't shirk his duties as supreme elder. And more pressingly, he didn't trust this world's Heaven's Will to ignore an interloper like himself. Eventually, he would have to face more tribulations sent by the Will of this world. Hiding would only delay the inevitable.

The scariest tribulation is a cultivator manipulated by Heaven's Will . . .

"Supreme Elder." Grand Elder Tenzin's voice jarred Slifer from his thoughts. He looked up to see the elder waiting patiently.

"Tenzin, come in, take a seat," Slifer said, waving the man over. Best to continue to build goodwill with one of the few elders who was trying to gain his favor.

They made small talk about sect affairs until Grand Elder Lydia glided in. Slifer greeted her as well and directed her to have a seat. Lydia inclined her head politely, face unreadable as always. She rarely spoke during meetings, seemingly content to simply observe.

Finally, Grand Elder Wyatt arrived, out of breath and red-faced. Slifer noted with satisfaction that he must have rushed all the way here. *Serves him right after his past attempts to trip me up. Let him stand awkwardly while the others sit. It's like owning a dog: you need to show them who the alpha is . . .*

Once Wyatt had caught his breath, Slifer cleared his throat. "Elders, I've called you here to discuss our next moves given recent events. The chaos caused by the Black Death Sect must be answered."

Tenzin nodded sagely. "Too right, too right. We cannot let such violence stand."

Wyatt quickly added, "With both the Black Heart and Black Death leaders gone, those sects will be directionless. Now is the time to assert dominance before they can regroup."

"Going to war would stretch our sect thin when we've already suffered losses," Tenzin cautioned.

Wyatt waved a hand dismissively. "This opportunity is too good to pass up. The heavens themselves have delivered our rivals into our hands. Together the three sects would be unstoppable. The three sects as one is how it was always meant to be."

"And how do you propose we manage three sects when we can barely handle one?" Tenzin countered, frowning. "The sect master is still in secluded cultivation, and we don't have enough manpower or resources to control an expanded territory."

"In time we can groom new elders from the conquered sects and extract greater taxes and tributes from the increased populace," Wyatt argued. "Without leaders to unify them, they will fracture and be easily dominated."

"I can't believe that I am saying this about you of all people"—Tenzin shook his head firmly—"but your thinking is dangerously shortsighted. The people will resent such heavy-handed occupation, and without the strength to enforce it, we'll face endless turmoil and rebellion."

As the two men debated, Slifer listened intently, weighing their words. Lydia sat silently, not bothering to give input one way or another.

When the arguing grew heated, Slifer held up a hand. "Enough. I will be making personal visits to both sects to assess the situation."

The elders lowered their heads. Dispatching an Ascendant cultivator like Slifer would certainly settle matters. None could hope to oppose someone so powerful. But it wasn't appropriate for them to suggest that the supreme elder himself act.

It'll be nice to get some fresh air . . . even if it is in another demonic sect.

In truth, Slifer would prefer relaxing in seclusion. But he couldn't pass up this opportunity. And entering the Black Death Sect's headquarters may reveal clues about Vowron's goals.

Decision made, Slifer stood up abruptly. The elders quickly followed suit. Without another word, Slifer retrieved the Divine Azerion Ark from his storage ring.

Just as he was about to jump on, a high-pitched voice called out, "Master, wait for me!"

Slifer turned to see Val soaring towards him. He smiled involuntarily at the sight of the bubbly creature.

Val sat down on his shoulder, scaly tail swishing in the air. "Where are we going? Is it a fun trip?"

"A quick business trip," Slifer clarified. At Val's crestfallen look, he relented. "But I suppose my fierce dragon bodyguard would be useful."

Val scrunched her snout. "Who're you calling fierce?" But she seemed pleased at the prospect of an adventure.

Wasn't she just trying to convince me she was fierce enough to scare Vowron? Why the sudden change?

Deciding there was no use trying to understand what was going on in the head of a baby dragon, Slifer moved to board the Ark once more. Val piped up again. "Oh, I brought a friend. Hope that's okay!"

Slifer raised an eyebrow. "Friend?"

"That would be me," a female voice answered. Slifer turned to see Leah, the young cultivator from the Black Heart Sect. The same girl Morvran had accidentally kidnapped when Slifer first arrived in this world, the girl he was supposed to be mentoring.

"Leah? What a . . . surprise," Slifer greeted awkwardly.

Leah bowed. "I wish to see my sect again after so long away. Can . . . can I join you?"

Seeing Slifer's hesitation, Val pleaded, "Come on, Master! The more the merrier."

Slifer chuckled inwardly. *Fine, the young disciple and cute dragon can come. They'll probably get into antics and misadventures, but things have been too tense lately. And maybe I will be able to finally convert her to the righteous side and get me that extra disciple slot.*

"Alright, welcome aboard."

CHAPTER FIVE

Zack soared through the sky on his flying sword following behind Hallibur and Mia. The unlikely trio made an interesting sight—the stern middle-aged cultivator, his arrogant disciple, and the mysterious young man from "distant lands."

Mia kept twisting around on her sword to shoot probing glances at Zack. He pretended not to notice, instead keeping his gaze fixed ahead as his lips curved in the hint of a knowing smile.

"So, Alfie . . ." Mia began, breaking the silence. "You never did mention where you're from. Some no-name backwater sect, I bet."

Zack offered the antagonistic girl a patient smile. "Just a small place in the Southern Region you probably haven't heard of. I'm afraid my origins aren't too exciting."

He had chosen the furthest region away from the north in the hopes that his answers wouldn't draw much suspicion even if there were inconsistencies.

Mia's lip curled in a smirk. "Hmph, just as I thought. Your sect probably kicked you out for having no talent. So, you came crawling to the Northern Wastes hoping to scavenge some treasures or techniques to bring back as an offering so they'll take you back."

"Mia, restraint," Hallibur uttered softly, though his gaze remained fixed ahead.

The rebuke made the girl duck her head. "Yes, Master." After a moment, she peered over at Zack again. "So, what made you leave your pathetic sect, anyways?"

Zack maintained his cheerful façade. This girl seemed intent on riling him up; she was likely jealous over the perceived threat to her standing with her master, or maybe this was her attempt at flirting.

With girls, one can never tell.

"Curiosity," he replied vaguely. "I wanted to see more of the world beyond my sect's lands. What better teacher than firsthand experience?"

Mia wrinkled her nose. "Why not just join a stronger sect, then?"

"I considered it," Zack admitted. "But my elders always said easy strength leads to complacency. If I joined some powerful sect, I'd probably grow lazy and entitled like those arrogant young masters . . ."

"Hmph, spoken like someone born without any real talent," Mia muttered. But Zack noticed she seemed thoughtful now rather than antagonistic. His words had given her something to chew on.

Time to divert this conversation before she started questioning his backstory too closely.

"Enough about me," Zack said breezily. "I'd love to hear more about the Northern Region from you both. Are there many sects around here?"

Mia brightened at the chance to show off her knowledge. She launched into a lecture about the local sects, seeming to forget her suspicions for now.

"There are five major sects that control the Northern Region. The most powerful is the Moon God Sect, which rules over all the others from their capital city, Taiya. My master and I are from the Sun Palace Sect." She turned to give Zack a smirk.

Zack's brow furrowed in thought. *Interesting how freely she volunteers such information. Aren't they supposed to be wary of outsiders?*

"What sets the Moon God Sect apart from the others?" he asked.

Mia preened, happy to play lecturer. "The Moon God Sect has nine Nascent Soul elders and three Origin Realm experts. The sect master is even rumored to be at the Peak of the Origin Realm!"

Zack's eyes widened convincingly. "A Peak Origin Realm expert oversees the entire region?"

Inwardly he scoffed. His true body could crush any Origin Realm cultivator in this backwater place. Hell, even Ascendant cultivators weren't safe from him. But keeping up appearances as a wonderstruck junior was paramount right now, especially since he didn't have the System to back him up.

Mia nodded, thrilled to impress him with her knowledge. "That's right! So don't get any funny ideas about causing trouble." She leaned closer on her sword, somehow looking even haughtier than before. "In fact, the only reason the other four sects can even survive is by paying huge tributes each month to the Moon God Sect."

Interesting. This place operates more like an empire, with the Moon God Sect extorting protection fees from the other players.

"That must be difficult for the other sects," Zack mused aloud. "Especially with Elder Hallibur and yourself to provide for." He glanced at the silent man. "Generating enough resources to satisfy Nascent Soul cultivators can't be easy."

For the first time, Hallibur spoke up. "The tributes are necessary for maintaining the balance of power. Without the Moon God Sect's oversight, the Northern Wastes would collapse into chaos and infighting."

His tone brooked no argument. Clearly the man was a loyalist who supported the status quo. Zack filed that tidbit away as he continued his line of questioning.

"Are there many rogue cultivators here? Do they trouble the sects?"

This time Hallibur remained silent, so Mia answered again. "There are always drifters and wandering cultivators passing through the Northern Wastes. Most know not to make trouble." Her lips curled up in a wicked smirk. "The foolish and desperate sometimes try raiding the sect caravans. But they don't last long against our enforcers!"

Zack laughed politely at the casual admission. "It seems quite a robust system you have here. Far more orderly than the chaotic Southern Region that I come from. The Northern Region seems a much safer place for a lone cultivator trying to improve his strength. Perhaps I'll stay here for a little while . . ."

Out of the corner of his eye, Zack noticed Hallibur's gaze linger on him for a fraction longer than before.

"You plan to remain in the Northern Region?" Mia asked, a complicated expression on her face.

Zack sensed Mia still saw him as a rival for Hallibur's attention. But his praise for the region's stability had softened her. She likely enjoyed enlightening an ignorant outsider about how things worked here.

"I do," Zack said. "It's better than wandering lost. Thanks to you both, I feel my journey has led me somewhere promising." He smiled warmly.

Mia huffed but looked pleased. "Just don't forget your place, outsider."

Zack bowed his head. "Of course. I'm in your debt for . . . educating me."

They continued traveling for some time, Zack asking a few more probing questions here and there about the various cities and strongholds that dotted the Northern Region.

As they flew, the scenery gradually transitioned from endless snowy plains to towering cliffs and labyrinthine canyons blanketed in fog.

Perfect terrain for an ambush, Zack noted warily.

But the journey continued uneventfully until a sprawling city carved into the mountainside came into view up ahead.

"There it is: Xairen, the Northern Region's greatest city," Mia declared proudly.

Xairen's towers and pagodas looked like giant icicles jutting out from the granite cliffs. Even from a distance, Zack sensed thousands of powerful cultivators living within.

"Magnificent," he whispered truthfully. It was the first honest thing he'd said all day.

Mia preened under the praise. "Just wait until you see the inside! My master knows all the best—"

"Mia," Hallibur interrupted, speaking for the first time in over an hour. "Go on ahead to the guest quarters and let the attendants know we will be having a guest join us."

Mia whipped her head towards her master in surprise.

"What? But, Master, I wanted to show our new friend around the markets and arena."

Though she tried to keep her tone even, Zack heard the reluctant whine creeping in. Clearly, she had looked forward to playing tour guide.

Hallibur's expression softened, though his eyes remained stern.

"I'm sure you can do so later, but for now, go and make the arrangements."

Mia bit her lip, a crease forming in her brow. She shot a quick sideways glare at Zack, as if this were somehow his fault. But under her master's expectant gaze, she stifled any further complaints.

"Yes, Master," Mia said with a bow before shooting forward towards the city on her sword.

"Is something wrong, Senior?" Zack raised an eyebrow.

Hallibur studied him for a long moment before responding.

"Not at all. I merely wished to speak with you privately before bringing you into the city."

Zack tensed imperceptibly. *Here it comes.*

Hallibur's eyes bored into him. "I admit, when we first crossed paths, I did believe your story. But now . . . not so much."

Zack's eyebrows shot up in feigned surprise.

"Oh? Was my acting that poor?" He let out an awkward chuckle.

Hallibur's lips quirked upwards for a split second. "Not bad, but I've cultivated long enough to notice certain inconsistencies."

Zack sighed. "I see. So, what gave me away?"

Hallibur ticked off points on his fingers.

"First, while you might show off the aura of an Early Core Formation cultivator, your reactions during the battle against the dragon were too quick, too refined. You were clearly holding back."

Zack shrugged, not bothering to deny it. No point maintaining a flimsy charade under this level of scrutiny.

"Second, while your spiritual pressure could pass for Core Formation, your actual qi flow patterns do not match. You are likely at the Nascent Soul stage."

Qi flow patterns? That's the first I'm hearing of this . . .

Hallibur eyed him meaningfully.

"And finally, you show no indications of originating from any of the great sects within the Sealed Realm, never mind the Southern Region. That can only mean one thing—"

"That I'm an outsider," Zack finished. He sighed and gave a small resigned smile. "You have me figured out it seems."

Hallibur considered him silently for another long moment, then said, "I understand why one in your position would be inclined towards discretion." His voice turned grave. "However, Xairen is dangerous for outsiders."

Zack's eyes narrowed warily. "How so?"

"The king has placed a substantial bounty on any outsiders. They must be brought before him, dead or alive."

So, this is what was meant by "They don't like outsiders." Zack stroked his chin thoughtfully. *But who is this king? And what's his problem with outsiders?*

"I see. Thank you for the warning, Senior." He clasped his hands together respectfully. "If you would still let me in your city, I promise not to cause you any trouble."

Hallibur paused before responding. "As much as I would like to, I cannot allow you entry into Xairen."

Zack's back stiffened. He kept his tone measured. "Why?"

Hallibur looked regretful yet resolute. "If anyone found out I assisted an outsider, the king would have my head. Even my own sect would not defend me." He spread his hands apologetically. "I wish things were different, but you just being here endangers us all."

Zack's lips pressed into a thin line as he processed this new information, his mind racing to recalibrate his plans. Getting driven away from the nearest major city was an annoying setback. And who knew what danger awaited him out here . . .

Hallibur eyed him warily, likely prepared to take action at the first sign of resistance.

Zack exhaled slowly. As much as he disliked this, provoking unnecessary conflict over access to one city would be shortsighted. This changed nothing about his overarching goals.

"You make a fair point," Zack conceded diplomatically. "I'll continue my travels elsewhere."

He gave a deep bow, which Hallibur returned.

"You show wisdom beyond your years, my friend," Hallibur said, relaxing his posture. "I wish you safe journeys. Perhaps our paths will cross again."

Zack smiled. "I hope so. Farewell for now, Senior."

He pivoted his sword around preparing to look for somewhere else to stay the night. But before he could leave, Hallibur suddenly thrust his sword forward and impaled Zack through the heart from behind.

"My apologies. But I'm afraid this is the end of your journey," Hallibur said coldly.

Zack froze, coughing up blood. But then he smirked. "Too predictable."

His form blurred and dissolved into wisps of black smoke.

"What?" Hallibur's eyes widened in shock.

The smoke solidified back together behind him to reveal Zack with his sword already mid-swing, aiming for Hallibur's back.

CHAPTER SIX

Zack's sword sliced through the air as Hallibur blurred out of sight. The elder cultivator had narrowly avoided what would have been a lethal blow.

Peak Nascent Soul experts are faster than I expected, Zack thought. *But not fast enough!*

With a thought, Zack's body transformed into a bolt of lightning and streaked across the sky towards Hallibur's new position. The elder raised his hands and summoned an ice shield just in time to block Zack's electrically charged palm strike.

The Thunderclap Palm, enhanced by the Nascent Soul Armor, exploded against the barrier in a flash of blue light. Hallibur slid back several meters but managed to keep his shield intact through pure force of will. Sweat beaded his brow from the effort of blocking such a powerful attack.

Not bad, old man, not bad. Zack smiled.

Hallibur's expression remained impassive, betraying none of the uncertainty he felt inside. This boy's strength exceeded what he had anticipated. He had assumed the outsider was only at the early stages of the Nascent Soul Realm.

Battle prowess at the Peak Nascent Soul Realm . . . Hallibur gritted his teeth. A young genius from the outside couldn't be spared.

He sent his shield spinning towards Zack in a deadly icy buzzsaw. At the same time, he drew his sword and launched himself forward, intending to catch Zack off guard between two attacks.

Instead of dodging, Zack's arms moved in a flurry, his sword becoming a silver streak, and he batted aside the icy projectile. Without missing a beat, he spun and met Hallibur's charge head-on.

Their blades collided in a flash of sparks. Zack's blow carried enough force to stop Hallibur's charge cold. The elder only narrowly twisted his sword aside before Zack could overpower him completely.

Gotta keep him off balance. Can't let him mount an effective counterattack.

Capitalizing on the momentary opening, Zack stepped forward and unleashed a devastating twelve-hit combo, his sword dancing through the air too fast to follow.

Hallibur's eyes widened. It was taking all his concentration just to track the angle of each strike, let alone attempt to block or evade them. He managed to parry the first few blows through pure instinct. But the onslaught was relentless.

Soon a gash opened on Hallibur's shoulder as a strike slipped through his guard. Then another slash landed across his thigh, which made him stumble. Hallibur realized he was being slowly whittled down by this assault.

Just a bit more should do it, Zack thought as he poured more power into his final strike. His plan had been to go fast and hard and not give his opponent the chance to counter.

Hallibur, sensing the killing blow coming, let out a roar and hastily activated his best defensive technique. Azure battle armor covered his body and a freezing aura erupted from within. Jagged spikes of ice jutted out from the armor at every joint.

Zack's sword strike clashed against the icy shell but failed to penetrate. At the same time, Hallibur's fist crashed into Zack's midsection and blasted him backwards.

Zack coughed, feeling as if he'd been hit by a battering ram. But aside from a few cracked ribs, his smoky armor still held.

Okay, that caught me off guard. Ice element armor technique. Very effective defense but looks like it drains him fast, judging by that labored breathing.

Hallibur stood firm, covered in a chilling aura. The brief break had allowed him to catch his second wind. They were back to square one.

Neither spoke as they circled each other warily. Zack kept his face an impassive mask, betraying none of his thoughts. But inside, his mind raced.

This is taking too long. I only have sixty seconds total of the Nascent Soul Armor before it disperses. Only twenty seconds left . . .

Zack's dark, smoky battle armor was a temporary boost at best, buying him time to finish the fight quickly. But Hallibur was proving more stubborn than expected.

I'll have to change strategies. Take him by surprise.

Decision made, Zack abruptly turned and shot into the sky, unfurling his wings again. Hallibur's eyes widened, then his face twisted into a savage grin.

"Fleeing won't save you now!"

The elder gave chase, propelling himself upwards in pursuit. He drew back his fist for an overhead punch intended to drive Zack straight back into the earth.

"Gotcha."

At the last second before impact, Zack's wings folded and he dropped in a blur of motion. Hallibur's fist swiped through empty space. Before he could react, Zack had slipped inside his guard and smashed an electrically charged palm straight into the elder's chest.

The blow crunched through the icy armor and jolted Hallibur violently. He let out an involuntary gasp as the air was blasted from his lungs. Zack gave him no chance to recover.

In a burst of shadow, he teleported behind Hallibur and delivered a vicious two-handed sword strike aimed at severing his spine. But the elder managed to twist just enough to avoid being sliced in half.

Now's my chance, while he's reeling!

Zack's free hand slipped into his robe and retrieved a small black seed. With a flick of his wrist, he sent it sailing towards Hallibur's back.

"What . . . is this . . ." Hallibur gasped out. Before he could react, the seed began rapidly swelling and split open to reveal a writhing mass of thorny black vines. In seconds, they had encased Hallibur's body in a tangled prison, leaving only his face exposed.

"A Genesis Vine—clever trick," Hallibur grunted, straining against the bindings. But the more he struggled, the tighter they constricted him.

Zack sighed in relief as the smoky armor finally dissipated, no longer able to maintain Peak Nascent Soul battle prowess.

The fight was over. He had won.

Despite being immobilized and at Zack's mercy, Hallibur's face remained expressionless. He gazed back at Zack silently as the youth walked closer.

"Did you really think I wouldn't see through such an obvious assassination attempt? After all that talk of duty and honor? Please," Zack said. Hallibur's eyebrow twitched but he held his tongue. "In any case, nothing personal"— Zack waved a hand—"but I'm afraid I can't let you live now that you know who I am."

At that, Hallibur finally spoke. "If you plan to kill me, outsider, my sect will scour these lands until they find and eliminate you." His voice held no fear, only absolute certainty in his words.

Zack shrugged, unimpressed by the threats.

"Yeah, that all sounds super scary. I'm absolutely quaking in my boots here," he drawled sarcastically. "Buuut . . . that's assuming you actually manage to escape and expose me. Which, no offense, Sensei, just isn't gonna happen. You just had to stick your nose into my business and then try ganking me when my back was turned. I was perfectly happy to walk away." Zack sighed. "But nope! You just couldn't leave me alone!" He threw his hands up dramatically. "And now, here we are. So, better start making your peace, Gramps."

Hallibur's breath grew ragged. For the first time in over five centuries, the elder actually felt an emotion he had nearly forgotten—raw terror. After analyzing their battle, Hallibur now understood he had been outmatched from the start against this mysterious cultivator's secret techniques and treasures.

Hallibur frantically reviewed his dwindling options before deciding to change tack. If force failed, then perhaps diplomacy and bribery might still spare his life . . .

"Spare me and whatever you want is yours!" the elder pledged desperately. "Sect treasures, spirit herbs, cultivation arts—name your price!"

Zack crossed his arms, looking more amused than tempted. The old man had too many faces to be trusted. He knew that as soon as he let him go free, he would send a hunting squad after him. With other Legacy Disciples to compete with, Zack didn't have the time to waste on these people.

"Nah, hard pass on the empty promises, buddy," he scoffed. "But there actually is something else you could provide that I'd find quite useful . . ."

Hallibur's blood ran cold. Whatever this outsider had planned, it could not be good.

Zack stepped closer and placed a hand on Hallibur's head almost gently. Hallibur flinched but could do nothing to stop him.

"Stay still, this won't take long," Zack murmured. Before Hallibur could respond, Zack activated the Soul Search technique.

Hallibur's body spasmed as he felt Zack's spiritual sense plunge into his soul and ruthlessly sift through his memories and experiences. He desperately tried to resist, to keep his mind intact, but against this brutal assault, his struggles were useless.

With an agonized scream, Hallibur's eyes rolled back, and his head slumped forward. Zack maintained the technique a moment longer before finally releasing him. His smile was gone now, his face once again an impassive mask.

"There, that wasn't so bad," he whispered, looking down at the corpse. "Sorry, but I don't plan on dying here." With a wave of his hand, he dismissed the vine bindings and moved the body into his storage ring.

What he had done was risky but worth it. He was glad that the Main Body had learned the Soul Search technique. Now that all of Hallibur's knowledge and secrets were his, including valuable insights into the Northern Region's politics and inner workings, he had all the information he needed to act as a native.

With this advantage, infiltrating the city would be child's play, but that girl would probably come searching for her master soon . . .

Even though she is kind of annoying, she doesn't deserve to die. Zack shook his head. He would need to find an alternative solution.

CHAPTER SEVEN

Deep within the halls of the Black Heart Sect, three grand elders gathered around a large obsidian table, their faces grim. Crimson tapestries bearing the sect's emblem, a bleeding heart pierced by a dagger, adorned the chamber walls.

The first was a bald man with a thick white beard that fell to his waist. His wrinkled face was creased in a permanent scowl, one milky white eye glaring while the other stared sightlessly at nothing. This was Elder Magnus, as bad-tempered as he was ancient. The centuries had done nothing to improve his sour disposition.

Across from him sat Elder Vesper, prim and proper as always. She wore an elegant burgundy robe, her iron-gray hair pulled back in a tight bun. Vesper had an air of noble refinement about her. Her posture was pin-straight and her hands were folded neatly in her lap as she looked at her fellow elders.

At the head of the table, looking utterly bored, slouched Elder Damien. He was absently picking at his jagged black nails with a dagger. Damien's youthful features seemed out of place when compared with the other elders, but the cold calculation in his coal-black eyes betrayed his centuries of experience.

"This is pointless," Magnus growled, breaking the tense silence. "We all know what must be done: gather our forces, march on the Black Rose pigs, and raze their precious sect to the ground!" He slammed his fist on the table.

Vesper arched an eyebrow. "And die in the attempt? Be reasonable, Magnus. Without the sect master, we don't have the strength to oppose them."

"Kaelius will return—he has to!" Magnus insisted. But the desperation in his voice betrayed his doubts. Their sect master had vanished without a trace weeks ago after visiting the Black Rose Sect. Foul play was suspected, but nothing could be proven.

"If he still lived, he would have returned by now," Vesper said gently. Magnus's face flushed with anger, but he held his tongue. Arguing with Vesper was pointless; she was far too pragmatic.

Damien idly inspected his dagger as he spoke. "While I admire your enthusiasm, Magnus, we must play the long game here. Open war would be . . . unwise."

Magnus spat on the floor. "You young folks. No backbone! In my day we would have slaughtered those Black Rose maggots by now."

Vesper exchanged a weary look with Damien. They had been enduring Magnus's bluster for centuries now. Once he had been a fearsome warrior, but time had withered his body, if not his temper.

"We face dark days ahead," Vesper said heavily. "Without Kaelius, the other sects will view us as weak. The vultures will soon circle, righteous and demonic alike."

Damien nodded. "We must present a united front. Squabbling with each other will only hasten our demise."

A heavy silence fell as the elders contemplated this grim possibility. The balance of power between the three main demonic sects had always been tenuous at best, but Sect Master Kaelius's strength had kept the other sects in check. Without him . . .

The Black Rose Sect had two Ascendants now, and one was even able to dominate others at the same cultivation realm; it was an unprecedented concentration of power for a demonic sect. And the situation with the righteous sects was no better. They would use any excuse to wipe out a demonic sect and seize their resources. Truly, it seemed the heavens themselves had turned against the Black Heart Sect.

Magnus grumbled under his breath but held his tongue for now. Without Kaelius, Damien and Vesper were in control. And open war with the Black Rose Sect was clearly suicidal.

"Then, what do you propose?" Magnus asked. "We cannot win a war on two fronts."

Before Damien could respond, there was a weak knock at the door. The elders exchanged glances as they sensed the aura of the pathetic worm on the other side.

"Enter," Damien called out lazily. He couldn't be bothered to remember the names of anyone below the Nascent Soul Realm.

A young disciple scurried in, his robes askew and chest heaving as if he'd run all the way here. He prostrated himself before the elders and stuttered out, "H-Honored Elders! A report from the perimeter!"

"Out with it, then!" Magnus's qi flared. "What could be so important you'd interrupt—"

"A massive ark approaches the sect!" the disciple blurted. "It flies with no banners but . . . but judging from its size and splendor, the scouts suspect it belongs to the Black Rose Sect!"

The temperature in the room plummeted as killing intent leaked from the three elders. The disciple trembled, sweat beading his brow at the terrifying pressure.

"Leave us," Vesper ordered, voice hard as diamond. The disciple couldn't scramble away fast enough, and the door slammed shut behind him.

Damien rose to his feet, the chair scraping against stone. "It seems our guests have arrived sooner than expected." His eyes met Magnus's and Vesper's in turn. Unspoken understanding passed between them.

Between one breath and the next, the three vanished in a swirl of shadow.

In the courtyards and halls of the Black Heart Sect, disciples went about their daily training and duties. Some sparred in groups, the clang of weapons and grunts of exertion filling the air. Others sat in quiet meditation, honing their demonic qi.

A group of young disciples, barely in their teens, huddled together whispering excitedly. They were supposed to be practicing their sword forms, but the absence of the elders made them bold.

"Did you hear? The sect master has been gone for weeks now!" one boy said, eyes wide.

"I heard he went to the Black Rose Sect for the Inter-Sect Tournament and never came back," another added. "You don't think . . . something happened to him, do you?"

"Don't be stupid, our sect master is an Ascendant! Those Black Rose dogs wouldn't dare touch him."

"But what if they did? I heard they have two Ascendants now. Two!"

The kids shuddered at the thought. Thanks to the intervention of the righteous sects, a demonic sect having more than one Ascendant was rare. It was said Ascendants could slaughter Origin Realm experts like cattle. What chance would their sect have against that?

Suddenly, a looming shadow fell over the courtyard. The disciples looked up, confused. Their sect was high in the mountains, untouched by clouds. So what . . . ?

Screams rang out as an enormous black ark came into view, blotting out the sun. It was massive, easily dwarfing their sect in size.

"W-what is that thing?"

"Are we under attack? Quick, sound the alarm!"

Panic spread like wildfire as disciples scattered in all directions. Some ran for weapons, others for cover. In the chaos, no one noticed three figures rise into the sky to meet the approaching ship—the grand elders.

From his place on the Ark, Slifer watched the pandemonium below with amusement. *I remember reading these kinds of scenes. I can't lie, it's not a bad feeling. I really should make trips like this more often.*

The three grand elders hovered high in the air above the Black Heart Sect.

Vesper gritted her teeth as she took in the Divine Azerion Ark rapidly approaching from the horizon, a behemoth that dwarfed the mountain peaks below. Only an expert at the Peak stage of the Ascendant Realm could possess such a treasure.

Damien followed her gaze, frowning. "It's as we suspected, then. The supreme elder of the Black Rose Sect graces us with his presence."

A muscle ticked in Magnus's jaw as he struggled to rein in his battle lust. The urge to draw his greatsword and charge the incoming ship was nearly over-whelming. Only the presence of his two fellow elders kept him in check . . . for now. Starting a fight with an Ascendant was suicidal.

But as the Ark grew larger, eclipsing the sun, a strange scene reached their eyes. What appeared to be a tiny black dot was circling the Ark, dipping and wheeling in wild loops.

Vesper squinted, hardly believing what she was seeing. "Is that . . . a baby dragon?" The creature was far too small to be a mature drake, but there was no mistaking the sinuous body and bat-like wings. It tumbled through the air in an oddly playful manner.

Damien noticed something else that gave him pause. There, standing at the bow of the ship, was a figure he recognized: the young disciple Leah. She was the daughter of Olakin, a former grand elder killed by Slifer himself.

She should be confined in the Black Rose Sect as a hostage. What in the world was she doing accompanying Slifer here? Had she betrayed the sect?

The elders exchanged uneasy glances as the Ark drew close enough to make out the figure at the helm. His orange robes wafted in the breeze, and his sharp eyes seemed to stare right through them even at this distance.

There was no mistaking it—the Black Rose Sect's supreme elder himself had come to the Black Heart Sect.

Magnus clenched his fists until his knuckles cracked. Vesper's face was perfectly blank, but Damien noticed a tightness around her eyes. And he himself felt perspiration dampen his palms despite the chill mountain air.

They were three of the Black Heart Sect's greatest experts, a hair's breadth from the Ascendant Realm. Yet the thought of facing the supreme elder was enough to intimidate them.

The Ark came to a stop and hovered over the sect's grand hall, while Val glided in merry circles around it. Leah stood at the prow, her eyes wide as she took in the dark majesty of her former home.

Never thought I'd be back here, she mused. As the daughter of a grand elder, she had been treated as a princess in the sect. However, with her father dead and no one to protect her, she was no longer able to return. *To think that the one who took everything away would be the one to bring me back.*

Speaking of her captor . . . Leah looked over to where Slifer lounged on a golden throne, one leg thrown over the armrest making him look every inch the honored supreme elder.

Only, Leah got to see the dopey grin he couldn't quite hold back as he watched Val's aerial stunts. The dragon was happily showing off for her audience of one.

It's hard to be properly intimidated by him when I know just how much his disciples mean to him, Leah thought wryly. Her younger self would have exploited that weakness of his, but the righteous lectures that the supreme elder delivered along with the time she spent with the baby dragon had changed her. And maybe for the good. *For all his fearsome reputation and overwhelming power, the great Slifer is not as heartless as one might think.*

With a grand gesture, Slifer levitated off his throne, then descended onto the ship's deck, robes swirling around him. Val swooped down to sit on his shoulder while Leah stepped up beside him.

The three grand elders remained hovering several hundred yards away, their postures tense. Slifer could practically smell their fear. He smirked. *Good, let them simmer a bit before I make my grand entrance.*

He raised an arm and Val launched herself off it with a joyful trill. She zipped close to the grand elders, mischief glinting in her big eyes.

"Boo!" She blew a tendril of azure fire towards Magnus and cackled when he flew back. "Aww, don't tell me Big Bad Cultivator is scared of little ol' me?" Val pouted, giving her best puppy-dog eyes.

"Val, quit tormenting the inmates and get back here," Slifer called, not bothering to hide his grin.

"You're no fun, Master." She stuck her forked tongue out at the fuming grand elder before gliding back to Slifer's shoulder. Leah pinched the bridge of her nose, already feeling a headache coming on.

Slifer turned to face the elders fully. "I believe we have matters to discuss. Should we go inside?" It wasn't a request.

Without waiting for a response, he stepped off the ship onto empty air. Violet qi gathered under his feet and formed a transparent platform. He walked towards the grand hall, forcing the elders to fall in line behind him or be left gawking.

Yes, Slifer thought smugly as he felt the elders' qi spike with alarm. Flying was something anyone above the Core Formation Realm could do, but manipulating qi to create platforms? They had never witnessed anything like it. Such an ability could only be performed by those on the brink of the Immortal Realm. *The thousand Karmic Credits to buy this treasure was so worth it.*

As Slifer landed in front of the grand double doors, they creaked open as if by an unseen hand. He stepped into the hall, eyes flicking from the decadent tapestries to the rows of blood-red pillars. He sniffed disdainfully.

"Your interior decorator needs to be fired. Ever heard of color theory? Pairing that particular shade of red with those black undertones is a crime against aesthetics."

Val nodded her head up and down. "You're right, Master. This place feels icky. They should make the walls orange like me so it's not so dark and scary."

Slifer hummed thoughtfully. "Good idea, my dear disciple. Perhaps some nice murals too. Really lighten the place up."

"Ooh, and some comfy armchairs in a cozy reading nook!"

"Of course, of course, every good dungeon needs an evil overlord's personal library."

Behind them, the three grand elders shared incredulous looks. Were the honored guests . . . criticizing their decor? In front of their faces? While disregarding them entirely?

It was so preposterously brazen that for a moment they could only gape in stunned offense, all thoughts of their missing sect master gone. Just who did these impudent fools think they were?

Finally, Magnus could take no more. "You dare—!" he roared, blotchy red creeping up his neck.

Slifer and Val turned to him slowly, blinking as if just recalling that the elders were still there. "Hmm? Did you say something?" Slifer asked lightly, head cocked. "Sorry, I was distracted with planning how I'm going to refurbish this dreary place once I take over."

"You—! You—!" Magnus spluttered, saliva flying from his lips as a vein throbbed in his temple. Vesper laid a warning hand on his arm, but he shook her off, too incensed to consider the consequences of provoking an Ascendant Realm expert.

He pointed a finger at Slifer, eyes blazing. "Unbridled arrogance! You walk in here uninvited, insult our hall, and talk so glibly of conquest? I should cut you down where you stand!"

A heavy pressure descended, as if a mountain had materialized above their heads. Magnus froze, the words dying in his throat as killing intent blasted him.

Slifer smiled pleasantly. "By all means, cut me down," he invited, spreading his arms. "I could use the exercise."

"Now, now, let's not be hasty," Damien cut in through gritted teeth. Sweat dripped down his back, and his knees felt like jelly under that suffocating qi. A qi that surpassed even their sect master's. "Supreme Elder, you say you have matters to discuss? Then let us go somewhere more private."

Slifer considered the elder, his gaze heavy and piercing. Just when it seemed the pressure would crush the man, Slifer released his aura with a chuckle. "I suppose I can spare you lot a few minutes of my valuable time." He flapped a hand at Magnus dismissively. "Lead the way, then, before I grow bored."

Damien bowed his head, not daring to show his relief. He turned and marched stiffly towards a side chamber, praying Magnus would have the sense to keep his mouth shut for once.

Vesper followed on his heels, her eyes never leaving Slifer's back, as if expecting him to strike at any moment. Magnus clenched his fists as he stomped after them, his face an alarming shade of purple.

Slifer meandered behind the elders with Val still draped across his shoulders. Leah walked beside them.

"Did you have to rile them up so much?" she murmured.

I would rather use up an Ascendant Aura Card worth five thousand Karmic Credits to intimidate them than get into a drawn-out battle and waste who knows how many credits. But it was not like he could tell Leah that.

"Of course! I have a reputation to uphold." Slifer chuckled. "An aloof and overweening attitude generates a special sort of dread, you know?"

"Well, your special sort of dread nearly got us skewered," Leah deadpanned. "You really are a master at the Dao of Pissing People Off."

"I prefer to think of it as the Dao of Establishing Dominance," Slifer sniffed. "Either way, it's a very potent cultivation method. You could stand to learn it."

"What, so I can be killed that much faster? I think I'll pass."

Their whispered exchange cut off as they entered a smaller chamber hung with more tastefully macabre paintings. A black jade table surrounded by chairs that looked like they were made from human bones took up the center of the room.

Slifer eyed the chairs dubiously before shrugging and plopping himself down at the head of the table, lounging as if he were presiding over his own throne room instead of the heart of a hostile sect.

Val coiled in his lap, yawning to show off a mouthful of needle-sharp teeth. She had insisted that she be in her larger form for the meeting, but Slifer didn't think a Nascent Soul dragon would have any effect on an Origin Realm expert, no matter how scary she may seem.

The grand elders took their seats, Vesper and Damien flanking Magnus in a transparent attempt to keep him in check.

Leah stood behind Slifer knowing that it would be rude of her to sit in the presence of the elders.

Slifer crossed his arms and gave the elders a smile that was all teeth. "Now then, let's *chat* about your missing sect master and what that means for your sect, shall we? I'm *very* curious to hear what you have to say on the matter."

The elders held their postures high, refusing to be cowed. But a thread of unease coiled in their guts as those sharp eyes pinned them in place. It was going to be a tense conversation.

CHAPTER EIGHT

The three grand elders of the Black Heart Sect sat across from Slifer. An uncomfortable silence stretched between them; the only sound was Val's tail swishing in the air.

"So," Slifer drawled, breaking the silence. "Your sect master has gone missing, and you suspect my sect had something to do with it. Is that about the gist of it?"

Elder Damien cleared his throat. "With all due respect, Supreme Elder, the timing of Sect Master Kaelius's disappearance is . . . suspicious. He vanished immediately after visiting your sect for the Inter-Sect Tournament."

"And he has not been seen or heard from since," Vesper added, her tone carefully neutral. "Even for a reclusive cultivator of his level, such an extended absence is concerning."

"It's not concerning, it's downright unacceptable!" Magnus slammed a fist on the table. "Our sect master would never abandon his duties like this. The Black Rose Sect must have done something to him!"

Slifer raised an eyebrow. "Those are bold accusations to throw around, Elder Magnus. I don't suppose you have any actual evidence to back them up?"

Magnus flushed an ugly purple. "We don't need evidence! It's obvious—"

"What Elder Magnus means," Damien cut in smoothly, shooting the other man a look, "is that the circumstances are highly suspect. And with our sect master gone, we find ourselves in a precarious position."

"A precarious position?" Slifer feigned ignorance, blinking innocently.

Vesper sighed. "Come now, Supreme Elder. Surely you're not so naive. With no Ascendant to defend us, the righteous sects will see us as easy prey. They smell blood in the water. They've been looking for an excuse to wipe us out for centuries. Without Sect Master Kaelius here, they may just try it."

"They're no better than a pack of hyenas," Magnus spat. "Circling, waiting for us to show weakness before they pounce."

"Can you blame them?" Vesper asked tiredly. "Demonic sects aren't exactly known for playing nice with others. We've all got blood on our hands."

Val perked up. "Blood? Where?" She looked around eagerly.

Slifer patted her head. "Figure of speech, my dear disciple."

Though, knowing demonic sects, it could be literal too . . .

"And it's not just the righteous sects we have to worry about," Vesper continued. "The Black Death Sect has also been eyeing our territory. With their Half-Step Immortal leader sealed by you, Supreme Elder, they are also vulnerable. But that . . . only makes them more desperate and dangerous."

Slifer stroked his chin, humming thoughtfully. "It seems you lot are stuck between a rock and a hard place. Enemies on all sides, both righteous and demonic. And with no Ascendant to protect you . . . Well, it's not looking good for the Black Heart Sect, is it?"

Magnus bristled. "We are not so weak as that! We still have three Origin Realm elders—"

"Who will be slaughtered like pigs the moment an Ascendant enters the fray," Slifer said bluntly. "Face it, without your sect master, you're sitting ducks. Lambs to the slaughter."

"What do you propose, then, Supreme Elder?" Damien asked, his eyes narrowed.

"Yeah, what's your angle?" Magnus demanded. "You didn't come all this way just to gloat, so spit it out already!"

"Magnus! Mind your tongue!" Vesper hissed. But her own eyes were wary as they darted between Slifer and the fuming elder. She didn't know how long she could hold Magnus back; that fool seemed adamant about getting them killed.

"Master isn't gloating," Val yawned, sounding bored. "He is saying the truth. You bad men are in big trouble, and you know it."

"What does a baby lizard know—" Magnus started hotly, but he choked on his words as Slifer flared his aura.

The temperature plummeted and the elders' breath misted before their faces. Damien and Vesper froze, not daring to move a muscle.

"Careful," Slifer said softly. "That's my disciple you're insulting. And I don't take kindly to rudeness towards what's mine."

Magus shrank back, all the fight draining out of him. He ducked his head and mumbled an apology.

Slifer let him stew for a moment longer before reining in his aura. The elders released a collective breath, their shoulders slumping.

Damien was the first to recover. He looked at Slifer intently. "You have a proposal for us," he stated. It wasn't a question.

Slifer's lips curved. "I do." He leaned forward. "The way I see it, you have two options. Option one: continue as you are and pray to whatever twisted gods you worship that the righteous sects and your demonic rivals will take pity on you. Spoiler alert: they won't."

The elders exchanged grim looks but didn't interrupt.

"Option two . . ." Slifer paused for effect, his smile widening. "Ally with a power strong enough to keep your enemies at bay. A power so overwhelming, none would dare challenge you."

Magnus frowned. "You mean the Black Rose Sect." His voice dripped with disdain.

"No." Slifer's eyes gleamed. "I mean me."

It was silent as the elders stared at him blankly.

Then Magnus broke out in a laugh. "You? What's the difference? You're the supreme elder of the Black Rose Sect. Allying with you is the same as allying with them!"

Slifer tsked. "I don't mean an alliance. I mean"—he spread his hands—"handing over control of your sect to me. Making me your new sect master."

Magnus shot to his feet spluttering incoherently. Vesper and Damien looked poleaxed.

"You can't be serious!" Magnus roared, his face turning an alarming shade of purple. "We would never submit to an outsider! The Black Heart Sect bows to no one!"

"Sit down, Magnus," Damien said tightly. He waited until the apoplectic elder had thrown himself back into his seat before turning to Slifer. "What you propose is . . . unprecedented. No sect has ever had an outsider as sect master."

"There's a first time for everything," Slifer said cheerfully. "Think about it. With me as your sect master, no one would dare touch you. The Heavenly Light Sect, Pure Soul Sect, White Tiger Sect . . . they'd all have to back off. Same goes for the Black Death Sect or any other demonic upstarts."

"And what of your current position in the Black Rose Sect?" Damien frowned. "Surely you don't intend to abandon them . . ."

Slifer waved a hand. "Of course not. I'll simply have to split my time between the two sects. With the elders handling day-to-day affairs, it shouldn't be an issue."

Vesper pursed her lips. "That still sounds suspiciously like the Black Heart Sect being annexed by the Black Rose Sect."

"Not at all!" Slifer said. "The two sects will remain separate entities. I'll just happen to be in charge of both. Really, it's the best of both worlds. You get my protection and guidance while maintaining your autonomy . . . mostly."

Damien rubbed his chin. "It's an . . . intriguing proposition," he allowed. "But the details—"

"Intriguing?!" Magnus exploded. "It's insanity! Handing over our sect to this—this—" He jabbed a finger at Slifer, apparently too enraged to come up with a proper insult.

Slifer inspected his nails, unfazed by the outburst. "You're welcome to refuse my generous offer," he said mildly. "Of course, that means you'll be left to fend for yourselves against the circling wolves. I'm sure that will end well for you—especially since there's already one in your den."

Magnus opened his mouth, then closed it, teeth grinding audibly.

"I think Master's idea is great! You guys clearly need all the help you can get," Val chirped. "Think of all the fun joint events the sects could hold! Talent competitions, night hunts, demonic beast races . . ." Her eyes sparkled.

Leah, who had been standing silently behind Slifer, struggled to keep a straight face. Imagining the bloodthirsty Black Heart Sect disciples participating in peppy inter-sect activities was too absurd.

Damien held up a hand before Magnus could have another outburst. "Supreme Elder Slifer. You have given us much to consider. Can we have some time to discuss this amongst ourselves?"

Slifer shrugged. "By all means. Take all the time you need." He flashed a toothy grin. "Just don't take too long. My patience, like my mercy, has limits." With that ominous statement hanging in the air, he rose to his feet. Val scampered up to perch on his shoulder. "Oh, and one more thing," Slifer said, pausing in the doorway. "Do try to keep this little chat between us, hmm? I'd hate for word to get out prematurely. It could make things . . . messy."

The unspoken threat was clear. The elders paled but nodded stiffly.

"Wonderful!" Slifer clapped his hands together. "I look forward to hearing your decision." He walked out, Leah trailing behind him.

The moment the door closed, Magnus whirled on his fellow elders. "Don't tell me you're actually considering this madness?"

Damien pinched the bridge of his nose. "What choice do we have, Magnus? You heard him. Without an Ascendant's backing, we're as good as dead."

Vesper's lips thinned. "I don't like it, but I fear Damien is right. At least this way we retain some measure of control. The alternative is to be carved up like a roast duck by our enemies."

Magnus ground his teeth but couldn't argue against their logic. As much as it burned him, Slifer's offer was looking more and more like their only viable option.

As Slifer walked through the corridors of the Black Heart Sect, a blue box appeared before him.

> *Ding!*
> New Mission: Acquire the Black Heart Sect by becoming their new sect master.
> Rewards: 10,000 Karmic Credits, Unlocking of Sect Management Interface

A bit late to give this as a mission . . . Slifer's breath caught when he saw the reward. *Ten thousand credits? That is an incredibly generous bounty. And the Sect Management Interface sounds intriguing . . .*

As if sensing his thoughts, the System continued:

> The Sect Management Interface will allow you to oversee and adjust various aspects of the sects under your control, including, but not limited to, Disciple Recruitment and Training, Resource Allocation, Laws and Punishment, Karmic Affinities, and more!
> With the Black Heart Sect under your banner, you will be in a position to begin mass conversion of the demonic cultivators.

I expected as much. Converting the demonic sect into a righteous sect would be far more efficient than trying to strong-arm one stubborn disciple at a time.

He had already done all he could. Now he just needed to wait for the grand elders to cave to the inevitable.

Val flew in excited loops around his head. "I can't wait to whip those Black Heart meanies into shape!" she chirped. "Ooh, I'm gonna make them do so many trust falls and group hugs, they won't know what hit them!"

Slifer chuckled and reached up to scratch under her chin. "That's my girl. Just make sure to leave them some dignity. We want allies, not broken shells."

"No promises!" Val said cheerfully.

Leah, who had been quietly observing, murmured, "You realize the disciples will resent you at first, right? Demonic cultivators are a prideful lot. They won't take kindly to an outsider coming in and upending their way of life."

Slifer shrugged. "They'll get over it. Or they won't, and I'll make an example of the troublemakers. Either way, they'll fall in line."

Leah suppressed a shiver, reminded once again that for all his irreverent quirks, Slifer was not a man to be trifled with.

The next hour passed in a blur. The grand elders secluded themselves, no doubt arguing in circles about Slifer's "offer."

Slifer himself spent the time exploring the sect grounds with Val and Leah and noticing the areas that could use improvement. *A training field expansion here, a meditation grotto renovation there . . . Being a sect master is going to mean a lot of infrastructure management, isn't it?* Slifer mused wryly. *Oh well, at least I can delegate most of the grunt work . . .*

Soon enough, a disciple ran up to summon them back to the meeting chamber. Slifer walked in to find the grand elders awaiting him, their faces dark but resigned.

"Supreme Elder Slifer," Damien began. "After much deliberation, we have decided to accept your proposal."

Magnus looked like he'd swallowed a lemon, but he held his tongue.

Vesper continued, "We will acknowledge you as the Black Heart Sect's new sect master."

"Ha ha, you made the right choice. The Black Heart Sect is now under my wing. I'll defend it—and its members—as my own."

"Thank you . . . Sect Master." Damien stood and bowed deeply, and the other elders followed suit.

I . . . I could get used to this. Slifer held back a smirk. Outwardly, he inclined his head magnanimously.

Ding!

Mission Complete

You have gained 10,000 Karmic Credits. The Sect Management Interface is now unlocked.

Congratulations!

You have taken your first step towards unifying the demonic sects under the banner of righteousness.

Yeah . . . that's exactly *why I did it.*

CHAPTER NINE

Slifer lounged on the plush cushions of his new throne, a smirk playing across his lips. The sect master's chambers were every bit as rich as he had hoped—obsidian walls inlaid with precious gems, flowing silk tapestries, and, of course, a throne that could make an emperor jealous.

Sure, the decor was a bit macabre for his tastes, with all the bleeding hearts and impaled skulls, but hey, when in a demonic sect, do as the demons do, right?

A chime interrupted his musings. Slifer sat up straighter as a glowing panel materialized before him.

Sect Management Interface: Black Heart Sect
Disciples:
Outer Disciples: 567
Inner Disciples: 152
Core Disciples: 42
Legacy Disciples: 5
Elders: 10
Grand Elders: 3
Resources:
Spirit Stones: 1,348,204
Artifacts: 217
Medicinal Herbs: 8,394

Alchemy Materials: 3,562
Reputation:
Infamy: 7,893
Karmic Affinity: -5,621

Slifer whistled, impressed despite himself. The Black Heart Sect was no lightweight: these assets were nothing to scoff at. However, that Karmic Affinity . . . yikes. He had his work cut out for him turning these demonic cultivators to the light.

Ding!

A new notification popped up.

As sect master, your disciples' actions reflect upon you. For every evil deed committed, you will lose 1 Karmic Credit. Guide them well.

Slifer grimaced but nodded. It was a fair trade-off considering the credits he stood to gain by setting these wayward souls on the righteous path. Still, reforming an entire demonic sect was easier said than done.

He had cowed the Black Rose Sect's Disciplinary Hall through sheer power and intimidation. But they were already half-tamed compared to these Black Heart lunatics with their depraved rituals and cutthroat politicking.

Think, Slifer, think! He rapped his knuckles against his forehead. *How do I turn a pack of rabid wolves into fluffy lambs?*

Ding!
In light of the Black Heart Sect's . . . proclivities, you will be granted a one-month grace period before penalties for disciples' misdeeds take effect. However, Karmic Credits earned from righteous acts will be halved during this time. Make it count!

"Well, how generous of you," Slifer drawled. But he breathed a little easier. A month wasn't much, but it was a start.

Slifer glanced over to see Leah staring, no doubt puzzled by his reactions to seemingly thin air.

"Ah, Leah! Just the person I wanted to see." He clapped his hands together. "I need you to send a message to the Black Rose Sect. Tell Morvran to get his stern, rule-abiding backside over here, pronto."

Leah's brows shot up. "You want Morvran . . . here? At the Black Heart Sect?"

"I need his help whipping these delinquents into shape. It'll be like the Disciplinary Hall but supersized!"

Leah looked dubious but she bowed. "As you command, Sect Master. I'll go to the messaging chamber now."

Ah yes, the messaging chamber. A staple of every self-respecting sect. Using formations and runes, qi-infused messages could be sent vast distances nearly instantaneously. Highly convenient for coordinating between sects . . . or in Slifer's case, summoning his favorite enforcer.

With Morvran's iron fist and my dazzling charisma, we'll have these Black Heart hooligans toeing the line in no time! Slifer's eyes gleamed as he envisioned the impending disciple wrangling. Oh, the Karmic Credits he would reap!

Ding!
New Mission: Mentor the unrighteous.
Lead misguided disciples onto the path of virtue. The more sect members you reform, the greater your reward.
Rewards:
Outer Disciples: 50 Karmic Credits per disciple
Inner Disciples: 100 Karmic Credits per disciple
Core Disciples: 300 Karmic Credits per disciple
Legacy Disciples: 500 Karmic Credits per disciple
Elders: 1000 Karmic Credits per elder
Grand Elders: 2,000 Karmic Credits per grand elder

Slifer rubbed his hands together, a wicked grin stretching his face. While these disciples wouldn't be his personal students, not in the System's "hallowed" opinion, anyways, he could still rack up some sweet, sweet Karmic Credit guiding these lost lambs.

A twinge of unease crept through his mirth. He had subjugated the grand elders sure enough, but what about the rank-and-file disciples? Were there any hidden thorns among the roses? Potential rivals or, heaven forbid, protagonists?

Bah, I'm just being paranoid! Slifer shook off the thought. *What kind of xianxia protagonist gets his sect stolen by a quirky old man? Ha ha . . . ha. Oh heavens, I hope I didn't just flag death.*

A hesitant knock at the door blessedly interrupted his spiraling thoughts.

"Enter," Slifer said as he straightened his robes and schooled his features into a stern mask. Image was everything!

Damien shuffled in, bowing deeply at the waist. "Sect Master, the disciples have been gathered as you ordered. We await your address in the grand courtyard."

Showtime. Slifer rose to his feet, squaring his shoulders. "Very good. You're dismissed, Damien. I'll be along shortly."

The elder backpedaled out, his head still lowered. Once alone, Slifer checked his reflection in the wall-mounted spirit beast's fangs—*I, talk about gauche decor*—and fussed with his hair and robes.

The trick is to look imposing yet genial. Strict but benevolent. A real "kneel before me, but feel free to grab a snack after" sort of vibe.

Satisfied he looked appropriately imposing, Slifer strode out, a maniacal glint in his eyes. Time to bring the circus to these unwashed masses!

Elarkin shifted uncomfortably in the grand courtyard of the Black Heart Sect trying to see over the sea of dark robes and hear over the muttered curses of his fellow disciples. Just his luck to be a bit on the short side in a sect full of beefcakes.

The low buzz of hundreds of whispered conversations swelled around him, and Elarkin found himself straining to pick up tidbits here and there.

"I'm telling you, it's gotta be some kind of declaration of war," one burly disciple grunted.

His companion shook his head. "Use your brain, dimwit. Why would the supreme elder of the Black Rose Sect come alone if he wanted to start a fight?"

"Well, excuse *me* for not being a tactical genius, oh wise one," the first snapped back. "You come up with a better reason, then."

The other disciple hesitated. "Maybe . . . maybe it's about what happened to Sect Master Kaelius?"

A tense hush fell over their little group. The disappearance of their sect master was the demonic elephant in the room that no one wanted to acknowledge.

Rather than get drawn into that potential quagmire, Elarkin let his attention drift, his mind churning over his own predicament.

It had been a little over a year since he had come to the Black Heart Sect, a scrawny refugee from a poor mountain village that had been razed by rogue cultivators in one of their petty squabbles. He still remembered the acrid scent of smoke and blood and the way his mother had shoved him into a hidden cellar moments before their home collapsed in flames around her . . .

No. He couldn't think about that now. The past was dead and gone. All that mattered was clawing his way to power so that he'd never be weak and helpless again. And the Black Heart Sect had seemed like the perfect ruthless crucible to forge himself into the ultimate cultivator.

Oh, he'd been so naive back then. Eating up all the honeyed words the recruiters spouted about how "might makes right" and the glory of the demonic path, how "the strong feast on the flesh of the weak."

That youthful idealism quickly curled up and died during his first month as an outer disciple. Nothing but drudge work and vicious hazing from dawn to dusk, scrabbling for the dregs of cultivation resources like a pack of starving dogs.

And when Elarkin finally saw his chance to rise to inner disciple, to escape the constant grind of petty chores and brutal beatings, he had grabbed it with both hands . . . only to choke on the bitter ashes of betrayal.

Apparently his "friend" Jagim didn't share Elarkin's touching notions of loyalty and was perfectly happy to stab his bunkmate in the back—metaphorically and literally—to secure that one spot of promotion.

Elarkin absentmindedly rubbed the ragged scar along his ribs, jaw clenching at the phantom pain. Yet another reminder seared into his flesh of this cruel world he'd dedicated himself to.

Which brought him to his current dilemma as he lurked in the grand courtyard waiting for the mysterious supreme elder to unveil his purpose here. Should he cut his losses and run while everyone was confused? Try to book it to another demonic sect before this whole ship sank?

No . . . no, that would be the coward's way out. He was done being the heavens' punching bag. One way or another, Elarkin swore he would climb to the peak of power on the demonic path, even if he had to stain his hands red with the blood of so-called "allies."

So, Elarkin held his tongue and faded into the background like he always did, cold eyes assessing and calculating behind a mask of perfect blankness, just another faceless drone in a sea of black robes. Waiting, watching, biding his time until opportunity smiled upon him once more.

A sudden hush rippled through the crowd and Elarkin turned his head as the huge obsidian doors of the main hall were blown open.

He watched the three grand elders walk out and line up like an honor guard for . . .

His eyes widened fractionally as they landed on the fourth figure, the one who could only be the infamous supreme elder.

Unlike most of the other disciples, Elarkin had been training when the supreme elder arrived, so he had missed the commotion. This was his first time setting eyes on the number one cultivator of the Black Rose Sect.

The old man moved with an otherworldly grace, his feet not quite touching the ground. He had a smirk playing about his lips as if he found the entire

room vastly entertaining. And was that . . . Was that a tiny dragon perched on
his shoulder?

What in the nine hells . . .

The supreme elder came to a stop, hands clasped before him in a decep-
tively casual stance. And then it hit Elarkin like a spirit beast's backhand: the
pure, blinding aura rolling off the man, heavy as a physical weight, pressing
down on every disciple in the hall.

So, this is the might of an Ascendant cultivator . . . Elarkin thought, bones
aching under the invisible pressure. It was all he could do not to keel over like
some of the weaker disciples.

The grand elders stood stiffly to either side of their guest, faces pale. Even
the normally blustering Elder Magnus had been reduced to little more than a
quivering mass of mangy beard and shaky knees.

But all that was secondary to the bomb that the supreme elder was about
to drop on their heads.

"I will keep this brief as I'm sure you're all eager to get back to . . . whatever
it is you people do around here," the man said with a careless wave of his hand.
"I am the supreme elder of the Black Rose Sect, Slifer." His smirk widened as
he paused to let them stew in anticipation. "And, as of today . . . your new
sect master."

Elarkin nearly choked on his own tongue. *Wait, what did he just say?*

The rest of the disciples apparently shared his shock, as the grand courtyard erupted into a roar of startled exclamations and heated conversations.

"Is this a joke?"

"The supreme elder is our new sect master?"

"What about Sect Master Kaelius? What happened to him?!"

"This must be a trick! The Black Rose Sect is trying to swallow us whole!"

"We've been conquered? I knew it!"

The clamor rose to a deafening pitch, the mob seconds away from explod-
ing into violence—like that would actually change anything. The supreme
elder just stood there unruffled amidst the growing storm, that smirk still on
his face.

Through it all, Elarkin remained frozen, his mind whirling. This was . . .
unprecedented. A hostile sect takeover without bloodshed? What could have
brought the proud grand elders to surrender so abjectly? Especially someone
like Grand Elder Magnus?

Something's not right, his instincts screamed. *No one man should wield such
influence, not without a trump card so devastating it's not even worth fighting.*

But what manner of hellish trump card could—

His spiraling thoughts came to a standstill as a nova of qi exploded through the courtyard. Elarkin's knees buckled and he hit the floor, gasping like a landed fish.

All around him, disciples crumpled like rag dolls, pinned under the titanic spiritual pressure. Even the grand elders staggered, barely keeping their feet.

Cold sweat slicked Elarkin's face as he struggled to raise his head a fraction, fighting the force bearing down on him. His eyes widened, limbs trembling with animalistic terror.

A colossal projection loomed over the hall: a blood-red titan in Slifer's image. Blazing qi roared off it like solar flares threatening to incinerate Elarkin's mind.

An Ascendant avatar, Elarkin realized with numb horror. Only Immortal Realm experts could project such manifestations of their might. This old man was an *Immortal*.

The thought rattled around his skull as darkness crept into the edges of his vision. Some distant part of him snorted derisively at how easily he'd dismissed the danger of the situation.

No one could stand against an expert of this level, not the grand elders, not the disciples, not even the late sect master. The Black Heart Sect was well and truly conquered.

As his consciousness guttered out, one final thought drifted through Elarkin's mind.

Well . . . so much for slipping away quietly, eh?

Then he blacked out.

CHAPTER TEN

Slifer sat cross-legged in the center of the vast courtyard with nearly a thousand Black Heart Sect disciples fanned out before him in neat rows. A handful of Nascent Soul elders had also joined, but the grand elders were absent.

He shook his head wryly as he remembered their faces when he first subjugated the sect. That little stunt with the Susanoo-like avatar, courtesy of a pricey Immortal Avatar Aura Card, sure did the trick.

The despair in their eyes as they realized an "Immortal" had them by the spiritual bits . . . Ah, priceless. Worth every one of those ten thousand Karmic Credits.

Had he merely shown Ascendant-level strength, they would have still been hoping that their missing sect master, Kaelius, might return to save them. Now, they knew they were well and truly conquered.

Speaking of grand elders . . . Slifer's eyes narrowed as he considered Damien. *What a sneaky fellow, hiding his Half-Step Ascendant cultivation. The others actually bought his "Peak Origin Realm" act. Guy definitely has plots brewing behind that pretty face of his.*

Well, no matter. Slifer had him cowed for now with the Immortal ploy. If Damien still wanted to tango after that display, then he was a few spirit stones short of a core.

As he surveyed the sea of expectant faces, Slifer let his mind wander. He'd been putting on the wise Immortal act for a while now, dispensing cryptic wisdom and stern rebukes in equal measure. But honestly? It was starting to wear thin.

All this flowery language and profound-sounding nonsense . . . It just wasn't him. Slifer was a straightforward guy, always had been. This xianxia elder shtick was as ill fitting as a hairshirt.

But then again, who was going to call him out on it? He was an "Immortal" now, with the Karmic Credits to back it up. If he wanted to drop the stern sect master façade and be more of his true self, who could stop him?

Immortals were known for being eccentric, after all. A little quirk here, a spot of irreverence there . . . It would only add to his mystique. If anything, it would be more suspicious if he didn't change up his act.

Yeah, that's the ticket! Slifer thought with a grin. *Time to let me be me, not some cookie-cutter xianxia NPC.*

Slifer's attention snapped back to the present as a disciple stepped forward, bowing low. The young man launched into an account of his recent breakthrough to Core Formation, his voice gradually gaining confidence as he went.

". . . and as I circulated my qi through the sixty-fourth meridian, I felt a buildup of pressure in my dantian. It was as if a great serpent was coiling tighter and tighter, ready to strike! I knew I had to redirect the flow before . . ."

Slifer nodded along, only half listening as he mentally dissected the disciple's experience. More details to add to his growing repository of knowledge. Zack's insights alone weren't enough to prepare for his own impending tribulation, not with the ungodly lightning that was sure to rain down on his head courtesy of being a transmigrator. His own tribulation would likely give these kiddos a heart attack.

Assembling these disciples for story time was a stroke of genius, if I do say so myself.

He glanced to the side where Morvran stood with his arms folded. The Disciplinary Hall master had arrived two days ago, and already the disciples were scurrying about like whipped puppies. Slifer almost felt bad for them. Almost.

Better a few bruises now than losing Karmic Credits for their stupidity later, he reasoned. Maintaining his public Immortal façade was significantly easier than micromanaging the little monsters. He'd leave the tedious bits to Morvran.

The disciple finished his story and Slifer turned expectantly to the elders. There was an awkward pause before a man who looked to be in his forties, but was probably centuries old, coughed and stood up.

"This unworthy one broke through to Core Formation some three centuries ago, back when he was a mere wandering cultivator," the elder began, his reedy voice filling the courtyard. "I secluded myself in the Reaving Demon Caves, and on the thirty-seventh day of my meditation . . ."

Slifer settled in as he listened with half an ear, making appropriately sage noises at intervals. The Nascent Soul elder's experience was more polished than the disciple's novice fumbling, but no less valuable for his purposes.

When the elder finished, the others chimed in one by one, and a chorus of droning voices recounted, step by step, their breakthroughs from long ago. Slifer took it all in, assembling the puzzle pieces in his mind's eye.

After some time, Slifer blinked and suddenly realized that days had passed. *Stupid cultivator time dilation.* Now he got why xianxia novels could spend a dozen chapters on these enlightenment infodumps.

He glanced over the sea of glazed eyes and slack jaws and noted that the Core Formation disciples and above seemed mostly cognizant while those at Foundation Establishment and below looked ready to keel over.

Right, time to throw 'em a bone.

Slifer clapped his hands, jolting the crowd to attention. He smiled at their startled faces.

"I think that's enough of the appetizers," he announced. "How about we get to the main course, hmm? This old man will share his own insights on Core Formation, accumulated over countless years. Get your jade slips ready!"

The disciples scrambled for their writing tools, their exhaustion vanishing. Even the drowsiest outer disciples perked up, eyes gleaming. Slifer preened a bit at their awed expressions. How often did an Immortal drop cultivation gems?

In the back row, Elarkin leaned forward intently. This was just the break he needed. Sure, the lecture was a few realms above his Peak Qi Refining stage, but surely he could glean some wisdom to drive his own advancement, right?

Slifer launched into his carefully prepared speech, rattling off nuggets he'd pilfered from Heaven Rank manuals in the System Shop. The teaser text alone gave him plenty of ammunition.

"Now, during Foundation Establishment, you need to construct pillars of qi. Well, more isn't always merrier! Nine is the perfect number for optimal stability."

A disciple piped up. "This humble one understands fewer pillars means weaker foundations, so surely more can only strengthen the base?"

"Common misconception!" Slifer waggled a finger. "Too many and your cultivation will be about as stable as a one-legged chicken. Sure, you'll have qi for days, but you'll waste more energy than a leaky spirit stone. Bigger isn't better if you can't use it right."

Several disciples made faces like Slifer had insulted their ancestors. Clearly, size was a touchy subject for these macho demonic types. Slifer cheerfully soldiered on.

"Now, when it comes time to condense your core, location is key. You want to seek out a place counter to your cultivation path. A fire cultivator, for example, would go frolic in the ocean."

One skeptical voice called out, "I've always heard it's best to hunker down in places aligned with your element for breakthroughs. That's why we've got all those shiny elemental caves, right?"

Slifer nodded sagely. "Ah, but that's just begging your qi to run amok! Foreign surroundings will keep your energy on a tighter leash as it coalesces. Toss a fish in a volcano and it'll have to adapt or burn. Same principle."

Shocked exclamations echoed around the courtyard. Several Nascent Soul elders looked befuddled as they had flashbacks of their own breakthroughs. Clearly, this clashed with conventional wisdom, but from their knitted brows, it seemed to align with their experiences.

Slifer held up a hand. "Now, let's delve into the nitty-gritty of Core Formation itself. Not all cores are created equal!" He began to pace, hands clasped behind his back in a lecturing pose. "At the bottom of the barrel, you have your mixed cores. Ugly little things, all a mishmash of impurities and conflicting elements. Might as well be cultivating with mud for all the good they'll do you."

The disciples leaned forward hanging on his every word. Slifer smirked.

"A step up from that sorry lot are the mid-grade cores. You can tell them by their color—green, purple, red, what have you. Decent enough if you don't mind being stuck in the kiddie pool of potential." He paused to let the anticipation build. "But if you want to swim with the big boys? You'll need to set your sights on the cream of the crop, the ultimate prize . . . the Golden Core!"

Gasps rippled through the audience, their eyes wide with awe. Slifer nodded sagely.

"Mm-hmm, that's right. The shinier and sturdier the core is, the more qi you can pack in there. A Golden Core expert would wipe the floor with any other Core Formation cultivator, no contest."

A disciple shot to his feet, unable to contain his excitement. "Sect Master, what about the mythical cores of legend? The Frozen Core, the Crimson Core, the Core of Chaos? This humble one has heard tales of their world-shaking might!"

Oh heavens, the plot-device cores. Slifer froze, his smile going rigid. He hadn't gotten round to checking if the System mentioned anything about them. *Quick, deflect!*

He cleared his throat and put on a stern expression. "Now, now, let's not get ahead of ourselves. Those exotics are the stuff of rumor and hearsay. Worry about the core in front of you, not the pipe dreams of madmen."

"Of course, Sect Master," the disciple said, wilting. "This one . . . spoke out of turn."

Crisis averted. Slifer breathed an inwards sigh of relief. The last thing he needed was some upstart elder calling him out on his ignorance. Immortal Aura could only bluff so far.

"As I was saying," he continued smoothly, "the path to a Golden Core requires an impeccable foundation and a top-notch cultivation method. Skimp on either and you'll be stuck in the chromatic dregs with the rest of the chumps." He leveled a piercing stare at the disciples and was gratified to see them shrink back. "So, unless you want to be the laughingstock of the Core Formation Realm, you'd best put your nose to the grindstone and cultivate like your life depends on it. Because—mark my words—it does."

The disciples hastily bowed, cowed by the weight of his gaze. "Yes, Sect Master!"

Slifer nodded, satisfied he'd put the fear of the Heavenly Dao in them. And the fear of Slifer, of course. Always good to hammer home who was top dog around here.

"Lastly, the most vital piece: Heavenly Tribulation. Contrary to what many believe, the lightning is not a punishment but a test. A chance for the worthy to refine their Dao. The stronger the tribulation, the greater the reward."

Slifer outlined the five grades of tribulation. The first three grades were well known, but by the time he had introduced the fourth grade, his audience was hanging on his every word. And when he moved onto the mysterious Grade 5 Celestial Prism, their jaws were practically on the floor.

"Sect Master!" a voice called. Slifer glanced over to see the only disciple he had identified with stats that could compete with his own disciples trembling with excitement—Elarkin. "Have you experienced the legendary Grade 5 tribulation?"

All eyes snapped to Slifer. He smiled enigmatically, neither confirming nor denying it. Let them stew on that little tidbit. It would only feed his growing legend.

I barely survived the Grade 4 Foundation Establishment tribulation, and that's only because I had some OP cards! Slifer mentally scoffed. Grade 5 tribulation at the Core Formation Realm or higher would vaporize him in an instant, critical block cards be damned.

Still, judging by the speculative whispers, they had bought his implied feats hook, line, and sinker. *Disciples are so easily impressed. Throw around some mystique and they'll write the tall tales for you,* Slifer thought smugly.

Just then, a series of System alerts popped up in his periphery.

Ding!
You have enlightened 350 Outer Disciples.
Reward: 17,500 Karmic Credits
Ding!
You have enlightened 150 Inner Disciples.
Reward: 15,000 Karmic Credits
Ding!
You have enlightened 30 Core Disciples.
Reward: 9,000 Karmic Credits
Ding!
You have enlightened 4 Legacy Disciples.
Reward: 2,000 Karmic Credits
Ding!
You have enlightened 8 elders.
Reward: 8000 Karmic Credits

Slifer nearly tripped over. Heavens above, he could get used to these kinds of karmic windfalls. Sure, he hadn't enlightened everyone, but over 50,000 credits was nothing to sneeze at. It took some of the sting out of creating that expensive Ascendant avatar.

Basking in his success, a realization hit Slifer like a spirit beast's backhand. He had dawdled in this sect long enough. He still had a trip to make to the Black Death Sect, and he couldn't afford to let those righteous bores get there before him.

It was time for this bodhisattva to grace the next batch of unruly disciples with his merciful tutelage. After pilfering their sect's manuals for Core Formation tips, of course.

Truly, doing evil for the greater good is such tireless work!

"Right, then!" He clapped his hands, the sound echoing like thunder. "I trust I've given you lot plenty to chew on. Meditate on these profound truths, plumb their depths . . . and maybe you'll scrape together something resembling a proper Golden Core. Stranger things have happened." He turned on his heel, robes swirling dramatically. "Class dismissed. Now scram, the lot of you. Teacher's got places to be and faces to frighten."

The disciples scattered like startled rabbits, more than one tripping over their feet in their haste to obey. Slifer watched them go with a smirk playing about his lips.

Ah, to be the unquestioned authority figure.

CHAPTER ELEVEN

Zack walked towards the city gates of Xairen, his white robes fluttering in the chilly mountain breeze. To any passerby, he looked like just another young cultivator visiting the great city.

Gotta play it cool, act like I belong here, Zack thought, keeping his expression neutral. *At least until I cement my position. Then Mia's accusations won't matter.*

Fabricating a cover story had been child's play with Hallibur's memories. Zack now knew enough about the Northern Region to pass as a native. He just needed to sell the lie.

"Halt! State your name and purpose," a burly guard barked when Zack reached the gates.

"This one is Alfie," Zack bowed. "A rogue cultivator seeking to mend his ways and join a righteous sect."

The guard sneered. "A rogue? Hmph, we'll be watching you closely, then. Cause any trouble and you'll be dead before you know it."

Zack raised his hands. "I assure you, those days are behind me. I only wish to start again in your magnificent city."

With a disinterested look, the guard waved him through. "See that you do. The king of the Moon God Sect has no patience for troublemakers."

Neither do I, Zack mused.

Stepping into Xairen, he took in the sprawling metropolis of ice and stone. Pagodas stood like frozen sentinels amidst a sea of slate-roofed buildings.

Thousands of cultivators filled the streets haggling with merchants or hurrying to unknown destinations.

Zack extended his senses as he tried to locate Mia's aura. *There! Near the central pavilion.* In a burst of speed, he blinked through the crowds and appeared behind the oblivious girl.

"Hey there, Mia! Miss me already?"

"Gah!" Mia spun around, nearly decking Zack. "Alfie! Don't sneak up on me like that!" Then her eyes narrowed. "Wait, where's Master? Why are you here alone?"

Showtime. Zack put on a serious expression.

"About that . . . I'm afraid I have concerning news. Your master tasked me with passing on an urgent message."

Her eyes widened. "What? What message?"

Zack glanced around as if wary of eavesdroppers. "Not here. Let's find somewhere private to talk." They ducked into a deserted alley. Zack continued, lowering his voice, "Your master uncovered a conspiracy within your sect. Traitors in league with the Frozen Lotus Sect are planning to undermine the Sun Palace's position. He's gone to investigate further and root them out."

Mia paled. "Traitors? In our sect? But why not tell me himself?"

Zack shook his head. "He feared the conspirators might have eyes and ears everywhere. By sending an outsider like me, he avoided arousing their suspicion." He gripped her shoulders, his expression intense. "Master Hallibur instructed you to return to the Sun Palace Sect immediately. Speak of this to no one. Act as if everything is normal. He will contact you once he's dealt with the traitors. But for now, you must not let them know he's on to them."

Mia swallowed hard, then straightened with resolve. "I understand. I . . . I will do as Master instructs."

Zack nodded. "Good. Now go, before anyone becomes suspicious. Your master is counting on you."

Pulling out her flying sword, Mia prepared to take off, but Zack stopped her.

"Whoa there, you might want to reconsider that. Flying is forbidden in the city for anyone below the Origin Realm."

Mia scoffed. "Please, I'm a disciple of the Sun Palace Sect. They wouldn't dare stop me."

With that, she shot into the sky and sped off towards the southern horizon. However, she didn't get far before a group of city guards on flying swords intercepted her.

"Stop right there! Get down immediately or face the consequences!" one of the guards shouted.

Mia's face reddened with indignation. "Do you know who I am? I'm Mia, disciple of Elder Hallibur of the Sun Palace Sect!"

The guard remained unmoved. "I wouldn't care if you were the sect master's daughter. The law applies to everyone. Now get down before we make you."

Grumbling, Mia reluctantly descended back to where Zack stood shaking his head at her actions.

"Told you so," he said with a smirk.

Mia glared at him. "Oh, shut up. I guess I'll just have to walk out of the city like a commoner." She gave Zack a final nod. "Take care of yourself, Alfie. I'll be back to check on how you're doing once everything is sorted."

With that, she strode off towards the city gates, her flying sword tucked away.

Zack watched her go, a faint smile on his lips. *Spoiled little sect princess. She's in for a rude awakening if she thinks her status means anything outside these walls. But that's not my problem.* Shaking his head, Zack turned and continued into the city proper. *That should keep her out of my hair for a while. By the time she gets back, it'll be too late.*

He turned and melted back into the crowd. It was time to get down to business.

Zack made his way deeper into the city, keeping his senses alert. Thanks to Hallibur's memories, he now knew Xairen like the back of his hand. Every hidden alleyway, every shady tavern, every secretive information broker—all of it was laid bare in his mind.

So many useful tidbits floating around in that old man's head, Zack mused. *Almost makes me feel bad for killing him. Almost.* He chuckled darkly to himself. A passing merchant gave him an alarmed look before scurrying away.

Zack paid the man no mind as he arrived at his destination: the Drunken Immortal Inn.

It wouldn't be a true xianxia unless there was a Drunken Immortal Inn. They probably have one in every realm.

To the uninitiated, the inn looked like any other seedy watering hole. But those in the know understood it was a hub for all manner of illicit activity.

The inn was built right up against the city's walls. According to Hallibur's memories, a secret tunnel from the cellar led directly outside, bypassing the gates entirely. Useful information if he ever needed a quick escape.

Zack pushed open the door and stepped inside. Shady looking men huddled around rickety tables, muttering to each other. A bored barmaid wiped down some dirty glasses.

Only a few customers bothered to glance up at Zack's entrance. He wasn't worried. They likely dismissed him as just another young rogue cultivator. His simple robes and lack of flashy artifacts helped him blend right in.

Zack made his way to the bar and ordered a cup of wine. The barmaid slid it over wordlessly before turning back to her cleaning.

As Zack sipped the sour alcohol, he expanded his spiritual sense and began picking up snatches of hushed conversation.

". . . damned Moon God Sect, squeezing us for every last spirit stone . . ."

". . . new batch of everblood flower just came in, expensive as hell . . ."

". . . Sect Master Helios must be shitting himself, what with the tribute deadline coming up . . ."

Zack filed away each tidbit for later. He never knew what seemingly random piece of information might prove valuable.

After finishing his drink, he climbed the creaky stairs to the second floor and rented out a room from the apathetic innkeeper. Fortunately, spirit stones were a universal currency.

Once inside, Zack pulled out two talismans from his storage ring and placed them strategically around the room.

First, he placed the Shroud of Spiritual Obscurity to the door. This jet-black talisman would create an impenetrable barrier against spiritual sense below the Ascendant Realm, effectively hiding Zack's presence from prying eyes. As he activated it with a flick of his spiritual energy, the talisman emitted a faint pulsing red light.

The Main Body really came through with this one, Zack mused, admiring the talisman's handiwork. *With this, I can scheme in peace without worrying about nosy cultivators poking around in my business.*

Next, he placed the Aegis of Profound Protection in the center of the room. This gold talisman would generate a powerful defensive field capable of withstanding a single attack from a Nascent Soul cultivator. As Zack activated it, a shimmering dome of energy sprang into existence, bathing the room in a soft golden glow.

And if someone does try to get the drop on me, this little beauty will buy me enough time to mount a counterattack or escape, Zack thought with a smirk. *The Main Body sure knows how to pick 'em.*

With his preparations complete, Zack sat down on the cultivation pillow.

Okay, so I've successfully infiltrated Xairen. That annoying girl is out of the way. Time to figure out my next move.

Zack's eyes narrowed in thought as he recalled why he was sent to this realm in the first place. Many disciples from the outside mistakenly believed the greatest treasures of the Sealed Realm were its secret techniques, rare resources, and ancient artifacts.

But those were mere trinkets compared to the true ultimate prize: the

Realm's Blessing. It was a little-known secret, passed down only to the Legacy Disciples. The blessing manifested for those who performed grand acts that benefited the Sealed Realm as a whole. Not piddly little good deeds, but true large-scale development that advanced the realm closer to generating a true Heaven's Will.

Because, of course, this backwater dimension can't manage a real Heaven's Will, Zack scoffed mentally. *It's just a half-assed imitation that needs outsiders to do its job for it.*

Still, therein lay the opportunity. By receiving the Realm's Blessing, one could receive unique abilities and use the realm's qi to break through.

And I intend to claim that blessing for myself, Zack declared silently. *I just need to figure out what this pseudo-Will wants . . .*

He began brainstorming possibilities.

Maybe he could help reform the sects and bring about a new era of cooperation and unity? Nah, too idealistic. These factions were too set in their ways.

Perhaps he could lead a crusade against the rogue cultivators and wipe them out to usher in an age of peace? Tempting, but ultimately it would just be putting a bandage on the underlying issues.

No, no, I'm thinking about this all wrong, Zack realized. *I need to look for signs of where the Will is already nudging things, then give it a push in that direction.*

Closing his eyes, Zack delved into Hallibur's memories once more to look for patterns and clues.

The noble sects constantly warring for dominance, resulting in a tense, uneasy stalemate . . .

Rogue cultivators rising up in response to this imbalance, disrupting the tribute system . . .

And the king of Xairen, ruling with an iron fist, oppressing all beneath his heel . . .

Slowly, an idea began to take shape in Zack's mind. A grin spread across his face.

Of course! It's so obvious! The Will wants a total upheaval of the status quo. And I'm just the man to make that happen.

But he couldn't be too hasty. He would need to insert himself into the current power structure first and gain influence while assessing the lay of the land.

And to do that, he needed to join a sect.

Joining one of the top-tier sects was out of the question. With his current cultivation, he'd just end up as some low-ranking inner disciple or guest elder at best.

No, what he needed was a sect on the decline, one he could "help" in exchange for slowly taking control behind the scenes. Becoming a shadow sect master would grant him a power base to work all sorts of schemes.

A wry smile appeared on Zack's face as he remembered how the Main Body had strong-armed the Black Heart Sect into submission. *Guess we're just a couple of sect-stealing bastards, aren't we? Must run in the, uh, blood? Soul? Whatever. Now, time to find a suitable target.* Zack sifted through Hallibur's knowledge until the perfect target jumped out at him: the Fiery Mist Sect.

Once a powerful faction, the Fiery Mist Sect had fallen on hard times. Their former sect master recently fell in battle, and his replacement was still solidifying his position. They were struggling to meet their tribute demands to the Moon God Sect, and their numbers had dwindled to an all-time low.

They were teetering on the brink, desperate for any lifeline. A vulnerability Zack fully intended to exploit.

Time to pay my new friends a visit.

Whistling a tune, Zack strolled out of the Drunken Immortal Inn, just another unassuming young cultivator out to make his mark on the world.

CHAPTER TWELVE

Finick, the new Sect Master of the Fiery Mist Sect, paced restlessly in his quarters. His hands trembled as he clenched them into fists, trying to stop them from shaking. He had never wanted this role, had never been prepared for it. And now, with the news of his father's death on the southern battlefront, the weight of leadership fell on his shoulders.

I'm not ready for this, he thought, panic rising in his chest. *I can't do this. I'm not strong enough, not wise enough. I'm just a spoiled young master who only knows how to drink and chase women.*

His father, Ignius, had been a powerhouse: a Late Nascent Soul expert who commanded respect through his strength and wisdom. Under his leadership, the Fiery Mist Sect had prospered and become one of the top sects below the five major powers in the Northern Region.

But now . . . now Ignius was gone, fallen in battle against the forces of the Central Region. And Finick was left to pick up the pieces, to somehow fill the void left by his legendary father.

How could this happen? Finick thought, sinking into his chair, head in his hands. *Father was invincible. I always thought . . . I never imagined he could actually die.*

A bitter laugh escaped his lips. He had grown up believing his father to be an undefeatable god, an immovable mountain. To have that illusion shattered so brutally left Finick reeling, lost and unsure.

A sudden knock at the door startled him from his spiraling thoughts.

"C-come in," he called, trying to gather his composure.

A nervous-looking disciple entered, head bowed. "Sect Master, apologies for the intrusion, but the Moon God Sect representative has returned. He . . . he is demanding an increase in our tribute payment."

Finick gritted his teeth, a flash of anger burning through his grief and self-pity. That smug bastard from the Moon God Sect, always swaggering around like he owned the place, extorting them for every last spirit stone. It made Finick sick.

But what can I do? he thought bitterly. *I may only be a half step away from the Nascent Soul Realm, but he is a genuine Nascent Soul cultivator—it is not even comparable. Without Father, we have no one who can stand up to him.*

A wry smile twisted his lips as he remembered all the times he himself had bullied those weaker than him, reveling in his status as the sect master's son. How the tables had turned.

"Give him what he wants," Finick said with a sigh, waving a dismissive hand.

The disciple's eyes widened. "But, Sect Master, we don't have the resources to—"

"Find a way!" Finick snapped, slamming his fist on the table. "Sell some treasures, dig into our reserves, I don't care. Just make it happen."

The disciple swallowed hard but bowed his head. "Y-yes, Sect Master." He scurried out of the room leaving Finick alone with his misery once more.

I'm a failure, he thought, burying his head again in his hands. *A useless, pathetic failure. I've always relied on Father for everything. And now, when the sect needs me most, I have nothing to offer.*

"It looks like you could use some help," a voice suddenly said from the shadows.

Finick leapt to his feet, his qi flaring defensively, and whirled to face the intruder. His eyes widened as a figure stepped out from the corner of the room encased in swirling gray armor that obscured its features.

"W-who are you?" Finick demanded, trying to keep his voice steady. "How did you get in here?"

The question felt stupid the moment it left his lips. He could feel the powerful aura rolling off the stranger in waves: the pressure of a Peak Nascent Soul Realm expert, even greater than his own father had been.

The armored man chuckled, a deep, resonant sound that seemed to fill the room. "I am your help, your guide, your mentor. I can give you everything you need to save your sect."

Finick swallowed hard, mind racing. This had to be some kind of trick, a trap. No one offered something for nothing, especially not someone this powerful.

"And why would you help me?" he asked warily.

The figure spread his hands. "Because I see potential in you, Finick. I see a leader waiting to be born. But you're lost, directionless. You need someone to show you the way."

He stepped closer, looming over Finick. "Without me, you will drive the Fiery Mist Sect into ruin. All your father's hard work, all he sacrificed and bled for, will be for nothing. Is that what you want?"

Finick flinched as if struck. The stranger's words cut deep, voicing all the doubts and fears swirling inside him.

"N-no, of course not. But I . . ." He trailed off, looking away in shame.

The armored man placed a hand on his shoulder, his grip firm but not painful. "I know you've grown accustomed to a certain lifestyle, Finick. The wine, the women, the luxury. And I can help you keep all of that. All you need to do is listen to me and follow my guidance. Can you do that?"

Finick hesitated, a chill running down his spine. This felt wrong, dangerous. Like he was making a deal with a devil, bargaining away his soul for fleeting pleasure and power.

But what choice do I have? he thought desperately. *I can't do this alone. I need help, need someone to tell me what to do.*

His father's final words echoed in his mind, a last fading whisper of the man he had been. *Grow up, Finick. Become the man I know you can be. The sect will one day be yours. Don't let me down.*

With a shaky breath, Finick met the stranger's gaze and nodded. "I . . . I'll do it. I'll follow your lead."

The man smiled, a flash of white teeth in the shadows of his helmet. "Excellent. You've made the right choice."

He waved a hand and the gray armor dissipated like smoke on the wind to reveal a handsome young man underneath. Finick blinked in surprise. If he hadn't just witnessed that overwhelming aura, he never would have believed this youth possessed such power.

He must be one of those ancient monsters, the ones who can change their appearance at will, Finick realized with a shiver. *Just how old and strong is he really?*

Another knock sounded at the door making Finick jump. He glanced uncertainly at his new "mentor."

The young man smirked, waving a hand lazily. "You'd better answer that."

Finick cleared his throat. "Come in!"

The same disciple as before entered, looking even more harried and agitated.

"What is it?" Finick asked, frowning at the panic on the man's face.

The disciple's eyes darted between Finick and the strange youth, clearly uncertain if he should speak in front of an outsider. Finick gestured impatiently for him to continue.

"It's the M-Moon God Sect representative again," the disciple stammered. "H-he says he's growing tired of the insults and delays. He's demanding that you, the sect master, go to him and . . . and kowtow to show your obedience and fealty to the Moon God Sect."

Finick's face flushed red with humiliation and fury. To kowtow to that smirking, imperious bastard, debasing himself before all his subordinates . . . Just the thought made his blood boil.

But what can I do? The now familiar refrain of helplessness echoed in his mind. *He holds all the power here. If I refuse, he'll . . .*

A sudden laugh interrupted his racing thoughts. Finick turned to see his newfound ally grinning, a fierce light in his eyes.

"Don't worry," the young man said as he clapped Finick on the shoulder. "I'll deal with this arrogant fool. Just follow my lead and watch how a real master handles things."

With that, the enigmatic cultivator strode out of the room leaving a stunned Finick to hurry after him.

What have I gotten myself into? he wondered as he followed the confident figure. *Who is this man really? And what does he truly want from me?*

But even as doubt gnawed at him, a flicker of hope sparked to life in Finick's heart. Maybe, just maybe, with this mysterious powerhouse on his side, the Fiery Mist Sect stood a chance. Maybe he wouldn't fail his father after all.

I guess I'll find out soon enough, he thought grimly as they approached the courtyard where the Moon God Sect representative awaited. *One way or another, things are about to change around here.*

When the group arrived at the courtyard, they found the Moon God Sect representative standing there with an oily smile on his face. He wore flowing silver robes adorned with crescent moon emblems, and his graying hair was slicked back into a topknot. Behind him stood a group of a dozen black-clad cultivators, hands resting on the hilts of their swords.

"Ah, Sect Master Finick," the representative, Elder Marius, called out in a mocking tone. "So good of you to finally grace us with your presence."

Finick gritted his teeth, fury and humiliation warring within him. He took a step forward, ready to unleash a scathing retort, but a firm hand on his shoulder stopped him.

"Allow me," his mysterious ally murmured, then glided past him with a confident stride.

Elder Marius's eyes narrowed as he took in the young man. "And who might you be?" he demanded. "I don't remember seeing you around the Fiery Mist Sect before."

The youth smiled, a cold, sharp thing that didn't reach his eyes. "I am Alfie, Sect Master Finick's new advisor. I'll be handling this . . . negotiation on his behalf."

Marius scoffed, his lip curling in disdain. "An advisor? How quaint. As if I would lower myself to deal with an outsider."

He pointed a finger at Finick. "Now, kneel and kowtow as you've been instructed, boy. It's time you learned your place."

Finick's face burned with shame and anger. His fists clenched at his sides as he fought the urge to lunge at the sneering elder, to wipe that arrogant look off his face. But he knew it would be futile. Marius was a Nascent Soul expert, as far beyond Finick as the heavens were above the earth.

Zack, however, seemed utterly unfazed by the threat. He crossed his arms and cocked his head to the side as if examining a mildly interesting insect.

"Kneel?" he repeated, a hint of amusement in his voice. "Now, why would the Sect Master of the Fiery Mist Sect kneel to a lowly representative like you?"

Marius's face purpled with rage. "Lowly? You insolent whelp, I am an elder of the exalted Moon God Sect! Your master is merely the puppet ruler of a second-rate power, clinging to relevance only by our good graces!"

Zack yawned theatrically as he examined his nails. "Is that so? From where I stand, it looks more like the Moon God Sect is a pack of bullies, extorting and oppressing those it should be protecting. Hardly behavior befitting the 'exalted' sect, wouldn't you say?"

Marius sputtered, spittle flying from his lips. "You . . . you . . . How dare you speak such slander!"

His hand shot out and a blinding bolt of ice qi screeched towards Zack's heart. Finick cried out in alarm, sure he was about to watch his only hope perish before his eyes.

But as the deadly blast neared, a swirling vortex of gray smoke suddenly enveloped Zack's form. The ice qi slammed into the smoky barrier and shattered into a million glittering shards, then dissipated harmlessly.

Zack emerged from the smoke unscathed, his expression almost bored. "Tsk tsk," he chided, wagging a finger as if scolding a misbehaving child. "Attacking a guest in your host's own home? How unseemly. Is this how the Moon God Sect treats its neighbors?"

Marius gaped, stunned at how easily his attack had been nullified. Behind him, his retinue shifted uneasily, uncertainty creeping into their expressions.

Zack sighed and shook his head in disappointment as the smoky armor continued to swirl around him. "It seems you are unwilling to see reason, Elder Marius. A pity. I had hoped we could resolve this like civilized men." His eyes flashed with a sudden terrifying light. "But if you insist on using force, then I'm more than happy to oblige."

The air around Zack shimmered and distorted, and his armor pulsed with an otherworldly energy. He extended a hand, palm facing outwards, and his eyes burned brighter.

"Void Piercer."

The words were softly spoken, but they seemed to echo in the sudden silence of the courtyard. A dark swirling vortex appeared before Zack's palm, crackling with power. The gray smoke from his armor flowed into the vortex and turned it a deep malevolent black.

Finick found himself instinctively holding his breath, transfixed by the sight.

For a moment nothing happened. Marius sneered, his face twisted with vindictive glee. "Ha! All bark and no bite, just as I thought—"

His words cut off with a choked gurgle. Slowly, disbelievingly, he looked down at his chest, where a tiny inconspicuous hole had appeared right over his heart. A thin trickle of blood leaked from the wound and was staining his immaculate silver robes crimson.

"W-what . . ." Marius lifted a trembling hand to the hole, his fingers coming away wet and red. "H-how . . ."

Zack lowered his hand, his expression cold and remote. "The Void Piercer technique manipulates space itself. It phases through all barriers, all defenses to strike at the target's most vital point."

He took a step forward, and though his voice remained calm, the air seemed to tremble with the weight of his presence. "You made a grave mistake in challenging me, Elder Marius. One that you will not live long enough to regret."

As if on cue, Marius crumpled to his knees as blood poured from his mouth and nose. His eyes rolled back in his head, and he toppled face-first to the ground, limbs twitching spasmodically.

Behind him, his retinue stood frozen in shock and horror, their faces drained of color. Several took stumbling steps back, hands shaking as they gripped their swords.

Zack turned his burning gaze on them, and they flinched as if struck. "Let this be a message to your masters in the Moon God Sect," he declared, his voice ringing out like a clarion call. "The Fiery Mist Sect is not to be trifled with. We will not bow to your tyranny any longer."

He made a dismissive gesture. "Now, get out of my sight. And take that trash with you." He flicked a finger towards Marius's still-twitching corpse.

The Moon God Sect cultivators didn't need to be told twice. They scrambled forward, scooped up their fallen elder with shaking hands, and fled the courtyard as if the hounds of hell nipped at their heels.

Finick watched them go, his mouth hanging open in disbelief. He turned slowly to Zack, shock and awe warring on his face.

"You . . . you killed him," he whispered hoarsely. "Just like that. A Nascent Soul elder."

Zack shrugged and dusted off his hands as if he'd just finished a mildly strenuous chore. "He was courting death with his arrogance. I merely obliged him."

He turned to face Finick fully, his eyes intense and searching. "This is the kind of strength you will need to lead the Fiery Mist Sect into a new era, Finick. The strength to stand up to tyrants and bullies, to forge your own path." As the smoky armor dissipated, he placed a hand on the young sect master's shoulder. "And I can help you attain that strength if you're willing to learn. But for the moment, all you need to do is rely on me."

Finick gulped, his heart racing. As he looked into the young man's calm eyes, he felt like he was on the brink of a cliff, wavering between his past and an uncertain future ahead.

Do I dare take that leap? he wondered silently.

CHAPTER THIRTEEN

Zack lounged in his quarters savoring the roast duck and crispy pork belly the Fiery Mist Sect had provided. The food here was first-rate, a definite step up from the trail rations he'd been living off recently. He had to hand it to Finick—the young sect master knew how to treat an honored guest.

Not bad, he mused. *The quarters are comfy too. That Finick kid sure is trying to butter me up.*

The formerly arrogant young master had practically begged Zack to take over the sect master's chambers, but Zack had politely declined. No need to ruffle the old fogies' feathers just yet by staging an overt takeover.

Besides, subtlety is key when trying to build your own little empire, he reminded himself with a chuckle.

Zack wasn't entirely certain if this whole "overthrowing the status quo" gig was what the pseudo-Heaven's Will had in mind, but hey, no harm in consolidating some power in the meantime, right? Play the long game and all that.

He picked at his teeth idly as he pondered his next move. If he could just wrangle some top-notch treasures out of the old man, he could turn this backwater sect into a regional powerhouse. Strong enough to make the Moon God Sect think twice about messing with them.

Well, for a little while at least.

Just as he was contemplating the finer points of cultivator politics, a familiar voice echoed in his soul. *You know how many credits it takes to send you those "trinkets"?*

Zack smirked. Nothing like a little ribbing from yourself to brighten the day.

Apologies, not all of us have a System to speed things up, Zack sent back, not sounding sorry at all. *But hey, you saw the memory. I need the stuff. Gotta put on a good show, y'know?*

A disgruntled snort. *Yeah, yeah. Quit yer yapping. The stuff's in your ring.*

Zack grinned, giving his storage ring a little pat. The "old" man always came through in the end.

With an elegant flick of his wrist, he summoned the treasures, each one hovering in the air before him. Zack let out a low whistle of appreciation. The Main Body sure hadn't skimped this time.

First up was the Aegis Bastion Formation, a handy little setup that could tank an attack from an Ascendant Realm big-shot—provided you had enough peons fueling it with their qi. Good thing minions grew on trees around these parts. Though, like most formations, it became a fancy light show if you ran out of fuel.

Next was a Spirit Vein, a rare and precious resource that could speed up cultivation. This particular beauty was only High Earth Rank; apparently, springing for Heaven Rank would've put too much of a dent in the karma credit card. Still, considering that the Fiery Mist Sect's current collection topped out at Low Earth Rank, this was quite the upgrade. *Should get the old coots off my back for a bit.* Say what you will about cultivators, but nothing says "I come in peace" like cold hard resources.

And last but not least was a snazzy black cloak that would make Harry Potter green with envy. Not only could it hide his stunning features from sight, but it also cloaked his aura from anyone under the Ascendant Realm. The perfect accessory for late night strolls and political skullduggery.

Zack admired his new toys, but a sudden thought made him pause and shake his head. Knowing the typical xianxia plot, there was probably some Half-Step Immortal Realm geezer lurking in the shadows, secretly running the show. The kind of guy who'd burn down a whole realm for a tiny power-up.

I shouldn't laugh, he mused soberly. *Knowing my luck, that cliché is spot on.*

A soft knock at the door interrupted his musings. "Enter," Zack called out as he tucked the cloak away for now.

Finick shuffled in looking equal parts awed and terrified in Zack's presence. Zack had to suppress a smirk. The kid thought he was some mysterious old monster in disguise. If only he knew . . .

"How may I assist you today, Sect Master Finick?" Zack asked in his best "wise senior" voice.

Finick gulped, head bowed. "S-Senior, this unworthy one seeks your guidance. Now that we've offended the Moon God Sect, they're sure to send someone even stronger. What . . . what should we do?"

Zack smiled, holding up a hand. "Peace, young sect master. The Moon God Sect is as predictable as they are arrogant. They'll send their attack dog, we'll put it down, and so on until they finally take us seriously." He gestured to the artifacts. "And with these little beauties, we'll be more than ready for them."

Finick's eyes nearly bugged out of his head as he looked at the legendary treasures up close. "Are . . . are those . . . ?" He actually reached up to rub his eyes, as if dispelling an illusion. When the items stubbornly remained, he sank to his knees. "Senior . . . I don't . . . How . . ."

Zack enjoyed watching the youth grapple with his own cognitive dissonance for a moment longer, then took pity on him. He clapped a hand on Finick's shoulder.

"Rise, Sect Master. You'll be in no state to oversee implementation of these gifts if you pass out from shock."

Nodding dumbly, Finick clambered to his feet as he visibly struggled to compose himself. His impression of Zack's "seniority" was clearly rising by the second. He stared at the Spirit Vein in particular, marveling at the High Earth Rank quality.

Zack could practically see the questions burning on the boy's tongue, but to his credit, Finick kept his mouth shut. *Smart lad. Rule one of Cultivator Club: don't ask where the mysterious experts get their shiny toys.*

"The Spirit Vein will help our long game," Zack explained. "Elders will advance, disciples will grow. In time, the qi here will be worthy of an elite sect."

He made a show of wrinkling his nose and glancing around disdainfully. *Seriously, the ambient energy here is barely a step up from mortal air. How do they cultivate in this?*

Finick ducked his head, ears pink with embarrassment. Clearly, he'd picked up on Zack's unspoken distaste. When his gaze fell on the formation disc, he cocked his head quizzically.

Zack grinned, always happy to educate an avid student. "That, my dear sect master, is the Aegis Bastion Formation," he declared grandly. "Once properly set up and powered, it can block an attack from an Ascendant Realm expert."

Finick made a strangled noise, his eyes practically bulging out of his head. "A-A-Ascendant?" he stammered. "With that protecting us, the Fiery Mist Sect would be untouchable!"

The young man fell to his knees, kowtowing repeatedly. "Senior is as generous as he is mighty! This Finick can never repay such a debt!"

Zack waved off the flowery praise, secretly preening inside. Oh yes, he could get used to this "wise master" gig. The Main Body had his fair share of it; now it was his turn.

"Think nothing of it. I'm merely fulfilling my duty to set this sect on the right path. Which reminds me: we have preparations to make. Go brief the elders on how to operate the formation. I expect our 'visitors' will arrive within two days."

Finick nodded vigorously, then snatched up the formation disc and scurried away with a breathless string of "Yes, Seniors."

As the door clicked shut, Zack collapsed back into his seat with a smug grin, basking in the sound of Finick barking orders and of feet scrabbling to obey in the courtyard.

For all his bravado, he knew the next couple days would make or break his gambit. If he succeeded, he'd have the Fiery Mist Sect in his back pocket, a first step to shaking up the realm's status quo. If he failed . . . Well, there were fates worse than death for an upstart protagonist in a xianxia world.

On that note, perhaps I should direct some of the sect's resources into establishing a proper intelligence network. One never knows when a choice bit of blackmail or a well-placed spy might come in handy . . .

CHAPTER FOURTEEN

Finick wiped the sweat from his brow as he finished explaining the formation to the last group of disciples. Two days of nonstop drills had everyone on edge as they waited for the inevitable retaliation from the Moon God Sect. The tension hung thick in the air, like a heavy fog before a storm.

"I still say we should have just kept our heads down," Elder Balthus grumbled. "No good ever came from poking a dragon."

Finick shot the old man a sharp look. Balthus had been a thorn in his father's side for years, always questioning his decisions and undermining his authority. If only Finick could expel the troublesome fossil—but an Early Nascent Soul elder was not so easily cast aside.

"Enough of that coward talk!" Elder Jayna snapped. "We've been under the Moon God Sect's boot for too long. It's high time we stood up for ourselves!" A fiery glint entered her eyes as she turned to face the disciples. "Not like that coward Ignius, content to lick the Moon God Sect's boots . . ."

Finick felt his ears burn. While he appreciated Jayna's support, did she have to disparage his late father in the process? The man had done his best in an impossible situation.

The disciples huddled in nervous clumps, whispering amongst themselves.

"Who do you think that mysterious expert was? The one who killed the Moon God elder?"

"I heard he's a rogue cultivator come to destroy the sects!"

"No, no, he's a hidden master here to guide us to glory!"

"I heard he's an outsider! Came from beyond the Northern Wastes to stir up trouble!"

"Don't be stupid. An outsider would never risk going against the Moon God Sect . . ."

The wild speculation and bickering flared, growing louder and more agitated by the second. Finick watched the rising chaos with a sinking feeling in his gut.

They're scared, he realized. *They're looking for anything to latch on to, any scrap of hope or intrigue to distract from the danger ahead. I need to get them focused, united. I need to lead.*

Squaring his shoulders, Finick gathered his qi and released a wave of Early Nascent Soul aura, letting it wash over the courtyard like a crashing wave. The babble died instantly as every eye turned to him, wide and startled.

Project confidence, Alfie's advice echoed in his mind. *Even if you don't feel it, make them believe it. That's what a real sect master does.*

Finick took a deep breath and forced his voice to come out strong and steady. "I know you have questions about Senior Alfie," Finick said. "And I understand your suspicion. But consider this: a cultivator of his level has no need for a sect like ours. He has gifted us with treasures and knowledge while asking nothing in return. If we repay his generosity with ingratitude, then we have only ourselves to blame when he withdraws his support."

The elders' eyes widened as they no doubt recalled the ease with which Alfie had dispatched the Moon God elder. A few disciples gulped audibly.

Finick pressed on, hoping his voice sounded more confident than he felt. "With Senior Alfie as our patron, we have nothing to fear—not even the Moon God S—"

"Is that so?" The voice cut through Finick's speech like a bolt of icy lightning. The words seemed to shake the very heavens, reverberating through the courtyard with unnatural force.

Finick's head snapped up. Hovering above the sect grounds was a figure that appeared no older than a child of ten. But the sheer pressure emanating from his little form left no doubt—this was no mere child, but an ancient master of the Origin Realm.

The figure sneered down at them as his voice echoed across the distance. "Care to repeat those words to my face?"

A gasp rippled through the crowd as they recognized the newcomer: not just an Origin Realm expert, but the Moon God sect master's right-hand man—Norion!

Norion's cultivation was rumored to be in the Mid-Stage of the Origin

Realm. An Early Origin Realm expert would fall to a cultivator of Norion's level nine times out of ten. It would be like an amateur challenging a seasoned gladiator. Against such an opponent, what hope did they have?

Finick felt his knees tremble as Norion casually tapped the purple barrier that sprang up around the sect.

Norion clicked his tongue. "This toy might withstand three of my attacks. Maybe four. And then"—he smiled, a cold, terrifying expression—"you all die."

Finick felt his tongue turn to lead in his mouth and his earlier bravado wither under the crushing weight of Norion's aura. He opened his mouth to reply, to say something, anything, but no words came out.

I can't do this, he thought desperately. *I'm not ready. I'm not strong enough. Father, what would you do? What would you say to this monster in a child's skin?*

But his father was gone, and Finick was alone, drowning in his own inadequacy. He could feel the eyes of his sect upon him, could sense their mounting panic as they saw their leader falter.

It's over, a voice whispered in his mind. *We're doomed. I've doomed us all with my arrogance, my stupidity. I should have listened to Balthus. I should have—*

A hand clasped his shoulder. Firm. Reassuring.

Alfie.

Relief flooded through Finick at the sight of his mentor standing tall and unafraid before Norion's might. With Alfie here, they had a chance. They had to.

Alfie leaned in close, his voice low and urgent. "Get the formation ready. I'll handle our guest."

Finick nodded jerkily, his brain kicking into gear. He spun to face the stunned crowd. "Elders! Disciples! Take your positions! We activate the formation on my mark!"

As they scrambled to comply, Norion's gaze locked onto Alfie. His eyes narrowed. "You! You're the one who killed an elder from my sect? Bold of you to show your face."

"Killed one elder so far," Alfie corrected. "But don't worry, I'm always happy to add to my tally. Maybe I'll start a collection: delusional man-children who don't know when to quit."

"You dare?" Norion hissed, his small hands clenching into fists. "You dare mock me, you insignificant worm?"

"Oh, I dare," Alfie retorted. "I dare to see you for what you are: a bully and a coward, hiding behind your master's robes. Tell me, does he let you sit on his lap during sect meetings, or do you have your own special cushion?"

Norion's face turned an interesting shade of purple. With a snarl, he thrust out his hand. The very air seemed to crystallize around him as freezing mist swirled into a perfect sphere above his palm.

Finick watched in horrified awe as the ice orb began to glow, tongues of crimson fire flickering to life within its heart. The clashing energies of hot and cold qi intertwined, contained within a prison of Norion's will. The power radiating from that condensed sphere of elements tripped every danger sense Finick possessed. If that struck the barrier before the formation was active . . .

Two strikes. Maybe three. And then oblivion.

As if in slow motion, Finick saw Norion rear back his arm. The sphere rocketed from his hand and struck the barrier with a blinding flash. Light skittered across the dome as it struggled to absorb the impact. The entire sect trembled. For one terrifying heartbeat the barrier flickered, guttering like a candle flame in a hurricane.

And held. Barely.

"How much longer?" Alfie's tone was mild, as if asking about the weather rather than their imminent destruction.

Finick glanced at the elders frantically pouring their energy into the formations. Beads of sweat gathered on his brow. "A few minutes. Maybe five?"

Alfie sighed and turned back to face Norion. "Guess I'm on toddler duty till then."

Finick winced. Taunting a berserk Origin Realm expert—was that really wise? But he didn't dare question his mentor now. Not with their lives on the line.

Zack sighed heavily as he watched the Moon God Sect elder float menacingly outside the barrier. If the Fiery Mist Sect disciples couldn't get the grand formation up in time, he would have no choice but to step in and personally hold back this Origin Realm powerhouse.

Not exactly my idea of a good time, he mused wryly. *Facing down an Origin Realm expert without any Critical Block Cards? Talk about feeling exposed!*

He patted the storage pouch at his waist and hoped the treasures the Main Body had provided would be enough to force a stalemate, if it came to that. In theory, they should be able to deal with an Origin Realm expert. But Zack wasn't keen on testing that theory. If the enemy pulled out some kind of last-ditch suicide move . . . Well, Zack had no intention of being taken down with him.

Zack shook his head. Like he always said, he was far too young and pretty to die.

"Looks like we're doing this the hard way," he announced, cracking his knuckles. "Fair warning, kid: I may not be able to go all out without bringing this whole mountain down on our heads . . . but I've got more than a few tricks up my sleeve."

"You think your parlor tricks can stand against the might of a true Origin Realm expert?" Norion spat. "I'll grind you to dust and scatter your remains across the frozen peaks!"

Alfie's grin turned sharp, predatory. "Big words, tiny terror. Let's see if you can back them up."

"Why don't you step outside that flimsy barrier, boy? We will see if you dare talk a big game then!"

Zack had to laugh at that. This arrogant little twerp really thought he could goad him into leaving the protective formation? Not a chance. The whole advantage of a sect barrier was that it stopped enemies from attacking those inside while still allowing the defenders to project their attacks outwards. Which meant Zack could blast away at this Moon God goon to his heart's content without having to worry about a single hair on his own handsome head getting singed.

No way was he going to throw away that edge by playing the reckless hero. Maybe in cheap cultivation novels, the dashing protagonist would leap out to duel the wicked invader in honorable single combat. But this was real life. And in real life, tactically sound choices tended to trump grandstanding heroics.

Zack raised his right hand and pointed his index finger directly at Norion like the barrel of a gun.

At first, nothing happened. But then a minuscule mote of light began to gather at the tip of Zack's finger. It swelled rapidly and enlarged from a mere pinprick to an orb the size of a melon in the span of a single breath. And still it continued to grow, radiating power as it ballooned to the dimensions of a small house.

Just when it seemed the sphere couldn't possibly expand any further without detonating, it suddenly stopped and began to contract, collapsing in on itself like a dying star. In a matter of moments, it had shrunk back down to a pulsing pinhead of pure energy hovering an inch away from Zack's outstretched finger.

Norion gaped at the display, his face draining of color faster than a Qi Refining cultivator's robes in a rainstorm. "H-how . . . how is this possible?" he sputtered as real fear leaked into his voice for the first time. "Your aura is only at the Core Formation Realm! At best, a monstrous genius at your level could hope to defeat Nascent Soul experts. But channeling an attack with Origin Realm power? Impossible!"

Zack didn't bother to reply. Why waste time with words when he could just let his actions speak for themselves?

What Norion couldn't possibly realize was that Zack himself wasn't doing much of anything at all. The dazzling light show was entirely the work of the black ring on his index finger: a Heaven Rank treasure capable of discharging a devastating cannon blast equivalent to the full might of an Origin Realm cultivator.

Too bad it only had a limited number of uses before crumbling into worthless scrap. Actually, to be specific, the particular ring Zack currently wore was a single-shot variant. Meaning he'd have exactly one chance to ruin this Moon God Sect stooge's whole day before the powerful tool disintegrated into sparkly dust.

Ah well. If he had to burn a Heaven Rank artifact on a two-bit chump like Norion, so be it. The look of sheer pants-pissing terror the little runt would inevitably spray across his smug face would make it all worthwhile.

I guess this is what they mean when they say "Pay to win."

"Bang," Zack whispered, and with a gunslinger's motion, he flicked his wrist and sent the condensed qi bullet flying straight as an arrow towards Norion's heart.

The little elder was fast, Zack had to give him that much. Moving with the honed reflexes of an Origin Realm ace, Norion managed to jerk his body sideways at the last instant, causing the energy blast to miss his vitals by a hair's breadth.

Unfortunately for him, "missing the vitals" was not the same thing as "missing entirely."

Instead of achieving a perfect heart shot fatality, Zack's qi bullet slammed into Norion's shoulder with all the force of an angry minor deity. There was a meaty *thunk*, a flash of white light, and then . . .

Norion screamed.

It was a thin, reedy sound, more befitting a kicked puppy than the venerated elder of a powerful sect. But then, that tended to happen when someone's arm spontaneously exploded at the joint, spraying the surrounding air with a viscous slurry of pulped flesh and powdered bone fragments.

For a long moment, Norion simply hovered there, stock-still, his remaining hand clutching spasmodically at the ragged, oozing stump where his right arm used to be. Dark blood jetted from the wound in erratic spurts, splattering the immaculate jade tiles of the sect courtyard.

He stared at Zack, his eyes wide and glassy with disbelief, as if he couldn't quite process the fact that a Core Formation pipsqueak had just casually blown his limb off.

Zack beamed back at him, the very picture of innocence. "Well, now, that looked like it stung a bit. Ready for another?"

He leveled his finger-gun at Norion once more, never mind that the spent Heaven Rank ring had already crumbled into a sad little pile of glittery ash around his feet. What Norion didn't know wouldn't hurt him.

"Y-you're an Origin Realm expert?"

CHAPTER FIFTEEN

Zack smirked at the dumbfounded man-child, but before he could deliver another witty quip, a golden dome blinked into existence around the Fiery Mist Sect. The Aegis Bastion Formation had finally activated, encasing the sect grounds in an impenetrable barrier.

Norion gaped at the sudden obstacle, his remaining hand clenching into a fist. He glared murderously at Zack.

"You . . . you think this will stop me?" he snarled, spit flying from his lips. "I was about to unleash my full fury and tear you limb from limb!"

Full fury? Zack raised an eyebrow. "Oh really? By all means, don't let this flimsy barrier stop you. I'm sure it'll shatter like glass against your mighty . . . um, remaining arm."

Norion's face turned an interesting shade of purple. He opened his mouth, closed it, then opened it again. No words came out, just an incomprehensible sputtering of rage.

The things these old monsters will do to save face, Zack mused, shaking his head. *It would be funny if it wasn't so sad.*

"How about this," Zack said, his tone turning serious. "The Fiery Mist Sect is under my protection now. Fly on back to your king and give him a message from me: back off. This isn't his playground anymore."

Norion looked like he'd swallowed a live toad. "You . . . you upstart! The king will never stand for this!"

"Then I suggest you get very good at standing. On one leg." Zack wiggled his pinkie in the direction of Norion's stump and then his leg.

Not wanting to lose another limb, Norion spun in the air and shot off. Zack watched him go, a faint smile playing on his lips.

"Senior Alfie, that was incredible!"

Zack turned to see Finick staring at him, eyes shining with something uncomfortably close to worship. The other elders and disciples were in a similar state, alternating between gaping at Zack and cheering at Norion's retreat.

"Truly, Senior Alfie is invincible!"

"The Fiery Mist Sect is saved!"

"We'll never have to bow to the Moon God Sect again!"

Zack waved a hand. "Yes, yes, I'm amazing, I know. But this is just the beginning. The king won't give up so easily, mark my words." He turned to Finick. "Double the patrols, fortify the defenses. I want this place locked up tighter than your great aunt's"—he paused, remembering his audience—"coin purse."

Finick nodded vigorously. "Yes, Senior! Right away!" He scurried off, barking orders at the disciples.

Watching the disciples scrambling to follow orders, Zack allowed himself a small chuckle. The Moon God Sect would certainly come for revenge, but for now, he would enjoy this little victory.

And who knows? Maybe next time he'd take more than just an arm.

A few days later, Zack sat on his throne, his chin resting on his hand as he stared moodily off into space. There had been no further word from the Moon God Sect. It seemed they were content to bide their time, licking their wounds in silence.

For now, Zack thought darkly. *But how long will that last?*

He knew the Moon God Sect's king wasn't the type to let an insult slide. Sooner or later, he'd make his move. And when he did . . .

Zack sighed, drumming his fingers on the armrest. *I need intel*, he mused. *Some way to keep tabs on those old monsters and figure out what they're planning.*

A sudden knock at the door startled him out of his brooding. Zack quickly straightened up to look sage-like.

"Enter," he called out.

Finick shuffled in looking equal parts nervous and excited. "Senior Alfie, there's been some news regarding what you instructed us to look for."

Zack leaned forward, his interest piqued. He had ordered his new minions to be on the lookout for any signs of outsiders—people with strange accents or mannerisms that didn't fit the norm for the Northern Realm. Not to engage them, but to report back immediately.

"Oh? And what did you find?" Zack asked.

"Our scouts have returned with news of an outsider in the northern city of Frostholm. A young man, by all accounts. And his speech . . . Well . . ."

Zack cocked an eyebrow. "His speech?"

"They say he talks like his mouth is full of porridge," Finick blurted out. "All slurred and strange, like nothing they've ever heard before."

Zack had to fight the urge to slap his forehead. *Yeah, that sounds like a mainlander, alright.*

Anyone from beyond the Sealed Realm was referred to as an outsider or mainlander. He recalled his own mainlander "accent," a clumsy slurring of syllables that made him sound like a brain-damaged duck to the inhabitants of the Sealed Realm. It was only through Hallibur's memories that he'd managed to pick up the proper dialect of this world.

Good thing too, Zack mused. *Otherwise, I'd be drawing just as much attention as this poor sap.*

He plastered on a thoughtful look. "Yes, those outsiders do have some peculiar dialects. Good catch."

Finick leaned in, lowering his voice. "Word is, the Moon God Sect has taken an interest in this outsider. They're sending a team to 'collect' him as we speak. Led by an Origin Realm elder, no less."

"An Origin Realm expert? To snatch up some random outsider?"

He stroked his chin thoughtfully. *So, it's true, they really do take hunting outsiders seriously . . . I wonder which disciple it is . . . Could it be someone from the Black Rose Sect?*

Zack had little interest in aiding anyone from an enemy sect but if it was someone from his own sect, one of his own disciples, then he wouldn't hesitate to step in and help. He rose from his throne and said, "You've done well to bring me this information, Finick. I'll handle it from here."

Finick bowed again, even lower this time. "Of course, Senior. I live to serve."

"Live to serve," Zack thought with a raised eyebrow. *Guess those How to Grovel 101 lessons are paying off already.*

As the young sect master scurried out, Zack summoned his invisibility cloak with a flick of his wrist. He draped the fabric over his shoulders, feeling the familiar tingle as it settled into place.

Time to play the mysterious stranger, he thought with a grin as he disappeared from sight, then slipped out of the sect like a ghost in the shadows.

Misery. That was the only word to describe Lucious's experience since entering this wretched Sealed Realm. When he exited the portal, he had emerged in the middle of a frozen wasteland, right in the eye of a snowstorm.

It had taken days of travel just to reach the first sign of civilization: a small ramshackle village huddled at the base of an icy mountain.

Lucious had tried to keep a low profile, speaking as little as possible to avoid drawing attention to his foreign accent and mannerisms. He already knew that the natives of this realm spoke a different dialect, and even the slightest slip could expose him as an outsider.

That would be an unacceptable risk. He had already risked drawing attention by killing a traveler and stealing their clothing just to blend in. The rough furs and sturdy boots were a far cry from his usual silk robes, but he had to make do.

The only bright spot so far had been his successful cultivation breakthrough. He had been a monster in his own realm at the Peak stage of Core Formation. But now . . .

Lucious closed his eyes and sensed the Nascent Soul that pulsed within him: the manifestation of his cultivation base, the true mark of an elite expert. It opened its eyes, and he felt a surge of power rush through his body.

A smile tugged at his lips, but it quickly faded. He had foolishly assumed that reaching Nascent Soul would allow him to dominate anyone in this Sealed Realm, to crush all opposition as long as it wasn't another Legacy Disciple.

But as soon as he had broken through, he sensed several powerful auras fixate on him like hawks spotting a rabbit. Most were clearly in the Origin Realm, far beyond his current level. And one . . . one might have even been an Ascendant, an existence at the level of his own sect master.

Lucious shook his head. If there truly was an Ascendant here, then drawing attention would be suicidal. No, he would need to rely on his true talent: scheming and manipulating from the shadows.

He trudged onwards into the village, shivering despite his thick cloak and his cultivation base to shield him. A stall caught his eye as the savory aroma drifted towards him—a vendor selling meat buns.

Lucious's stomach rumbled. *When was the last time I ate?* He couldn't actually remember. Cultivation breakthroughs had a way of making one forget mundane concerns. As a Nascent Soul cultivator, he had no real need for food, but that didn't mean he wouldn't indulge every now and then.

He approached the stall, fishing in his pocket for the unfamiliar currency. The shopkeeper, an old man, squinted at him suspiciously.

"Haven't seen you around before," he said gruffly. "You a traveler?"

Lucious nodded, not trusting himself to speak. He pointed at the buns and held out a handful of coins.

The old man harrumphed but took the money and passed him a greasy bundle. "Enjoy," he muttered.

Lucious retreated to the edge of the square and tore into the food with a ferocity that he assumed beggars possessed. As a senior brother and Legacy Disciple, he usually had to maintain an air of unfathomable superiority, but now, he was playing the role of a peasant.

He was so focused on portraying the stereotypical image of a starving beggar that he almost missed the figure tailing him from the shadows.

Almost.

Pausing mid-bite, Lucious extended his senses. Sure enough, someone was following him. Their cultivation base flickered at the Mid-Core Formation stage. They were clearly trying to mask their presence, but to a newly minted Nascent Soul expert like Lucious, they might as well have been waving a flag and shouting.

Outwardly, Lucious showed no sign of noticing his stalker. He continued to eat and stroll casually through the village as if he didn't have a care in the world. The figure shadowed him from a distance, always staying just out of easy detection range for an average cultivator.

But Lucious was far from average. He would deal with this little problem swiftly and decisively.

He turned down a narrow alley between two ramshackle huts, a dead end hidden from prying eyes. The moment his tail stepped around the corner, Lucious struck.

His Nascent Soul surged forth and a tsunami of power crashed into the Core Formation cultivator before they could even react. Lucious's palm slammed into the man's chest and sent him flying back into the alley wall with a sickening crunch.

It was over in an instant. The man crumpled to the ground, blood trickling from his mouth and nose. His eyes were wide and glassy with shock, the light fading from them rapidly.

Lucious knelt beside the corpse and riffled through his robes until he found what he was looking for: a communication talisman. It had an intricate sigil depicting a crescent moon cradling a radiant pearl.

So, his arrival had been noticed, and he was being watched. That changed things.

The emblem of the Moon God Sect?

Before entering the Sealed Realm, he had read up on the known powerhouses. The latest information on the Moon God Sect implied that their sect master, better known as their king, was an Early Origin Realm cultivator.

But after so many years, I wouldn't be surprised if that's changed.

The talisman flared with light, likely projecting the scene back to the sect.

Lucious cursed under his breath and crushed the talisman in his fist to cut off the transmission. He had to move—now—before more of them came.

He stood and glanced back at the village square, where a crowd was starting to gather, drawn by the commotion. They pointed at him, whispering frantically.

"Murderer!" one woman cried. "Someone call the guards!"

Lucious sighed. So much for stealth. It seemed his welcome had just run out.

He turned on his heel and sprinted out of the village, not bothering to look back as the shouts and alarms rose behind him. He had to find somewhere to lay low and plan his next move.

Or else he'd be dead before he ever got a chance to scheme at all.

CHAPTER SIXTEEN

Lucious shot through the sky like an arrow loosed from a bow, the wind whipping at his face. He had to put some distance between himself and that cursed village before whoever it was that was monitoring him caught up.

As a newly minted Nascent Soul cultivator, flight came as naturally to him as breathing. No clumsy swords or artifacts needed—his own power was more than sufficient to propel him through the air at breakneck speeds.

A smug grin tugged at his lips. Even outside this backwater realm, his cultivation would make him an elder in any top sect and a leader in any of the weaker ones.

But his self-congratulatory musings were cut short as a familiar prickle ran down his spine: the unmistakable aura of a Nascent Soul cultivator, hot on his trail. Lucious frowned. How had they caught up to him so quickly? He'd assumed he would have more of a head start.

Gritting his teeth, he poured more energy into his flight, determined to shake off his tail. He had no doubt he could handle a single Nascent Soul expert in a fight . . . but if he got bogged down now, it would only give the others time to catch up. And if an Origin Realm powerhouse entered the fray, even he would be hard-pressed to emerge unscathed.

No, better to run now and fight on his own terms later. Lucious pushed himself to fly even faster, the landscape blurring beneath him into a sea of white.

But no matter how much distance he put between them, that nagging sense of being watched never quite faded. If anything, it only seemed to grow stronger with each passing moment.

Lucious extended his spiritual sense, probing his surroundings for any signs of—

There! To the left, right, front, and back—four blazing auras flared to life, locking onto him like a pack of wolves cornering a wounded deer. How was this possible? They had him completely surrounded!

A wave of confusion washed over Lucious, tinged with the first inklings of a feeling he had not experienced in a long time—fear. He knew the people of this realm weren't exactly fond of outsiders . . . but to coordinate such a sophisticated ambush in so short a time spoke of something more than simple xenophobia.

Just what in the nine hells is going on here?

Lucious shook himself. It was clear now that escape was off the table—these bastards had him well and truly boxed in. His only choice was to stand his ground and fight.

Gritting his teeth, Lucious angled himself into a steep dive and arrowed down towards a barren plateau that seemed as good a place as any to make his last stand. He could only pray that the Origin Realm expert he knew was coming would be delayed long enough for him to deal with these small fry.

The moment his feet touched the ground, four figures emerged from the blizzard: three men and one woman, all radiating the power of Early Nascent Soul—except the leader, a man with a long mustache. He was a step above, at the Mid-Nascent Soul stage.

"Well, well, well. I have to say, I'm impressed," Lucious called out, his voice cutting through the howling wind. "Didn't think you lot would be able to track me down so quickly. Care to share your secret?"

The four cultivators looked at each other, then back at Lucious. Their expressions were cold, tinged with disdain and something else . . . Disgust? They regarded him as one might regard a cockroach scuttling across a temple floor.

The leader spoke, his voice flat and hard. "We have nothing to say to you, outsider. Your kind are a plague upon our realm, and it is our duty to expunge you."

Lucious felt his eye twitch. This was the first time that anyone had dared to look down on him.

"Fine, then," he spat. "If you won't talk, then I'll just have to make you scream."

He reached into his robes, brought out a fistful of blood-red seeds, and threw them to the ground at his feet. The seeds had been nourished with his demonic energy, and they sprang to life as a tangle of writhing, thorn-covered vines.

The legacy technique of the Black Rose Sect was as versatile as it was horrifying. Illusions to cloud the mind, lashing tendrils to tear flesh from bone, even snapping jaws to devour victims whole—the vines of the Black Rose could do it all. And Lucious, as a Legacy Disciple, was a true master of their power.

Lucious thrust out his hand and sent the vines surging towards the woman. The flowers bloomed in a dizzying kaleidoscope of colors before bursting, enveloping her in a cloud of pollen.

The woman reeled back coughing and rubbing at her face as the hallucinogenic spores took hold. She screamed and began to claw at her face. Lucious did not want to know what she was seeing.

The mustached expert reacted instantly with a hail of razor-sharp icicles that sliced through the air towards Lucious. But Lucious was already in motion, and a wall of crimson vines erupted from the ground to intercept the frozen projectiles.

Rolling out from behind his leafy barrier, Lucious summoned a swarm of thorny rose pellets with a silent gesture. With a sharp thrust of his arm, he sent the deadly spheres hurtling towards his enemies in a high-speed barrage.

The other two cultivators managed to put up their defenses in time—one a crackling shield of electricity, the other a wall of solid stone. The rose pellets that struck these barriers shattered into clouds of needling thorns. But those that found flesh burrowed deep, and the wounds instantly began to fester with vicious poison.

Lucious allowed himself a cold smile as he heard their shouts of pain. He had never been one to play fair.

His satisfaction was short-lived. A massive claw of ice exploded from a nearby snowdrift and nearly took his head as he threw himself to the side. The mustached expert had used the chaos of the melee to maneuver behind him.

Lucious hit the ground rolling and slammed his palms to the dirt. A dense web of vines burst from the earth to form a living barrier.

The ice claw ripped into the mass of vegetation and shredded the vines but failed to break through to Lucious. Seizing the chance, Lucious pushed more energy into his technique and commanded the vines to lash out and ensnare the frozen limb.

In seconds, the icy construct was immobilized, trapped in a strangling cocoon of vegetation. But Lucious wasn't finished.

"Bind!" he snarled. At his command, the vines contracted with crushing force, reducing the ice claw to glittering powder.

The mustached expert leapt back with a curse, barely avoiding the vines that lunged after him. Pure hatred burned in the man's eyes, but he kept his distance; one little mistake could bring the battle to an end.

The strength of these Northern Realms masters is laughable. Lucious smirked. Even this mighty expert of the Mid-Nascent Soul stage was hesitant to engage him directly.

Lucious's vines swarmed the battlefield in an unending tide that kept the four experts off balance and on the defensive, unable to mount a coordinated counterattack.

Minutes dragged by in furious struggle, but the conclusion was inevitable. The woman and one of the men were the first to fall, succumbing to the poison and madness racking their bodies.

The earth-wielding cultivator tried to tunnel to safety. It was a fatal mistake. He had barely descended a handful of meters before vines speared through the ground above him and dragged him back to the surface in bloody pieces.

The mustached expert lasted the longest, weaving walls of slicing ice and frigid wind to keep the tide of plants at bay. But it was a losing battle. For every vine he cut down or froze, dozens more took its place.

Steadily, inexorably, the vines closed in, hemming the expert in on all sides. Cornered and desperate, he roared the words of an ultimate technique: "Frozen Lotus Entombment!"

A massive lotus of purest ice bloomed around him and sealed him completely in a hardened cocoon. For a second, there was silence.

Then a hundred-foot-long vine reared up and pierced through the icy shell like a spear through rotten wood. It punched out the opposite side in a spray of crystalline shrapnel and bloody mist. The frozen flower collapsed to reveal the broken, skewered corpse within.

"Im-impossible," the expert choked out with his dying breath. "An outsider . . . this powerful . . . It cannot . . . be."

And just like that, it was done. Lucious stood alone amidst a circle of Nascent Soul corpses. He was barely even winded.

"Pathetic," Lucious muttered, petting one of the vines. Was this truly the limit of Sealed Realm Nascent Soul cultivators? He'd hoped for better from opponents of this level.

Movement caught his eye—the woman somehow still clung to a faint spark of life.

Well, that can be rectified easily enough . . . But first, perhaps this fool might have some information to share.

Lucious knelt over the dying cultivator and pressed his palm to the woman's forehead. "Soul Scour Surge," he whispered.

His spiritual sense plunged into the cultivator's mind like a spike, ripping and tearing, searching for useful knowledge. Soul-searching techniques were difficult to master, and Lucious's Mortal-grade version was far from perfect, but even fragments might prove valuable.

An image flashed behind Lucious's eyes: a sprawling complex of majestic palaces and temples, all carved from flawless white jade that glowed under the moon's silver light. At the heart of it all stood a tower. It was magnificent, and its peak appeared to pierce the very heavens.

Then another vision: a figure sat on a throne, his ageless face both beautiful and terrifying. Power rolled off him in suffocating waves as he gazed down at the ranks of kneeling disciples.

A name drifted through the chaotic whirl of stolen thoughts: Moon God Sect. And then another name . . . the Moon God King.

Pain. Fear. A desperate urge to fight, to flee, to live. The expert's mind was collapsing. Lucious tore his hand away with a frustrated hiss as the light left the woman's eyes and her soul burned to ash.

Barely anything. Just a sparse handful of hints and fragments, useless without—

A crushing pressure descended, nearly driving Lucious to his knees. He swore viciously even as a knot of dread coiled in his gut—he knew that sensation all too well. The sheer crushing weight of an Origin Realm aura . . .

Lucious looked up as a figure flew down from the heavens to touch down lightly on the far side of the plateau. At first glance, he appeared to be little more than a young boy, his youthful features set in an arrogant smirk.

But the overwhelming pressure radiating from his sleight frame told a different story. This was no mere child, but a monster wearing human skin.

The boy cocked his head as he studied Lucious with a kind of detached amusement. "Well, now, isn't this a pleasant surprise?" he drawled. "I was hoping for something to take my mind off . . . recent disappointments. And here you are, a new chew toy dropped right into my lap. It's like the heavens want me to work out my frustrations!"

The boy—no, the Origin Realm expert—raised his arm in a clawing motion. Lucious barely had time to curse before a wind scythe, sharp enough to split a mountain, came screaming towards him.

A circular barrier of crimson light snapped into place before him just in time for the wind blade to crash against it with a sound like breaking glass. The barrier held . . . then shattered, a spider web of cracks radiating from the point of impact as it drained the killing force from the attack.

One of Lucious's lifesaving treasures, burnt out in a single use. He fought down a surge of relief and frustration—of course he was happy to be alive, but to expend such a rare treasure so early in the fight . . . !

The arrogant child clicked his tongue. "Of course. You outsiders always have such interesting trinkets. But I wonder . . . How many of those do you have left?"

Lucious gritted his teeth; he knew that despite being able to handle multiple Nascent Soul cultivators, an Origin Realm cultivator was a different beast. He slipped his hand into his robe to grip the pendant hanging against his chest, the absolute last resort: a vessel containing a single strike from a living Ascendant, Lucious's own master.

Once unleashed, that power could crush an Origin Realm expert into a bloody smear . . . but it would also mean that Lucious would not have any other treasures that could threaten a higher realm cultivator. Not ideal . . . but better than dying here and now!

But just as he started to channel qi into the treasure, he noticed the expert's eyes lock onto something over his shoulder. Confusion, then shock, then pure hatred flashed across the child cultivator's face.

"You?" he spat. "What in the heavens are you doing here?"

Lucious turned to see a black-cloaked figure standing behind him. A bone-white mask, its surface etched with crimson tattoos, covered their face.

The cloaked man tilted his head. "Now, now, what's with that scary face, Norion? I just stopped by to see my favorite raging midget. Is that so wrong?"

CHAPTER SEVENTEEN

Norion's face twisted with fury. "You dare mock me?" He raised his arm to gather qi for another attack . . .

The figure pointed his finger at Norion in a gun-like motion.

The Origin Realm expert flinched, his eyes widening.

"Well, would you look at that," the figure drawled, his tone dripping with mock surprise. "Seems like you got your arm back. Fancy another go? I'd be more than happy to relieve you of it again."

Norion's face contorted as rage and fear warred across his childlike features. He took an involuntary step back, his hands clenching into fists.

Lucious watched the exchange with confusion. It was clear that this Norion, despite his Origin Realm cultivation, was intimidated by the masked figure in black. No, more than intimidated—he was terrified.

Just who is this guy? Lucious wondered, his grip tightening on his lifesaving treasure. *If he can scare off an Origin Realm expert with a mere gesture, he must be at the Peak of the Origin Realm himself. Maybe even . . . an Ascendant?*

The thought sent a chill down Lucious's spine. He'd thought himself powerful, a big fish in this backwater pond. But now, faced with these monstrous existences, he felt like a minnow among sharks.

Norion seemed to come to a decision.

"I won't forget this!" With a last venomous glare at the figure, he turned on his heel and shot into the sky, fleeing with as much dignity as he could muster. Which, given the circumstances, wasn't much.

The figure watched him go, a smirk playing on his lips beneath the mask. Then, slowly, he turned to face Lucious.

Lucious fought the urge to squirm under that inscrutable gaze. His hand never left his medallion, ready to activate it at a moment's notice. If this came to a fight . . .

"Alfie," the masked man said abruptly. "You can call me Alfie."

Lucious blinked. *Alfie?* What kind of name was that for an apex predator?

"What do you want from me?" Lucious asked warily.

"Want from you?" Alfie laughed. "My dear boy, I want nothing *from* you. Rather, I want *for* you."

At Lucious's blank look, he elaborated. "The Moon God Sect is after you, outsider. If it weren't for my timely intervention, you'd be on your knees before their king right now."

Lucious's face darkened at the thought. He, Lucious, Legacy Disciple of the Black Rose Sect, kneeling before some two-bit ruler from a backwater realm? The very idea was ridiculous.

"That king of theirs," Alfie continued, his tone almost conversational, "he has a real bee in his bonnet about you outsiders. Seems determined to get his hands on you, dead or alive."

"Why?" Lucious asked despite himself. "Why does he care about outsiders?"

Alfie was silent for a long moment, and Lucious got the distinct impression he was being studied, assessed. Weighed and measured like a prized steer at market.

"That," Alfie said at last, "is a very good question. One you will have to find an answer for yourself." He shook his head, as if to dismiss the thought. "But that's a matter for another day. Right now, we need to focus on keeping you alive and out of the Moon God Sect's clutches."

"And how do you propose we do that?" Lucious asked, a note of challenge entering his voice.

Alfie laughed again. "Simple. A Nascent Soul cultivator like yourself, all alone in this big bad realm? You might as well paint a target on your back." He paused, letting the implication hang in the air. "But if you were to join me . . . Well, no one would dare trouble you then."

Lucious's eyes narrowed. This was starting to sound suspiciously like a recruitment pitch. "And just who are you, exactly, that you can make such bold promises?"

The masked man spread his arms wide, as if presenting himself for inspection. "Like I said, I'm Alfie."

That doesn't answer my question at all, Lucious thought irritably. But something told him pushing further would be unwise. This Alfie seemed like the type to share information on his own terms, if at all. Lucious sighed and released his grip on the lifesaving treasure. "Fine," he ground out, the word tasting like ashes in his mouth. "I'll come with you. For now."

Beneath the mask, Zack smirked. *Hook, line, and sinker.*

With a casual flick of his wrist, Zack tore a portal in the very fabric of space. Lucious stared at the shimmering rift, his eyes wide—such a feat should be impossible for anyone below the Immortal Realm.

Zack gestured towards the portal with a mocking half-bow. "After you, oh mighty Legacy Disciple."

Lucious shot him a dirty look but stepped through the portal without another word. Zack followed a heartbeat later, the rift sealing shut behind them like a closing eye.

While Lucious was being shown around the Fiery Mist Sect, no doubt probing for information about his mysterious benefactor, Zack sat on his throne, lost in thought.

The people of this realm are nothing more than pieces on a chessboard, he mused, tapping his fingers against the armrest. *And those from the Main Realm? They're the more powerful pieces. The rooks, the knights, the bishops.* A slow smile spread across his face. *And now, I've secured myself a bishop in Lucious. Oh, he's not fully under my control yet. That will take time, and more than a little careful manipulation.*

But Zack knew the ways of demonic cultivators. Knew that above all else, they respected strength. As long as he maintained the façade of the mysterious, all-powerful senior, Lucious would not dare to openly defy him.

It's a start, he thought with satisfaction. *A foundation upon which to build my—*

An urgent knocking at the chamber door interrupted his musings. Zack straightened up, schooling his features into a mask of inscrutability.

"Enter," he called.

The door burst open and Finick rushed in, his face flushed with excitement and anxiety. "Senior, I bring news!"

Zack raised an eyebrow. "Oh? Pray tell, what has you in such a tizzy, Sect Master Finick?"

"There's been unusual activity in the border region between the Sun Palace and Celestial Blade Sects."

Zack cocked an eyebrow. "Unusual how?"

"A dramatic increase in security, as if they're guarding something of great value. Our spies have noticed covert troop movements, whispered conversations . . . It's like they're preparing for an attack. Or perhaps hiding some new treasure."

Zack tapped his fingers on the arm of his throne, frowning thoughtfully. He recalled a piece of knowledge gleaned from Hallibur, one that seemed especially relevant now.

Whenever outsiders entered the Sealed Realm in significant numbers, it was said that long-lost inheritances would reveal themselves: ancient cultivation sites and secret scriptures, hidden caches of spirit stones and rare herbs—all manner of priceless resources.

While these so-called treasures were ultimately just a smokescreen to mask the realm's true value, they were, nonetheless, power and assets Zack couldn't ignore. If Sun Palace and Celestial Blade really had stumbled across some newly emerged inheritance . . .

He rose from the throne, his black and silver robes swirling around him like a living shadow. "Finick, gather our top Core Formation disciples. Have them prepare for an expedition." He paused, considering. "Oh, and inform Lucious that his presence is required as well."

Finick bowed again, so low his forehead nearly brushed the floor. "As you command, Senior!"

As the sect master scurried out, Zack reached for his mask and settled it over his features with practiced ease. It wouldn't do for Lucious to realize that the mighty Alfie and the Black Rose disciple Zack were one and the same, now, would it?

CHAPTER EIGHTEEN

Slifer sat on his throne aboard the Divine Azerion Ark, legs kicked up and arms folded behind his head. He watched with amusement as Val zipped around the deck, her scales flashing in the sunlight.

Leah stood at the prow with her eyes fixed on the horizon. "There it is," she said. "The Black Death Sect."

Slifer glanced over to take in the sprawling sect grounds. Unlike the Black Heart Sect with its jagged obsidian walls, the Black Death Sect was shrouded in an eerie mist. Skeletal trees dotted the landscape, their gnarled branches clawing at the sky.

Charming place, Slifer thought wryly. *Real welcoming vibe they've got going on.*

Of the three major demonic sects, the Black Death Sect had always been the most mysterious. Where the Black Rose Sect reveled in turning over a new leaf and the Black Heart Sect wore their cruelty like a badge of honor, the Black Death Sect . . . were an enigma wrapped in shadows.

Val swooped down to sit on Slifer's shoulder, her claws digging in a little too tightly to be entirely comfortable. "Master, this place feels . . . wrong. Like something rotten and hungry." She shivered, tucking her wings close. "I don't like it. It scares me."

Slifer reached up to stroke her head. "There, there. Nothing to fear while I'm here."

But even as he comforted Val, Slifer's eyes narrowed. *If even a dragon at the Nascent Soul stage is unsettled, something is very rotten in the state of the Black Death Sect.*

He thought back to their recent conquest of the Black Heart Sect. Sure, that place had been gloomy and a bit murdery, but it hadn't felt intrinsically wrong like this. There was something deeply, fundamentally off about the Black Death Sect, and Slifer assumed it was related to demons.

As the Ark approached the border, a shimmering barrier sprung up, stopping their advance. Slifer raised an eyebrow. *Well, well, seems they don't want uninvited guests. Too bad for them I'm notoriously hard to refuse.*

A figure in black robes flew up from within the sect and came to a stop on the other side of the barrier. He was a middle-aged man with a hawkish face and cold eyes.

"Supreme Elder Slifer," the man greeted. "I am Mortis, the new Sect Master of the Black Death Sect."

Slifer raised an eyebrow. "Actually, it's Sect Master Slifer now. Of the Black Heart Sect, that is."

Mortis's eyes narrowed slightly at this revelation, but he remained silent. His face was an impassive mask, betraying none of his thoughts.

Slifer leaned back and took stock of the elders and the disciples gathered below. Unlike the quaking disciples at the Black Heart Sect, these folks seemed . . . unruffled by his presence.

Hmm, either they're putting on a brave face or they really don't give a fig about little ol' me, Slifer mused. *Insight!*

But what he saw made his blood run cold.

How in the nine hells are there so many demons in the Mortal Realm? Slifer thought, reeling. *This isn't some piddly little infestation like I thought. This is a full-blown invasion force! There must be a portal to the Nether Realm hidden somewhere in the sect . . . It's the only explanation.* He swallowed hard, keeping his expression blank even as his mind raced. *Change of plans. Sweet talking these freaks won't cut it. Looks like it's time for a bit of good old-fashioned intimidation, demonic style. Whip 'em out and measure, as they say.*

Slowly, deliberately, Slifer reached into his spatial ring. Val and Leah tensed, ready to leap into action at a moment's notice. But instead of a weapon, he withdrew a small urn carved from black jade. He opened it to reveal a pile of ashes—all that remained of Vowron, the previous Sect Master of the Black Death Sect.

"Since I killed your sect master," Slifer said casually, "I'll be taking this sect for myself now." He closed the box with a snap and returned it to his ring. *Never know when the remains of a Half-Step Immortal might come in handy for alchemy.*

Mortis's eyes widened slightly at the sight of Vowron's ashes. They knew

Slifer had captured him, but to think he had actually succeeded in killing a cultivator at the Half-Step Immortal stage . . . That was no mean feat.

But the surprise faded quickly and was replaced by a placid mask. "With all due respect, Supreme Elder, the Black Death Sect has no need of . . . outside leadership. We manage quite well on our own."

Translation: Thanks, but no thanks. Now, buzz off, Slifer thought dryly.

Out loud, he said, "Funny, I wasn't asking for permission. See, if I can singlehandedly crush a Half-Step Immortal . . . Well, I doubt this little barrier of yours will give me much trouble."

To make his point, Slifer reached out and tapped the barrier with one finger. Ripples spread from the contact point.

Mortis's lips thinned. "I've heard tales of your prowess, Supreme Elder. But there are some things even you may not wish to meddle in. Consider this a . . . friendly warning."

Just then, a System alert pinged in Slifer's mind.

Ding!

New Mission: Investigate the Black Death Sect's secrets and eliminate the demonic threat.

Reward: 25,000 Karmic Credits

Failure: -10,000 Karmic Credits

Of course. It's never simple, is it? Slifer complained. But he knew he couldn't back down now, not with the System breathing down his neck.

Unlike the Black Heart Sect, where a flashy show of force had been enough, it seemed the Black Death Sect would require a more . . . hands-on approach.

Slifer sighed and slid open the System Shop interface. His eyes skimmed the list of available cards until he found what he was looking for.

Name: Heaven's Unraveling Card

Rank: Heaven

Description: Instantly dismantle any spirit barrier or formation below the Immortal Realm.

Cost: 15,000 Karmic Credits

Expensive, but cheaper than brute-forcing my way in, Slifer reasoned. He purchased the card and felt the credits drain away.

Mortis watched him like a hawk, clearly expecting some kind of attack. Slifer just smiled, all teeth.

He pressed his palm against the barrier and channeled Heaven's Unraveling. The barrier shuddered as cracks spiderwebbed out from Slifer's hand. With a sound like shattering glass, the barrier collapsed into motes of light.

Mortis reeled back, shock plain on his face. Then his expression twisted into a snarl.

"You can't enter!" he spat as black qi gathered around his hands. He thrust his palms forward and launched a roiling wave of necrotic energy at Slifer. But before it could land, a portal opened up and swallowed the attack whole.

A heartbeat later, the portal reopened behind Mortis. His own death qi blast slammed into his back and sent him tumbling from the sky with a scream.

Slifer dusted off his hands, not a hair out of place. *At this level, the Barrier Reflection Card is more useful than a Critical Block Card. Works for both offense and defense!*

He then leveled a flat stare at the shocked sect members below.

"Last chance," Slifer said coolly. "Submit or face the consequences."

For a moment, everything was quiet. Then, all at once, the eyes of every disciple and elder turned bright red. Their human forms melted away to reveal their true demonic nature. Demonic qi burst out and changed into something much darker and fouler. The air itself seemed to pull away and was filled with a sickening smell of sulfur and rot.

Val watched in terror as the cultivators transformed into horrible monsters. Their skin split open, exposing scales, fur, and insect-like armor underneath. Their faces stretched into animal-like snouts filled with sharp teeth. Horns grew from their heads like terrible crowns. Hands turned into claws, feet into hooves or insect legs.

In just a few seconds, the human-looking cultivators had become a horde of demons, their real selves now visible to everyone.

Val stumbled back, her eyes wide with shock and disgust. "Master . . . those are . . . those are demons!" she cried out, her voice shaking with fear.

Beside her, Leah recoiled, her face twisting with a mix of shock, revulsion, and raw terror. In all her years as a demonic cultivator, she had never seen anything like this. Demonic cultivators, for all their wicked ways, were still human at their core. They pursued power through unsavory means, true, but they were a far cry from the soulless abominations that now stood before her.

These were true demons, born of the Nether Realm itself. The sworn enemies of all life in the Mortal Realm. Even the most depraved demonic cultivator would balk at cooperating with such vile creatures.

Slifer sighed. He wasn't surprised but was still sickened by the ugly sight. *I should have known it wouldn't be that easy.*

He looked at Leah and Val, his face serious. "Stay on the ship, you two. Things are about to get ugly."

Val lashed her tail and smoke came from her nose even as she shook. "But, Master, I can help! I'm not scared of a few weak demons!"

But Slifer shook his head, his voice firm. "Not this time, my little fireball. These aren't your snacks."

Val shrank back, her courage fading, when she saw how serious Slifer was. She had never seen real demons before, only heard scary stories about how cruel and evil they were. Seeing such a horrible thing for herself . . . It shook her to her very core.

Slifer turned back to the mass of demons, his eyes hard as stone. He could feel their bloodlust washing over him, a sickening feeling that threatened to choke the life from the air.

These weren't the weak, half-formed demons that sometimes crawled into the human world. No, these were born in the Nether Realm, soaked in the evilest qi.

And they were hungry, so very hungry. Slifer could see it in their glowing red eyes: a terrible desire to rip and tear until nothing was left but blood and ruin.

Well, who am I to say no to their last meal?

But before Slifer could make a move, a voice cut through the tense atmosphere. "Supreme Elder Slifer, why am I not surprised to see you here?"

Slifer froze, caught off guard by the sudden presence so close to him. Hiding his surprise, he turned to face the speaker. There, standing in the air beside him, was a young man clad in pristine blue and white robes. His white hair was tied back in a simple topknot, secured with a white jade pin. The man's face was youthful, with delicate features that belied the overwhelming power radiating from him. His eyes, a striking pale blue, seemed to stare straight into Slifer's soul.

Slifer plastered on a smile, falling back on his usual confident demeanor. "Ah, you must be the master of the Heavenly Light Sect . . ."

CHAPTER NINETEEN

nsight!

Name: Ace
Realm: Half-Step Immortal
Known Techniques: N/A
Known Affiliations: Heavenly Light Sect
Disposition: N/A

A Half-Step Immortal . . . As expected from the sect master of the number one sect in the Mortal Realm, Slifer thought, suppressing a grimace. *This could get messy.*

The Heavenly Light sect master's lips curved into a polite smile. "Let me take care of this little problem for you."

With a casual wave of his hand, the white-haired youth unleashed a torrent of pure, radiant energy. Slifer watched as the demons began to scream, their bodies consumed by holy fire. They writhed and thrashed as their forms crumbled to ash in mere seconds.

Well, that's one way to make an entrance, Slifer mused, eyebrows raised. *Note to self: don't piss off the guy who can turn demons into barbecue with a flick of the wrist.*

As the last echoes of demonic shrieks faded, Ace turned to face Slifer. His blue eyes sparkled as he offered a slight bow. "I believe proper introductions are in order. I am Ace, Sect Master of the Heavenly Light Sect. It's a pleasure to finally meet you, Supreme Elder Slifer. Or should I say Sect Master Slifer?"

Slifer clasped his hands and returned the bow, his mind racing. *The presence of the Heavenly Light Sect Master changes everything. I barely scraped by against Vowron, and that was with the System's help and the element of surprise. Ace knows I've defeated a Half-Step Immortal, so he won't let his guard down.*

He forced a pleasant smile onto his face. "The honor is mine, Sect Master Ace. I've heard much about the Heavenly Light Sect."

And none of it good, if you're asking the demon crowd, he added silently.

A flicker of surprise crossed Ace's features. "I must admit, I didn't expect the master of two demonic sects to be quite so . . . courteous."

Slifer's smile widened. "Ah, you know how rumors can be. Greatly exaggerated, I assure you."

I'm only being nice because I don't want to waste credits fighting you, he thought wryly.

Ace's eyes twinkled with amusement. "Indeed. You know, little Zofia has said some rather interesting things about you."

Yeah, I bet she has. That first supreme elder of yours is one vindictive woman. Still can't get over her defeat, can she?

"Oh?" Slifer said out loud, keeping his tone light. "All good things, I hope?"

Ace's smile widened. "She mentioned that you might even be a match for me."

A chill ran down Slifer's spine as those piercing blue eyes bore into him. *Why do all the powerful cultivators have to be the crazy ones?*

Before Slifer could respond, Ace's smile vanished. His gaze snapped towards the depths of the Black Death Sect, his expression hardening. A moment later, Slifer felt it too: a massive surge of demonic qi so potent it made the air itself feel heavy and oppressive.

"It seems there's a gateway between the Nether World and the Mortal Realm," Ace said, his voice low. "We should cut off the connection." Without another word, he shot off in the direction of the energy pulse.

Slifer turned to Leah and Val, who had been watching the exchange with wide eyes. "Stay inside the Ark," he ordered. With a wave of his hand, a purple barrier sprang to life around the vessel. "This should protect you against anything short of an Ascendant Realm attack."

At least I hope so, he thought as he took off after Ace. *Who knew that tinkering with that old relic would actually pay off?*

As Slifer caught up to the Heavenly Light sect master, the oppressive aura of demonic energy grew stronger. It was a cloying, sickening presence that made his skin crawl. They came to a stop and hovered in the air before a sight that made Slifer's jaw drop.

A massive portal hung suspended in space, its edges flickering and warping. Through its swirling surface, Slifer caught glimpses of a hellish landscape—rivers of fire, mountains of obsidian, and skies choked with ash and lightning.

"Is this your first time seeing a portal to the Nether Realm?" Ace asked, his voice soft.

Slifer nodded, unable to tear his eyes away from the nightmarish scene.

Ace sighed. "It's quite a sight, isn't it?"

That's one way of putting it, Slifer thought. *"Terrifying beyond all reason" would be another.*

Ace turned to face Slifer, his expression serious. "We need to enter and find what's keeping the portal open on the other side. Once we break that connection, the portal will become unstable and collapse."

Slifer frowned as he eyed the flickering edges of the gateway. "It already looks pretty unstable. Doesn't seem like the brightest idea to just walk right in."

Ace shook his head. "We've cut the connection on our side, but it'll remain usable until we destroy the anchor on the other side. That's the only way to shut it down permanently." His eyes narrowed slightly. "Unless . . . you never planned to deal with this portal?"

Slifer felt the weight of Ace's gaze. *All I wanted was to subjugate another sect, gain some credits, and figure out what's been going on with these demons pretending to be Black Death Sect members. I wasn't planning on world-hopping again. Been there, done that, got the T-shirt.*

Not wanting to draw anymore suspicion onto himself, Slifer shrugged. "I didn't know what to expect when I came here," he said carefully. "But even as a demonic cultivator, I have some morals. I know better than to let the Nether Realm invade the Mortal Realm."

Ace nodded, a hint of approval in his eyes. "If only other demonic sect masters thought the same," he murmured. Then, almost to himself, he added, "It's been a while since I paid the Nether World a visit."

Wait, what? Slifer's eyes widened. *He's been there before?*

Before he could voice his surprise, Ace turned to him. "Are you ready?"

Slifer took a deep breath and steeled himself. *No, not really. But when has that ever stopped me?* He nodded, and without another word, they stepped into the portal together.

The transition was jarring. One moment, Slifer was surrounded by the misty gloom of the Black Death Sect. The next, he was assaulted by a wave of scorching heat.

As his vision cleared, Slifer found himself standing on a ledge overlooking a vast, hellish landscape. Rivers of molten lava snaked through jagged canyons of black rock. The sky above was a roiling mass of dark clouds, occasionally split by flashes of crimson lightning.

"Charming place," Slifer muttered. "Really nails that 'eternal damnation' vibe."

Ace, standing beside him, let out a soft chuckle. "The Nether Realm isn't known for its hospitality," he said, his eyes scanning the horizon. "We need to find the anchor point quickly. The longer we stay here, the more attention we'll attract."

Slifer nodded, trying to ignore the oppressive weight of the demonic energy that saturated the very air. "Any ideas on where to start looking?"

Ace pointed to a towering spire of obsidian in the distance. Its surface seemed to pulse with an eerie red light. "There. That's likely where they've set up the anchor."

"Of course it is," Slifer sighed. "Because it couldn't be somewhere nice and accessible, could it?"

As they began to make their way towards the spire, Slifer couldn't shake the feeling that they were being watched. The hairs on the back of his neck stood on end, and he found himself constantly glancing over his shoulder.

"So," Slifer said, partly to distract himself from the creeping dread, "you've been here before?"

Ace nodded, his eyes never ceasing their vigilant scan of their surroundings. "A few times. The Heavenly Light Sect has been fighting against demonic incursions since the Great War. And sometimes that means taking the fight to their home turf."

"Huh. And here I thought you righteous types just sat around meditating and spouting wisdom all day."

That earned him another chuckle from Ace. "We do that too. But someone has to keep the balance between realms."

As they picked their way across the treacherous landscape, Slifer's mind raced. *This is way above my pay grade. I'm supposed to be reforming demonic sects, not hopping between dimensions!*

Suddenly, Ace held up a hand, signaling Slifer to stop. In the silence that followed, Slifer heard it—a low rumbling growl that seemed to come from everywhere at once.

"We've been noticed," Ace said, his voice low. "Prepare yourself."

Before Slifer could ask what exactly he should be preparing for, the ground beneath their feet began to tremble. Cracks spiderwebbed across the obsidian surface, and with a deafening roar, a massive form burst from the earth.

It was a demon, but one unlike any Slifer had ever seen. Its body was a nightmarish fusion of molten rock and living flame, easily the size of a small mountain. Multiple heads, each crowned with twisted horns, swiveled to fix their gaze on the two intruders.

Name: Tachion Demon
Realm: Peak Ascendant
Known Techniques: N/A
Known Affiliations: N/A
Disposition: N/A

"Oh, come on!" Slifer exclaimed as he backed away from the monstrosity. "That's just excessive!"

Ace, however, seemed unperturbed as he slid into a fighting stance. "I'll handle this."

Before Slifer could protest—not that he was planning to—Ace sprang into action. His movements were a blur as he wove between the demon's massive limbs, each dodge seeming to defy the laws of physics.

Slifer watched in awe as Ace unleashed a barrage of attacks. Blades of wind sliced through the demon's rocky hide. Bolts of lightning struck with pinpoint accuracy, causing the creature to bellow in pain. Pillars of earth erupted from the ground and momentarily trapped its limbs.

So, this is the power of a Half-Step Immortal, Slifer thought, his eyes wide. *He's not even breaking a sweat against a Peak Ascendant demon!*

Ace's expression remained calm and focused as he danced around the demon's attacks. It was like watching a master artist at work—each movement precise, each technique flowing seamlessly into the next.

The demon, for all its size and ferocity, couldn't land a single blow on the Heavenly Light Sect Master. Its roars of rage turned to howls of pain as Ace systematically dismantled it, piece by piece.

Finally, with a gesture that looked almost casual, Ace called down a massive bolt of lightning from the roiling sky above. It struck the demon dead center and, for a moment, the entire area was bathed in blinding white light.

When Slifer's vision cleared, all that remained of the demon was a smoking crater.

Ace landed lightly beside him, not a hair out of place. "Shall we continue?" he asked, as if they had merely paused for a brief rest.

Slifer blinked, still trying to process what he had just witnessed. "Uh, yeah. Sure. Let's . . . let's do that."

As they resumed their journey towards the obsidian spire, Slifer couldn't help but think about what he had just seen. *If that's what Ace can do to a Peak Ascendant demon, what chance would I have against him?*

The thought was sobering. For all his schemes and System-granted abilities, Slifer knew he was out of his league here. As long as he was without a card that could one-shot a Half-Step Immortal, he'd have to tread very carefully.

"I must admit," Ace said as they walked, breaking the silence, "you're really not quite what I expected, Slifer."

Slifer raised an eyebrow. "Oh? And what did you expect?"

Ace's lips quirked into a small smile. "Based on the reports I've received, I was prepared to meet a bloodthirsty tyrant. Someone whose very purpose was embroidered in chaos and destruction." He glanced at Slifer. "Instead, I find someone who seems . . . reasonable. Cautious, even."

If only you knew, Slifer thought wryly. Aloud, he said, "Like I mentioned before, the rumors of my villainy have been greatly exaggerated. I may be a demonic cultivator, but that doesn't mean I want to see the world burn."

"Interesting," Ace mused. "And what do you want, Slifer? What drives you to accumulate power and conquer sects?"

It was a loaded question, and Slifer knew he had to choose his words carefully. "I suppose you could say I'm trying to change things," he said slowly. "The demonic sects have been stuck in their ways for too long. All that infighting and backstabbing . . . It's counterproductive."

Ace's eyebrows rose slightly. "You seek to reform the demonic sects?"

Slifer shrugged. "Reform, unite, improve—call it what you will. I just think there's a better way to do things."

For a long moment, Ace was silent, his blue eyes studying Slifer intently. Finally, he nodded. "A noble goal, if true. Though, I imagine it's not an easy path you've chosen."

You have no idea, Slifer thought. *Try explaining to a bunch of bloodthirsty demons that maybe murder and mayhem aren't the answer to everything. It's like herding cats. Extremely violent, power-hungry cats.*

Their conversation was cut short as they reached the base of the obsidian spire. Up close, it was even more imposing—a twisting monolith of black glass that seemed to devour the light around it. The pulsing red glow they had seen from a distance was stronger here and was emanating from symbols etched into the surface of the spire.

"This is it," Ace said, his voice low. "The anchor point. We need to disrupt those runes to destabilize the portal."

Slifer nodded as he eyed the complex array of symbols. "Any ideas on how to do that without, you know, blowing ourselves up in the process?"

Ace's brow furrowed in concentration. "The array is intricate but not impenetrable. If we can identify the key nodes and—"

He was cut off by a bone-chilling screech from above. Slifer looked up to see a swarm of demons descending upon them. Their leathery wings blotted out what little light filtered through the ashen sky.

Ace's expression hardened. "We don't have time for this. Slifer, can you hold them off while I work on disrupting the array?"

Slifer's eyes widened. "Me? But you're the one who—"

"I need to focus on the runes. Every moment we delay, more demons will go through the portal to the Mortal Realm. Can you do it?"

Slifer swallowed hard as he looked up at the approaching swarm. *All at the Early to Mid-Ascendant Realm. Just how many credits would that be?*

"Alright," he said, sighing to himself. "I'll keep them busy. Just . . . work fast, okay?"

Ace nodded, already turning his attention to the glowing runes.

Slifer flew up to face the oncoming horde of demons. He took a deep breath, centering himself.

Okay, System. Let's see what you got.

CHAPTER TWENTY

As if responding to his thoughts, a series of options appeared in front of Slifer.

Name: Exorcist's Fury Card
Description: Channels the wrath of ancient exorcists and releases a torrent of spiritual energy that severely damages and weakens all demons, up to the user's cultivation realm, within range for 60 seconds. Warning: this technique does not work on Immortal Realm demons.
Cost: 20,000 Karmic Credits

Name: Starfall Arrow Card
Description: Fires an arrow imbued with the power of a falling star. Early Ascendant level attack.
Cost: 20,000 Karmic Credits

Name: Phoenix Feather Barrage Card
Description: Releases a storm of flaming phoenix feathers that home in on the target. Mid-Ascendant level attack.
Cost: 25,000 Karmic Credits

Name: Soul-Devouring Flames Card
Description: Engulfs the target in flames that consume both body and soul,

ensuring complete annihilation and preventing resurrection. Flames can affect multiple targets. Late Ascendant level attack.
Cost: 30,000 Karmic Credits

Slifer quickly dismissed the Soul-Devouring Flames Card. *Nope, too expensive and way overkill. I just need to stop them, not erase them from existence. Save that for a rainy day.*

He also ruled out the Starfall Arrow Card. *Single target? Against this swarm? No thanks.*

The Phoenix Feather Barrage Card seemed promising at first, but Slifer shook his head. *Mid-Ascendant level might not cut it. If even one of these ugly bat-wannabes dodges it and gets close, I'm toast.*

That left the Exorcist's Fury Card. Slifer raised an eyebrow. *Exorcists? In a xianxia world? What's next, vampire cultivators?* He shook his head and pushed the thought aside. The demons were getting closer, their ugly features becoming clearer by the second.

Well, beggars can't be choosers, Slifer thought with a resigned sigh. *System, I'll take the Exorcist's Fury Card.*

A confirmation message popped up in his mind. Slifer grimaced as he felt the 20,000 credits drain away. *This better work.*

As the demons came within striking distance, their faces twisted with bloodlust, Slifer raised his hand. A subtle golden light emanated from his palm and quickly expanded outwards to engulf the entire swarm.

The effect was instantaneous and terrifying.

The demons' screeches of bloodlust turned to wails of agony and fear. Their powerful auras, once oppressive and intimidating, flickered and dimmed like candles in a storm. Slifer watched with wide eyes as the demons' cultivation bases plummeted from Ascendant Realm to . . . Foundation Establishment?

Holy crap, it actually worked! Slifer thought, a grin spreading across his face.

One of the demons, a particularly ugly creature with bat-like wings and the face of a deformed bull, snarled in a guttural language that Slifer could barely understand. "What . . . what is this? My power . . . it's gone!"

Another demon, this one resembling a twisted hybrid of a snake and an eagle, hissed in panic. "Flee! We must flee before—"

But it was too late. Slifer's smoky Nascent Soul Armor materialized around him, and he shot forward like a bullet. His sword flashed and the snake-eagle demon's head went flying.

Ding!

> You have killed an Early Ascendant Demon
> You have gained 2000 Karmic Credits

Two thousand credits? Last time I killed an Early Ascendant, it was only one thousand . . . Is there a two-times modifier for killing demons?

Such a thing wouldn't surprise Slifer; the System did seem to have a personal vendetta against anything demonic.

"Sorry, no fleeing allowed," Slifer quipped, turning his attention back onto his prey. "You guys wanted a piece of me? Well, come and get it!"

What followed was less of a battle and more of a slaughter. With their cultivation bases reduced to Foundation Establishment, the demons were no match for Slifer's speed and power. He darted between them, his sword a blur of motion, and left dismembered limbs and severed heads in his wake.

A demon with the body of a man and the head of a wolf lunged at Slifer, claws extended. "Die, human scum!"

Slifer sidestepped the attack easily. "You know, that might have been scary a minute ago. Now? Not so much." His sword flashed and the wolf-headed demon fell in two pieces.

> *Ding!*
> You have killed an Early Ascendant Demon
> You have gained 2000 Karmic Credits

As he continued his deadly dance among the demons, Slifer couldn't help but feel a bit . . . disappointed? *Is this really what Ascendant Realm cultivation is like?* he wondered. *Being able to swat aside enemies like flies? No wonder cultivators are always so arrogant.*

A group of demons tried to gang up on him, surrounding him from all sides. Slifer just smirked. "Nice try, guys. But I've played enough video games to know how to handle a mob."

He spun in a circle, his sword leaving a trail of golden light. The demons fell back as their bodies dissolved into ash.

Man, if only the guys back in my old world could see me now, Slifer thought. *From living in my mother's basement and entering pie-eating competitions to being a bona fide demon slayer. Talk about a career change.*

As the last demon fell, Slifer landed lightly on the ground, his bloody sword resting casually on his shoulder.

> *Ding!*

> You have killed a Mid-Ascendant Demon
> You have gained 3000 Karmic Credits

Slifer dismissed the multiple notifications and turned to Ace, who was still focused intently on the runes covering the obsidian spire.

"You about done down there?" Slifer called out. "Because I'm all out of demons to kill up here."

Ace looked up, his eyes widening slightly as he took in the carnage around Slifer. "Hmm, as expected," he said, his tone neutral. "And yes, I've nearly finished. We need to reach the portal now. It will collapse any second. If we don't make it in time, we'll be trapped here."

Slifer's smug grin vanished. *You've got to be kidding me. A little warning would have been nice!*

"Right," Slifer said aloud, trying to keep the panic out of his voice. "Let's go, then."

They both took to the air and flew towards the shimmering portal that would take them back to the Mortal Realm. Slifer pushed himself to fly faster, acutely aware that Ace was holding back to stay with him.

Come on, come on, Slifer urged himself. *I have no idea if level two of Dimensional Slide will work in the Nether Realm, and I definitely did not come all this way just to get stuck in demon hell forever!*

They were almost there when the ground beneath them erupted. A massive form burst from the earth, sending debris flying in all directions. Slifer came to an abrupt halt, narrowly avoiding a chunk of obsidian the size of a car.

As the dust settled, Slifer got a good look at their new obstacle. It was a demon with the body of an enormous rat, easily the size of a house, with patchy fur that seemed to writhe and move on its own. Its face was a nightmarish fusion of rat and human features with bulging red eyes and teeth like jagged daggers.

Oh, come on! Slifer thought, exasperated. *What is this, the final boss?*

He quickly used his Insight skill, hoping to gauge the threat level of this new enemy. What he saw made his blood run cold.

> Name: Unknown
> Realm: Half-Step Immortal
> Known Techniques: N/A
> Known Affiliations: N/A
> Disposition: Hostile

You have got to be kidding me, Slifer thought, his mind racing. *A Half-Step Immortal? I don't have anything that can even scratch something that powerful!*

He glanced at Ace, whose eyes had narrowed at the sight of the rat demon. Slifer could practically see the gears turning in the Heavenly Light Sect Master's head.

The rat demon's bulbous eyes fixed on them and its mouth split into a grotesque grin. "Well, well," it said, its voice a grating squeak that somehow managed to convey both amusement and malice. "What do we have here? Two little cultivators, so far from home."

Slifer swallowed hard. *Okay, think. There's got to be a way out of this. Maybe if we—*

His thoughts were cut short as Ace suddenly burst into motion. The Heavenly Light Sect Master's body blazed with the aura of five elements—fire, water, earth, wind, and lightning. He moved so fast that Slifer could barely track him with his eyes.

One moment, Ace was beside Slifer. The next, he was behind the rat demon.

There was a moment of absolute stillness. Then, slowly, the rat demon's massive head slid from its shoulders and fell to the ground with a sickening thud.

Slifer stared, his jaw hanging open. *What . . . what just happened?*

The rat demon's body swayed for a moment before collapsing and sending up another cloud of dust and debris. When it cleared, Ace was standing there looking as calm and composed as ever.

"We need to hurry," Ace said, his voice betraying no sign of exertion. "The portal won't stay open much longer."

Slifer nodded dumbly, once again trying to process what he had just witnessed. As they resumed their flight towards the portal, his mind was in turmoil.

That . . . that was insane, he thought. *He took out a Half-Step Immortal like it was nothing. Is Ace actually an Immortal? No, no, that can't be right. It must be some kind of special technique. Yeah, that's it. Something he can't use too often. Because if he can . . .*

Slifer shuddered, not wanting to complete that thought. The implications were too terrifying to contemplate.

They were almost at the portal now. Its swirling surface seemed to pulse and waver, as if it was struggling to maintain its form. Slifer could see glimpses of the Mortal Realm through it—the misty landscape of the Black Death Sect was so much more welcoming now than it had seemed before.

Almost there, Slifer thought, relief washing over him. *Just a few more seconds and we'll be—*

Suddenly, a pressure unlike anything Slifer had ever felt before slammed down on them. It was as if the very air had turned to lead, crushing down on him from all sides. Slifer gasped, finding it difficult to even breathe.

What . . . what is this? he thought, panic rising in his chest. *It feels like I'm being crushed by a mountain!*

With tremendous effort, Slifer managed to lift his head. What he saw made his blood run cold.

High above them, impossibly large and terrifyingly real, a massive red eye had opened in the sky. It stared down at them with an intensity that made Slifer feel like an insect under a microscope.

Beside him, Ace's eyes widened in shock and . . . was that fear? "Immortal!" the Heavenly Light Sect Master exclaimed, his usual calm demeanor cracking for the first time.

What? Slifer thought, his mind reeling. *An actual, honest-to-goodness Immortal? Here? Now?* It would be his first time in the presence of a genuine Immortal since he arrived in this xianxia world. *What kind of dog-shit luck is this? Insight!*

Name: Unknown
Realm: Immortal
Known Techniques: N/A
Known Affiliations: N/A
Disposition: Hostile

I-Immortal . . .

Before either of them could react further, the massive eye blazed with crimson light. A beam of energy as wide as a building and blindingly bright shot towards them.

Oh shit, Slifer thought. *Let's hope that Critical Block Card is as "critical" as advertised. Would be nice if it worked against Immortal-level attacks too!*

The energy beam struck and the world exploded into light and heat. Slifer felt himself being flung backwards into the portal.

If I survive this, I'm definitely leaving a five-star review for that card . . .

CHAPTER TWENTY-ONE

For a moment, everything went dark. Then Slifer found himself sprawled on the ground back in the Mortal Realm. The mist-shrouded landscape of the Black Death Sect surrounded him once more.

Slifer blinked, disoriented. He patted himself down, checking for injuries. *No holes, no missing limbs. That Critical Block Card really pulled through.* He glanced around and spotted Ace nearby. The Heavenly Light Sect Master was already on his feet looking completely unruffled. Not a hair out of place or a speck of dust on his pristine robes. *How does he do that? Some secret Immortal-level technique?*

Ace met Slifer's gaze, his eyes widening slightly. For the first time since they'd met, there was a glimmer of something like respect in the sect master's expression.

"You withstood that attack," Ace murmured. "Impressive."

Slifer shrugged, trying to appear nonchalant. "What can I say? I'm full of surprises." *And literal cheat cards. Can't forget those.*

Ace's lips twitched into the ghost of a smile. "Indeed. It seems the rumors about you weren't entirely exaggerated after all."

So, he has been analyzing me this whole time. Interesting.

Slifer pushed himself to his feet, brushing dirt from his robes. He kept his tone casual as he asked, "That power . . . Was that really an Immortal?"

Ace nodded solemnly. "Yes. I take it this was your first encounter with one?"

"You could say that," Slifer replied, his mind racing. *Time to fish for some information.* "I've heard stories, of course, but to actually feel that level of power . . ." He let his voice trail off, hoping Ace would fill in the blanks.

The Heavenly Light Sect Master's gaze grew distant. "Before them, we are nothing more than ants. Even though we stand half a step from the Immortal Realm, it may as well be the distance between the heavens and the earth."

Slifer swallowed hard as he remembered the overwhelming pressure of that massive red eye. "Well, as long as that thing stays inside the Nether Realm, we're not completely defenseless, right? I mean, there must be ways to . . . prepare for such encounters." He watched Ace carefully, hoping his probing wasn't too obvious.

"True enough," Ace said with a slight nod. "If the Immortal demons become directly involved, the Immortal cultivators will step in to maintain the balance. As for preparation . . ." He paused, studying Slifer. "The best defense is to avoid their notice altogether."

Great. So, we're just pawns in some cosmic chess game. And apparently, the winning move is not to play.

Slifer pressed on, his curiosity getting the better of him. "But surely there are techniques, artifacts that can offer some protection? I mean, we managed to survive that attack . . ."

Ace's eyes narrowed slightly. "There are . . . methods. But they come at great cost and are far from foolproof. It's best not to dwell on such things unless absolutely necessary."

Translation: Stop asking questions you're not ready to handle. Message received. But Slifer simply nodded and said aloud, "I see. Well, let's hope it doesn't come to that again anytime soon." *Though, knowing my luck, I'll probably have an Immortal breathing down my neck by next Tuesday.*

Ace shook his head as his expression turned serious, his brow furrowing. "There's more. While we were in the Nether Realm, I detected hints of other portals connecting to the Mortal Realm."

Slifer's eyes widened. "Other portals? You mean there are more of those things?"

Ace nodded. "It seems this plot runs deeper than I initially suspected. We can't trust the other sects. Just as a portal was hidden beneath the Black Death Sect, there may be others concealed elsewhere."

"Which sects are hiding them?" Slifer asked, his mind racing.

"That," Ace said, "is what we need to find out."

Slifer eyed the Heavenly Light Sect Master warily. "And you're telling me this because . . . ?"

Ace's eyes locked onto Slifer's. "Because I believe you can be of use in uncovering the truth."

Slifer raised an eyebrow. "Me? The leader of a demonic sect? I'm flattered, but aren't you worried I might be part of this . . . scheme?"

"Are you?" Ace asked, his tone neutral.

Slifer snorted. "If I was, do you think I'd tell you?"

A hint of a smile flickered across Ace's face. "Perhaps not. But your actions speak louder than your words. Your performance during the Inter-Sect Tournament, and now here . . . They paint an interesting picture."

"Oh?" Slifer said, keeping his voice casual. "And what picture is that?"

Ace took a step closer, his voice low. "One of a man playing a dangerous game. A man with secrets, certainly, but also with . . . unexpected principles."

Well, that's uncomfortably perceptive, Slifer thought. Aloud, he said, "You're making a lot of assumptions based on very little information, Sect Master Ace."

"Am I?" Ace countered. "Then tell me, Slifer, why did you really come to the Black Death Sect? Was it truly just to expand your power base?"

Slifer hesitated, choosing his words carefully. "Let's just say I had my suspicions about certain . . . irregularities within the demonic sects. I came to investigate."

"And you found far more than you bargained for," Ace finished.

Slifer nodded slowly. "You could say that."

They stood in silence for a moment, each sizing the other up. Finally, Ace spoke again. "We find ourselves at an impasse, Slifer. I don't fully trust you, and I'm certain you don't trust me. But the threat we face is greater than our individual suspicions."

"So, what do you propose?"

Ace reached into his robes and pulled out a small jade talisman. He held it out to Slifer. "A temporary alliance. This is a communication talisman. I'll be in touch when I have more information."

Slifer eyed the talisman warily. "And what do you expect in return?"

"Information," Ace said simply. "Your unique position gives you access to circles I cannot easily penetrate. Share what you learn, and I'll do the same."

Slifer considered for a moment, then reached out and took the talisman. It was warm to the touch and thrummed with spiritual energy. "Alright. I suppose we have a deal."

Ace's lips curved into a small smile. "Let's call it a mutually beneficial arrangement. For now."

As Ace prepared to depart, Slifer couldn't resist one last question. "Why me? Why not work with other righteous sects?"

Ace paused, his gaze distant. "Because sometimes, Slifer, it takes a bit of darkness to illuminate the truth." With that cryptic statement, he took to the air, his form blurring into a streak of white and blue, and quickly disappeared into the mist.

Slifer stood there for a moment turning the talisman over in his hands. *Well, this is certainly going to complicate things,* he thought wryly. *I came here to annex a sect, and instead I got to visit demon hell, almost got obliterated by an Immortal, and ended up in a secret alliance with the most powerful cultivator in the Mortal Realm. Just another Tuesday in the life of Slifer, I guess.*

He looked around at the remains of the Black Death Sect. The once imposing buildings were now little more than rubble, and the mist that had shrouded the grounds now dissipated to reveal a desolate landscape.

So much for annexing this place, Slifer thought with a sigh. *Can't rule over a pile of rocks.*

He shook his head, trying to focus. There would be time to dwell on missed opportunities later. Right now, he needed to get back to his own sect and figure out his next move.

Slifer flew back to the Ark. "Val! Leah!" he called out. "Time to go!"

The barrier around the Ark dissipated, and moments later Val came zooming out, her scales flashing in the light. She circled Slifer excitedly.

"Master! You're okay!" she chirped as she landed on his shoulder. "I was so worried! There was this big boom, and then everything went all wobbly and—"

"Easy there, little fireball," Slifer said, patting her head. "I'm fine. Just had a bit of . . . an adventure."

Leah emerged from the Ark more slowly, her face pale and her eyes wide. "Sect Master," she said, her voice shaky, "what . . . what happened out there?"

Slifer sighed. "It's a long story. I'll explain everything once we're back at the Black Rose Sect. For now, let's just say our plans have . . . changed."

He waved his hand, and the Divine Azerion Ark shrunk back down to its miniature size. Slifer tucked it back into his spatial ring, then turned to face his companions.

"Alright, gather close," Slifer said. "We're heading home."

Val clung tighter to his shoulder, and Leah stepped closer, her eyes still wide with a mix of fear and curiosity. Slifer took a deep breath and focused his qi. He reached out with his senses and felt for the familiar energy signature of the Black Rose Sect. Once he had a lock on it, he began to channel his power.

Dimensional Slide, don't fail me now, Slifer thought as he gathered his energy. *I really don't want to explain to these two why we're suddenly in the middle of the ocean or something. That would be embarrassing . . .*

With a tearing gesture, Slifer opened a hole in space. The air in front of them shimmered and warped to reveal a swirling vortex of darkness.

"Hold on tight," Slifer warned. Then, without further hesitation, he stepped into the portal, pulling Val and Leah along with him.

The world blurred around them as they traveled through the dimensional rift. For a brief disorienting moment, Slifer felt as if he was everywhere and nowhere at once. Then, with a lurch, they emerged on the other side.

Slifer blinked as his eyes adjusted to the sudden change in light. They were standing in the courtyard of the Black Rose Sect. The familiar sight of blooming black roses surrounded them.

Home sweet home, Slifer thought with a mixture of relief and weariness. *Now to figure out what the hell I'm going to do next. This is all too much for a mere Foundation Establishment cultivator to deal with . . .*

CHAPTER TWENTY-TWO

Val, still perched on Slifer's shoulder, chirped excitedly. "We're back! That was so cool, Master! Can we do it again?"

Slifer chuckled and patted the little dragon's head. "Maybe later, Val. Right now, we have work to do."

Leah stumbled slightly, looking a bit green. "Sect Master, I don't mean to complain, but . . . could we maybe use a more conventional method of travel next time?"

"What, you don't enjoy bending the fabric of space and time?" Slifer asked with a grin. "Kids these days. No sense of adventure." His expression grew serious. "Alright, listen up. What happened at the Black Death Sect stays between us for now. We need to be careful about who we trust with this information."

Leah nodded, her face pale but determined. "Of course, Sect Master. But . . . what exactly are we going to do?"

Good question, Slifer thought. *I'm kind of making this up as I go along.*

"For now," he said aloud, "we prepare. Something big is coming, and we need to be ready."

As if on cue, a familiar figure came hurrying across the courtyard towards them. Morvran, Slifer's right-hand man, looked as unflappable as ever in his bulky robes, his bald head gleaming in the sunlight.

"Welcome back, Master." Morvran bowed. "I trust your mission was successful?"

Slifer raised an eyebrow. "That depends on your definition of success, Morvran. How did things go with the Black Heart Sect after I left?"

A slow, innocent smile spread across Morvran's face. "Oh, they've been . . . properly disciplined, Master. I ensured that they understand the consequences of disobedience."

I bet you did, Slifer thought, suppressing a shudder. *Note to self: never get on Morvran's bad side.*

"Good work," Slifer said aloud. "But we have a new priority now. I want you to screen the entire sect for any trace of demon energy. Every disciple, every building, every nook and cranny. If you find even the slightest hint of demonic qi, I want to know about it immediately."

Morvran's brow furrowed. "Demon energy? But, Master, we're a demonic sect. Wouldn't that be . . . normal?"

Slifer shook his head. "Not the kind I'm talking about. Trust me, you'll know it if you find it. It's . . . different to demonic qi. More potent. More dangerous."

And, I hope, not here at all, Slifer added silently. *But after what I saw at the Black Death Sect, I can't take any chances.*

"I understand, Master," Morvran said, though his expression suggested he didn't quite grasp the gravity of the situation. "I'll get right on it. Anything else?"

Slifer nodded. "Yes. I want you to adjust the training regimen for all disciples. From now on, we're going to focus more on combat skills."

Morvran's eyebrows shot up. "Combat? But, Master, our sect has always prioritized cultivation techniques over fighting. Are you sure—"

"I'm sure," Slifer said, cutting him off. "Times are changing, Morvran. We need to be prepared for anything."

Morvran nodded slowly. "As you wish, Master. I'll make the necessary arrangements. But may I ask why? Is there something we should be worried about?"

Slifer paused, considering his words carefully. "Let's just say I've received some . . . concerning information. It's better if we're prepared, even if nothing comes of it."

"I see," Morvran said. "Well, you can count on me, Master. I'll get started right away."

"Good." Slifer clapped him on the shoulder. "And Morvran? Keep this between us for now. No need to cause unnecessary panic among the disciples."

"Of course, Master."

As Morvran hurried off to carry out his orders, Slifer turned back to Leah and Val. "Alright, you two. Get some rest. We'll talk more later."

Val nuzzled against Slifer's cheek before flying off, probably in search of something shiny to add to her hoard. Leah hesitated for a moment before speaking up.

"Sect Master . . . are we in danger?"

Slifer paused. "We're cultivators, Leah. We're always in danger. But knowledge is power, and now we know more than we did before. We'll face whatever comes together."

And, hopefully, by "we" I mean "someone else entirely," Slifer thought.

With that, Leah left, leaving Slifer alone in the hall. The Supreme Elder of the Black Rose Sect sighed, feeling the weight of responsibility on his shoulders.

Time to level up. If I'm going to have any chance of surviving in this world of Immortals and demon invasions, I need to get stronger. Fast.

In a courtyard not so far away from Slifer, his disciple Fenlock paced back and forth, his hands fidgeting nervously. The gentle fragrance of blooming flowers filled the air, but it did little to calm his nerves. His gaze kept darting to the entrance of the garden as anticipation and anxiety warred within him.

She'll be here any moment now, he thought, his heart racing. *What if she changed her mind? What if—*

His thoughts were interrupted by the soft sound of footsteps. He turned, and his breath caught in his throat.

Approaching him was Lenvari, a vision of beauty that never failed to take his breath away. Her long raven-black hair flowed like silk in the gentle breeze, and her jade-green eyes sparkled with curiosity. She wore a simple yet elegant white robe that seemed to accentuate her graceful movements.

"Senior Brother," she called out, a smile lighting up her face. "I hope I didn't keep you waiting too long."

Fenlock felt his face heat up. "N-not at all, Junior Sister Lenvari," he stammered. "I, uh, I just got here myself."

Lenvari's smile widened as she came to stand before him. "Is everything alright? You seem . . . nervous."

Nervous? Me? I'm just about to introduce the girl I love to my terrifying master. Why would I be nervous? Fenlock thought sarcastically. Out loud, he said, "I'm fine, really. It's just . . . Well, meeting Master Slifer is a big deal."

Lenvari reached out and gently took his hand, her touch sending a jolt through his system. "Senior Brother, breathe. It's going to be alright. From everything you've told me about your master, he seems like a reasonable person."

Fenlock couldn't help but chuckle at that. "Reasonable isn't exactly the word I'd use to describe Master Slifer. He's . . . unique."

"Unique how?" Lenvari asked, her head tilting slightly in curiosity.

Fenlock paused, trying to find the right words. "Well, he's not like other sect masters. He doesn't really care about all the formal stuff. And sometimes he says the strangest things . . ."

"Like what?" Lenvari prompted, her eyes sparkling with amusement.

"Well, there was this one time during training," Fenlock began, a smile tugging at his lips despite his nervousness, "when he told us to 'cultivate like your lives depend on it, because they probably do.' Then he muttered something about 'plot armor' not being thick enough yet."

Lenvari laughed. "He sounds interesting, at least. Not at all like the stuffy old masters I've heard about in other sects."

"Oh, he's far from stuffy," Fenlock agreed. "There was the time he tried to explain the concept of Dao comprehension using food analogies. He said understanding the Dao was like trying to describe the taste of water to someone who's never had it. Then he spent the next hour trying to get us to 'taste the Dao' in various snacks he'd brought."

"Did it work?" Lenvari asked.

"Well, I'm not sure if I understood the Dao any better, but I did develop a new appreciation for spicy cultivated snake chips."

Lenvari giggled. "He certainly sounds creative in his teaching methods."

Fenlock nodded, feeling some of his tension ease. "He is interesting. And powerful. You should see him in action, Lenvari. It's . . . amazing."

"I've only seen him from afar. I'm looking forward to finally meeting him." Lenvari gave Fenlock's hand a reassuring squeeze. "But, Fenlock, you still haven't told me why you're so nervous. Is there something else?"

Fenlock swallowed hard, his mouth suddenly dry. *It's now or never,* he thought.

"Junior Sister, I . . . There's something I need to tell you," he began, his voice shaky.

Lenvari's expression turned serious. "What is it, Senior Brother? You know you can tell me anything."

Fenlock took a deep breath. "I . . . I have feelings for you. Strong feelings. I think . . . I think I'm in love with you." There was a moment of silence that felt like an eternity to Fenlock. He stood there, his heart pounding, waiting for her response.

Then, to his surprise and delight, Lenvari's face broke into a radiant smile. "Oh, Fenlock." She said his name softly. "I was wondering when you'd finally say it."

Fenlock blinked, stunned. "You . . . you knew?"

Lenvari laughed, the sound filling the garden. "Senior Brother, you're many things, but subtle isn't one of them. I've known for a while now. I don't know anyone who hasn't noticed . . ."

"And . . . and how do you feel?" Fenlock asked, hardly daring to hope.

In response, Lenvari leaned in and pressed a soft kiss to his cheek. "Does that answer your question?" she asked, her cheeks tinged with a delicate blush.

Fenlock felt as if he could fly without using any cultivation techniques. "Junior Sister, I . . . I don't know what to say."

"You don't have to say anything," Lenvari replied, her eyes twinkling. "But maybe we should focus on meeting your master first? We can talk more about . . . us . . . after that."

Fenlock nodded, feeling as if a great weight had been lifted from his shoulders. "You're right. Let's go meet Master Slifer. Just . . . be prepared for anything, okay?"

"Like what?" Lenvari asked, a hint of nervousness creeping into her voice for the first time.

Fenlock thought for a moment. "Well, he might ask you to demonstrate your cultivation techniques. Or he might quiz you on obscure cultivation theories. Or . . ."

"Or?" Lenvari prompted when Fenlock trailed off.

"Or he might challenge you to a pie-eating contest," Fenlock finished with a straight face.

Lenvari stared at him for a moment before bursting into laughter. "A pie-eating contest? Really? That sounds like a mortal thing to do."

Fenlock shrugged, grinning. "With Master Slifer, you never know. He once said that a true cultivator should be able to channel their qi to expand their stomach capacity."

"Well," Lenvari said, still giggling, "I suppose I'd better be prepared for anything, then. Lead the way, Senior Brother."

As they walked arm in arm towards Slifer's quarters, Fenlock couldn't help but feel that no matter what happened next, everything was going to be alright. With Lenvari by his side, he felt like he could face anything—even his master.

Slifer sat cross-legged in his private chambers, his eyes closed in deep meditation. The events of the past few days weighed heavily on his mind, but he knew he couldn't afford to dwell on them. There were more pressing matters at hand.

It's time, he thought, opening his eyes. *I've put this off for too long. If I'm going to face whatever's coming, I need to be stronger. Core Formation, here I come.*

He stood up and stretched his limbs. "Morvran!" he called out.

A moment later, there was a knock at the door, and Morvran's bald head poked in. "You called, Master?"

Slifer nodded. "I'm going to be busy for a while. Make sure no one disturbs me, no matter what. Understood?"

Morvran's eyes widened slightly. "Are you . . . are you going to break through to the Immortal Realm, Master?"

Slifer froze, his mind racing. *Immortal Realm? Oh crap, that's right. They all think I'm some kind of cultivation prodigy. How do I play this off?*

"Immortal Realm? Uh, yeah . . . that's the plan," Slifer replied, trying to keep his voice steady. He laughed nervously and rubbed the back of his neck. "You know how it is. Always reaching for the next level, right?"

Smooth, Slifer. Real smooth. Maybe I should just fake my own death and start a new sect at this point.

Morvran's face lit up with awe and excitement. "That's incredible, Master! To think I'll be witness to such a momentous occasion! Is there anything you need for your breakthrough? Sacred artifacts? Rare herbs? The blood of a thousand virgins?"

Slifer blinked, taken aback. *Blood of a thousand virgins? What kind of cultivation novels has this guy been reading?*

"No, no, nothing like that," Slifer said hastily. "Just . . . peace and quiet. You know, for concentration and stuff. Very important for reaching the, uh, Immortal Realm."

Morvran nodded vigorously. "Of course, Master! I'll make sure no one comes within a hundred meters of your chambers. Not even a fly will disturb your breakthrough!"

"Great, that's . . . great," Slifer said, forcing a smile. "Just remember, no matter what you hear or sense, do not enter this room. The process of becoming an Immortal is, uh, very delicate." *And by "delicate" I mean "completely made up on the spot."*

"Understood, Master!" Morvran said with a salute. "Good luck with your breakthrough! The whole sect will be celebrating your ascension soon!"

As Morvran left, closing the door behind him, Slifer let out a long shaky breath. *Well, that's one way to raise the stakes. Now I really can't afford to fail this Core Formation breakthrough. Talk about performance pressure.*

He slumped back down onto his meditation mat and ran a hand through his hair. *Alright, System. Let's see what you've got for me. Because apparently, I've got an Immortal Realm breakthrough to fake.*

With a mental command, Slifer opened the System Shop interface. His eyes widened as he scrolled through the available items, and he stopped when he came across something unexpected.

Name: Core Formation Celestial Lotus Pill Recipe
Description: A high-level alchemical recipe for crafting pills to aid in breaking through to the Core Formation Realm. Increases success rate by 50% and reduces cultivation time by 30%.
Cost: 5000 Karmic Credits

Slifer's eyebrows shot up. *A Core Formation pill recipe? And one our sect doesn't have? This could be a game changer.*

He quickly checked the price of pre-made Core Formation pills in the Shop and let out a low whistle when he saw the cost.

Thirty-five thousand credits for a single pill? That's highway robbery! Slifer thought indignantly. *But if I can make them myself . . .* A slow smile spread across his face as an idea began to form. *Who says I can't be an alchemist? It's not like I haven't picked up new skills in this world before. And having a reliable source of high-level pills could be invaluable.*

Decision made, Slifer purchased the recipe. A flood of information filled his mind—ingredients, proportions, refining techniques. It was overwhelming at first, but as he sorted through the knowledge, he found himself growing excited.

This could work, he thought. *And hey, who doesn't want to be friends with the guy who can make powerful cultivation pills? Might help smooth over some of those . . . strained relationships I've been developing lately. Plus,* he thought with a wry smile, *no one wants to be enemies with the guy who can make their breakthrough pills. It's like being the only person with snacks at a party: suddenly, everyone's your best friend.*

With renewed enthusiasm, Slifer began browsing the materials section of the Shop. He carefully selected the ingredients needed for the Core Formation Celestial Lotus Pill.

Name: Celestial Lotus Petal
Description: Rare petals from lotuses grown in celestial springs. Enhances spiritual energy absorption.
Cost: 500 Karmic Credits per petal

Name: Nine-Tailed Fox Essence
Description: Concentrated essence from a nine-tailed fox. Improves energy control and stability.
Cost: 500 Karmic Credits per vial

Name: Thunderbolt Fruit
Description: Fruit infused with the power of lightning. Strengthens the body's meridians.
Cost: 1000 Karmic Credits per fruit

Name: Dragon's Breath Crystal
Description: Crystallized dragon's breath. Acts as a catalyst for spiritual energy transformation.
Cost: 1000 Karmic Credits per crystal

Name: Void Lotus Root
Description: Root of a lotus grown in the void between realms. Enhances spatial awareness and control.
Cost: 1000 Karmic Credits per root

Slifer purchased enough materials for three attempts, wincing slightly at the total cost but reminding himself of the potential benefits.

Five thousand credits for the recipe and four thousand per attempt versus thirty-five thousand for a single pill, he mused. *Even if I mess up a few times, I'll still come out ahead. Assuming I don't blow myself up in the process, of course.*

With everything prepared, Slifer reached into his spatial ring and pulled out the green cauldron he had acquired earlier and set it down beside him.

Alright, Slifer thought, cracking his knuckles. *Time to see if I've got what it takes to be an alchemist. How hard can it be, right? Just throw some ingredients in a pot and hope for the best.*

As he began arranging the materials around the cauldron, a memory from his old world flashed through his mind: a high school chemistry class where he'd nearly set the lab on fire. He chuckled nervously.

On second thought, maybe I should start with some safety precautions . . .

Slifer spent the next hour setting up protective barriers around his workspace, just in case things went south. Better safe than sorry, especially when dealing with volatile spiritual ingredients.

Finally satisfied with his preparations, Slifer took a deep breath and faced the cauldron.

"Alright," he muttered to himself. "Let's do this."

CHAPTER TWENTY-THREE

Fenlock's heart raced as he and Lenvari approached Slifer's courtyard. The Black Rose Sect's grounds were always beautiful, but today they seemed especially vibrant. Perhaps it was just his heightened emotions coloring everything.

"Are you sure about this, Senior Brother?" Lenvari asked, her voice tinged with nervousness.

Fenlock squeezed her hand reassuringly. "Of course. Master Slifer may be . . . unique, but he's fair. I'm sure he'll approve of us."

As they neared the entrance to Slifer's private courtyard, a familiar figure came into view. Morvran, Slifer's right-hand man, stood guard with his arms crossed.

Oh no, Fenlock thought. *This might complicate things.*

"Boss Morvran," Fenlock called out, bowing respectfully. "We're looking for an audience with Master Slifer."

Morvran's eyes narrowed as he looked them over. "Master Slifer is not to be disturbed. He's in the middle of an important breakthrough."

Fenlock blinked in surprise. "Breakthrough? To what realm?"

A hint of pride crept into Morvran's voice. "To the Immortal Realm, of course. Did you expect anything less from our master?"

Lenvari gasped beside him. Fenlock felt his own jaw drop. "The . . . Immortal Realm? Are you certain?"

Morvran nodded sagely. "Master Slifer himself told me. He's not to be disturbed under any circumstances."

Fenlock's mind raced. *The Immortal Realm? But that's . . . that's impossible, isn't it? Even for Master Slifer . . .*

"How long will this take?" Lenvari asked, her curiosity overcoming her shyness.

Morvran shrugged. "Who can say? The journey to immortality is not a simple one. It could be days, weeks, months, or even years."

Fenlock's brow furrowed as he processed Morvran's words. A thought struck him, and he couldn't help but ask, "Boss Morvran, do you intend to stand guard here the entire time? Even if it takes years?"

Morvran nodded as if Fenlock had just asked him whether the sky was blue. "Of course. It is my duty to protect Master Slifer during this crucial time. I will remain here, unwavering, for as long as it takes."

Lenvari's eyes widened in amazement. "But . . . what about food? Or rest?"

"Such mortal concerns are beneath me," Morvran declared proudly. "My cultivation method has prepared me for just such trials."

Fenlock's heart sank as the reality of the situation set in. He had been so excited to introduce Lenvari to his master, to seek his blessing for their relationship. Now it seemed they might be waiting for a very, very long time.

Years of Morvran standing guard? Fenlock thought incredulously. *Surely Master Slifer's breakthrough can't take that long . . . can it?*

"Is there no way we could speak with him, even for a moment?" Fenlock pleaded. "It's quite important."

Morvran's expression softened slightly. "I understand, young Fenlock. But Master Slifer's orders were clear: no disturbances, no matter what. The process of becoming an Immortal is very delicate."

Lenvari tugged gently on Fenlock's sleeve. "It's alright, Senior Brother. We can wait. Your master's breakthrough is far more important."

Fenlock nodded reluctantly. "You're right, of course. Boss Morvran, could you at least let Master Slifer know we came by? When he's . . . finished?"

Morvran stroked his chin thoughtfully. "I suppose I could do that. What is this about?"

Fenlock felt his face heat up. He glanced at Lenvari, who gave him an encouraging nod.

"Well, you see . . ." Fenlock began, his voice slightly shaky, "Junior Sister Lenvari and I . . . we've developed feelings for each other. We wanted to seek Master Slifer's blessing for our relationship."

Morvran's eyebrows shot up. He looked between Fenlock and Lenvari as a slow smile spread across his face.

"Ah, young love," he said, his voice uncharacteristically wistful. "It reminds me of my own youth, before I dedicated myself to the Way of the Cock."

Fenlock and Lenvari exchanged a confused glance. *The way of the what now?* Fenlock thought.

"That's . . . nice?" Lenvari said hesitantly.

Morvran nodded, lost in his memories. "Indeed, it was. But such worldly attachments can be a distraction from true cultivation. Are you sure this is the path you wish to take?"

Fenlock straightened his shoulders. "Yes. My feelings for Junior Sister Lenvari only strengthen my resolve to become a better cultivator."

"And I feel the same," Lenvari added, squeezing Fenlock's hand.

Morvran studied them for a long moment, then sighed. "Very well. I will inform Master Slifer of your visit and your . . . situation . . . once his breakthrough is complete. In the meantime, I suggest you focus on your cultivation. The path of dual cultivation can be treacherous for the unprepared."

Fenlock's face burned even hotter. "D-dual cultivation? We haven't . . . I mean, we're not . . ."

Lenvari giggled beside him, clearly enjoying his discomfort.

Morvran waved a hand dismissively. "No need to explain. Just be careful. And perhaps consult some manuals before attempting anything . . . strenuous."

I think I'm going to die of embarrassment right here, Fenlock thought.

"Thank you for your . . . advice," Lenvari said, barely containing her laughter. "We'll be sure to study diligently."

Morvran nodded approvingly. "See that you do. Now, if there's nothing else . . ."

Fenlock bowed quickly. "No, nothing else. Thank you for your time, Boss Morvran."

As they turned to leave, Morvran called out, "Oh, and Fenlock?"

Fenlock looked back nervously. "Yes, Boss?"

A hint of a smile played at Morvran's lips. "Congratulations. Master Slifer will be pleased to see you growing up." With that, he turned and resumed his guard position, leaving Fenlock and Lenvari to make their way back through the courtyard.

Once they were out of earshot, Lenvari burst into giggles. "Oh, Senior Brother, your face! I thought you were going to burst into flames!"

Fenlock groaned. "Was it that obvious?"

Lenvari nodded, still laughing. "You looked like a tomato with hair!"

Despite his embarrassment, Fenlock found himself chuckling along with her. Her laughter was infectious, and he couldn't help but feel lighter.

"Well, I'm glad my discomfort amuses you so much, Junior Sister."

Lenvari's laughter died down, but her eyes still sparkled. "I'm sorry, I couldn't help it. But you have to admit, it was pretty funny. The Way of the Cock? What kind of cultivation technique is that?"

Fenlock shook his head. "I have no idea, and I'm not sure I want to know. Sometimes it's best not to question Boss Morvran's . . . eccentricities."

They walked in silence for a moment, hand in hand. Despite the setback, Fenlock felt content. Being with Lenvari just felt right.

"So," Lenvari said after a while, "what do we do now? It could be a long time before your master finishes his breakthrough."

Fenlock considered this. "Well, we could follow Boss Morvran's advice and focus on our cultivation. Or . . ."

"Or?" Lenvari prompted, a hint of mischief in her voice.

Fenlock grinned. "Or we could go for a walk in the Black Rose Garden. I hear the night-blooming roses are particularly beautiful this time of year."

Lenvari's face lit up. "That sounds wonderful! I've always wanted to see them up close."

As they changed direction, heading towards the famous garden, Fenlock felt a surge of happiness. Things might not have gone exactly as planned, but he was with the girl he loved in a place of beauty and wonder. For now, that was enough.

Master Slifer, he thought, *I hope your breakthrough goes well. And I hope you'll approve of us when you return.*

Little did Fenlock know, his master's "breakthrough" was taking a very different form than he imagined.

Inside his private chambers, Slifer stared at the green cauldron before him, a mixture of excitement and trepidation coursing through him. The ingredients for the Core Formation Celestial Lotus Pill were arranged neatly around the cauldron.

Alright, he thought, *time to see if I've got what it takes to be an alchemist.*

Slifer picked up the Celestial Lotus Petal and marveled at its beauty—it was otherworldly. It seemed to shimmer with an inner light, pulsing in time with his own heartbeat.

"Okay," he muttered to himself, "according to the recipe, I need to infuse this with my spiritual energy before adding it to the cauldron."

He closed his eyes and concentrated on channeling his qi into the delicate petal. It was harder than he expected: the spiritual energy of the petal seemed to resist his efforts, slipping away like water through his fingers.

After several frustrating minutes, Slifer finally felt the petal accept his qi. He opened his eyes to find the petal glowing brightly, its color deepened to a rich, vibrant hue.

"One down, four to go," he sighed as he reached for the vial of Nine-Tailed Fox Essence.

As he worked his way through the ingredients, Slifer found himself gaining a new appreciation for the art of alchemy. Each component required a different approach, a unique touch. The Thunderbolt Fruit crackled with electricity as he infused it, sending little shocks through his fingers. The Dragon's Breath Crystal nearly burned his hand with its intense heat.

By the time he reached the Void Lotus Root, Slifer was sweating profusely, his concentration pushed to its limits.

No wonder alchemists are so respected, he thought as he struggled to imbue the root with his qi. *This is harder than any cultivation technique I've tried.*

Finally, after what felt like hours, all five ingredients were prepared. Slifer took a deep breath and steeled himself for the next step.

"Alright," he said aloud, his voice echoing in the empty chamber. "Time to put it all together and hope I don't blow myself up."

He carefully added each ingredient to the cauldron, following the precise order specified in the recipe. As the last component, the Void Lotus Root, fell into the mixture, the contents of the cauldron began to swirl of their own accord, colors blending and separating in a hypnotic dance.

Slifer watched in fascination as the mixture began to glow, first a soft blue, then a vibrant green, and finally a deep, pulsing red. The air around the cauldron shimmered with heat and spiritual energy.

So far, so good, he thought cautiously. *Now for the tricky part.*

According to the recipe, he needed to carefully regulate the spiritual fire beneath the cauldron while simultaneously stirring the mixture with his qi. It was a delicate balance: too much heat would ruin the pill, too little would fail to properly combine the ingredients.

Slifer took another deep breath and centered himself. He extended his hand over the cauldron and channeled his spiritual energy to create a steady flame beneath it. With his other hand, he began to stir the mixture using a tendril of pure qi.

At first, things seemed to be going well. The contents of the cauldron bubbled gently and the colors swirled together in a mesmerizing pattern. Slifer allowed himself a small smile of satisfaction.

Maybe I've got a talent for this after all, he thought.

No sooner had the thought crossed his mind than things started to go wrong. The mixture suddenly began to churn more violently, the colors separating instead of blending. Slifer frantically tried to adjust the heat and his stirring technique, but it was like trying to control a wild horse with dental floss.

"No, no, no," he muttered, sweat beading on his forehead. "Come on, work with me here!"

But the alchemical mixture seemed to have a mind of its own. It bubbled and frothed as it rose higher and higher in the cauldron. Slifer could feel the spiritual energy within it growing unstable as it pulsed erratically.

This is bad, he thought, a hint of panic creeping into his mind. *Really bad. I need to—*

Before he could finish the thought, the mixture exploded. There was a blinding flash of light, a deafening boom, and Slifer found himself thrown backwards, slamming into the wall of his chambers.

For a moment, he sat there, dazed and disoriented. His ears rang, and his vision swam with afterimages of the explosion. As his senses slowly returned, he became aware of a peculiar sensation all over his skin.

Slifer looked down at himself and groaned. Apparently, the System hadn't categorized that as an attack and hadn't activated the Critical Block Card, so he was now covered from head to toe in a sticky, multicolored substance that sparkled faintly with residual spiritual energy.

"Well," he said aloud, his voice hoarse, "I guess that's what they call a critical failure."

As if in response to his words, a System message appeared before his eyes.

Ding!
Your Alchemy skill has increased.
Alchemy Level 1 (30%)

Slifer blinked in surprise. *Wait, I actually gained experience from that disaster? Huh. I guess there's something to be said for learning from your mistakes.*

He struggled to his feet, wincing at the various aches and pains making themselves known. The chamber looked like a technicolor tornado had torn through it. The cauldron was miraculously intact, but everything else—including Slifer himself—was coated in the failed alchemical mixture.

At least the protective barriers held, he thought, noting with relief that the chaos seemed to be contained within his personal space. *I'd hate to have to explain this mess to the rest of the sect.*

As he surveyed the damage, Slifer couldn't help but chuckle at the absurdity of the situation. Here he was, supposedly a powerful sect elder, covered in magical goop, like a child who had gotten into the finger paints.

"I don't think I'm cut out to be one of those genius alchemists who get it right on the first try," he mused aloud as he tried to wipe some of the sticky substance from his face. "Maybe I should start with something simpler. Like . . . boiling water."

A thought struck him, and he groaned. "The ingredients . . . All those expensive materials wasted on this mess. At this rate, I'll probably bankrupt myself before I ever make a successful pill."

Slifer sighed and ran a hand through his goopy hair. "I hate to admit it, but I think I need help. There's got to be an alchemist in the sect who can teach me the basics. It'll probably be embarrassing, but it's better than blowing myself up again."

Decision made, Slifer began the arduous process of cleaning himself and his chambers. It took far longer than he expected—the failed alchemical mixture seemed resistant to both mundane and spiritual cleaning methods.

By the time he had made himself and his surroundings somewhat presentable, Slifer was exhausted. But he knew he couldn't put off facing the world any longer. Morvran would be wondering what had happened, and there were probably sect matters that needed his attention.

"Alright," he said to his reflection in a newly cleaned mirror. "Time to go out there and pretend I'm a competent sect elder who definitely wasn't just defeated by a cauldron."

Slifer took a deep breath, straightened his robes, and opened the door to his chambers. He stepped out into the courtyard, blinking in the bright sunlight.

As his eyes adjusted, he became aware of a strange scene before him. Morvran, his trusted right-hand man, was . . . sitting on someone? And not just anyone—it appeared to be Fenlock, Slifer's disciple. Beside them stood a young woman Slifer didn't recognize shaking her head in what looked like a mixture of amusement and exasperation.

Slifer blinked, wondering if perhaps he had hit his head harder than he thought during the explosion. But no, the scene remained unchanged.

Well, he thought, *at least I'm not the only one having an interesting day.*

"Morvran," Slifer called out, keeping his voice steady despite his confusion. "Care to explain why you're using my disciple as a chair?"

Morvran looked up, his expression brightening. "Ah, Master Slifer! You've emerged from your breakthrough! How did it go? Are you now an Immortal?"

"Not . . . exactly," Slifer said, barely managing to keep a straight face. "But never mind that for now. Why are you sitting on Fenlock?"

CHAPTER TWENTY-FOUR

Morvran blinked, as if just realizing his current position. He quickly stood up and allowed Fenlock to scramble to his feet. "Ah, my apologies, Master. After I told them you were not available, I caught these two lurking around your courtyard. I assumed they were trying to sneak in and disrupt your breakthrough."

Fenlock, his face red with embarrassment, bowed deeply. "Master, it's not what it looks like! I was just showing Junior Sister Lenvari around the sect. We had no intention of disturbing you!"

Slifer's eyebrows rose. *Junior Sister Lenvari? So, Fenlock finally made a move, huh?* He turned his attention to the young woman, who bowed respectfully.

"It's an honor to meet you, Supreme Elder," she said, her voice soft but clear. "I apologize for any misunderstanding we may have caused."

Slifer waved off her apology. "No harm done. Though, I'm curious, Fenlock. When did you finally gather the courage?"

Fenlock's blush deepened. "Well, Master, you see . . . Junior Sister Lenvari and I . . . we've been spending a lot of time together lately, and I . . ."

"We're courting, Supreme Elder," Lenvari finished for him, a small smile on her face. "We hoped to seek your blessing."

Courting? The way this kid acts, it's like she's been his wife for centuries, Slifer thought, amused. Out loud, he said, "I see. And you thought the best time to ask was when I was supposedly in the middle of a breakthrough?"

Fenlock looked mortified. "No, Master! We didn't know you were . . . I mean, we wouldn't have . . . It's just that Boss Morvran said you might be in there for years, and we didn't want to wait that long, and—"

Slifer held up a hand to stop Fenlock's rambling. "Years? Morvran, what exactly did you tell them?"

Morvran straightened, a hint of pride in his voice. "I informed them that you were undergoing a breakthrough to the Immortal Realm, Master. Such a monumental achievement could take an indefinite amount of time."

Oh boy. This is going to be fun to explain, Slifer thought. "I see. Well, I appreciate your . . . enthusiasm, Morvran. But perhaps in the future we should be a bit more careful about spreading such information."

"Of course, Master," Morvran said, bowing deeply. "I apologize if I overstepped."

Slifer turned his attention back to Fenlock and Lenvari. He took a moment to really look at the young woman, and he had to admit she was quite beautiful. Her jade-green eyes sparkled with intelligence, and her long raven-black hair flowed like silk down her back.

Damn, Fenlock. Nice catch, Slifer thought, then immediately felt a pang of envy. *Why can't I have any luck like that in this world? Stupid System, putting me in an old man's body. Even my clone, Zack, has girls drooling over him!*

Pushing aside his personal frustrations, Slifer addressed the young couple. "So, you two want my blessing, huh?"

Fenlock nodded eagerly. "Yes, Master. It would mean the world to us."

Slifer pretended to consider for a moment, enjoying the way Fenlock squirmed nervously. Finally, he smiled. "Well, who am I to stand in the way of young love? You have my—"

Before he could finish, a familiar blue screen suddenly appeared before his eyes.

Ding!
New Task: Guide the young couple to create a unique dual cultivation technique. Upon completion, their cultivation speed will be doubled when practicing together.
Reward: Every time they dual cultivate, you will receive a boost to your own cultivation

---

Slifer blinked, momentarily caught off guard. *Really, System? Right now? Talk about timing.* He glanced at the eager young couple before him, his mind racing. *Well, well. Looks like Fenlock might be more important to this story than I thought. A unique dual cultivation technique, huh? That's definitely the kind of thing that makes a protagonist OP later on. Hmm, and it'll benefit my own growth . . . Not bad.*

Clearing his throat, Slifer adopted a serious expression. "Fenlock, Lenvari, I'm glad to see your relationship blossoming. However, before I can give you my full blessing, there's a task you must complete."

Fenlock's shoulders slumped slightly, and he let out a small sigh. "I knew it," he muttered under his breath. "Master always has some strange quest . . ."

Lenvari squeezed his hand reassuringly. "It's okay, Senior Brother. Whatever it is, we'll complete it together."

Slifer pretended not to notice their reactions. "As cultivators, your path forward must be one of mutual growth and understanding. Therefore, to prove your compatibility and commitment, I want you to work together to create a unique dual cultivation technique."

Fenlock's eyes widened in surprise. "A . . . dual cultivation technique, Master? But that's—"

"Challenging? Unconventional? Perhaps even a bit scandalous?" Slifer finished for him, a mischievous glint in his eye. "Precisely. This task will test not only your cultivation skills but also your ability to work together harmoniously."

And it'll probably make for some entertaining scenes later in the story, Slifer thought to himself, suppressing a grin.

Lenvari's face had turned a delicate shade of pink, but her eyes narrowed with determination. "We accept your challenge, Supreme Elder. Right, Senior Brother?"

Fenlock nodded, his initial reluctance fading in the face of Lenvari's enthusiasm. "Yes, we do. We won't let you down, Master."

Slifer nodded approvingly. "Excellent. Take as much time as you need. I'll let you know when you've completed the task."

Fenlock's brow furrowed in confusion. "You'll let us know, Master? But . . . how will you know when we've finished?" Fenlock's face turned an even deeper shade of red than Lenvari's. "Master," Fenlock said hesitantly, "you're not . . . I mean, you won't be . . . observing us, will you?"

Slifer blinked, momentarily taken aback by the question. Then he burst out laughing. "Heavens, no! What do you take me for, some kind of creepy old man?" *Though, I suppose I am technically an old man in this body.* Slifer held back a sigh. "No, no," he continued, waving his hand dismissively. "I have my ways of knowing these things. Trust me, when you've created a truly unique dual cultivation technique, I'll be aware of it."

Fenlock let out a sigh of relief, though he still looked slightly skeptical. "If you say so, Master."

Lenvari tugged gently on Fenlock's sleeve. "Come on, Senior Brother. We have a lot of work to do."

As the young couple bowed and prepared to leave, Slifer added, "Oh, and Fenlock? Remember what I taught you about thinking outside the box. Sometimes the most powerful techniques come from unexpected places."

Like protagonists. Slifer smiled. *Always pulling game-changing abilities out of nowhere.*

Fenlock and Lenvari bowed once more before hurrying off, their heads already bent together in discussion.

Morvran, who had been silent throughout the exchange, finally spoke up. "Master, isn't creating a dual cultivation technique a bit . . . advanced for disciples their age?"

Slifer waved his hand dismissively. "Nonsense, Morvran. It's never too early to start pushing one's boundaries. Besides," he added with a cryptic smile, "I have a feeling those two will come up with something amazing."

As Morvran nodded, Slifer turned his gaze to where Fenlock and Lenvari had disappeared. *Alright, System. Let's see what kind of protagonist-level nonsense those kids can come up with. This should be interesting.*

"They make a good pair," Morvran observed, breaking into Slifer's thoughts.

"They do," Slifer agreed. He shook his head and refocused on more pressing matters. "Morvran, I have a question for you."

"Of course, Master. What do you need?"

Slifer hesitated for a moment, wondering how to phrase his request without raising suspicion. "Who would you say is the best alchemist in our sect?"

Morvran's brow furrowed in thought. "That would undoubtedly be Elder Feng, Master. He's a Nascent Soul cultivator who's been with us for over seven hundred years. His skill in alchemy is unparalleled within the Black Rose Sect. It's just unfortunate he hasn't been able to break into the Origin Realm."

As Morvran spoke, memories from the original Slifer began to surface in his mind. *Elder Feng . . . Oh great, the original and that old coot didn't get along at all. Something about the original stealing a pill recipe . . .*

"I see," Slifer said carefully. "And where does Elder Feng stay these days?"

"He stays in the Misty Cauldron Cave, on the eastern edge of the sect grounds," Morvran replied. "But, Master, why are you looking for him? If you need any alchemical products, I'd be more than happy to get them for you."

Slifer waved off the offer. "No, no. I have some . . . personal matters to discuss with Elder Feng. Thank you for the information, Morvran. You're dismissed for now."

Morvran bowed deeply. "As you wish, Master. Please let me know if you need anything else."

As Morvran walked away, Slifer took a deep breath and steeled himself for what was sure to be an interesting encounter. *Well, I'm the supreme elder now. Hopefully, that counts for something with the old alchemist.*

With that thought, Slifer set off towards the eastern part of the Black Rose Sect's grounds. The path was lined with the sect's namesake flowers, and as he walked, he couldn't help but marvel at the beauty.

I really don't appreciate this place enough. It's like something out of a fantasy novel, Slifer thought, then chuckled at the irony. *Well, I guess it technically is. Still, it's nice to appreciate the scenery once in a while.*

As he neared the eastern edge of the sect grounds, the landscape began to change. The well-manicured gardens gave way to wilder growth, and a light mist began to swirl around his feet. In the distance, Slifer could make out the entrance to a cave partially obscured by the mist.

That must be the Misty Cauldron Cave, he thought. *Fitting name, I suppose.*

As Slifer approached the cave entrance, he heard a commotion from inside. Suddenly, a body came flying out of the cave and landed with a thud on the ground just a few feet away from him. The young man, clearly a disciple, groaned in pain. His robes were singed and torn. Despite his obvious discomfort, he immediately began to kowtow towards the cave entrance.

"I'm sorry, Master Feng!" the disciple cried out. "I'll do better next time, I promise!"

Slifer raised an eyebrow. *Well, I guess this isn't a good time for a visit. Maybe I should come back later . . .*

Before he could make a decision, another disciple emerged from the cave. This one looked nervous, his eyes darting between Slifer and the cave entrance.

"M-Master Feng," the disciple called out, his voice shaky. "The supreme elder is here to see you."

There was a moment of silence, then a cranky voice echoed from within the cave, "Eh? What does he want?"

Slifer suppressed a sigh. *This is going to be fun,* he thought sarcastically. Raising his voice, he called out, "Elder Feng, I was hoping we could have a word. If you're not too busy, that is."

Another pause, then the sound of shuffling footsteps. A moment later, an old man emerged from the cave. His long white beard nearly touched the ground. Despite his age, his eyes were sharp and alert, and he was sizing up Slifer with obvious suspicion.

"Supreme Elder," Elder Feng said, his tone neutral. "To what do I owe this . . . honor?"

Slifer put on his most charming smile. "Elder Feng, I was hoping to discuss a matter of some importance with you. Perhaps we could speak privately?"

Elder Feng's eyes narrowed. "Hmph. I don't trust you, not after last time. But I guess I can't say no to the supreme elder. Come in, then. But touch nothing! My experiments are delicate."

As Slifer followed the old alchemist into the cave, he couldn't help but feel like he was walking into the dragon's den. *Well, here goes nothing. Time to see if I can charm this old coot into teaching me alchemy.*

The interior of the Misty Cauldron Cave was a sight to behold. Shelves filled with jars of mysterious ingredients and glowing pills lined the walls. Cauldrons of various sizes were scattered throughout the space, some bubbling with strange concoctions, others lying dormant.

Elder Feng led Slifer to a small clearing in the center of the cave, where two simple stone stools sat. The old alchemist settled onto one and gestured for Slifer to take the other.

"Well?" Elder Feng grumbled. "What's this important matter you wanted to discuss?"

Slifer took a deep breath, choosing his words carefully. "Elder Feng, I'll be direct. I find myself in need of some . . . alchemical expertise. And I've been told you're the best our sect has to offer."

Elder Feng's eyebrows rose slightly. "Oh? And what sort of 'expertise' does the great supreme elder require? Surely one as powerful as yourself has no need for my humble skills."

Is that sarcasm I detect? Slifer thought. *This old man's got some bite to him.*

"On the contrary," Slifer said aloud, "I have great respect for the art of alchemy. In fact, I've recently taken an interest in learning more about it myself."

Elder Feng snorted. "You? Learn alchemy? At your age?" He shook his head. "Alchemy is not something you can pick up on a whim, Supreme Elder. It takes years of study, centuries of practice. It's not for dabblers or dilettantes."

Slifer felt a flicker of annoyance but pushed it down. *Keep calm. You need this cranky old man's help.*

"I understand that, Elder Feng," Slifer said, his voice level. "I'm not expecting to become a master alchemist overnight. But everyone has to start somewhere, right? I was hoping you might be willing to . . . guide me in the basics."

Elder Feng stared at Slifer for a long moment, his expression unreadable. When he finally spoke, his voice was dripping with skepticism. "And why, pray tell, has the supreme elder suddenly developed an interest in alchemy? Surely you have more important matters to attend to."

Slifer hesitated. He couldn't very well tell the truth—that he'd nearly blown himself up trying to refine a pill. No, that was too embarrassing. But he needed a convincing reason . . .

"The world is changing, Elder Feng," Slifer said after deciding to play to the old man's pride. "I believe that to lead our sect effectively, I need to understand all aspects of cultivation. Alchemy is a crucial part of that. And who better to learn from than the most skilled alchemist in our sect?"

Elder Feng's expression softened slightly at the praise, but suspicion still lingered in his eyes. "Flattery will get you nowhere, Supreme Elder. But . . . I admit, your reasoning is not entirely without merit."

He stroked his long beard thoughtfully. "Very well. I will give you a test. If you pass, I may consider teaching you the basics of alchemy. If you fail . . ." He grinned, revealing a mouth full of surprisingly sharp teeth. "Well, let's just say you'll wish you'd never set foot in my cave."

Slifer swallowed hard. *What have I gotten myself into?*

"I accept your challenge, Elder Feng," Slifer said, trying to sound confident. "What is this test?"

Elder Feng's grin widened. "Oh, nothing too difficult. I simply want you to identify these."

He reached into his robes and pulled out a small pouch. From it, he produced three small objects and placed them on a nearby table.

Slifer leaned in to get a better look. The first object was a leaf, deep green in color with jagged edges. The second was a small round seed that seemed to glow faintly. The third was a piece of what looked like ordinary bark.

"Well?" Elder Feng prompted. "What are they?"

Slifer stared at the items, his mind racing. He had some knowledge from the original Slifer's memories, but it was fragmented and incomplete. He'd have to rely on his own observations and deductions.

Or I can just rely on the Insight skill . . .

CHAPTER TWENTY-FIVE

Slifer focused his attention on the leaf first and activated the Insight skill.

Name: Thunderleaf

Description: A rare herb that grows only in areas frequently struck by lightning. Contains trace amounts of electric energy. Commonly used in pills to strengthen the body's meridians.

Interesting, Slifer mused. *That could be useful for more than just pills.* He turned his attention to the glowing seed next.

Name: Starlight Seed

Description: Seed from the Celestial Starfruit tree. Absorbs and stores starlight energy. Often used in pills to enhance spiritual perception and connection to celestial energies.

Celestial energies, huh? I wonder if that has anything to do with those Immortal Realm cultivators I keep hearing about.

Finally, he examined the piece of bark.

Name: Ironbark

Description: Bark from the Iron Oak tree. Extremely durable and resistant to both physical and spiritual attacks. Used in protective pills and talismans.

Slifer allowed himself a small smile. *Not bad, Insight skill. Let's see if we can impress the old man.* He looked up at Elder Feng, who was watching him with narrowed eyes.

"Well?" the old alchemist prompted. "What are they?"

Slifer pointed to each item in turn. "This leaf is Thunderleaf, often used in pills to strengthen meridians. The seed is a Starlight Seed from the Celestial Starfruit tree, used for enhancing spiritual perception. And this bark is Ironbark from the Iron Oak, used in protective concoctions."

Elder Feng's eyebrows shot up in surprise. "Well, well," he muttered. "It seems you're not completely ignorant after all."

Was that . . . almost a compliment? Slifer wondered.

"Now you can teach me, right?" Slifer asked, trying not to sound too eager.

Elder Feng's eyes narrowed again. "Not so fast, Supreme Elder. That was just a warm-up." He reached into his robes and pulled out another pouch. "Let's see how you fare with these."

He emptied the pouch onto the table and revealed five more objects: a fiery feather, a small red fruit, a chunk of what looked like crystal, a vial of silvery liquid, and a dried flower.

Looks like the old man's not giving up so easily, Slifer thought. *Fine by me. Let's see how long before he gives up.*

He focused on the feather first.

Name: Phoenix Plume
Description: A feather from a lesser phoenix. Contains trace amounts of fire and rebirth energy. Used in pills for cleansing impurities and promoting regeneration.

Slifer's eyes widened slightly. *A phoenix feather? Now that's impressive.*
He moved on to the fruit.

Name: Blood Apple
Description: Fruit from the Blood tree, which grows only in places of great bloodshed. Enhances blood essence and vitality.
Caution: Addictive if consumed raw.

Well, that's suitably creepy for a demonic sect, Slifer thought.
Next, he examined the crystal.

> Name: Void Quartz
> Description: Crystal formed in areas of distorted space. Enhances spatial manipulation abilities when used in pills or talismans.

Spatial manipulation? Now that could be useful.
He turned his attention to the vial of liquid.

> Name: Moonsilver
> Description: Liquid metal that absorbs and stores moonlight. Used in pills to enhance yin energy and promote calm states of mind.

Calm states of mind, huh? Maybe I should keep some of that around for when my disciples return.
Finally, he looked at the dried flower.

> Name: Timeblossom
> Description: A flower that only blooms for one second every hundred years. Rumored to have time-altering properties when used in high-level pills.

Slifer's eyebrows rose. *Time-altering properties? Intriguing.*

He looked up at Elder Feng, who was watching him with growing agitation. Slifer couldn't help but feel a bit smug.

"Well?" Elder Feng demanded. "What are they?"

Slifer pointed to each item in turn and recited their names and primary uses. With each one he got correct, Elder Feng's face grew redder.

"The Phoenix Plume for cleansing and regeneration, the Blood Apple for enhancing vitality—though, I'd be careful with that one: it's addictive when raw. The Void Quartz for spatial manipulation, Moonsilver for enhancing yin energy and promoting calm, and Timeblossom, which I hear has some interesting temporal properties in high-level pills."

Elder Feng's mouth opened and closed several times, though no sound came out. Finally, he sputtered, "How . . . how did you . . ."

Slifer shrugged, trying to look nonchalant. "I've picked up a few things over the years." *And by "picked up" I mean "just learned about five seconds ago, thanks to this handy Insight skill."*

Elder Feng slumped onto his stool, looking deflated. "Fine," he grumbled. "Your alchemy knowledge is . . . adequate. If barely." He straightened up and fixed Slifer with a glare. "But knowing ingredients is just the beginning. Let's see if you can keep up with the real lessons."

Slifer nodded, suppressing a grin. *Challenge accepted, old man.*

"Before we begin," Elder Feng said, stroking his beard, "it's important you understand the different levels of alchemists. There are six main ranks: Novice, Intermediate, Advanced, Expert, Master, and Grandmaster."

Slifer nodded. This much he remembered from the original Slifer's memories. But as Elder Feng continued, he realized there was much more to learn.

"Novice alchemists can create simple pills and elixirs, mostly for healing minor injuries or providing small boosts to cultivation. They work with common ingredients and basic equipment." Elder Feng paused, eyeing Slifer. "I assume you're at least beyond this level?"

Slifer coughed, thinking of his earlier disastrous attempt at pill-making. "Of course," he lied smoothly. "Please, continue."

"Intermediate alchemists," Elder Feng went on, "can create more complex concoctions. They work with rarer ingredients and can produce pills that aid in breaking through to higher cultivation realms, though the success rate is . . . variable."

Variable, huh? Sounds like a polite way of saying "Expect a lot of explosions."

"Advanced alchemists," Elder Feng said, puffing up slightly, "can create high-level pills consistently. We work with rare and sometimes dangerous ingredients to craft pills that can significantly boost cultivation speed or grant temporary special abilities."

Slifer nodded, impressed despite himself. "And the Expert level?"

Elder Feng's expression soured slightly. "Experts can create pills that alter the very essence of a cultivator. They work with the rarest of ingredients and can even craft unique, one-of-a-kind pills tailored to specific individuals."

"Sounds impressive," Slifer said. "But I assume you're past that level, given your reputation in our sect?"

Elder Feng's face reddened. "As much as I'd like to brag about being a Master, I am merely at the Advanced stage," he admitted grudgingly.

Slifer blinked in surprise. "But . . . you're the best alchemist in our sect, aren't you?"

Elder Feng laughed. "In our sect, yes. But in the entire Mortal Realm? The highest rank you'll find here is Expert. And there's only one of those: Alchemist Xiao of the Heavenly Light Sect."

Heavenly Light Sect? Slifer thought. *Guess they're not the number one sect for nothing.*

"This Alchemist Xiao," Slifer said carefully, "must be quite powerful."

Elder Feng nodded grudgingly. "An Ascendant Realm cultivator, of course. You see, to become an Expert alchemist, one must generally be an Ascendant. Alchemy is tied closely to one's cultivation level."

He paused, a sly look crossing his face. "Of course, there are rare exceptions when one can go beyond their cultivation realm in alchemy. I, for instance, am an Advanced alchemist despite being only at the Nascent Soul Realm."

Ah, Slifer thought. *So that's what's got him all puffed up.*

"Most other Advanced alchemists are at the Origin Realm," Elder Feng continued, his voice taking on a haughty tone. "But I assure you, they're no better than me despite their higher cultivation."

Slifer nodded, trying to keep his expression neutral. *Someone's got a chip on their shoulder.* Aloud, he said, "I see. And what of the Master and Grandmaster levels?"

Elder Feng waved a hand dismissively. "Those are beyond the Mortal Realm. Master alchemists can create pills that fundamentally alter reality itself. And Grandmasters?" He shook his head in wonder. "It's said they can create pills that grant immortality or even ascension to higher realms of existence."

Slifer's eyes widened. *Immortality pills? Now that's something to aim for.*

"Fascinating," he said. "So, where do we begin?"

Elder Feng grinned, a slightly wicked gleam in his eye. "Oh, I very much doubt your claim of being a Novice alchemist, so we'll start with the basics. Can't have the great supreme elder blowing himself up, now, can we?"

CHAPTER TWENTY-SIX

Over the next few hours, Elder Feng took Slifer through a whirlwind tour of basic alchemy. They covered everything from proper cauldron selection to flame control techniques. Slifer found himself genuinely fascinated and was absorbing the information like a sponge.

"Now," Elder Feng said as he gestured to a row of small cauldrons, "each of these is suited for a different type of pill. This jade one is excellent for pills dealing with wood-element energy. The copper one is best for fire-based concoctions."

Slifer examined each cauldron carefully. "And this black one?" he asked, pointing to an ominous-looking cauldron at the end of the row.

Elder Feng's eyes gleamed. "Ah, that's for more . . . specialized pills. The kind our sect is known for."

Right, Slifer thought. *Demonic cultivator stuff. I should probably learn that too, even if I don't plan on using it.*

As they moved on to ingredient preparation, Slifer couldn't help but ask, "Elder Feng, how did you become interested in alchemy?"

The old man's expression softened slightly. "It was many years ago," he said, his voice taking on a distant quality. "I was but a young disciple, not much older than your Fenlock. There was an epidemic sweeping through our sect, and our alchemists were working day and night to produce enough healing pills." He paused, a faraway look in his eyes. "I was fascinated by their work, by the way they could take simple herbs and minerals and create something that could save lives just as well as take them away. From that day on, I knew what my path would be."

Apart from the "take lives" bit, the old coot isn't so bad after all, Slifer thought.

Elder Feng seemed to snap out of his thoughts, his usual gruff demeanor returning. "Yes, well, enough of that. Let's move on to pill formation techniques."

As the lesson continued, Slifer found himself gaining a new appreciation for the complexity of alchemy. It wasn't just about throwing ingredients into a pot and hoping for the best. There was a rhythm to it, a delicate balance of energy manipulation and precise timing.

"The key," Elder Feng explained while demonstrating with a small flame dancing above his palm, "is to maintain consistent heat while gradually infusing your own spiritual energy. Too much at once and you'll destabilize the entire mixture."

Slifer watched closely as he tried to memorize every detail. *This is way more complicated than I thought. No wonder I nearly blew myself up earlier.*

As the day wore on, Elder Feng covered topics ranging from ingredient compatibility to the finer points of pill condensation. Slifer's head was swimming with information, but he found himself eager to learn more.

Finally, as the light outside the cave began to dim, Elder Feng stepped back from the workbench. "Well," he said, eyeing Slifer critically, "you've absorbed more than I expected. Perhaps you're not entirely hopeless after all."

Coming from Elder Feng, Slifer realized this was high praise indeed. "Thank you for your instruction, Elder Feng," he said, bowing slightly. "I've learned a great deal."

Elder Feng harrumphed, but Slifer could see a glimmer of satisfaction in the old man's eyes. "Yes, well, don't get too full of yourself. You've barely scratched the surface of true alchemy." He paused, stroking his beard thoughtfully. "Still, I suppose you've earned a demonstration of real skill. Choose any pill that is Nascent Soul or below, and I'll show you how a true master works."

Slifer held back a smirk as he thought of an idea. "Well, I've always been curious about the Core Formation Celestial Lotus Pill. I've heard it's quite challenging to create. Perhaps you could demonstrate that one?"

Elder Feng's eyebrows shot up, his eyes widening in surprise. A moment later, his face flushed red with embarrassment. He coughed, averting his gaze.

"The Core Formation Celestial Lotus Pill? That's . . . Well . . ." Elder Feng mumbled, now stroking his beard nervously. "I'm afraid I don't have that recipe. In fact, our sect doesn't possess it either."

Slifer feigned innocence. "Oh? I thought surely a skilled alchemist like yourself would know such a renowned pill."

Elder Feng's eyes narrowed suspiciously. "How do you even know about that pill, Supreme Elder? It's not common knowledge." He studied Slifer's face intently, then his expression darkened. "Wait a moment . . . You didn't . . . steal it, did you?"

"I'm not sure what you mean, Elder Feng," Slifer said carefully.

The old alchemist snorted. "Don't play coy with me. It wouldn't be the first time you've acquired things that don't belong to you. Need I remind you of the Frost Phoenix Elixir incident?"

Oh great, Slifer thought. *The old man still hasn't gotten over that. Why was the original such a thief?*

Elder Feng leaned in close, his voice low and urgent. "Listen well, Supreme Elder. Whoever had that pill recipe won't have a simple background. If you've taken it from someone powerful, you could be bringing down a world of trouble on our sect." He straightened up, his expression serious. "I won't ask where you got it, but be careful. Don't drag the Black Rose Sect into your schemes this time."

I didn't think he'd jump to such a conclusion, Slifer thought, his mind racing. *Well, this complicates things. But maybe I can still turn it to my advantage.*

"Your concern is noted, Elder Feng," Slifer said. "But let's say, hypothetically, that I did have access to this recipe. Would you be interested in working together to create it?"

Elder Feng's eyes narrowed, a mix of suspicion and intrigue dancing across his face. He stroked his beard and eyed Slifer with a calculating gaze.

"Collaborate, you say?" he mused, his voice low. "That's a dangerous game you're proposing, Supreme Elder. The Core Formation Celestial Lotus Pill isn't just any pill. It's the stuff of legends."

Slifer leaned in, keeping his voice steady. "And who better to bring a legend to life than the most skilled alchemist in our sect?"

Elder Feng's chest puffed up slightly at the compliment, but his eyes remained wary. "Flattery will get you nowhere, Supreme Elder. But . . ." He paused, clearly torn between caution and curiosity. "If you truly have access to this recipe, it could revolutionize our sect's standing."

Now we're getting somewhere, Slifer thought. "It really could," Slifer agreed aloud. "Imagine the power our disciples could attain with such a pill at their disposal."

Elder Feng nodded slowly, his eyes taking on a distant look. "The success rate for Core Formation would skyrocket. We could produce more high-level cultivators than any other sect in the region."

"Exactly," Slifer said, pressing his advantage. "And you, Elder Feng, would be the one to make it all possible."

Elder Feng studied Slifer for a long moment, his expression unreadable. Finally, he sighed. "I must be going senile to even consider working with you. But . . . very well. If you can produce this recipe, I'll work with you on creating the Core Formation Celestial Lotus Pill."

Slifer allowed himself a small smile. "Excellent. I knew I could count on your expertise, Elder Feng."

"Don't get ahead of yourself," Elder Feng grumbled. "I haven't agreed to anything beyond examining the recipe. If I deem it too risky, or if I suspect it's a forgery, the deal's off. Understood?"

Slifer nodded solemnly. "Of course. I wouldn't expect anything less from an alchemist of your caliber."

Elder Feng harrumphed, but Slifer could see a glimmer of excitement in the old man's eyes. "Well then, Supreme Elder. Let's see this miraculous recipe of yours."

Slifer reached into his spatial ring and retrieved the recipe he had purchased from the System Shop. He handed it over to Elder Feng and watched closely as the alchemist's eyes scanned the contents. Elder Feng's eyebrows rose higher and higher as he read. His fingers trembled slightly, and Slifer could practically see the gears turning in the old man's mind.

"This . . . this is . . ." Elder Feng muttered, his voice filled with awe. "It's genuine. I can hardly believe it, but . . . this is the real Core Formation Celestial Lotus Pill recipe." He looked up at Slifer, his eyes wide with a mix of excitement and trepidation. "Do you realize what you've brought me, Supreme Elder? This isn't just a powerful pill recipe. It's a game changer. With this, our sect could . . ." He trailed off, shaking his head in wonder.

Slifer nodded, attempting to look wise and all-knowing. "I understand the significance, Elder Feng. That's why I brought it to you. I know you have the skill to bring this recipe to life."

Elder Feng clutched the recipe tightly, his eyes darting around as if expecting someone to leap out and snatch it away. "We'll need to be careful. Very careful. The ingredients alone will be a challenge to gather without raising suspicion."

"Leave that to me," Slifer said confidently. *After all, I've got a handy System Shop to supply whatever we need.* "And, of course," he added, "I'll need you to continue teaching me the art of alchemy. If we're to work together on this, I'll need to understand the intricacies of pill creation."

Elder Feng nodded absently, his attention still focused on the recipe. "Yes, yes, of course. We'll need to . . . Wait." He looked up sharply at Slifer. "Is that what this is about? You're bribing me with this recipe to teach you alchemy?"

Slifer held up his hands defensively. "Not at all, Elder Feng. Think of it more as a mutually beneficial arrangement. You get access to a legendary pill recipe, and I get to learn from the best alchemist in our sect. Everybody wins."

Elder Feng snorted, but Slifer could see the corners of his mouth twitching upwards. "Flattery and bribery. You're a piece of work, Supreme Elder."

"I prefer to think of it as resourcefulness," Slifer said with a grin.

Elder Feng shook his head, but there was a glimmer of amusement in his eyes. "Fine. We have a deal. But don't think this means I'll go easy on you. If you want to learn alchemy, you'll work for it. Understood?"

Slifer bowed slightly. "I wouldn't have it any other way, Elder Feng."

CHAPTER TWENTY-SEVEN

Slifer smiled, pleased that his plan was coming together. "Shall we get started?"

Elder Feng blinked, and his eyebrows furrowed in confusion. "Get started? What do you mean?"

"Well, I thought we'd make the pill now," Slifer replied, as if it were the most obvious thing in the world. "We have the recipe, after all."

The old alchemist stared at Slifer for a moment before bursting into laughter. His shoulders shook as he wheezed and clutched his stomach.

"Oh, Supreme Elder," Elder Feng said, wiping a tear from his eye. "You truly are something else. Does it look like I have the ingredients for such a pill just lying around?"

Geez, it wasn't that funny. Slifer rolled his eyes internally at the old man's extreme reaction. *These cultivators and their dramatics.*

"Actually," Slifer said, reaching into his storage ring, "I do have the ingredients."

Elder Feng's laughter cut off abruptly, and his eyes widened as Slifer began pulling out various items and placing them on the workbench.

"Impossible," the old alchemist muttered, leaning in to examine the ingredients. "I know you said you would bring the ingredients, but how did you already . . . Where did you . . ."

Slifer shrugged, trying to appear nonchalant. "I have my sources." *And by "sources" I mean "a convenient interdimensional shopping system,"* he added silently.

Elder Feng picked up the first ingredient, a delicate petal. "A Celestial Lotus Petal," he whispered. "I've only seen these drawn out in my master's books."

Slifer watched, feeling slightly awkward as the old man cradled the petal like it was a newborn child. *Is this normal behavior for alchemists?* he wondered.

Elder Feng moved on to the next ingredient, a small vial. "Nine-Tailed Fox Essence," he murmured, holding the vial up to the light. "Legend has it that this essence can grant a cultivator unparalleled control over their spiritual energy." He then held up a fruit that crackled with tiny sparks. "Thunderbolt Fruit! Oh, the power contained within . . . I've always wanted to work with one of these!"

As the old alchemist continued to salivate over each ingredient, Slifer found himself torn between fascination and discomfort. On one hand, Elder Feng's knowledge was impressive and Slifer could see the value in learning about these rare materials. On the other hand . . .

He looks absolutely crazy, Slifer thought, watching as Elder Feng practically cooed at the ingredients. *Is this what I'd turn into if I became an alchemist? This old man seems one step away from talking to the walls!*

"And this!" Elder Feng exclaimed, holding up a glowing crystal. "Dragon's Breath Crystal! Do you know how rare these are? It takes a hundred years for a single crystal to form from a dragon's exhalations!"

A hundred years of dragon morning breath. Lovely, Slifer thought, suppressing a grimace.

Finally, Elder Feng picked up the last ingredient. "Void Lotus Root," he breathed heavily. "Grown in the spaces between realms . . . I never thought I'd see one with my own eyes."

As the old alchemist continued to fawn over the ingredients, Slifer found himself reconsidering his career choices. *If becoming an alchemist means turning into this, maybe I should stick to cultivation.*

After what felt like an eternity of ingredient worship, Elder Feng finally seemed to remember Slifer's presence. He cleared his throat, composing himself. "We must begin immediately! But first, we need the proper equipment."

The old alchemist hurried to a nearby shelf and pulled out various tools and instruments. "We'll need my finest mortar and pestle for grinding the Celestial Lotus Petal," he muttered, more to himself than to Slifer. "And a crystal vial for the Nine-Tailed Fox Essence . . ."

After a few minutes, Elder Feng returned to the workbench, his arms full of various tools and instruments. He set them down carefully, then turned to Slifer with a proud grin.

"Now, Supreme Elder, let me show you the pride of my collection," Elder Feng said as he gestured to a row of cauldrons against the far wall. "These are no ordinary pill-refining vessels. Each one is specially crafted to enhance certain aspects of the alchemical process." He pointed to a cauldron made of what looked like polished jade. "This one amplifies wood energy. Perfect for pills that promote growth and healing." Then he indicated a copper cauldron with flame patterns etched into its surface. "And this beauty is ideal for fire-based concoctions. The patterns help circulate heat evenly, reducing the chance of overheating."

Slifer nodded politely, trying to show interest. *I suppose every profession has its tools of the trade. Though, I doubt blacksmiths get quite this excited about their hammers.*

"For the Core Formation Celestial Lotus Pill," Elder Feng continued, "we'll need something truly special. Perhaps the silver cauldron with celestial runes, or maybe the one forged from meteorite iron . . ."

As the old alchemist debated with himself over which cauldron to use, Slifer had an idea. *If he's this excited about his cauldrons, I wonder what he'll think of mine.*

"Actually, Elder Feng," Slifer interrupted, "I have a cauldron we might use." He reached into his storage ring once more and pulled out a beautiful green cauldron. Elder Feng turned to look, and his words died on his lips as he saw the cauldron in Slifer's hands. The old man's face went pale and his eyes widened to an almost impossible degree.

"Elder Feng?" Slifer asked, concerned by the alchemist's reaction. "Are you okay?"

Elder Feng stumbled backwards and caught himself on the edge of the workbench. "That . . . that can't be," he whispered, his voice trembling. "The Jade Skyfire Cauldron? Here?"

"You know about this cauldron?" Slifer blinked in surprise.

Elder Feng nodded slowly, his eyes never leaving the green vessel. "I . . . I have heard rumors," he whispered. "Whispers that you possessed the Jade Skyfire Cauldron, but I thought . . . well, I assumed it was exaggeration. Most things related to you tend to be, after all."

Slifer raised an eyebrow at that last comment. *Most things related to me are exaggerations? I'm not sure if I should be flattered or offended.*

Elder Feng approached slowly with his hands outstretched, as if he were approaching a wild animal. "May I . . . may I touch it?" he asked.

Slifer nodded, holding out the cauldron. Elder Feng's hands shook as he ran them over the smooth surface, tracing the intricate patterns etched into the green material.

"Incredible," Elder Feng murmured. "The stories don't do it justice. This cauldron . . . It's said to increase the success rate of pill refinement by eight times! And the purity of the resulting pills . . . They say it's one of the top ten cauldrons of the Immortal Realm."

Slifer's eyebrows shot up in surprise. *Eight times? I knew it was special because it could contain Vowron, a Half-Step Immortal, but this? I can't believe even with such an OP cauldron I failed that badly. Maybe I'm worse at alchemy than I thought.*

Elder Feng continued to caress the cauldron, his eyes shining with excitement. "The Jade Skyfire Cauldron was said to be created in the earliest days of cultivation, when the boundaries between the Mortal and Immortal Realms were still blurred. It's said that the cauldron can even refine heavenly materials that would destroy lesser vessels."

He looked up at Slifer with crazy eyes. "We must use this for the Core Formation Celestial Lotus Pill. With this cauldron, our chances of success are practically guaranteed!"

Slifer nodded, secretly relieved. *At least now I won't have to worry about blowing us both up. Hopefully.*

"Alright," Slifer said, "let's get started, then. What's the first step?"

Over the next few hours, Slifer acted as Elder Feng's assistant, following the old alchemist's instructions to the letter. They carefully measured out each ingredient and prepared them according to the recipe.

"Now, gently crush the Celestial Lotus Petal," Elder Feng instructed. "We want to release its essence without damaging the delicate structures within."

Slifer complied, using a jade mortar and pestle to carefully grind the petal. As he worked, he felt a strange tingling in his fingers, as if the petal's celestial energy was seeping into his skin.

Huh, maybe there's something to all this alchemy stuff after all, he thought.

Next came the Nine-Tailed Fox Essence, which Elder Feng insisted on handling himself. "One must approach this with the utmost caution," he explained. "A single misplaced drop could imbue the entire pill with chaotic fox energy." Slifer watched closely as the old alchemist carefully measured out three drops of the silvery liquid.

As they continued through the process, Slifer found himself becoming more and more invested. There was a rhythm to alchemy, a dance of elements and energies that he hadn't fully appreciated before.

"Now, Supreme Elder," Elder Feng said, his voice tense with concentration, "we come to the most crucial step. We must combine the Thunderbolt

Fruit with the Dragon's Breath Crystal at precisely the right moment. Too soon and the energies will clash. Too late and they'll fizzle out."

Slifer nodded, feeling a bead of sweat form on his brow. *No pressure or anything.*

Elder Feng began to chant as his hands moved in intricate patterns over the cauldron. Slifer watched in fascination as tendrils of energy began to swirl within the vessel, forming a miniature vortex.

"Now!" the old alchemist cried.

Slifer dropped the Thunderbolt Fruit into the cauldron, followed immediately by the Dragon's Breath Crystal. For a heart-stopping moment, nothing happened.

Then, with a blinding flash and a crack of thunder, the cauldron erupted with power. Slifer stumbled back, shielding his eyes.

"Yes!" Elder Feng crowed. "Perfect fusion! Oh, I haven't felt such a rush in centuries!"

As the light faded, Slifer blinked the spots from his vision. The cauldron now glowed with an inner fire, pulsing with barely contained energy.

"What now?" Slifer asked, his voice hoarse.

Elder Feng grinned, a manic glint in his eye. "Now we add the final ingredient: the Void Lotus Root." With extreme care, the old alchemist lowered the root into the cauldron. As soon as it touched the swirling energies within, it began to dissolve, spreading threads of void-like emptiness throughout the mixture. "And now," Elder Feng said, his voice dropping to a whisper, "we wait."

For the next hour, Slifer and Elder Feng sat in tense silence watching the cauldron. The energies within continued to swirl and pulse as they slowly coalesced into a single point of light.

Just when Slifer thought he couldn't take the suspense any longer, Elder Feng leapt to his feet. "It's ready!"

With practiced movements, the old alchemist began the final steps of the refinement process. Slifer watched in awe as Elder Feng's hands blurred as he channeled spiritual energy into the cauldron with incredible precision.

Finally, with a sound like a distant bell, a single pill rose from the cauldron. It hovered in the air for a moment glowing with an inner light, then gently settled into Elder Feng's outstretched palm.

A blue box appeared before Slifer's eyes.

Ding!
You have gained 200 Karmic Credits for breaking through to Level 2.
You have gained 400 Karmic Credits for breaking through to Level 3.

You have gained 800 Karmic Credits for breaking through to Level 4.
Congratulations!
You have broken through to Intermediate Alchemy.
Intermediate Alchemy (Level 4):
Can create pills up to Nascent Soul Realm with a 40% success rate
70% success rate for Core Formation pills and below
Can work with materials of up to 3rd-grade rarity with 50% reduced risk
of waste
Ability to infuse pills with up to 2 complementary attributes
Can identify common ingredient interactions with 80% accuracy
30% increase in pill potency compared to Novice level
Able to sense and correct minor imbalances during pill formation

Three levels at once? That's unexpected. Slifer blinked in surprise. *Wait . . . If I jumped three levels just by assisting in making this pill, there's no way I could have crafted it myself. It would have been completely impossible. If I'd tried this pill on my own, I wouldn't have just ended up covered in sticky ingredients,* he thought. *Best case, I'd have reduced the entire sect to rubble. Worst case? I might have opened a portal to who-knows-where and gotten sucked into the void between realms. Thank the heavens I decided to seek out Elder Feng.* A wave of relief washed over him. *Not only did I get the pill, but I've learned more in one session than I probably would have in years of fumbling around on my own.*

"We've done it," the old alchemist breathed, bringing Slifer out of his thoughts. "The Core Formation Celestial Lotus Pill. In all my years, I never thought I'd see one, let alone create it myself."

Slifer leaned in to examine the pill. It was smaller than he'd expected, no larger than a grape, but it radiated an aura of power that made the hair on the back of his neck stand up.

"Can I see it?" Slifer asked, holding out his hand. Elder Feng hesitated for a moment, clearly reluctant to part with his creation. But after a brief internal struggle, he carefully placed the pill in Slifer's palm. "Fascinating," Slifer murmured, turning the pill over in his hand. Then, without warning, he slipped it into his storage ring.

Elder Feng's jaw dropped. "W-what are you doing?" he sputtered.

Slifer blinked innocently. "Storing it for safekeeping, of course."

The old alchemist's face cycled through a range of emotions—shock, confusion, anger, and, finally, resignation. "I . . . I suppose I shouldn't be surprised." He sighed. "But why would you want it? Surely an Ascendant Realm cultivator like yourself has no need for a Core Formation pill."

Slifer shrugged, trying to look nonchalant. "It never hurts to be prepared."

Elder Feng frowned, his brow furrowing in thought. After a moment, his eyes widened in realization. "Oh," he said softly. "I didn't think you cared so much about your disciples."

I need it a lot more than my disciples, Slifer thought. Aloud, he said, "A sect master must look out for his own."

Elder Feng nodded, a hint of newfound respect in his eyes. "Well, I'm afraid it will be some time before we can make another. Gathering ingredients of this caliber is no easy task."

Slifer nodded, already planning his next shopping spree in the System Shop. "I understand. Thank you for your help, Elder Feng. I don't think I'd have been able to do it without you."

The old alchemist puffed up at the praise, his earlier disappointment forgotten. "Yes, well, with a cauldron like that, even a Novice could work wonders."

At the mention of the cauldron, Slifer realized he should probably put it away. He reached out and grasped the Jade Skyfire Cauldron, preparing to store it in his storage ring.

Elder Feng's reaction was immediate and extreme. His face drained of color and his eyes bulged as if he might have a heart attack on the spot. He reached out with trembling hands, making small, distressed noises.

Slifer took a step back, genuinely concerned. *Geez, what's his problem now?* "Elder Feng?" he asked cautiously. "You okay there?"

The old alchemist's eyes had taken on a crazed, desperate look. "The cauldron," he croaked. "You can't . . . you can't just take it away!"

Slifer glanced down at the cauldron, then back at Elder Feng. An idea began to form in his mind. *He really wants to use this thing, huh? I bet I could work out a deal here . . .*

"You know, Elder Feng," Slifer said casually, "I might be willing to loan out the cauldron from time to time."

The old alchemist's head snapped up, hope blooming in his eyes. "Truly? You would . . . you would allow me to use the Jade Skyfire Cauldron?"

Slifer nodded slowly, as if considering. "On one condition."

"Anything!" Elder Feng blurted out, then quickly composed himself. "I mean, what did you have in mind, Supreme Elder?"

"It's simple," Slifer said. "You agree to make any pill I want, free of charge. I'll provide the ingredients, of course."

Elder Feng's eyes widened. For a moment, Slifer thought he might refuse. But then the old alchemist nodded vigorously. "Yes! Yes, of course!" he exclaimed. "It would be my honor to craft pills for you, Supreme Elder. With the Jade Skyfire Cauldron, we could create wonders beyond imagination!"

As Elder Feng continued to ramble about the possibilities, Slifer found himself wondering if he should have asked for more. *Maybe I could have gotten him to throw in some cultivation resources too. Oh well, there's always next time.*

"Excellent," Slifer said, cutting off the old alchemist's excited babbling. "I'll leave the cauldron with you for now, then. I'm sure you're eager to experiment with it."

Elder Feng nodded enthusiastically, already reaching for the cauldron. "Oh yes, Supreme Elder. I have so many ideas . . . so many possibilities to explore! I might even be able to finally become an Expert alchemist!"

Slifer nodded absently, already inching towards the cave entrance. The thought of listening to another hour of alchemical theories made his newly acquired Intermediate Alchemy knowledge recoil in horror.

"That's . . . great," Slifer said, forcing a smile. "I look forward to seeing what you come up with. But for now, I should really be going. Sect business and all that." As Elder Feng opened his mouth, likely about to launch into another lecture about pill formation or cauldron maintenance, Slifer quickly added, "I'll be in touch when I need more pills. Good day, Elder Feng."

Without waiting for a response, Slifer turned and almost ran out of the cave, breathing a sigh of relief as the fresh air hit his face. Behind him, he could still hear Elder Feng's excited muttering echoing from the cave.

Slifer shook his head as he turned his focus to his next step of action. *Time to break through to the Core Formation Realm!*

CHAPTER TWENTY-EIGHT

Slifer sat cross-legged on a cultivation pillow in his room, his eyes closed in deep concentration. Outside in the courtyard, Morvran stood vigilant, waiting for the start of his master's tribulation.

Alright, time to level up, Slifer thought as his eyes flashed open. *Let's hope this goes smoother than last time.*

He took a deep breath and centered himself as he prepared for the task ahead. Breaking through to the Core Formation Realm was no small feat, even for someone as resourceful as Slifer.

It feels like ages since I broke through to Foundation Establishment, he mused. *Like it happened in a whole different book. Now look at me, about to form a core.*

Focusing his mind, Slifer began to review the various levels of breakthrough he might face. *First up, Azure Pinnacle Tribulation. Sky-blue clouds, three lightning strikes. Sounds manageable. Then there's Crimson Wave Tribulation. Five simultaneous lightning bolts, but hey, at least you get a twenty to thirty percent boost in qi quality and quantity. Risk versus reward, I guess. Golden Crown Tribulation brings nine lightning strikes to the party. But you might gain enlightenment and master some techniques, so that's cool. And finally, Obsidian Monarch Tribulation. Thirteen lightning strikes and a chance at a bloodline. Because who doesn't want to get zapped over a dozen times for some mystery DNA?*

Slifer's brow furrowed as he remembered his previous breakthrough. What had started as a relatively tame event had quickly escalated into an Obsidian Monarch Tribulation.

"Still haven't unlocked that bloodline," he muttered aloud. "What a rip-off! What's the point of nearly getting fried if I can't even use the reward?" *But let's hope history doesn't repeat itself. I don't fancy another Obsidian Monarch Tribulation. And this time, I don't even have my protagonist disciples here to shield me with their plot armor . . . I mean, luck.*

Deciding it was better to be overprepared than under, Slifer accessed his System interface. The familiar blue screen materialized before his eyes, displaying various options and his current stats.

> Name: Slifer
> Race: Human
> Alignment: Demonic
> Spiritual Cultivation: Peak Foundation Establishment
> Body Cultivation: Peak Foundation Establishment
> Lifespan Remaining: 100 years
> Karmic Credits: 51,970
> Skills: Insight (Intermediate), Nascent Soul Armor (Level 2), Phase Ability (Level 1), Void Being Aura (Level 1)
> Items: Reversal Card, Peak Slifer Card, Caelum Card, Hughie Card, Critical Block x3, Reflection Barrier Card x3, Thunderblast Card x2, Critical Heal x3, Time Reversal Card, One Minute Rewind Card x2, Mimicry Card x3, Teleportation Marker x3
> Affinities: Light (25%), Fire (15%), Space (20%), Lightning (10%)
> Abilities: Firebreath, Mirror Mastery (Level 2)
> Techniques: Sunrise Slash (Level 3), Stellar Nova Strike (Level 2), Dimensional Slide (Level 2), Nascent Soul Armor (Level 1), Void Piercer (Level 1), Soul Search (Level 2)
> Weapon Mastery: Sword (20%)
> Perks: Dual Cultivator Perk

Time to go shopping, Slifer thought. As he scrolled through the available items in the System Shop, his eyes settled on the Critical Block Cards. Each card could protect against one critical strike during his tribulation.

Let's see . . . The maximum number of strikes I could face is probably around thirty, and that's if I encounter each tribulation one after another. But surely my luck isn't that bad.

After a moment's hesitation, Slifer decided to err on the side of caution. He selected thirty-five Critical Block Cards and winced slightly as he confirmed the purchase.

A System message popped up.

> *Ding!*
> Purchase successful
> You have gained 35 Critical Block Cards.
> 31,500 Karmic Credits deducted
> Current Karmic Credit balance: 20,470

Slifer sighed as he watched his hard-earned Karmic Credits dwindle. "Better poor than dead," he muttered, trying to reassure himself. "I'll make it back quickly enough from the Disciplinary Hall and Black Heart Sect anyways."

With his safeguards in place, Slifer turned his attention to the main event. He reached into his storage ring and brought out a small glowing pill—the Core Formation Celestial Lotus Pill.

As he held the pill up to the light, Slifer's thoughts turned to the different types of cores cultivators could form.

Let's see if I remember this correctly, he mused. *At the bottom of the barrel, you've got mixed cores, a jumble of various elements and impurities. Not ideal, but better than nothing, I guess. Then there are the mid-grade cores, each defined by a specific color based on the cultivator's primary method: green, purple, red—cultivation's own rainbow connection. The purer the core's color and the more robust its structure, the greater the qi capacity and quality. It's like the difference between a rusted-out junker and a high-performance sports car.*

For the cream of the crop, those with an impeccable foundation and a Heaven Rank method might form a legendary Golden Core. In all those xianxia novels I read back on Earth, it was always the top disciples of the big sects who managed that feat. The original Slifer formed a Golden Core, so both me and Zack should at minimum be capable of the same.

A spark of ambition flared in Slifer's eyes. *But why stop there? There are rumors of even more exotic cores—Frozen Cores, Crimson Cores, Cores of Chaos. Now that would be something to brag about.* He looked down at the pill in his hand. *Zack already formed a Golden Core. With this pill, I might have a shot at one of those rare variants. The boost might be tiny, but hey, I'll take any edge I can get.*

After taking a deep breath, Slifer popped the pill into his mouth and swallowed. The effect was almost immediate and a surge of energy coursed through his body.

Here goes nothing, he thought as he closed his eyes and began to circulate his qi. In his mind's eye, Slifer could see the nine Foundation Establishment pillars within his dantian. *Time for some renovations,* he thought with a hint of amusement.

One by one, he began to destroy the pillars. It was a delicate process that required precise control to channel the released energy correctly. A small lapse in control could easily lead to qi deviation.

As each pillar crumbled, the qi it contained joined with the energy from the pill swirling in a vortex at the center of his dantian. Slifer felt a bead of sweat form on his brow as he concentrated. The amount of power coursing through him was staggering and threatened to overwhelm his senses.

Stay focused, he reminded himself. *You've got this.*

As the final pillar collapsed, the maelstrom of energy in Slifer's dantian reached a fever pitch. He could feel the qi condensing, growing denser and more potent with each passing moment.

Slowly but surely, a sphere began to take shape within the swirling energies. At first, it was no larger than a marble, but it steadily grew in size and complexity. Intricate patterns formed on the surface of the nascent core. Slifer could feel his connection to the world around him changing and deepening in ways he couldn't fully articulate. As the core neared completion, Slifer allowed himself a small smile of satisfaction. The sphere now hovered at the center of his dantian, radiating power.

Ninety-nine percent there, he thought, examining his handiwork. *Not bad, if I do say so myself. Once the tribulation's over, we'll see what color this bad boy turns out to be.*

Just as Slifer was about to congratulate himself on a job well done, a low rumble of thunder shook the room. His eyes snapped open, and a mixture of excitement and apprehension flashed across his face.

"Showtime," he muttered, rising to his feet.

Slifer took a moment to stretch, working out the kinks from sitting still for so long. He glanced around his room, taking in the familiar surroundings one last time before the impending tribulation.

Better head to the courtyard, he thought. *I'd rather not have to redecorate if things get a little . . . zappy in here.*

As he made his way to the door, Slifer couldn't help but feel a twinge of nervousness. Heavenly Tribulations were no joke, after all. But there was excitement too, and the thrill of pushing himself to new heights.

The original went through an Origin Realm tribulation in that courtyard, and it's still standing, Slifer reassured himself. *If it can handle that, my little Core Formation breakthrough should be fine to do here.*

He paused at the threshold and took a deep breath to center himself. Outside, he could see Morvran standing at attention, ready to assist if needed.

Alright, world. Hit me with your best shot.

With that, he stepped out into the courtyard, ready to face whatever challenges lay ahead.

As Slifer's foot touched the stone pavement of the courtyard, a gust of wind swept through the area, rustling the leaves of nearby trees. The air felt charged with anticipation, as if the very world was holding its breath.

Morvran turned to face his master, a mixture of respect and concern evident in his expression. "Master," he said, bowing slightly. "The formations are ready. Is there anything else you require?"

Slifer shook his head and offered a reassuring smile to his loyal subordinate. "No, Morvran. You've done well. Just keep watch and make sure no one interrupts. This could get . . . interesting."

"Of course, Master." The bald man nodded. "I shall guard you with my life."

Always so dramatic, Slifer thought with a touch of amusement. *But I suppose that's par for the course in this world.*

As Slifer moved to the center of the courtyard, he took a moment to appreciate the formation patterns etched into the stone. The work was undoubtedly commissioned by the original Slifer—a masterpiece of protective arrays designed to withstand even the most powerful tribulations.

Whoever the original hired to create these formations really knew their stuff, Slifer thought, impressed. *Must have cost a fortune, but I guess when you're facing Origin Realm tribulations, no expense is too great.* He traced one of the patterns with his foot. *Good thing he was smart enough to invest in top-tier protection. I'd rather not have to explain to the sect why the house of their most powerful elder suddenly turned into a smoking crater.*

Another rumble of thunder echoed overhead, louder this time. Slifer glanced up at the sky to see the clouds gathering.

"Morvran," he called out, not taking his eyes off the sky. "What color are those clouds?"

The bald man squinted, shielding his eyes with one hand. "They appear to be . . . sky blue, Master."

Slifer nodded, a small smirk playing at the corner of his lips. "Azure Pinnacle Tribulation it is, then. Looks like we're starting off easy."

Three lightning strikes, he reminded himself. *Child's play compared to last time. Just stay focused and don't get cocky.*

CHAPTER TWENTY-NINE

Slifer stood in the center of the courtyard, his eyes fixed on the sky above. He could feel the hair on the back of his neck standing up. Three lightning bolts began to form in the air, their electric blue tendrils twisting and coiling like angry serpents.

Here we go, Slifer thought, bracing himself for the impact. *Three lightning strikes.*

But as he watched, something strange happened. The lightning bolts seemed to hesitate, as if unsure where to strike. Slifer's brow furrowed in confusion.

What's going on? This isn't how it's supposed to work.

Before his eyes, the three bolts of lightning began to merge, twisting and coalescing into a massive figure in the sky. A fully bearded face formed in the clouds and a single enormous arm extended from the mass of energy.

Well, this is new, Slifer thought, his eyes wide. *I don't remember reading about Zeus showing up for Core Formation tribulations.*

Nearby, Morvran stood watching, his mouth agape. This was his first time witnessing an "Immortal" tribulation, and it looked like his master was about to fight a deity.

"Master," Morvran called out, his voice trembling slightly. "Is this . . . normal?"

Slifer glanced at his subordinate. "Not exactly. This is something else."

Before Slifer could ponder further, the giant hand in the sky moved. In the blink of an eye, it appeared directly in front of him, its fingers outstretched to grab and crush him.

Oh, crap.

Just as the hand was about to close around him, an invisible barrier sprang into existence before him.

Ding!
Critical Block Activated

The lightning struck the barrier with a thunderous crack, sending sparks flying in all directions.

Thank you, System, for these Critical Block Cards, Slifer thought as he watched as the card's effect protected him from certain death.

But his relief was short-lived. The hand didn't disappear or retreat. Instead, it continued to squeeze the barrier, testing its strength.

This isn't good.

Slifer watched as another Critical Block Card activated, then another. Sweat began to bead on his forehead as he did some quick mental math.

Each Critical Block lasts about three seconds. I have forty-one cards left. That gives me . . . one hundred and twenty-three seconds before I'm out of protection.

The realization hit him like a ton of bricks. If the hand didn't dissipate in the next two minutes, he was going to die. And with the Shop on lockdown, he couldn't buy any more cards.

Just great. I finally make it to Core Formation and I'm about to be squished by a giant lightning hand. Slifer gritted his teeth and watched as card after card was used up. The barrier flickered each time a new one activated. *If all the Critical Blocks are used up, I'll have to use the Reflection Barrier Cards along with the Phase Ability. But after that . . . I'm not sure how I'll survive.*

As the seconds ticked by, Slifer found himself in a grim countdown to his death.

"Thirty cards left," he muttered. "Twenty-nine . . . twenty-eight . . ."

Meanwhile, Morvran watched the scene unfold with a mixture of confusion and awe. The aura emanating from the giant hand felt impossibly powerful, easily at the Origin Realm level. And yet, his master stood there seemingly unfazed by the cosmic forces trying to crush him.

Incredible, Morvran thought. *The supreme elder truly is on another level. This must be just the weakest attack. From here, even more powerful assaults will rain down, perhaps even reaching the Immortal Realm.*

As Morvran's imagination ran wild with visions of ever-escalating tribulations, Slifer continued his countdown.

"Twenty-five Critical Blocks left," Slifer said through clenched teeth. "Twenty-four . . . twenty-three . . ."

The pressure from the hand seemed to increase with each passing second. Slifer could feel the weight of it even through the barrier. It was like having a mountain slowly descend upon him.

Come on, come on. Dissipate already!

Just as the twentieth Critical Block Card was used up, something unexpected happened. The massive lightning hand began to flicker and fade as bits of electricity flew off in all directions.

Slifer, surprised by this, looked up at the sky. The face made of lightning was still there, but it was changing too. Its angry look turned into something else—like it was trying to speak.

The face's mouth moved, but Slifer couldn't hear anything. He squinted as he tried to understand what was happening. The face looked like it was fighting to stay together, really wanting to tell Slifer something.

Is it trying to talk to me? Slifer wondered, feeling a bit scared.

But before any words could come out, the face started to fall apart. Its features got blurry and started to disappear. With one last silent try, the face broke into sparks and vanished.

What was that about? Slifer blinked in confusion as the oppressive energy that had filled the air moments ago vanished as if it had never been there. *Is that it?* Slifer wondered, his brow furrowing in confusion. *As unexpected as that whole experience was, it wasn't nearly as bad as I thought it would be.* He looked around cautiously, half expecting another giant hand to pop out of nowhere.

"Master?" Morvran called out hesitantly. "Is it over?"

Slifer held up a hand, signaling for silence. He closed his eyes and focused his attention inwards to check on his dantian. What he saw made him frown.

In his mind's eye, Slifer could see his core. It was about the size of a marble and was floating in the center of his dantian. The core wasn't solid yet—instead, it looked like a swirling mix of colors that shifted and changed, never settling into a final form. The edges of the core were fuzzy, as if it was still trying to take shape. It pulsed gently, sending little waves of energy through Slifer's body. But it was clear the core wasn't done forming. It lacked the solid, stable feeling a finished core should have.

If the tribulation was complete, the core would be finished by now.

Slifer's eyes snapped open and narrowed as he scanned the sky once more. "It's not over," he said quietly. "Another tribulation is coming."

Morvran's eyes widened. "Another one? But the clouds have dissipated."

Slifer shook his head. "The heavens aren't following the usual playbook here. We need to be ready for anything."

As he spoke, Slifer's mind raced through the various types of tribulations he had read about in countless xianxia novels. *Lightning tribulation, check. Fire tribulation? Possible. Demon tribulation? God, I hope not. What else . . . Oh, right. Human tribulation.*

His thoughts were interrupted by a bloodcurdling scream that echoed across the courtyard. Slifer's head snapped up, searching for the source of the sound.

A figure appeared in the sky and was descending rapidly towards them. At first, Slifer couldn't make out who it was. The person seemed to be surrounded by a chaotic aura, their features distorted by rage.

As the figure drew closer, Slifer's eyes widened in recognition. "No way," he muttered.

It was the sect master, Malachar. But he looked . . . different. His usually neat appearance was in disarray, his hair wild and his eyes blazing with an unnatural light. The friendly, approachable face Slifer was used to had been transformed into a mask of fury.

A blue box appeared before Slifer's eyes.

Name: Malachar (True Name Unknown)
Realm: Half-Step Immortal Realm
Known Techniques: N/A
Known Affiliations: Black Rose Sect
Disposition: Berserk

Slifer blinked at the information, a sinking feeling in his stomach.

A berserk Half-Step Immortal. Just great.

"Master!" Morvran cried out, his voice filled with panic. "It's the sect master! But . . . but he looks—"

"Completely off his rocker?" Slifer finished, his eyes never leaving the approaching figure. "Yeah, I noticed. It seems to be part of the tribulation. The heavens are using him as a tool to test me." *Or to kill me,* he added silently. *Let's hope it's the former.*

Malachar landed in the courtyard with enough force to crack the stone beneath his feet. His eyes, usually so cunning and perceptive, now burned with mindless rage. He let out another scream, the sound more animal than human.

"Supreme Elder!" Malachar roared, his voice distorted and unrecognizable. "You dare! You dare to betray us!"

"Betray?" Slifer raised an eyebrow. "What are you talking about, Sect Master?"

But Malachar didn't seem interested in explanations. With a snarl, he lunged forward, moving so fast he seemed to blur.

In that split second, Slifer activated his Phase Ability. His body shimmered and became intangible just as Malachar reached him.

The berserk sect master passed right through Slifer as his momentum carried him forward, and Malachar's fist, crackling with barely contained power, slammed into the courtyard ground behind him.

The impact was catastrophic. Stone shattered like glass, sending shards flying in all directions. A spider web of cracks spread out from the point of impact and raced across the courtyard. The ground buckled and heaved and created a small crater where Malachar's fist had landed.

Okay, it looks like the heavens want to get rid of me for good. A Half-Step Immortal for a Core Formation tribulation is a death sentence!

Slifer's eyes darted around searching for Morvran. He released a sigh of relief when he spotted his right-hand man at a safe distance, having wisely retreated to the far edge of the courtyard.

Undeterred by his miss, Malachar whirled around, his eyes blazing with fury.

"Soul-Devouring Palm of the Nether Beast!" Malachar roared, and he swiped at Slifer, his hand wreathed in sickly purple qi. The attack passed through Slifer harmlessly, but the qi lingered and corroded the courtyard wall behind him.

"Blood-Boiling Kick of the Infernal Phoenix!" The sect master's leg ignited with crimson flames as he aimed a devastating roundhouse at Slifer's head. The kick missed and instead connected with a nearby pillar, turning it into ash.

"Thousand Curses of the Void Demon!" Malachar's fingers danced in a complex pattern as they summoned a storm of purple sigils that should have torn Slifer's soul apart. Instead, they passed through him and peppered the surrounding area with spots of decay and corruption.

For thirty seconds Slifer watched as Malachar's relentless assault devastated the courtyard. Walls crumbled, pillars toppled, and the ground became a patchwork of craters. The protective formations flickered and strained against the onslaught, wavering dangerously.

Just a second before Slifer's Phase Ability wore off, Malachar's latest attack, a wild "Crushing Fist of the Abyssal Tyrant," passed through him and obliterated a nearby statue, leaving a pool of hissing corrosive energy behind.

Holy crap, Slifer thought as he solidified. *Any one of those strikes could one-shot an Ascendant cultivator! If that had hit me . . . I'd be nothing but a smear on the ground right now.*

Ding!
New Mission: Survive the human tribulation.
Overcome the trial presented by berserk Sect Master Malachar and complete your breakthrough to Core Formation.
Rewards: Successful formation of your core and advancement to Core Formation Realm, 10,000 Karmic Credits
Failure: Death
Note: The sect master's attacks are part of your tribulation. Each blow you withstand brings you closer to forming your core. Find a way to endure long enough for your breakthrough to complete.

If this is all part of the tribulation, then maybe . . . Slifer's thoughts quickened. *Maybe once I complete my breakthrough, Malachar will regain his sanity and stop attacking me? But how can I survive long enough for that to happen?*

CHAPTER THIRTY

Morvran stood at the edge of the courtyard, his eyes wide with disbelief. The scene before him was unlike anything he had ever witnessed in all his three hundred years of cultivation. His master stood motionless in the center of the courtyard, facing off against the enraged sect master.

He couldn't help but flinch each time Malachar's fist or foot came within a hair's breadth of Slifer's face.

This can't be happening, Morvran thought, his bald head glistening with sweat. *The sect master has gone mad!*

Malachar was a blur of motion, his attacks coming from every conceivable angle. Yet, somehow, none of them seemed to land. It was as if an invisible barrier surrounded Slifer, deflecting each potentially devastating blow. It was as if he was merely watching a mildly interesting play rather than facing a berserk Half-Step Immortal.

How is this possible? Morvran wondered, his eyes darting between Slifer and Malachar. *Master isn't even moving, yet the sect master can't touch him.*

As Malachar's assault continued, Morvran's mind raced. He had served Slifer for years, had seen the supreme elder's power firsthand. But this . . . this was beyond anything he had imagined.

When was the last time anyone actually landed a hit on Master? Morvran wondered, squinting as he tried to recall. *It's been . . . months? Maybe even longer?*

The more he thought about it, the more certain Morvran became. No one had successfully struck Slifer in combat for a very long time, at least not to his knowledge. His master would always stand motionless as attacks would either pass right through him or be stopped by some invisible barrier.

Morvran had first assumed it was because of Slifer's breakthrough to the Ascendant Realm; after all, it wasn't strange for an Origin Realm cultivator to not be able to harm an Ascendant cultivator. However, now having seen both the tribulation and the sect master be unable to even land a hit, he had a new theory.

It must be some kind of formation technique, Morvran concluded, nodding to himself. *A barrier so advanced it can even deflect attacks from a Half-Step Immortal. I've never heard of such a thing!*

As the battle continued, Morvran found himself struggling to breathe. The sheer power radiating from Malachar was overwhelming even from his position away from the courtyard.

If I'm feeling this from here, what must it be like for Master? Morvran wondered as he wiped away the sweat from his brow. His admiration for his master was growing with each passing moment. *He's taking the full brunt of not just the aura but the attacks themselves, yet he looks completely unfazed.*

Suddenly, Malachar came to a stop opposite Slifer. The sect master's chest heaved. His eyes were wild with fury.

"Why won't you fight back?" Malachar roared, his voice distorted, sounding inhuman.

Slifer raised an eyebrow. "Because I can defeat you without lifting a finger."

Malachar's response was a bone-chilling howl. The red demonic qi surrounding him began to swirl violently, growing darker and darker until it was pitch black.

Morvran's jaw dropped as he watched the transformation unfold. Malachar's robes disintegrated, vaporized by the intense energy radiating from his body. His form began to change as he grew leaner and more bestial.

What in the name of the heavenly Dao is happening?

Wickedly curving black horns erupted from Malachar's head. His fingers elongated into sharp claws, and when he snarled, Morvran caught a glimpse of razor-sharp teeth.

"M-Master," Morvran stuttered, "the sect master . . . he's—"

"A demon," Slifer finished, his tone surprisingly casual. "Yeah, I noticed."

Morvran's mind reeled. *The sect master is a demon? But how? Didn't he fight against the demons thousands of years ago?*

As if reading his thoughts, Slifer spoke again. "Looks like our esteemed sect master has been keeping some secrets."

Morvran glanced at his master searching for any sign of surprise or concern. But Slifer's face remained impassive, almost bored.

Did he already know? Morvran wondered. *Is there anything Master doesn't know?*

The demon let out another roar, this one shaking the very foundations of the courtyard. "I'll devour your soul, human!"

Slifer yawned. "You know, I've heard that one before. Can't you demons come up with some new material?"

Malachar's response was to begin inhaling deeply, his chest expanding to an impossible size. Dark energy swirled around him, then condensed into a ball of pure destruction.

Morvran's eyes widened in horror. *That attack . . . If it hits, even Master might not survive!*

"Master!" he called out. "You must stop him!"

But Slifer remained still, watching Malachar with mild interest.

"Morvran," Slifer said calmly, "you might want to retreat even further."

Morvran hesitated for a moment, torn between obeying his master and trying to help. In the end, his loyalty won out, and he retreated further from the impending clash.

Malachar's body had swollen to twice its normal size and was pulsing with dark energy. With a final roar, he unleashed his attack. A torrent of black qi, wider than a house, shot towards Slifer. The air itself seemed to scream as the attack tore through it, leaving a trail of destruction behind.

Morvran's heart stopped. *This is it,* he thought. *Even Master can't possibly survive this.*

But just as the beam was about to strike Slifer, something incredible happened. An invisible barrier flickered into existence and caught the attack. For a moment, the black qi swirled against the barrier, trying to break through.

Then the barrier suddenly reflected the attack back at Malachar.

The sect master's eyes widened in shock, his demonic face twisting in disbelief. He had no time to dodge. The reflected beam struck him squarely in the chest and sent him flying backwards with tremendous force.

Malachar's body crashed through the walls of the supreme elder's house, disappearing into the structure.

For a moment, there was silence.

Then—*BOOM*—the house exploded.

Debris rained down across the courtyard. Dust and smoke filled the air, obscuring everything from view. Morvran threw up his arms to shield himself, coughing as the smoke reached his lungs.

As the dust began to settle, Morvran lowered his arms, and squinted through the haze to find his master. To his relief, he saw Slifer standing exactly where he had been before, completely unharmed.

Slifer brushed some dust off his shoulder, looking mildly annoyed. "Well, that's just great. Do you have any idea how much it costs to rebuild a house these days?"

Morvran couldn't help but chuckle as relief washed over him. If his master was joking, then surely the danger had passed.

He watched as Slifer's gaze drifted upwards and focused on something Morvran couldn't see. A small smile played across the supreme elder's lips.

What does he see? Morvran wondered, following his master's gaze but seeing nothing but empty sky.

Turning back to the ruins of Slifer's house, Morvran realized something was missing. There was no sign of Malachar's body among the debris.

The sect master . . . he's gone? Morvran thought, bewildered. *Did he flee? Or was he . . . destroyed?*

As Morvran stood there trying to process everything that had happened, memories of recent events flooded his mind. Just a few months ago, his master had struggled to break through to the Origin Realm. The failure had been devastating, and when Slifer had rushed off to stop his disciple Tyrus from leaving the sect, Morvran had feared the worst.

I thought that would be the last time I'd see him. His cultivation was crippled. I didn't think he could survive against Tyrus, let alone . . . this.

But Slifer had returned, and since then, everything had changed. His master seemed more powerful, smarter, and even . . . kinder?

As Morvran pondered these changes, Slifer turned to face him. "Well, Morvran," the supreme elder said with a wry smile, "it seems I'm in need of a new house. Any suggestions?"

Morvran blinked, caught off guard by the casual nature of the question after such an earth-shattering battle. "I . . . I'm sure we can arrange something suitable, Master," he stammered.

Slifer nodded, seemingly satisfied with this answer. "Good, good. Oh, and Morvran? Let's keep what happened here today between us, shall we? No need to cause a panic in the sect or alert the other sects about my tribulation. I'll release a statement after I consolidate my breakthrough."

"Of course, Master," Morvran agreed quickly. "But . . . what about the sect master? Should we pursue him?"

Slifer waved a hand dismissively. "No need. I have a feeling we won't be seeing Malachar for a while. Now, why don't you gather some disciples to help clean up this mess? And see if you can salvage any of my belongings from the rubble."

As Slifer turned away, Morvran found himself rooted to the spot, his mind still reeling from everything he had witnessed. With a shake of his head, Morvran set off to carry out his master's orders.

"You there!" he called out to a group of junior disciples who had gathered at the edge of the courtyard, drawn by the commotion. "Start clearing away the larger pieces of debris. Be careful not to disturb any formation remnants you might find."

As the disciples scurried to obey, Morvran found his thoughts drifting back to his master. *How did Master Slifer become so powerful in such a short time?* he wondered. *And why does he seem so . . . different?*

He remembered the Slifer of a few months ago—still formidable, but nothing like the invincible figure he had witnessed today. That Slifer had been more prone to outbursts of anger, more focused on personal gain and power. This new Slifer seemed calmer, more thoughtful, and, oddly enough, more human.

Morvran's thoughts were interrupted by the sound of loud chewing. He turned to see his disciple, Dusty, stuffing his face with a steamed bun, crumbs falling onto his robes.

"Master?" Dusty mumbled through a mouthful of food, his eyes wide as he looked at the destruction. "What happened here? We felt the ground shaking all the way in the dining hall."

Morvran's eye twitched at the sight of his disciple eating at a time like this. He hesitated, remembering Slifer's instructions to keep the incident quiet. "Just a small accident during the supreme elder's cultivation," he said finally. "Nothing to worry about."

Dusty swallowed hard, nearly choking on his bun. His eyebrows shot up in disbelief as he pointed at the aftermath. "A small accident? But the entire—"

"That's enough questions," Morvran cut him off, snatching the half-eaten bun from Dusty's hand. "And enough eating! This is no time for snacks. Make yourself useful and help with the cleanup."

Dusty's shoulders slumped as he watched his master toss the bun aside. "But, Master, I'm still hung—"

"Now!" Morvran barked, pointing towards the rubble. "Before I decide you need extra training on an empty stomach!"

Grumbling under his breath, the little fatty trudged off to join the cleanup efforts after casting one last look at his bun.

We have an Immortal, Morvran thought as his gaze drifted back to where Slifer stood amidst the rubble, a small smile playing on his master's lips. *Our very own Immortal in the Black Rose Sect.*

CHAPTER THIRTY-ONE

Well, that was . . . interesting," Slifer muttered, brushing debris off his robes as the dust settled from Malachar's explosive exit. "Though, I have to wonder if getting my house blown up was really necessary for character development."

He felt an odd tingling sensation in his dantian: the half-formed core that had been floating there began to pulse with an irregular rhythm, like a heart learning to beat for the first time. He could feel his core responding to the lingering demonic qi in the area, absorbing and transforming it in ways he'd never seen before.

"This definitely isn't your standard Golden Core formation," Slifer observed as he focused his attention inwards. The swirling colors within began to shift more rapidly as they created patterns that seemed to defy the laws of nature itself. "Unless Golden Cores typically look like a technicolor light show on steroids."

The core continued to evolve—its surface now resembled a miniature galaxy in constant flux. Where a normal core would maintain a stable color and energy signature, this one seemed to revel in chaos, shifting between various states of matter and energy with wild abandon.

A System notification suddenly appeared.

Congratulations!
You have successfully formed a Chaos Core.
Chaos Core: A legendary variant of the standard cultivation core that exists

in a state of perpetual flux. Unlike traditional cores, which specialize in specific elements or energies, a Chaos Core can adapt to and utilize any form of energy it encounters.
Advantages:
Universal energy compatibility
Enhanced energy conversion efficiency
Accelerated cultivation speed
Improved technique comprehension
Resistance to energy-based attacks
Disadvantages:
Requires constant energy input
Higher risk of qi deviation
Unstable during initial formation period
May cause unexpected side effects
Warning: Proper control of a Chaos Core requires exceptional mental fortitude and precise energy manipulation. Handle with care.

"Oh great," Slifer sighed. "So I've basically got a nuclear reactor for a core. No pressure."

Before he could fully process this development, another System notification appeared.

Requirements for Bloodline Awakening have been met.
Congratulations!
You have unlocked the Demonic Devourer Dragon Bloodline.
Congratulations!
You have gained 10,000 Karmic Credits.

Slifer's eyes widened as he felt a new power surge through his meridians. His blood began to boil and knowledge of his new abilities flooded his mind.

"Now this," he said with a grin, "I can work with."

Meanwhile, in the outer courtyard, a group of disciples had gathered to watch the cleanup efforts. Among them was a young outer disciple called Lin Yu.

"Something feels . . . different," she whispered to her fellow disciple. "The air . . . it's changing."

The disciple nodded, his face pale. "The demonic qi that was here during the supreme elder's breakthrough is disappearing."

They watched in amazement as streams of black energy began to flow through the air, all converging on a single point—their supreme elder. Slifer's body seemed to glow with an otherworldly light as he absorbed the demonic energy, his form gradually expanding like a balloon being inflated.

"Is . . . is he getting bigger?" Lin Yu stammered as she took an involuntary step back.

Slifer's frame was swelling visibly, his robes straining against his expanding form. The air around him rippled as he continued to devour every trace of demonic qi in the vicinity.

From his position near the rubble, Dusty dropped the piece of debris he'd been carrying, his mouth hanging open. "Master," he called out to Morvran, "the supreme elder is . . . um . . ."

"Quiet!" Morvran hissed, though his own eyes were wide with astonishment. "This is perfectly normal for a breakthrough of this magnitude."

The disciples weren't convinced, especially when Slifer's form doubled in size and his skin took on a faint purple hue. The sight of their normally composed supreme elder looking like an oversized grape might have been funny if it wasn't so terrifying.

This is ridiculous, Slifer thought as he looked down at his bloated form. *I look like I tried to cosplay as Violet Beauregarde.*

The System helpfully chimed in.

> *Ding!*
> Bloodline ability active: Demonic Qi Assimilation
> Current storage capacity: 94% full
> Warning: Approaching maximum safe storage limit.

"Yeah, thanks for that," Slifer muttered. "Any suggestions on what to do with all this extra qi?"

As if in response, he felt two distinct pathways open up within his body. One led to his spiritual core, while the other connected to his physical body's cultivation base.

"Oh, right. Two-way street. But if I dump all this into spiritual cultivation, I might overload my brand-new Chaos Core. Better play it safe and boost the body instead."

With that decision made, Slifer began channeling the stored demonic qi into his body cultivation. The effect was immediate and dramatic. His bloated form began to shrink as the energy was converted and absorbed; his muscle fibers strengthened, his bones densified, and his meridians expanded.

The System pinged again.

Breakthrough Detected

Body Cultivation has advanced to Core Formation Realm.

Name: Slifer

Race: Human (Demonic Devourer Dragon Bloodline)

Alignment: Demonic

Spiritual Cultivation: Early Core Formation (Chaos Core)

Body Cultivation: Early Core Formation

Lifespan Remaining: 300 years

Karmic Credits: 30,470

Skills: Insight (Intermediate), Nascent Soul Armor (Level 2), Phase Ability (Level 1), Void Being Aura (Level 1)

Items: Peak Slifer Card, Caelum Card, Hughie Card, Critical Block x6, Reflection Barrier Card x3, Thunderblast Card x2, Critical Heal x3, Time Reversal Card, One Minute Rewind Card x2, Mimicry Card x3, Teleportation Marker x3

Affinities: Light (25%), Fire (15%), Space (20%), Lightning (10%), Chaos (35%), Demonic (40%)

Abilities: Firebreath (Enhanced by Bloodline), Mirror Mastery (Level 2), Demonic Qi Assimilation (Bloodline), Purification Aura (Bloodline), Infernal Empowerment (Bloodline)

Techniques: Sunrise Slash (Level 3), Stellar Nova Strike (Level 2), Dimensional Slide (Level 2), Nascent Soul Armor (Level 1), Void Piercer (Level 1), Soul Search (Level 2)

Weapon Mastery: Sword (20%)

Perks: Dual Cultivator Perk

Note: Chaos Core grants +5% to all elemental affinities. Demonic Devourer Dragon Bloodline grants +40% affinity to demonic energy.

As his body returned to its normal size, Slifer took a moment to examine his new stats. The bloodline abilities seemed straightforward enough: devour demonic qi, purify it, and use it for power-ups. But like any good power-up in a cultivation novel, there had to be a catch.

He didn't have to wait long to find out what it was. As soon as his body cultivation breakthrough stabilized, he felt a gnawing hunger deep in his core.

"Let me guess," he sighed. "The bloodline comes with an addiction mechanic?"

> The Demonic Devourer Dragon Bloodline requires regular consumption of demonic qi to maintain optimal functionality. Extended periods without consumption may result in:
> Decreased energy levels
> Weakened cultivation base
> Intense cravings
> Mood swings
> Current demonic qi requirements: 100 units per day
> Note: Requirements will increase with cultivation level.

"Fantastic," Slifer muttered. "I'm basically a qi vampire with a very specific diet."

Looking around at the now completely cleansed courtyard, he realized this might pose some logistical challenges. The disciples were still staring at him with a mixture of awe and terror, probably wondering if their supreme elder had just turned into some kind of demon-eating monster.

Which, to be fair, is exactly what happened.

"Ahem," Slifer cleared his throat, addressing the crowd. "As you were. This was simply a . . . unique aspect of my breakthrough. Nothing to be concerned about."

The disciples nodded nervously, though none of them seemed particularly convinced. Morvran, ever the loyal right-hand man, quickly took charge of the situation.

"You heard the supreme elder!" he barked. "Back to work! These ruins won't clear themselves!"

As the disciples scrambled to resume their tasks, Slifer took a moment to really process everything that had happened. He had achieved a dual breakthrough to Core Formation, unlocked a legendary bloodline, and somehow managed to make his cultivation even more complicated than it already was.

"At least the house insurance should cover demonic tribulation damage," he mused, looking at the ruins of his residence. "Though, I might have some trouble explaining the 'act of God' clause when the god in question was technically me."

Later that evening, after the initial excitement had died down, Slifer sat in one of the spare elders' quarters. He was attempting to meditate, but the constant gnawing hunger for demonic qi made it difficult to concentrate.

"Okay, let's review what we've learned," he said to himself. "Pros: got a fancy new core, cool dragon bloodline, and double breakthrough. Cons: need to eat demonic qi like it's breakfast cereal, have a core that's about as stable as a teenager's mood swings, and I'm homeless." He pulled up his System interface again to study the new additions to his status. "The chaos core is interesting. Universal energy compatibility could be incredibly useful, especially combined with the bloodline's ability to convert demonic qi. But that instability warning is concerning."

As if to prove his point, his core gave a sudden lurch and various objects in the shelter floated momentarily before crashing back down.

"Case in point." Slifer sighed and picked up a fallen teacup. "I'm going to need some serious practice controlling this thing." A knock at the door interrupted his thoughts. "Enter," he called out.

Morvran stepped in carrying a stack of papers. "Master, I've compiled a list of available residences within the sect that might suit your needs. Also, there are several reports about unusual energy fluctuations in the area that require your attention."

"Let me guess: all the demonic qi disappeared and now everyone's wondering why?"

"Precisely." Morvran nodded. "The other elders are particularly concerned. They're requesting an explanation."

Slifer leaned back, considering his options. "Tell them it was a side effect of my breakthrough. No need to mention the specific details yet. We'll save the 'Supreme Elder is now part dragon' reveal for a special occasion."

"As you wish, Master." Morvran bowed. "Though, if I may ask . . . How are you feeling?"

"Hungry," Slifer admitted. "Very, very hungry."

Morvran's eyes widened slightly. "Should I . . . arrange for some food to be brought?"

"Unless you've got some bottled demonic qi hiding in the kitchen, I don't think regular food is going to cut it." Slifer stood up, stretching his newly strengthened muscles. "I need to figure out a sustainable source of demonic qi. Can't go around devouring every trace of demonic energy in the sect—it might make people nervous."

"Perhaps the Disciplinary Hall?" Morvran suggested. "Many of the prisoners there cultivate demonic techniques."

"Good thinking." Slifer nodded. "Plus, it gives me an excuse to check up on our guests. Two birds, one stone."

As Morvran left to make the arrangements, Slifer caught his reflection in a nearby mirror. His eyes now had a subtle purple tinge to them, and when he smiled, his teeth seemed slightly sharper than before.

"Well," he said with a chuckle, "at least I'm still prettier than most dragons in cultivation novels. Though, I should probably avoid any dramatic lighting—don't want to accidentally look like the final boss."

The next few hours were spent experimenting with his new abilities. He discovered that his Purification Aura could be controlled with precise enough cultivation and allowed him to cleanse specific areas while leaving others untouched. The Infernal Empowerment ability proved to be particularly interesting. It could temporarily boost any of his existing techniques, though the enhancement came at the cost of increased demonic qi consumption.

It's like having a turbo button, Slifer mused as he practiced. *But the fuel efficiency is terrible.*

He also found that his new bloodline had some unexpected effects on his appearance. When actively using his abilities, faint scale patterns would appear on his skin and his shadow would sometimes take on a more draconic shape.

"Great," he muttered as he watched his shadow sprout phantom wings. "Because I really needed to look more intimidating. The disciples are already scared enough as it is."

Speaking of disciples, word of his unusual breakthrough had spread quickly through the sect. By nightfall, all sorts of rumors were circulating. Some said he had defeated a demon king in single combat. Others claimed he had ascended to a new realm entirely. A few even suggested he had become some sort of demon himself.

The funny thing is, Slifer reflected, *they're all kind of right, in a way.*

As he prepared for bed in his temporary quarters, Slifer couldn't help but wonder what other surprises his new powers might bring. The System had warned about potential side effects, but in his experience, those usually didn't show up until the most inconvenient possible moment.

"At least things can't get any more complicated," he said with a yawn as he settled onto his bed.

CHAPTER THIRTY-TWO

The next morning, Slifer sat cross-legged on a meditation mat. A communication talisman was pulsing with soft blue light as it floated before him.

Time to explain how I let a Half-Step Immortal demon escape without revealing I'm absurdly underqualified for this entire situation.

The talisman flared, and Ace's image materialized. The Heavenly Light Sect Master appeared as immaculate as ever in his pristine robes, his white jade hairpin catching the light.

"Sect Master Slifer, your message mentioned an urgent security concern."

"Ace." Slifer kept his tone measured. "We have a situation. Malachar has been exposed as a demon."

A flicker of surprise crossed Ace's face. "The Black Rose Sect Master? Are you certain?"

"He revealed his true nature during a . . . private cultivation session." Slifer's fingers traced the talisman's edge. "He's been masquerading as a human cultivator, likely for centuries." *And he picked the perfect moment to try crushing me like a bug.*

"A demon infiltrator at such a high level." Ace's voice carried dangerous undertones. "This explains certain patterns I've observed. Did you eliminate him?"

If by "eliminate" you mean "barely survived while he did his best to redecorate my courtyard with my remains."

Aloud, Slifer said carefully, "He escaped after our confrontation. His power was . . . considerable."

Ace's eyebrows rose fractionally. "You let him escape?"

"The situation was complex," Slifer replied, choosing each word with precision. "His reveal was unexpected, and he employed techniques I hadn't seen before." *Like the "try to squash a supposedly equal-level cultivator with demonic qi" technique. Very innovative.*

"This is troubling news." Ace's fingers drummed once on an unseen surface. "He must be found. The information he possesses about portal locations to the Nether Realm could be devastating if shared with other demon cultivators."

Portal locations are the least of my worries when there's a Half-Step Immortal demon who probably wants to use my spine as a back scratcher.

"I understand the urgency," Slifer said. "However, the Black Rose Sect requires immediate attention. Without a sect master, the power vacuum could destabilize the entire region."

"The broader threat takes precedence," Ace countered. "One sect's stability does not outweigh the risk to the cultivation world. You need to pursue him."

I'd rather try teaching a phoenix to swim.

"The sect's resources would be better utilized maintaining order," Slifer argued. "Any disruption here could create opportunities for other demon cultivators to take advantage."

Ace studied him for a long moment. "I see you won't be moved on this. Very well. I will handle the hunt for Malachar personally."

Relief flooded through Slifer, though he maintained his impassive expression. "Your assistance is appreciated. The Heavenly Light Sect's resources will be invaluable in this pursuit."

"Indeed." Ace's tone carried a hint of steel. "Though, I wonder if your reluctance stems from something else. Perhaps the confrontation revealed unexpected complications?"

You have no idea. My entire existence is an unexpected complication.

"My only concern is maintaining stability," Slifer replied smoothly. "The sect needs leadership during this transition."

"Of course." Ace's smile didn't reach his eyes. "We all have our priorities. I will keep you informed of any developments in the search. I trust you'll do the same if Malachar makes contact?"

"Naturally."

The projection flickered as Ace prepared to end the communication. "One last thing, Sect Master Slifer. Should I discover any other . . . surprises about the Black Rose Sect, I trust you'll have satisfactory explanations?"

"In this matter, the Black Rose Sect stands with the righteous path. Recent events have only reinforced our commitment to opposing demon cultivators."

Technically true, since I'm supposed to be converting or eliminating them. The fact that I'm now part demon myself is just an ironic bonus.

Ace nodded once before his image dissolved, leaving Slifer alone with his thoughts.

Well, that went about as smoothly as trying to convince a tiger you're also a tiger while wearing a clearly fake tiger costume.

The lingering energy from the communication talisman dissipated slowly. Having Ace hunt Malachar removed one immediate threat, though it potentially created others. The Heavenly Light Sect Master's resources and abilities made him a formidable tracker.

Better him than me. I'd rather face his suspicion than Malachar's demonic techniques again. At least Ace probably won't try to redecorate using my internal organs as paint. But I need to be careful. If Ace discovers I've gained a demonic bloodline, his suspicions will turn to certainty. Then I'll have two Half-Step Immortals wanting to rearrange my molecular structure.

A knock at the door interrupted his thoughts. "Enter," he called out as he dispersed the remnant energy from the communication talisman.

Morvran stepped inside and bowed deeply. "Master, the elders are assembled. They await your announcement regarding Sect Master Malachar's . . . departure."

"Departure. That's one way to put it." Slifer straightened his robes. "Have you prepared the statement we discussed?"

"Yes, Master. Though, some elders are already questioning the official version of events."

"Let them question. Better they focus on a sanitized story than learn the full truth." Slifer moved towards the door. "For now, we maintain the narrative that Malachar left to pursue a breakthrough opportunity. The fewer who know about his demon nature, the better."

"And if they ask about the destruction in the courtyard?"

"A simple sparring accident. Nothing more." Slifer's lips curved slightly. "After all, what else would you expect when two powerful cultivators exchange pointers?" *And by "exchange pointers" I mean "one tries to murder the other while the other desperately tries not to die."*

As they walked towards the meeting hall, Slifer considered the complexities of his position. Ace would hunt Malachar, which solved one problem but created new ones. The Heavenly Light Sect's investigation could uncover inconvenient truths about the Black Rose Sect—and about Slifer himself.

Ding!

> New Mission: Maintain cover.
> Prevent Ace from discovering your true cultivation level or demonic blood-line while he investigates the sect.
> Rewards: 15,000 Karmic Credits, advanced stealth technique
> Failure: Exposure of true identity, possible confrontation with Half-Step Immortal
> Time Limit: 30 days

I really need to stop tempting fate. Though, at this point, fate seems less like a cosmic force and more like a bored novelist throwing increasingly ridiculous challenges my way.

Slifer stared at his reflection in the mirror as he adjusted the formal black and red robes of the Black Rose Sect Master. The gold trim along the edges sparkled in the morning light streaming through his temporary quarters' windows.

I look like I'm cosplaying as a final boss, he thought, tugging at the high collar. *Though, I suppose that's kind of the point.*

The ceremony to formally install him as sect master would begin in less than an hour. After Malachar's dramatic exit—and subsequent property damage—the sect needed stability. At least, that's what Morvran kept saying whenever Slifer suggested they pick someone else for the job.

"Master?" Morvran's voice came from outside the door. "The elders are gathering in the main hall."

"Coming," Slifer called back, making one final adjustment to his robes. *Let's hope nobody notices I have no idea what I'm doing despite already being a sect master.*

The System chose that moment to chime in with a new notification.

> *Ding!*
> New Mission: Assume control.
> Successfully complete the sect master installation ceremony.
> Reward: 10,000 Karmic Credits
> Failure: Loss of sect stability, possible revolt
> Time Limit: 1 hour

No pressure or anything. It's not like the entire sect's future depends on me not messing this up.

He opened the door to find Morvran waiting, dressed in his finest robes. His right-hand man's usual intimidating presence was somewhat undermined by the fact that he'd polished his bald head to a mirror shine for the occasion.

"Master, you look . . ." Morvran paused, searching for the right words.

"Like I raided an evil emperor's closet?"

"Dignified," Morvran finished. "The robes of office suit you."

As they walked through the corridors towards the main hall, they passed groups of disciples, who quickly bowed and pressed themselves against the walls. Slifer noticed their wide-eyed stares and hushed whispers.

Great, they're already treating me like I might randomly decide to eat their souls. Though, after the whole "growing to giant size and devouring demonic energy" incident, I can't really blame them.

The main hall of the Black Rose Sect was packed when they arrived. Hundreds of disciples and elders filled the space, their black robes creating a sea of darkness broken only by occasional flashes of red trim.

At the front of the hall, a raised platform held the sect master's throne—a somewhat overdramatic piece of furniture carved from black jade and decorated with rose motifs. *Because subtlety apparently isn't in our sect's vocabulary,* Slifer mused as he approached.

A figure materialized from the shadows near the throne, causing even the elders to step back in surprise. Elder Taizhe, a name spoken only in the dustiest records of the sect's archives, had emerged from his centuries-long cultivation seclusion. His presence alone made the air feel thick with primordial qi, the kind that made Slifer's cultivation senses tingle with a mix of respect and mild existential dread.

Great, a Half-Step Ascendant who's been cooking in his own sauce of power for a few centuries. Just what this ceremony needed.

Slifer hadn't even known Elder Taizhe existed until this moment—the commotion from his earlier battle with Malachar must have been enough to draw this ancient powerhouse from whatever dimensional pocket he'd been cultivating in.

Elder Taizhe's eyes, looking like they'd witnessed the rise and fall of countless dynasties, surveyed the crowd. His white hair seemed to float in an invisible breeze, defying gravity in that classic "I'm too powerful for physics" way.

"Cultivators of the Black Rose Sect." His voice carried clearly through the hall. "We gather today to witness the installation of our new sect master. Following the . . . departure of Sect Master Malachar to pursue a breakthrough opportunity, the council has unanimously selected Supreme Elder Slifer to assume leadership."

Unanimous selection is easier when everyone's too scared to vote no, Slifer thought.

"Supreme Elder Slifer has proven himself through his wisdom, strength, and dedication to our sect's principles," Elder Taizhe continued. "Would anyone like to challenge his right to lead?"

The hall remained silent. A few elders shifted nervously, but no one spoke up. Even the usually ambitious elders seemed to be discovering a sudden interest in floor patterns.

Smart of them. Though, I'm pretty sure even these NPCs know it's suicidal to go against a supposed Immortal.

"Then let the ceremony proceed," Elder Taizhe declared. He turned to face Slifer while holding out a jade tablet inscribed with complex formations. "Do you swear to uphold the traditions of the Black Rose Sect, to guide our disciples on the path of cultivation, and to protect our sect's interests?"

Slifer placed his hand on the tablet and felt the ancient formations pulse with power. "I swear," he said clearly as he let his qi respond to the tablet's energy.

The formations flared with crimson light as they recognized and recorded his oath. Elder Taizhe nodded in satisfaction and stepped back with a gesture towards the throne.

Here comes the theatrical part, Slifer thought as he ascended the platform. He turned to face the crowd, trying to project an air of authority he definitely didn't feel.

"Kneel before your sect master," Elder Taizhe commanded.

The sound of hundreds of cultivators dropping to their knees filled the hall. Slifer sat on the throne, doing his best to look imposing rather than uncomfortable.

I really hope this chair doesn't have some kind of "only the worthy may sit here" enchantment, he thought. *That would be awkward.*

But the throne apparently didn't object to his presence. Elder Taizhe raised his hands, and his voice rang out. "All hail Sect Master Slifer!"

"Hail Sect Master Slifer!" the crowd echoed.

Ding!
Mission Complete
You have gained 10,000 Karmic Credits.

Well, that went better than expected, Slifer thought as he stood to address the crowd. *Now for the hard part—actually running this place.*

"Rise," he commanded. "The Black Rose Sect enters a new era today. There will be changes, but our core mission remains the same: to grow stronger, to protect our interests, and to uphold our principles." *Even if I'm not entirely sure what principles demonic cultivators have.* "You are dismissed," he finished. "Return to your duties."

The disciples and elders filed out, still whispering among themselves. Soon only the council members remained, along with Morvran, who stood vigilantly near the throne.

Elder Taizhe approached first, bowing deeply. "Sect Master, there are several matters requiring your immediate attention. The sect's defensive formations need updating, the monthly resource allocation needs approval, and I've been told by the elders that we have received messages from three other sects requesting meetings."

"Let's start with the defensive formations," Slifer said decisively. "Given recent events, that seems most urgent." *Plus, I really don't want Malachar sneaking back in to finish the job.*

Elder Taizhe nodded approvingly. "I took the liberty of contacting Master Hong, one of the most renowned formation experts in the region. He can arrive within three days to begin the work."

"Good. Make the arrangements." Slifer stood from the throne, already tired of its uncomfortable grandeur. "I'll be in my office reviewing the other matters."

Three days later, Slifer stood watching at the sect's main gates as a peculiar procession approached. Master Hong, the renowned formation expert, rode at the front on a sword-shaped flying boat. This would have been impressive if the sword hadn't been decorated with pink tassels and what appeared to be glitter.

Behind him came a train of disciples carrying boxes, scrolls, and various formation materials. They looked exhausted, probably from trying to keep up with their master's erratic flight path.

Well, this should be interesting, Slifer thought as the formation master landed, his robes somehow remaining perfectly pressed despite the wind.

"Master Hong," Slifer greeted him. "Welcome to the Black Rose Sect."

"Oh my, oh my!" Master Hong clapped his hands together, his eyes sparkling behind round spectacles. "The qi flows here are absolutely fascinating! Such potential for innovative formation work!"

The man practically bounced as he spoke, his enthusiasm apparently unlimited. He looked more like an excited teenager than a master of ancient arts.

Great, we hired the cultivation world's equivalent of a caffeinated hamster, Slifer thought.

"I understand you need new defensive formations?" Master Hong continued without waiting for a response. "The old ones are quite good, quite good indeed, but so traditional! We can do much better. Much, much better!"

He pulled out a jade slip and began projecting various formation diagrams into the air while talking rapid-fire about energy convergence points and resonance harmonics.

Slifer exchanged a glance with Morvran, who looked equally bewildered by the formation master's enthusiasm.

"Perhaps we should discuss the specifics in my office?" Slifer suggested.

"Oh yes, yes!" Master Hong agreed cheerfully. "But first, a quick scan of the current formations. Won't take but a moment!"

He pulled out what looked like a child's toy kaleidoscope and began peering through it at various points around the gate.

"Fascinating!" he muttered. "The primary defense matrix is linked to secondary containment fields through a modified Five Elements array, but the energy distribution is terribly inefficient. And look here—they've used a standard Spirit Gathering formation when clearly a Reverse Heaven and Earth pattern would work much better!"

I understood about three words of that, Slifer thought. *But he seems to know what he's talking about.*

"How long will the upgrades take?" he asked.

Master Hong lowered his kaleidoscope and pushed his glasses up his nose. "Oh, three days should do it! Unless you want the deluxe package with the extra-dimensional pocket spaces and automated intruder redistribution system?"

"The what now?"

"It sends unwanted visitors to random locations!" Master Hong beamed. "Very popular with sects that have trouble with door-to-door cultivation-manual salespeople. Though, there was that one unfortunate incident where it sent a Nascent Soul elder into a duck pond . . . But I've mostly worked out those bugs!"

"Mostly worked out those bugs" doesn't sound very reassuring, Slifer thought.

"Let's stick to the basics for now," he said. "Focus on keeping unwanted visitors out rather than redistributing them."

"Your loss!" Master Hong shrugged cheerfully. "But we can still make these formations sing! I'm thinking a triple-layered defense grid with cascading energy feedback loops and—oh! We could add a reality distortion field around the perimeter!"

"Reality distortion?"

"Makes everything look slightly wrong to intruders," Master Hong explained. "Trees bend the wrong way, shadows fall in impossible directions, that sort of thing. Very disconcerting! Though, it does occasionally give the local wildlife existential crises . . ."

This guy is either a genius or completely insane. Possibly both.

"Just focus on making the formations as secure as possible," Slifer instructed. "We need to be able to detect and repel high-level threats."

Master Hong's eyes lit up. "Ooh, high-level threats? How exciting! I have just the thing: my new Heavenly Thunder Attraction Array! It calls down lightning on intruders automatically."

"Wouldn't that damage the sect buildings?"

"Only a little bit. And think how impressive it would look!"

I've had enough of lightning for one lifetime, Slifer thought, remembering his recent tribulation.

"Perhaps something less . . . destructive?"

"Spoilsport." Master Hong pouted. "Fine, fine. I'll stick to the classics—detection barriers, repulsion fields, the usual boring stuff. But I'm still adding my signature rainbow effect to the spirit gathering formations!"

"Rainbow effect?"

"Makes the qi look pretty! Very aesthetic!"

Slifer pinched the bridge of his nose. "Master Hong, we're trying to maintain a certain image here. The Black Rose Sect isn't really known for . . . rainbows."

"Every sect could use more rainbows," Master Hong declared firmly. "But if you insist on being traditional, I suppose I could tone it down to a nice subtle aurora borealis effect?"

This is going to be a long three days, Slifer thought.

Over the next few hours, Master Hong flitted around the sect's perimeter like an overcaffeinated hummingbird as he took measurements and made excited noises about energy convergence points. His disciples trailed behind looking increasingly frazzled as they tried to keep up with his rapid-fire demands for different materials.

"Master," Morvran murmured as they watched the formation expert kiss a particularly large formation stone. "Are you sure about this? He seems a bit . . ."

"Eccentric?"

"I was going to say 'unhinged,' but yes."

"According to Elder Taizhe, he's the best in the business," Slifer replied. "Though, I'm starting to wonder if that's because all the sane formation masters retired early . . ."

Master Hong's voice carried across the courtyard. "Oh my! Would you look at this energy node? It's practically begging for a Reverse Heaven and Earth pattern! Quick, someone bring me the prismatic crystals! And the sparkly chalk! This is going to be gorgeous!"

At least life won't be boring, Slifer thought as he watched a disciple hurry past with an armful of what appeared to be glowing chalk in various colors. *Though, I might need to invest in sunglasses if he keeps adding "aesthetic enhancements" to everything.*

By sunset, the first phase of formation work was underway. Master Hong had covered half the outer wall with complex patterns that somehow managed to look both intimidating and slightly psychedelic. His disciples had collapsed in exhausted heaps around the courtyard, surrounded by empty energy crystal containers and used formation materials.

"Progress report?" Slifer asked as Master Hong finally paused in his work.

"Oh, splendid, splendid!" The formation master beamed. "The primary defense grid is coming along nicely. I've added some extra surprises for anyone trying to breach it. Nothing too lethal, just some mild reality warping and temporary spatial displacement. Though, I should warn you about the side effects."

"Side effects?"

"Well, the new formations might cause some minor temporal fluctuations in the immediate area. You might notice some days feeling longer than others or occasionally experience Tuesday twice in a row. But don't worry—it usually sorts itself out eventually!"

Usually sorts itself out eventually? Slifer fought the urge to bang his head against the nearest wall. *Why do I get the feeling I'm going to regret this?*

"Is that . . . normal for high-level formations?"

"Oh heavens, no!" Master Hong laughed. "But normal is boring! Trust me, these formations will be the talk of the cultivation world. No other sect has anything quite like them!"

That's what I'm afraid of, Slifer thought.

"Just . . . try to keep the reality warping to a minimum," he requested. "We want to keep intruders out, not break the laws of physics."

"If you insist." Master Hong sighed. "Though, I still think my Möbius strip barrier would have been more interesting . . ."

As the formation master wandered off, humming to himself and trailing sparkles of qi, Slifer turned to Morvran.

"Keep an eye on him. Make sure he doesn't add anything too . . . creative to the defensive systems."

"Define 'too creative,'" Morvran asked warily.

"If it involves breaking causality, alternate dimensions, or spontaneous rainbow generation, stop him."

"And the temporal fluctuations he mentioned?"

"Let's hope he was joking about that part."

CHAPTER THIRTY-THREE

T he morning mist clung to the Thousand Peaks mountain range like a jealous lover, refusing to let go even as the sun climbed higher. Deep within a hidden valley, members of the Wang Clan stood around a peculiar floating orb that pulsed with a green light.

"Steady now," Patriarch Wang Feng commanded. His Origin Realm cultivation was apparent in the way space itself seemed to bend slightly around him. His face creased with concentration as he directed the formation. "Ming'er, adjust your position three steps to the east. The spiritual convergence needs to be perfect."

Wang Ming, his youngest daughter and a promising Core Formation cultivator, quickly complied. Her long black hair was tied back with a simple azure ribbon, and sweat beaded on her forehead from maintaining the complex array. "Yes, Father. But the treasure's energy . . . It feels strange. Almost like it's alive."

Around them, twelve other clan members maintained crucial positions in the stabilization formation. The most notable were the three Nascent Soul elders—venerable cultivators who had each lived nearly a millennium.

Elder Sun, with his characteristic white beard and perpetual scowl, stood at the northern point. Elder Liu, whose beauty remained unchanged since her youth thanks to her cultivation, maintained the western position. And Elder Chen, who had once been a wandering sword cultivator before joining the clan, held the southern point.

"Patriarch," Elder Liu called out, "the Thunderhawk Sect's patrol will pass through this region soon. We should expedite the containment."

Wang Feng nodded grimly. The Wang Clan wasn't the strongest in the region—that honor belonged to the Thunderhawk Sect, with their three Origin Realm patriarchs and rumored Half-Step Ascendant ancestor in seclusion. Below them in power were the Blood Phoenix Pavilion and the Earth Dragon Association, both of whom would love nothing more than to snatch this treasure from a smaller clan like theirs.

"Let them come," one of the younger disciples, Liu Chen, boasted from his position in the formation. His Foundation Establishment cultivation flared with youthful confidence. "With Patriarch and the three elders here, even the Thunderhawk's young master would think twice!"

Elder Sun barked a laugh that carried centuries of experience. "Bold words from one who has yet to see true combat. The Thunderhawk Sect's young master killed three Nascent Soul cultivators last year alone. Know your place, junior."

Wang Feng allowed himself a small smile at the exchange. The Wang Clan had always valued unity over raw power. With barely two dozen core members and another fifty or so outer disciples, they survived through cunning and cohesion rather than force. This treasure, if properly harnessed, could change their fate.

"Father," Wang Ming spoke up again, "I've been studying the ancient records. Could this be the Sphere of Infinite Paths mentioned in the ancient scripture?"

The patriarch's eyes widened slightly. Trust his brilliant daughter to make that connection. "Perhaps. The descriptions match: a sphere that 'contains worlds within worlds, paths untrodden by Immortals.' If so, this could elevate our clan significantly."

Elder Chen shifted his stance, his movement as precise as his legendary swordplay. "The last time such a treasure appeared, it sparked a war that lasted fifty years. The Crystal Valley Clan was wiped out entirely."

"Times have changed," Wang Feng responded, though his voice carried a note of uncertainty. "This treasure could be what I need to complete my breakthrough—"

"Assuming we survive long enough to use it," Elder Liu interjected. Her fingers traced complex patterns in the air as she strengthened the containment formation. "I count at least three observation spells trying to pierce our privacy formation."

The patriarch nodded. They had chosen this valley carefully—the natural spiritual veins in the earth helped mask energy fluctuations, and the ancient privacy formations left by their ancestors still held strong. But nothing stayed secret forever in a world of cultivators.

Wang Ming's voice trembled slightly as she maintained her position. "Father, what about the Dragon's Breath Consortium? They've been expanding aggressively since taking over the spirit stone mines in the south."

"Let's focus on the task at hand," Wang Feng replied. The concern was valid: the political landscape in the Eastern Region had grown increasingly complex in recent years. Small clans like theirs survived by finding protection under larger sects or by making themselves useful through specialized skills. The Wang Clan had survived for fifteen generations through their expertise in spiritual herb cultivation and formation arrays.

"Formation stabilizing," Elder Sun announced. "Spiritual convergence at seventy percent and rising. Another hour and we can begin the binding process."

Wang Feng studied the floating sphere with intense concentration. Its surface rippled like liquid mercury and occasionally revealed glimpses of impossible landscapes within—mountains floating in a starlit void, oceans that flowed upwards, cities that seemed to fold in on themselves in geometry-defying ways.

"Young Mistress Ming speaks truth," Elder Chen mused. "This treasure doesn't feel like anything from our realm. The spiritual frequency is . . . off somehow."

The patriarch had noticed it too, but they had come too far to back out now. The Wang Clan needed this edge. Their spirit herb farms barely produced enough income to purchase cultivation resources for the younger generation, and their best formation arrays were centuries old. Without something to change their fortunes, they would eventually be absorbed by a larger sect.

"Steady now," he commanded as the sphere pulsed more intensely. "Begin the seventh sequence of the Binding Mandate. Channel your spiritual energy through the azure meridians first, then . . ."

The next few hours passed in focused silence, broken only by occasional technical adjustments and the distant cry of spirit beasts. The Wang Clan's future hung in the balance, and every member present felt the weight of that responsibility.

None of them noticed that the glimpses of other worlds in the sphere's surface were becoming more frequent or that the impossible geometries were beginning to leak into the space around them.

The first sign that something was wrong came when the sphere's steady pulse began to quicken, like a heart beating in panic. The mercury-like surface rippled more violently, and the glimpses of other worlds became longer, more substantial.

"Patriarch!" Elder Liu's normally melodious voice carried a sharp edge of alarm. "The spiritual convergence is exceeding safety limits!"

Wang Feng's brow furrowed as he tried to maintain control. The sphere's energy was becoming erratic, refusing to follow the careful patterns they had established. "Everyone, double your energy input! We need to stabilize the—"

He never finished the sentence. The sphere suddenly expanded, its surface stretching like elastic, before snapping back with a sound that shouldn't have been possible—a crack in reality itself. Several younger disciples were thrown back, their positions in the formation broken.

"Father!" Wang Ming cried out as strange forces began pulling at her robes, her hair. "Something's wrong with the spiritual convergence! The readings are impossible!"

Elder Sun's face had lost its usual stern expression, which was replaced by naked fear. "Patriarch, these energy levels are beyond Origin Realm! Beyond anything I've seen!"

Wang Feng tried to maintain order even as chaos erupted around them. "Main formation members, fall back! Outer disciples, clear the area! Elders, prepare the Emergency Sealing Array!"

But it was too late. Space itself seemed to shudder, and a tear appeared next to the sphere—not a normal spatial crack, but something fundamentally wrong, as if reality was being unwritten. The pressure that emerged from it brought even the Nascent Soul elders to their knees.

"Get back!" Elder Chen shouted as he pushed several younger disciples away from the distortion. But Wang Ming was too close, trying to maintain her crucial position in the formation. The spatial tear pulsed, and she vanished with a terrified scream.

"Ming'er!" Wang Feng's heart nearly stopped as his daughter disappeared. Elder Liu moved to help, but another pulse dragged her in as well. Even Elder Chen, with all his centuries of combat experience, couldn't resist when the tear reached for him.

The remaining clan members watched in horror as their comrades vanished. The pressure emanating from the tear was beyond anything they had ever experienced—beyond Origin Realm, beyond even what they imagined an Ascendant cultivator might possess. Wang Feng found himself shaking, his cultivation of several millennia feeling as insignificant as a candle before the sun.

And then . . . a foot stepped through the tear.

The woman who emerged looked young, but her eyes held the weight of eons. Her simple white robes seemed to shift between different styles with each movement, as if reality couldn't quite decide how to perceive her. Her first action was to frown, and even that simple expression carried enough force to make the remaining disciples step back in terror.

"How bothersome," she muttered, her voice carrying strange harmonics. "The spiritual restrictions in these lesser worlds are always so . . . limiting." She raised her hand and studied it with mild annoyance. "Origin Realm cap, naturally. It will take time to adapt my cultivation to even reach this realm's pathetic ceiling of Half-Step Immortal."

Several of the younger disciples, still running hot with emotion from watching their companions disappear, raised their weapons. Liu Chen, always the hothead, actually began to form a spiritual attack.

"You! What did you do to Young Mistress Ming and the elders?" His spiritual energy flared as he prepared to launch a technique that would have been impressive for a Foundation Establishment cultivator.

Wang Feng moved faster than he had in centuries as he crossed the space between them and delivered a sharp slap that sent Liu Chen stumbling back. "Fool!" he hissed. "Do you wish to die?"

Then, with grace practiced over centuries of political maneuvering, the patriarch turned and dropped into a deep bow before the woman. "This humble one is Wang Feng, Patriarch of the Wang Clan. May this one know your exalted name?"

The woman's gaze passed over them like a goddess examining insects, though there was something almost amused in her expression. "You may call me Lady Chi." Her eyes swept the valley, taking in the spirit herb farms and modest clan compounds in the distance. "This will serve as an adequate base of operations."

Her eyes flashed red, and Wang Feng felt something vast and ancient reach into his mind. He should have resisted—any cultivator worth their spirit stones knew the importance of maintaining mental integrity. But her power simply bypassed all his defenses as if they didn't exist. His eyes flashed red in return as new loyalty was written into his very core.

"You will all serve me in my task," Lady Chi declared, and it wasn't a command so much as a statement of fundamental reality. One by one, the remaining clan members' eyes flashed red as they fell under her control.

As the Wang Clan knelt before her, Lady Chi's expression darkened. "I will find you, killer of Darius," she whispered to herself, "even if I must tear apart every realm in existence."

Behind her, the spatial tear sealed itself, leaving no trace of its existence. The sphere that had caused all this floated serenely nearby. Its surface was now calm and mirror-like, reflecting a sky that belonged to no world known to the Wang Clan.

CHAPTER THIRTY-FOUR

Zack stood at the edge of a frozen cliff and watched as his disciples struggled through the knee-deep snow behind him. The bone-white mask hid his amused expression. He had forbidden the cultivators from using qi—any use of qi could alert the enemy to their presence.

"Senior Alfie," one of the Core Formation disciples called out between labored breaths, "how much further must we travel?"

Zack didn't immediately answer. Instead, he patted the storage ring on his finger, reassuring himself that the emergency supplies from the Main Body were still there. Three Ascendant-grade protective talismans, five escape talismans, and one particularly nasty offensive talisman that could temporarily boost someone to the Peak of Origin Realm. Not exactly an arsenal worthy of a supposed Ascendant, but enough to maintain his bluff if things went south.

"We're close," he finally answered. "The disturbance lies just beyond the next mountain range."

Behind him, twenty hand-picked Core Formation disciples from the Fiery Mist Sect continued their arduous march. They were the cream of the crop, each one capable of holding their own against cultivators several levels above their current realm. Not that Zack particularly cared about their individual power levels—they were here primarily as witnesses. After all, what good was pulling off impressive feats if no one was around to spread the tales?

At the front of the group walked Lucious, the Legacy Disciple's face set in what appeared to be a permanent scowl. Every few minutes, he would shoot a resentful glare at Zack's back, clearly unhappy about being dragged along on this expedition.

"This is beneath me," Lucious muttered, just loud enough for Zack to hear. "A Legacy Disciple of the Black Rose Sect, trudging through snow like a common courier . . ."

Zack allowed himself a small smirk behind his mask. "Did you say something?"

Lucious stiffened. "No, Senior Alfie. Nothing at all."

"I thought not." Zack paused, holding up one hand to signal the group to stop. "We're getting close to the disturbance zone. Everyone, mask your spiritual presence. We don't want to announce our arrival."

The disciples immediately began suppressing their qi, their auras dimming until they were barely noticeable against the natural spiritual energy of the mountain. Zack nodded approvingly—at least Finick had taught them the basics of stealth.

According to Finick's spies, both the Sun Palace and Celestial Blade Sects had been acting suspiciously in this region for the past week: increased patrols, covert troop movements, and most tellingly, the presence of multiple Nascent Soul experts.

Something valuable had appeared in this frozen wasteland, something worth fighting over. And wherever there was conflict between major sects, there was opportunity for someone clever enough to seize it.

"Hold," Zack commanded as they reached the base of a particularly steep ridge. "Beyond this point, we enter contested territory. If anyone wishes to turn back, now is the time."

None of the disciples moved. Even Lucious, for all his grumbling, stood firm. Their loyalty might have been born of fear and awe rather than genuine respect, but it would serve for now.

"Very well." Zack gestured towards the ridge. "Let's see what all the fuss is about, shall we?"

They ascended the ridge in silence and when they neared the top, the first sounds of battle reached their ears: the distinctive crack of spiritual energy being unleashed, accompanied by shouts and explosions that echoed off the surrounding mountains.

Zack reached the summit first, dropping into a crouch to minimize his silhouette against the night sky. The others quickly followed suit, arranging themselves along the ridgeline to observe the scene below.

The valley spread out before them was a battlefield. Two groups of cultivators clashed in the air and on the ground, their spiritual energy lighting up the night like competing fireworks displays. Golden light from the Sun Palace Sect cultivators met the silver radiance of Celestial Blade techniques, creating explosions wherever they connected.

At the center of all this chaos stood what appeared to be an ancient temple, half buried in the snow and ice. Its stone walls gave off an eerie blue light that marked it as one of the legendary inheritance sites that occasionally appeared in the Sealed Realm. The structure seemed to radiate an ancient power, like a sleeping giant slowly stirring from a long slumber.

"Impressive," Lucious whispered, his earlier disdain forgotten as he studied the battle below. "The Sun Palace and Celestial Blade Sects must really want whatever's inside that temple."

Zack nodded silently with his eyes fixed on the four most powerful figures in the valley. Two Nascent Soul cultivators led each side—the Sun Palace experts wielded rays of golden light that could melt through solid rock, while the Celestial Blade masters fought with impossibly sharp sword energy that could slice through spiritual barriers like paper.

"That's Hong Yan and Wei Ling from the Sun Palace," one of the Fiery Mist disciples whispered, pointing at two figures wrapped in golden robes. The male and female pair moved in perfect synchronization with their attacks, complementing each other. "They're said to be husband and wife, cultivating the same technique for over a century."

"And those must be the infamous Sword Twins from Celestial Blade," another disciple added, indicating the other two Nascent Soul experts. These two were identical in appearance: tall, thin men with long white hair and matching silver robes. They wielded slender swords that seemed to disappear and reappear as they moved, leaving trails of deadly sword energy behind them.

The four Nascent Soul experts clashed again and again, their attacks sending shockwaves through the valley that knocked lesser cultivators off their feet. Meanwhile, their Core Formation disciples fought below, trying to breach the temple's defenses while preventing their opponents from doing the same.

"Watch carefully," Zack instructed the disciples. "It's not often you get to see Nascent Soul experts fighting all out like this."

Lucious snorted. "If you call this 'all out.' In the Main Realm, even Core Formation disciples could—"

"Yes, yes," Zack cut him off. "Everything's better in the Main Realm. We're all very impressed. Now be quiet and observe."

Below, the battle was intensifying. Hong Yan raised her hands, golden qi swirling around her like a miniature sun. "Husband! Formation Three!"

Wei Ling immediately responded, his own qi merging with hers. Together, they began tracing complex patterns in the air, their synchronized movements creating a massive array of golden symbols.

The Sword Twins recognized the threat. "Mirror Sword Array!" they shouted in unison, and their blades blurred as they created a defensive formation of overlapping sword images.

The resulting clash lit up the entire valley. Golden light met silver sword qi in a devastating explosion that sent lesser cultivators tumbling through the air. Snow melted instantly in a wide radius around the combat zone, creating a perfect circle of bare earth.

"Impressive light show," Zack murmured. "But notice how they're all so focused on each other that they're barely paying attention to the temple anymore."

He was right. While the Nascent Soul experts battled above, their disciples had gradually shifted from trying to breach the temple to simply preventing the other side from doing so. The ancient structure stood largely ignored in the center of the battlefield, its blue glow pulsing like a heartbeat.

"Senior Alfie," one of the disciples whispered. "Should we . . . should we make our move?"

Zack held up a hand for silence. Something wasn't quite right. His instincts were screaming at him that they weren't alone.

A familiar prickle ran down his spine: the unmistakable sensation of being watched by powerful cultivators. His eyes scanned the opposite ridge, searching the tree line until . . . There. Partially hidden among a cluster of ancient pines, a group of black-robed figures stood perfectly still, their faces hidden behind silver masks shaped like crescent moons.

The Moon God Sect. But what were they doing here? And more importantly, why weren't they making any move towards the temple?

One of them held what appeared to be a compass made of black metal. Even at this distance, Zack could see the needle spinning wildly, pointing in different directions as if searching for something. The cultivator holding it kept adjusting some kind of setting, fine-tuning whatever tracking function it possessed.

"Interesting," Zack murmured. "Very interesting."

The battle below reached a new level of intensity. The Sword Twins had apparently tired of the stalemate and decided to risk everything on a single devastating attack. Their voices rang out in perfect unison as they shouted, "Heavenly Cross-Cut Formation!"

Their sword qi coalesced into a massive cross of silver energy, so bright it hurt to look at directly. The attack sliced through the air towards Hong Yan and Wei Ling, who were already moving to counter it.

"Solar Emperor's Final Judgment!" they shouted together, and their combined qi formed a sphere of golden light that rivaled the sun itself.

Zack saw his opportunity. "Everyone, stay here," he commanded. "No matter what happens, do not move from this spot."

Before anyone could respond, he activated one of his treasures: a movement technique that made him literally invisible to spiritual sense. One moment he was crouching on the ridge, the next he was inside the temple and moving so fast that even Nascent Soul experts would have trouble tracking him.

The interior of the temple was surprisingly well-preserved. Ancient formations, glowing with pale blue light, created barriers that would have taken hours or days to break through normally. But Zack had no intention of breaking them—he used his phase ability to simply slip between them.

The main chamber was a circular room dominated by a stone pedestal. Floating above it was an ancient jade slip covered in mysterious markings that seemed to shift and change as he watched. The amount of spiritual energy radiating from it was staggering—this was definitely no ordinary inheritance.

"Well, well," Zack murmured as he reached for the jade slip. "What secrets are you hiding?"

The moment his fingers touched it, the markings flared with a golden light. Information flooded into his mind: fragments of ancient techniques, half-formed mysteries, and, most intriguingly, what appeared to be a map showing locations of other inheritance sites.

Outside, the combined attacks of the Nascent Soul experts finally met. The explosion was deafening—a shockwave of pure spiritual energy actually cracked the temple's ancient walls. But by then, Zack was already gone with the precious jade slip tucked safely away in his robes.

He reappeared on the ridge just as the dust began to settle, looking for all the world as if he had never moved. The disciples stared at him with a mixture of awe and confusion, clearly sensing that something had happened but unsure exactly what.

Below, the battle had reached a temporary stalemate. Both sides had been thrown back by the explosion, and now they faced each other warily as they gathered their strength for another round.

But Zack's attention was fixed on the Moon God Sect members across the valley. Their compass was pointing directly at his group now, its needle unwavering. The cultivator holding it was making adjustments frantically, as if unable to believe what it was telling him.

Suddenly, one of them looked up. Through the trees, across the valley, a pair of silver eyes met Zack's masked gaze.

"My, my," the Moon God cultivator said, their voice carrying across the distance, "what an interesting group we have here."

The way they emphasized "interesting" while staring at him and Lucious told Zack everything he needed to know. Their fancy compass wasn't tracking the inheritance at all—it was tracking outsiders. And right now, it was pointing directly at his little group, which just happened to include a genuine article straight from the Main Realm.

The Moon God Sect members jumped into the air and began flying across the valley straight towards them.

Really, Zack thought, *they were trying a bit too hard with the whole "mysterious cultivator" aesthetic.* At least his mask had some personality.

"Senior Alfie," Finick whispered urgently, "they're approaching fast. Should we prepare for battle?"

Zack did some quick mental math. On one side: an unknown number of Moon God Sect cultivators who were specifically hunting outsiders. On the other: his own identity as an outsider, which he'd really rather keep under wraps, thank you very much. The solution was obvious, if not exactly heroic.

"Actually," Zack said casually, raising his hand, "I just remembered I have a very important . . . thing. At the sect. Right now."

"What?" Lucious turned to him. "What thing?"

"You know"—Zack waggled his fingers—"a thing. Very important. Can't be missed. Sect master stuff."

Before anyone could question his extremely legitimate excuse further, Zack tore open a portal. "Finick," he called out as he stepped towards the portal, "you're in charge. Try not to die. Oh, and if anyone asks why I left so suddenly, tell them I . . . saw a particularly interesting cloud. Yes, that'll do nicely."

"But Senior—" Finick's protest was cut off as Zack stepped through the portal, which snapped shut behind him with a sound suspiciously like a snicker.

The remaining cultivators stared at the empty space where their supposedly mighty senior had just pulled a tactical retreat.

"Did he just—" one of the disciples began.

"Abandon us completely?" Lucious finished drily. "Yes, yes he did."

The Moon God Sect members were much closer now, their silver masks gleaming in the moonlight. The one holding the compass pointed it directly at Lucious, and the needle began spinning wildly.

"Surround them," the leader commanded. "The outsider must not escape."

"Outsider?" Lucious's eyes narrowed. "I don't know what you're talking about. I'm just a humble cultivator who happens to have an extremely suspicious accent and mysterious background."

The Moon God cultivators spread out in a classic encirclement pattern. Clearly, this wasn't their first outsider hunt.

"You can't fool our tracking compass," the leader said. "It's specifically designed to detect the unique spiritual signature of those from beyond our realm. And you, 'humble cultivator,' are practically glowing."

CHAPTER THIRTY-FIVE

Lucious stood perfectly still as the Moon God Sect members circled him, his face a mask of cold disdain. These backwater cultivators dared to threaten him? Him, a Legacy Disciple of the Black Rose Sect?

"You will come with us." The Moon God cultivator tilted his silver mask. "Either quietly or in pieces."

Rage flashed across Lucious's face. No one spoke to him that way. Not in the Main Realm, and certainly not in this sealed backwater.

"Fiery Mist members," he commanded, not bothering to look at them, "stay back. I'll handle these insects myself."

The leader raised his hand and moonlight gathered at his fingertips. "Take him."

Three Moon God cultivators moved simultaneously, their movements perfectly coordinated. Silver beams of concentrated moonlight shot towards Lucious from different angles in a deadly triangle of attacks that were nearly impossible to dodge.

Nearly impossible for a normal cultivator, that is.

"Black Rose Art: Thorned Barrier!" Lucious snarled. Dark qi erupted from his body and formed a dome of writhing thorny vines. The moonlight struck the barrier and scattered, leaving only slight scorches on the vegetation.

But the Moon God members weren't finished. Two more cultivators appeared above, their hands forming complex seals. "Lunar Shadow Binding!"

Strips of silver light rained down like chains, trying to entangle Lucious's barrier. Where they touched the thorny vines, the vegetation began to wither and decay.

Lucious sneered. "Is that all? Let me show you true power. Black Rose Art: Blooming Death!"

The barrier exploded outwards and thorny vines lashed out in all directions. But these weren't ordinary vines: each thorn contained a concentrated drop of deadly poison, and the flowers that bloomed along their length released clouds of hallucinogenic pollen.

The two Moon God cultivators were too slow to dodge. The vines wrapped around their legs and the thorns pierced through their protective qi. They screamed as the poison entered their systems and their bodies began to convulse.

"Protect the compass!" the leader shouted as he cut through the approaching vines with a blade of moonlight. "We can't lose our only way of tracking outsiders!"

The cultivator holding the compass retreated, and four others moved to form a protective circle around him. Lucious filed that information away—the compass was clearly vital to their operation.

But he had no time to focus on it. The leader and three others were already launching their next attack. "Moonfall Crisis!"

The sky above seemed to darken as four miniature moons formed from pure qi. They descended towards Lucious with crushing force, their silver light so intense it hurt to look at directly.

Lucious's hands blurred through a series of seals. "Black Rose Art: Underworld Garden!"

The ground beneath his feet turned black as night, and roses of deepest crimson burst forth in an expanding circle. As the artificial moons descended, twisted plants reached up to meet them, then wrapped around the spheres of light and began to drain their energy.

But something was wrong. The moons weren't weakening fast enough, and maintaining the technique was costing Lucious more qi than it should have.

"Your Main Realm techniques are impressive," the leader called out, "but did you really think we wouldn't have countermeasures against outsider cultivation methods?"

The moons suddenly pulsed with blinding light. Lucious's plants withered instantly, leaving him exposed as the four spheres of crushing force bore down on him. He had just enough time to cross his arms in a defensive position before impact. The explosion lit up the entire valley and sent shockwaves through the snow-covered ground.

When the light faded, Lucious was still standing, but blood trickled from the corner of his mouth. His expensive robes were tattered, and his breathing came in harsh gasps.

"Impossible," one of the Moon God cultivators whispered. "He survived a direct hit from Moonfall Crisis?"

"As expected of an outsider," the leader said. "But you're weakening. How much longer can you last?"

Lucious wiped the blood from his mouth, his eyes burning with hatred. The leader was right—that last attack had done serious damage. Something about this realm was making his techniques less effective than they should be.

"Black Rose Art: Thousand Thorn Rain!"

He leapt into the air as dark energy condensed into thousands of needle-like thorns, then shot towards his enemies. But the Moon God Sect was ready.

"Lunar Shield Formation!"

Six cultivators moved in perfect sync, and their qi connected to form a dome of silvery light. The thorns struck the barrier and disintegrated, unable to penetrate the combined defense.

"Now!" the leader commanded. "Eight Trigrams Moonblade Dance!"

Eight cultivators moved to surround Lucious as they each drew a sword that gleamed with lunar energy. They began a complex series of movements, their blades leaving trails of silver light in the air.

Lucious recognized the danger too late. The trails of light weren't random—they were forming a massive array with him at the center.

"Die, outsider!"

The array activated, and eight crescent-shaped blades of concentrated moonlight converged on Lucious from all directions. He tried to dodge, but there was nowhere to go. The attacks struck home, and his scream of pain echoed across the valley.

Lucious crashed to the ground, blood flowing from multiple deep cuts across his body. His qi was dangerously depleted, and he could feel the lunar energy continuing to damage his meridians.

"Surrender," the leader said, stepping forward. "You've lost."

Lucious tried to stand, his legs shaking with the effort. He was a Legacy Disciple, trained since birth to be supreme among his peers. To submit to these inferior cultivators was unthinkable.

But before he could make his likely suicidal last stand, a massive explosion rocked the battlefield. Golden light suddenly filled the valley as Hong Yan and Wei Ling descended from above, their faces twisted with rage.

"Moon God dogs!" Hong Yan shouted. "First you steal our inheritance, and now you dare to fight in our territory?"

The Sword Twins appeared moments later, their silver blades humming with killing intent. "The treasure was meant for the Celestial Blade Sect! Return it now and we'll grant you a quick death!"

The Moon God leader cursed. "We don't have your precious inheritance! We're here for—"

He never finished the sentence. Both sides attacked simultaneously, not bothering with words anymore. The valley erupted into chaos as four Nascent Soul experts clashed with the Moon God forces.

"Young Master Lucious!" Finick appeared beside him to support his weight. "We need to go, now! While they're distracted!"

For once, Lucious didn't argue. He could barely stand, let alone continue fighting. With the help of the Fiery Mist members, he began retreating from the battlefield.

The Moon God leader noticed their escape but could do nothing about it. He was too busy defending against Hong Yan's Solar Emperor technique while simultaneously dodging the Sword Twins' attacks.

"After them!" he managed to shout. "Don't let the outsider escape!"

But his words were drowned out by the sound of battle. The three sects were fully committed now, their techniques lighting up the night sky like competing fireworks.

Lucious and the Fiery Mist disciples disappeared into the snowy forest, leaving chaos in their wake. They moved as quickly as they could, though Lucious's injuries slowed their pace considerably.

"That compass," Lucious muttered as they fled. "They can track outsiders with it. We need to get back to the sect before they regroup."

Finick nodded grimly. "Don't worry, young master. The sect's formation arrays will protect you. And Senior Alfie—"

"Don't," Lucious cut him off, his voice cold. "Don't speak of that coward."

The disciples exchanged worried looks but said nothing. They continued their retreat through the snow, the sounds of battle gradually fading behind them.

Lucious's mind raced despite his exhaustion. The Moon God Sect's ability to track outsiders changed everything. He would need to be more careful, more strategic. And as for Senior Alfie's convenient disappearance . . . Well, that was a debt that would need to be repaid. Eventually.

For now, though, survival was his priority. The Moon God Sect had proven far more dangerous than he'd anticipated. Next time, he would be better prepared.

If there was a next time.

* * *

From his perch on a distant peak, a masked figure watched as chaos unfolded in the valley below. Three sects clashed in a storm of golden light and silver blades while Lucious and the Fiery Mist disciples slipped away into the shadows.

"Hmmm," Zack murmured behind his bone-white mask, "it looks like the Moon God Sect will do anything to get their hands on outsiders."

He raised his hand and tore open a portal to his chambers. With one last glance at the battlefield, he stepped through. The portal closed behind him, leaving only falling snow.

Zack lounged on his throne in the Fiery Mist Sect's main hall, one leg casually draped over the armrest as he studied the jade he had taken from the inheritance site.

"Fascinating," he murmured to himself. "The ancients really had no concept of proper indexing. Would it have killed them to add a table of contents?"

The peaceful moment was shattered by the sound of doors being thrown open. Lucious stormed in, his once pristine robes now tattered and stained with blood. The Fiery Mist members trailed behind him looking like they'd just survived a particularly aggressive "friendly sparring session."

"Well, well," Zack drawled, not bothering to change his relaxed position. "Look who finally decided to join us. How was your evening stroll?"

Lucious's face turned an interesting shade of purple. "Stroll? *Stroll?* We were ambushed! By Moon God Sect cultivators with techniques specifically designed to hunt outsiders!"

"Oh?" Zack said. "That sounds rather inconvenient."

"Inconvenient?" Lucious slammed his hands on the throne's armrest, forcing Zack to finally look up at him. "Where were you? You disappeared the moment they showed up!"

"Did I?" Zack tapped his mask thoughtfully. "I seem to recall mentioning something about an important matter requiring my attention."

"You said you saw an interesting cloud!"

"And it was very interesting indeed."

Finick stepped forward, perhaps hoping to prevent bloodshed. "Senior Alfie, Young Master Lucious was grievously injured. The Moon God Sect's techniques—"

"Were specifically designed to capture those with foreign qi signatures," Zack finished, his tone suddenly serious. He stood up and threw the jade at Finick. "Show me."

Lucious stepped back, clearly wanting to refuse on principle, but the pain from his injuries won out. He pulled aside his torn robes to reveal angry silver marks across his skin where the moonlight blades had struck.

Zack circled him slowly as he studied the wounds. "Fascinating. These aren't just attacks meant to harm. They're designed to interfere with foreign qi circulation—to weaken and trap rather than to kill." He poked one of the marks, causing Lucious to hiss in pain. "They must've been hunting outsiders for a very long time to develop techniques this sophisticated."

"How very interesting for them," Lucious growled. "And how fortunate that you weren't around to experience their hospitality firsthand."

"Oh, come now." Zack waved a hand dismissively. "I'm not here to coddle you, young master. You're a Legacy Disciple of the mighty Black Rose Sect, aren't you? Surely you can handle a few backwater cultivators without running to Senior Alfie for help."

"I was outnumbered ten to one!"

"Then perhaps this will be a valuable lesson in picking your battles more carefully." Zack reached into his robes and pulled out a small jade bottle. "Though, I suppose I can't have you dying before you prove useful."

He tossed the bottle to Lucious, who caught it reflexively. "What is this?"

"A healing pill from my personal collection. It should counteract the effects of their moon-attributed techniques and restore your qi pathways." Zack's mask tilted in what might have been amusement. "Do note that it isn't free. Consider it a loan, to be repaid with appropriate interest."

Lucious studied the bottle suspiciously. "And what kind of interest does Senior Alfie charge?"

"Oh, nothing too excessive. Just some future favors, to be determined at my discretion." Zack settled back on his throne. "Unless you'd prefer to heal naturally, of course. Though, with those particular wounds, that could take . . . months? Years? Who can say?"

Lucious glared at the masked figure but eventually uncorked the bottle and swallowed the pill. Almost immediately, the silver marks began to fade and his qi circulation stabilized.

"There, isn't that better?" Zack's tone was insufferably smug. "Now, tell me more about this compass they used to track you. Every detail."

As Lucious described the Moon God Sect's tracking treasure, Zack frowned. The level of sophistication in their anti-outsider techniques suggested a very specific and long-standing purpose. This wasn't mere xenophobia or territorial defensiveness—they were hunting outsiders systematically with techniques and tools developed over generations.

But why? What could they possibly want with cultivators from the Main Realm? Unless . . .

"Senior Alfie?" Finick's voice broke into his thoughts. "What should we do? If they can track Young Master Lucious . . ."

"The sect's formation arrays will shield his qi signature," Zack replied absently, still lost in thought. "But more importantly, I believe we've stumbled onto something far more interesting than a simple case of interdimensional prejudice."

"What do you mean?" Lucious asked, the healing pill having restored enough of his energy for curiosity to overcome his anger.

Zack stood and began to pace. "Think about it. Why would a sect invest so heavily in techniques specifically designed to capture rather than kill? Why track outsiders with such dedication? There must be a purpose, a goal." He stopped, turning to face them. "And I intend to find out what it is."

"We," Lucious corrected firmly. "After what they did to me, I want answers too."

"Oh?" Zack's mask tilted. "And here I thought you were angry with me for abandoning you to their tender mercies."

"I am. Furious, in fact." Lucious straightened his now-healed shoulders. "But I'm also a Legacy Disciple of the Black Rose Sect. We don't forget insults . . . or debts."

"How delightfully ominous of you." Zack clapped his hands together. "Well, then, shall we begin plotting some elaborate revenge? I do so enjoy a good scheme, especially when someone else is doing most of the dangerous parts."

Lucious's eye twitched. "You're impossible."

"So I've been told. Frequently. Usually right before something extremely unfortunate happens to the person doing the telling." Zack settled back on his throne. "Now, let's discuss how we're going to turn this situation to our advantage, shall we?"

CHAPTER THIRTY-SIX

Ziven stood amidst the carnage casually wiping blood from his sword with a silk handkerchief. Around him, the bodies of local cultivators littered the ground, their faces still frozen in expressions of shock. They really shouldn't have tried to stop him from claiming the inheritance.

"Honestly," he muttered, kicking aside a corpse, "did they think Core Formation cultivators could stop someone like me? The sheer audacity of these backwater sects."

The inheritance site itself was rather underwhelming—just a small cave with some glowing formations. But the technique manual he'd found inside? Now that was worth the effort. Heavenly Light Mirror Formation—exactly the kind of righteous technique that would make his elders proud.

A twig snapped in the forest behind him.

Ziven turned lazily, expecting another minor sect member with delusions of grandeur. Instead, he saw a face he hadn't expected to find in this sealed backwater.

William, that sniveling little demonic cultivator from the Black Rose Sect, stood at the edge of the clearing. Their eyes met, and Ziven watched with satisfaction as all color drained from William's face.

"Well, well," Ziven drawled, his green eyes gleaming with predatory intent, "if it isn't the demon's little lapdog. Quite far from home, aren't we?"

William took one step back, then another. Smart boy—he knew exactly how outmatched he was.

"I . . . I was just leaving," William stammered, dark energy already gathering around him for a quick escape.

Ziven's face darkened. Just the sight of demonic qi made his blood boil. "Oh, I don't think so."

He moved faster than William could follow and crossed the clearing in an instant. His sword, still wet with the blood of lesser cultivators, sang through the air.

William barely managed to raise a barrier of thorny vines. The sword cut through it like paper and forced him to dodge desperately to the side.

"Running away?" Ziven called out mockingly. "How very like a demonic cultivator. No honor, no pride—just survival at any cost."

"Some of us prefer living to dying pointlessly!" William shot back as he sent a wave of poisonous thorns at Ziven.

Ziven snorted and raised his hand. Pure white light erupted from his palm and incinerated the thorns instantly. "Is that what you tell yourself to justify your cowardice?"

He pressed forward, each step casual yet inexorable. William's techniques, while impressive for a Core Formation cultivator, might as well have been a child throwing pebbles at a mountain.

"Heavenly Light Art: Divine Spear!"

A lance of concentrated light pierced through William's shoulder, pinning him to a tree. The demonic cultivator screamed as righteous energy burned through his meridians.

"You know what I hate most about your kind?" Ziven asked conversationally as he advanced on his trapped prey. "It's not the demonic techniques or even the lack of morals. It's how you corrupt everything you touch. Like a disease spreading through the cultivation world."

William tried to speak, but only blood came out. The divine spear was systematically destroying his qi pathways.

"I'm actually doing you a favor," Ziven continued as he raised his sword for the final blow. "Better a quick death than letting that corruption spread further, don't you think?"

But before he could strike, a familiar prickle ran down his spine: killing intent—and lots of it.

Ziven leapt back just as five figures descended from above, their black robes and silver moon masks marking them as Moon God Sect hunters. Two radiated Nascent Soul power, while the other three were Peak Core Formation.

"Well," Ziven said drily, letting his divine spear dissipate. William collapsed to the ground, forgotten for the moment. "Are you all also here to give your lives away?"

"An outsider," one of the Nascent Soul cultivators said, pointing some kind of compass at Ziven. "And a powerful one."

Ziven raised an eyebrow. "Outsider? Is that what we're calling righteously aligned cultivators these days? Standards really have fallen in this realm."

Instead of responding, the Moon God hunters spread out in a standard encirclement pattern. Ziven had to admire their efficiency, even if it was pointless.

"Since you're clearly not here for pleasant conversation," Ziven said, rolling his shoulders, "let me save us all some time."

His qi exploded outwards as he released his full power. A Nascent Soul emerged from his dantian, glowing with pure white light. The pressure alone drove the Core Formation hunters to their knees.

"Now, then." Ziven smiled, though it didn't reach his eyes. "Shall we dance?"

The five Moon God Sect hunters circled Ziven cautiously, their silver masks reflecting the glow of his Nascent Soul. He noticed with satisfaction that even the other Nascent Soul cultivators seemed taken aback by his power level.

"I'll give you credit," Ziven said, casually spinning his sword. "Most people wait until after I've thoroughly thrashed them to look that worried."

The leader of the group, a tall Nascent Soul expert, made a quick hand signal and said, "Formation Three!"

The Core Formation cultivators took supporting positions while the two Nascent Soul experts flanked Ziven. "Moonfall Crisis!" they shouted in unison and conjured four miniature moons that descended with crushing force.

"Really?" Ziven sighed. "Opening with your strongest technique? How disappointingly predictable." His sword blurred as he traced a complex pattern in the air. "Heavenly Light Art: Solar Dawn Shield!"

Pure white light erupted around him to form a dome of righteous energy. The artificial moons crashed against it with thunderous force, but the barrier held firm.

"My turn." Ziven smiled. "Heavenly Light Art: Divine Judgment Rain!"

Thousands of light arrows materialized above the battlefield and with a casual gesture, he sent them screaming towards his opponents.

The Moon God hunters scattered, their formations breaking apart as they desperately dodged the lethal barrage. Two of the Core Formation cultivators weren't quite fast enough—the light arrows caught them in the legs and shoulders, drawing pained screams as righteous energy burned through their qi.

"Come now," Ziven taunted, already preparing his next technique. "I thought you people were supposed to be expert hunters. Or do you only pick on weaker prey?"

The leader snarled something unintelligible and charged forward as moonlight gathered around his fist. "Lunar Impact Fist!"

Ziven met the attack head-on, his sword wreathed in brilliant white light. "Heavenly Light Art: Dawn Breaker Strike!"

The techniques collided with explosive force, sending both cultivators skidding backwards. But while the Moon God leader's arm trembled from the impact, Ziven looked completely unfazed.

"Not bad," he admitted. "But let me show you what real power looks like. Heavenly Light Art: Divine Spear Array!"

Multiple lances of concentrated light formed around him, each one as powerful as the spear he'd used on William. He sent them flying with pinpoint accuracy, forcing the hunters to expend precious qi defending themselves. One spear caught the second Nascent Soul expert in the side, drawing a pained grunt as it pierced through his defensive moonlight barrier.

The Moon God hunters regrouped; their masks hid any expression, but their body language screamed frustration. Good. Angry opponents made mistakes.

Out of the corner of his eye, Ziven noticed William trying to crawl away while everyone was distracted. Part of him wanted to finish what he'd started with the demonic cultivator, but these Moon God Sect members were proving to be far more interesting prey.

The leader raised his hand and revealed a black jade slip. "Enough games. Lunar Suppression Art: Outsider's Bane!"

Dark moonlight erupted from the talisman, flooding the battlefield with a strange, oppressive energy. Ziven felt his qi circulation suddenly become sluggish, as if he were trying to cultivate through mud.

"Oh?" He raised an eyebrow. "Now that's interesting. A technique specifically designed to counter foreign qi signatures? You really have put some thought into this outsider-hunting business."

The other Nascent Soul expert took advantage of his momentary distraction. "Moonlight Binding Chains!"

Silver chains materialized around Ziven, trying to entangle and restrict his movements. At the same time, the remaining Core Formation hunter began a complex sealing technique.

Ziven's eyes narrowed. The situation had suddenly become rather less amusing.

"Heavenly Light Art: Purifying Radiance!"

White light exploded outwards from his body and dissolved the moonlight chains. But the effort cost him more qi than it should have—that suppression technique was no joke.

"Finally taking this seriously, are we?" the leader asked, moonlight gathering around him in a deadly aura. "Good. Lunar Art: Crescent Guillotine!"

A massive blade of concentrated moonlight swept towards Ziven's neck. He deflected it with his sword, but the impact sent uncomfortable vibrations up his arm.

"You know," Ziven said, dropping into a defensive stance, "I'm starting to think you people might actually be worth my full attention." His Nascent Soul flared brighter as he channeled more power. "Heavenly Light Art: Divine Guardian Manifestation!"

An enormous warrior of pure light materialized behind him mimicking his movements. It was one of his trump cards: a technique that could double the power of any attack.

But the Moon God hunters didn't seem impressed. If anything, they looked . . . satisfied?

"Confirmed," the leader said, checking that strange compass again. "High-level outsider using primarily light-attributed techniques. Proceed with capture protocol seven."

The two Nascent Soul experts began moving in a complex pattern while the remaining Core Formation hunter provided support. Moonlight traced arcane symbols in the air as they prepared what was clearly a well-practiced combination attack.

"How flattering," Ziven drawled, though internally he was reassessing the threat level of these opponents. "You have a whole protocol for me?"

"Lunar Sealing Art: Heaven Defying Prison!"

The symbols they'd drawn suddenly connected to form a massive array. Ziven felt space itself beginning to warp around him as moonlight crashed down like a tidal wave.

His Divine Guardian construct raised its sword in perfect sync with him. "Heavenly Light Art: Dawn's First Ray!"

Pure white light met crushing moonlight in a clash that shook the entire forest. Trees were uprooted, boulders reduced to gravel, and somewhere in the chaos, William finally managed to slip away entirely.

"Your parlor tricks are impressive," Ziven murmured, "but ultimately futile. Allow me to demonstrate true power." Divine light erupted from his body as he channeled more energy into his Nascent Soul. The pressure alone caused the Core Formation hunter to stumble backwards. "Heavenly Light Art: Divine Sun Domain!"

The entire battlefield was suddenly bathed in white light so pure it seemed to reject the very existence of darkness. His domain, a technique that marked him as truly exceptional among his peers, expanded outwards like a miniature sun.

"Impossible!" the Moon God leader exclaimed. "A domain at Early Nascent Soul?"

Ziven didn't bother responding to their shock. Such reactions were beneath his notice. Instead, he launched his attack.

"Heaven Scorching Blade!"

His sword move was perfect, absolutely perfect. A crescent of divine light that could split mountains. But something was wrong. The moonlight suppression from earlier had spread throughout his domain, making his techniques cost far more energy than they should.

The Moon God hunters seized their opportunity. "Lunar Cross Seal!"

Four beams of moonlight struck him simultaneously, burning through his qi pathways with frightening efficiency. Ziven's face contorted with rage as he felt his cultivation base being forcibly suppressed.

"You dare?" he snarled, his usual composure cracking. "*You dare?*" He fought through the pain and forced more power into his techniques. "Divine Punishment Array!"

Pillars of light crashed down from above and scattered the Moon God formation. But they recovered quickly—too quickly. Their moonlight techniques seemed specifically designed to counter his righteous energy.

"Target is weakening," the leader called out. "Execute final binding!"

Chains of pure moonlight wrapped around Ziven's limbs while sealing arrays appeared beneath his feet. He burned through precious qi breaking free, but each movement was more difficult than the last.

A blade of moonlight slipped through his defenses and opened a deep gash across his chest. His pristine robes, marked with the Heavenly Light Sect's emblem, became stained with blood. The injury itself was nothing. He had suffered worse in training. But the implications . . . the sheer insult of these lesser cultivators actually wounding him . . .

"Enough!" Ziven roared, his voice carrying genuine anger for the first time. "I will not be humiliated by backwater insects!"

He prepared to unleash everything, to burn through his cultivation base if necessary, to destroy these impudent hunters. But before he could, the leader activated another talisman.

"Lunar Art: Great Moon Binding!"

A massive array materialized above, taking the form of a full moon. Its light pressed down with an impossible weight that interfered with Ziven's qi circulation at a fundamental level. Blood trickled from the corner of his mouth as he fought against the technique. His Divine Sun Domain flickered and shrank, unable to maintain its brightness under the overwhelming moonlight.

"How?" he demanded through gritted teeth. "How are your techniques so effective?"

The Moon God leader's voice carried a hint of smugness. "We've been hunting outsiders for generations. Did you think we wouldn't develop countermeasures for even the most talented among you?"

Ziven's eyes blazed with cold fury as he assessed his situation. His qi was dangerously depleted, his techniques were being countered, and for the first time since entering this realm, he faced the very real possibility of defeat.

The thought was intolerable.

He gathered what power he had left, preparing for one final, devastating attack. These insects had managed to wound him, to make him bleed. That alone earned them death sentences.

But first, he needed to survive. And that meant doing something he hadn't done since his battle with that annoying girl.

He needed to retreat.

The very thought made his blood boil with rage.

CHAPTER THIRTY-SEVEN

Zack was in the middle of decoding the stolen inheritance when Finick burst into his chambers, out of breath and looking like he'd just seen a ghost cultivator—or worse, his cultivation base's monthly bill.

"Senior Alfie!" Finick gasped, bowing so low he nearly headbutted the floor. "Urgent news from our scouts!"

"Unless someone's discovered a way to properly index ancient technique manuals," Zack replied without looking up, "I'm not sure how urgent it could be."

"The Moon God Sect has been spotted in force at the border between the Eastern and Northern Regions. There are reports of a massive spiritual energy disturbance!"

Now that got Zack's attention. He carefully placed a bookmark in the ancient text—because even mysterious masked seniors need to keep their place—and turned to face Finick.

"Define 'in force,'" he said, his bone-white mask tilting slightly.

"Nascent Soul experts, Senior! And they appear to be hunting something . . . or someone."

Or someone, indeed. Zack stood, and his black robes swirled dramatically. He'd been practicing that move in private—presentation was half the battle when playing the mysterious senior.

"Well, then," he said as he raised his hand to tear open a portal. "I suppose I should investigate this little disturbance. Stay here. I'll return shortly."

He walked through the portal to emerge high above the border region. The spiritual energy disturbance was immediately obvious—parts of the forest below looked like they'd been hit by competing natural disasters, all with a distinctive moon-themed aesthetic.

"Now, what do we have here," he murmured, scanning the area.

Movement caught his eye: a figure stumbled through the undergrowth trailing blood and what appeared to be badly suppressed demonic qi. Even from this distance, Zack could tell it was another Black Rose Sect member.

Well, wasn't this just perfectly convenient?

He appeared directly in the cultivator's path and caused the young man to nearly jump out of his spiritual skin.

"Peace," Zack said, raising his hands in what he hoped was a non-threatening manner. Though, with the bone-white mask and black robes, he probably looked about as peaceful as a demon lord at a righteousness convention.

"Stay back!" The cultivator—William, if Zack recalled correctly—tried to summon some thorny vines but only managed to produce a sad-looking sprout.

"Now, now," Zack said soothingly, "is that any way to greet a potential ally? Especially one who's already providing sanctuary to another Black Rose Sect member?"

William froze. "What?"

"Lucious. Perhaps you've heard of him? Quite the charming fellow, if you ignore the overwhelming arrogance and tendency to monologue about Main Realm superiority."

"You . . . You're sheltering Young Master Lucious?"

"'Sheltering' might be a strong word. 'Putting up with' might be more accurate." Zack gestured at William's injuries. "I see you've had an unfortunate encounter with our moon-loving friends."

William's face darkened. "They hunted me like a dog. Used techniques I've never seen before, specifically designed to counter foreign qi." He paused to spit blood. "If that righteously aligned bastard hadn't shown up first and weakened me . . ."

"Righteously aligned?" Zack's interest was piqued. "Do tell."

"That Ziven from the Heavenly Light Sect! Nearly killed me before the Moon God hunters showed up." William swayed on his feet. "I barely escaped while they were fighting each other."

"Well, then," Zack said as he tore open another portal. "How would you like to join your fellow sect member in my protection? The Fiery Mist Sect has excellent medical facilities and, more importantly, formation arrays that can hide foreign qi signatures."

William stared at the portal, then back at Zack. "Why would you help us?"

"Let's just say I have a vested interest in understanding why the Moon God Sect is so dedicated to hunting outsiders." Zack's mask tilted in what might have been amusement. "Besides, collecting arrogant young masters from the Main Realm is becoming something of a hobby."

"And what do you want in return?"

"Smart boy. Information, primarily. And perhaps some future favors, to be determined at my discretion." Zack gestured towards the portal. "Do we have a deal?"

William glanced over his shoulder, where the sounds of battle could still be heard in the distance. It wasn't much of a choice really.

"Deal," he said and limped towards the portal.

"Excellent! Just tell Sect Master Finick that Senior Alfie sent you. He'll get you settled in right next to your delightfully arrogant sect brother."

As William disappeared through the portal, Zack turned his attention back to the distant battle. The Moon God Sect's hunters were becoming more aggressive, and now a Heavenly Light Sect chosen was involved?

"I really should just head back to my nice, safe sect," he mused as he created another portal closer to the battle. "But then I'd miss out on valuable intelligence gathering. Yes, that's definitely why I'm going—pure strategic interest. Not at all because I want to see Mr. Righteous Light get his divine posterior handed to him."

He emerged on a cliff overlooking the battlefield and immediately cloaked himself in shadows. Below, the forest had been transformed into a war zone. Moonlight clashed with divine radiance to create a light show that would put most sect formation arrays to shame.

Ziven stood in the center of the destruction, his pristine robes now significantly less pristine. One of the Nascent Soul hunters lay dead at his feet—impressive, if slightly concerning from a self-preservation standpoint. However, the remaining hunters had him surrounded, their moonlight techniques slowly but surely wearing him down.

"You're supposed to be the unstoppable young master type," Zack muttered, watching Ziven barely dodge another moonlight blade. "The kind who pulls power-ups out of nowhere and tramples all opposition. Don't tell me you're going to disappoint genre conventions now?"

The battle intensified. Ziven's attacks were still devastatingly powerful, but they lacked their earlier dominance. The Moon God hunters' anti-outsider techniques were proving remarkably effective at suppressing his righteous energy.

"Heavenly Light Art: Divine Retribution!" Ziven roared, sending pillars of light crashing down.

The hunters scattered but quickly regrouped. "Lunar Sealing Art: Outsider's Cage!"

Silver chains of moonlight wrapped around Ziven, drawing a grunt of pain as they burned into his qi pathways. He broke free with raw power, but the effort seemed to cost him precious energy.

"Fascinating," Zack observed from his hidden vantage point. "Their techniques aren't just suppressing his qi—they're specifically targeting the foreign spiritual signature. I wonder . . ."

His analysis was interrupted by a sudden explosion. One of the Core Formation hunters, caught in the crossfire between Ziven's light attacks and his companions' moonlight techniques, went flying through the air like a particularly unlucky cultivation rocket.

Right towards Zack's hiding spot.

"Oh, come on," Zack sighed, then stepped aside as the unconscious hunter crashed into the ground beside him. "I try to watch one battle incognito and the universe decides to play cultivation pinball."

Below, Ziven had apparently decided that strategic retreat was the better part of valor. His face was a mask of pure fury as he gathered his remaining power.

"Remember this day," he snarled at the Moon God hunters, "for it marks the beginning of your sect's doom. I, Ziven of the Heavenly Light Sect, swear by my Dao that I will return. And when I do . . ."

"Yes, yes," Zack muttered. "Vengeance, destruction, eternal doom—we get it. Very protagonist-y of you."

Ziven disappeared in a flash of divine light, though not before unleashing one final attack that forced the hunters to defend rather than pursue immediately.

"Now that was actually clever," Zack admitted. "Maybe there's hope for him yet."

The remaining hunters regrouped, clearly preparing to chase their prey. But before they could move, that strange compass they carried suddenly lit up like a spiritual festival lantern.

"Another one?" the leader said, turning the device slowly. "Weaker cultivation, but the signature is clear . . ."

The compass was pointing directly at Zack's hiding spot.

"Well," Zack said cheerfully, "this is awkward."

The hunters' heads snapped up, and moonlight started gathering around their hands as they spotted him standing next to their unconscious companion. Who he had definitely been planning to kidnap for interrogation purposes.

"Would you believe," Zack called out, already opening a portal, "that he fell out of the sky and I was just about to call for medical assistance?"

"Capture him!" the leader shouted, but Zack was already moving.

He grabbed the unconscious hunter and gave the others a jaunty wave. "Love to stay and chat, but I have an appointment with some aggressive questioning that simply can't be rescheduled."

The portal snapped shut just as moonlight blades sliced through his previous location. The hunters' frustrated shouts cut off and were replaced by the familiar atmosphere of his sect chambers.

"Well," Zack said to his unconscious guest, "that was educational. Now, let's see what secrets you can share about these anti-outsider techniques, shall we?"

The Core Formation hunter, being unconscious, had no comment on this plan.

Zack sat cross-legged in his private chambers studying the unconscious Moon God hunter before him. He'd taken the precaution of binding the cultivator with several high-grade restriction talismans—the kind that made escape about as likely as a righteous sect elder admitting they were wrong about something.

"You know," he mused, adjusting his bone-white mask, "this would be much easier if you cultivators came with instruction manuals. *How to Extract Plot-Critical Information from Your Enemies for Dummies* would be a bestseller."

The hunter, still unconscious and thoroughly bound, offered no commentary on potential cultivation publishing opportunities.

Zack sighed. "Well, no help for it, then. Time for everyone's favorite morally questionable technique: soul searching!"

He placed his palm on the hunter's forehead and channeled qi in the precise pattern needed for the Soul Search technique. It wasn't his best skill—trying to navigate someone else's memories was like reading a book where all the pages had been scrambled and half of them were on fire.

"Now, let's see what secrets you're hiding behind that fancy mask . . ."

Images began flooding into his mind. Training sessions where Moon God Sect elders demonstrated specialized techniques for suppressing foreign qi. Hunting parties tracking down outsiders across the frozen landscape. A massive underground complex where captured cultivators were—

"Well, that's disturbing," Zack muttered as he watched memories of outsiders being systematically drained of their spiritual energy. But there was a pattern to it. The energy wasn't being stored randomly—it was being channeled into specific formations that looked eerily like . . .

"Root systems?" Zack leaned forward, forcing more power into the technique. "Why would they need to arrange spiritual energy like tree roots?"

The next memory nearly made him lose his concentration. A vast chamber deep beneath the Moon God Sect, where countless threads of stolen spiritual energy converged on a single point. At its center, surrounded by floating crystals that contained the essence of captured outsiders, stood their king.

"The power of those beyond the seal," the king's voice echoed through the memory, "is the key to breaking through. Their connection to the Main Realm . . . Yes, that's what we need. That's what we've always needed."

The Moon God Sect wasn't just hunting outsiders out of xenophobia or for their power. They were harvesting something fundamental about their very nature. Something connected to the barrier between realms.

They're trying to use outsider souls as a bridge, he realized. *A way to force open a path to the Main Realm.*

But why the tree pattern? What was the significance of arranging the stolen energy in rootlike formations?

Zack pushed deeper into the hunter's memories, searching for the location of their secret base. If he could find where they were storing all that spiritual energy . . .

Something dark stirred in the cultivator's mind. A massive tree appeared, its branches reaching towards a blood-red sky while its roots dug deep into the very foundations of reality. But this was no ordinary tree—its bark was carved with countless screaming faces, and its leaves dripped with what looked disturbingly like liquid qi.

"Oh, that's not ominous at all," Zack muttered. "Very subtle with the evil tree symbolism there."

He tried to push past the image, but the tree seemed to notice his presence. Its branches twisted towards him, reaching across the mental landscape with impossible speed.

"Nope, nope, absolutely not." Zack tried to withdraw from the memory, but the tree's presence had already latched onto his spiritual sense.

Pain exploded behind his eyes as the soul-searching technique backfired spectacularly. He was thrown backwards, his mask nearly flying off, and crashed into the wall.

"Right," he gasped, clutching his head. "Note to self: mysterious demon trees in people's memories are not to be trifled with. File that one under 'obvious things I really should have known better about.'"

The hunter remained unconscious, but a thin trail of black energy seeped from his closed eyes. Whatever that tree representation was, it had some serious spiritual defenses built into it.

"Well, that was educational," Zack said as he stood somewhat unsteadily. "Horrifying and potentially traumatizing, but educational."

He'd learned three critical pieces of information. One: the Moon God Sect was using outsider souls to try and break their king through to the Ascendant Realm. Two: they believed outsiders were somehow key to breaking the seal between realms. And three: there was something very, very wrong about that tree.

"The real question," he mused, "is whether they're actually onto something with this 'outsiders as realm-crossing bridges' theory, or if this is just another case of cultivation megalomaniacs and their unnecessarily complicated schemes."

The hunter stirred slightly, and the binding talismans flickered as they maintained their suppression.

"And you, my friend," Zack said, "are going to need much more thorough questioning once you wake up. Preferably about things that don't involve cosmic horror trees."

He paused, considering the implications of everything he'd learned. If the Moon God Sect's theory was correct, then every outsider in the Sealed Realm was potentially a key to breaking its isolation. No wonder they were hunting them so aggressively.

"But why arrange the energy in root patterns? What's the significance of the tree?" He paced the chamber, mind racing. "And more importantly, how many cultivation resources am I going to have to burn through to get rid of this splitting headache?"

The whole situation was developing classic "major plot point" energy, the kind that usually preceded either a significant power-up or a devastating revelation about the nature of reality itself. Possibly both.

"You know," he told his unconscious guest, "I really should have stuck to my original plan of laying low and accumulating power. But no, I had to get curious about mysterious sects and their outsider-hunting habits. This is exactly how cultivation protagonists get dragged into world-shaking events." He sighed and rubbed his temples where the backlash still throbbed. "Still, at least I'm genre savvy enough to recognize the signs. That has to count for something, right?"

The hunter, displaying a remarkable commitment to unconsciousness, declined to comment.

Zack settled back into his chair to review everything he'd learned. The Moon God Sect's true goals were far more ambitious—and potentially catastrophic—than anyone had suspected. Using outsider souls to break through to the Ascendant Realm was bad enough, but trying to forcibly break the seal between realms?

"That's the kind of plan that either works perfectly or ends with reality being torn apart," he mused. "And in my experience, it's usually the latter." He glanced at the hunter and noticed the black energy had stopped seeping from his eyes. "Well, my unconscious friend, I believe it's time to make you comfortable in one of our more secure guest rooms. We have so much more to discuss once you wake up."

Assuming, of course, that whatever mental defenses that tree had planted didn't completely scramble the hunter's memories. That would be just his luck: finally capturing someone with valuable information, only to have it protected by eldritch plant life.

"I really need to work on my information gathering skills," Zack muttered as he prepared to move his prisoner. "Preferably ones that don't involve diving into people's memories and finding cosmic horror waiting there."

But for now, he had planning to do. The Moon God Sect's goals were clear, but their methods—particularly that disturbing tree—suggested there was much more to this story.

And Zack had a feeling he wasn't going to like where this particular plot thread led.

CHAPTER THIRTY-EIGHT

Deep beneath one of the secret bases belonging to the Moon God Sect, in a chamber untouched by natural light, five figures gathered around a massive formation array.

At the center stood the Moon God King, his ageless face a mask of cold beauty. His white robes seemed to absorb the moonlight, making him appear more like a living shadow than a man.

"The time approaches," he said, his voice carrying that peculiar resonance of someone who has long since transcended normal human limitations. "Our research has finally yielded results."

Around him, his four most trusted advisors, all Peak Origin Realm cultivators, bowed their heads in acknowledgment. Each wore the silver moon masks that marked their status, though theirs were far more elaborate than those worn by common sect members.

"Show us the specimens, my lord," one of them requested.

The king gestured and part of the chamber wall became transparent. Two separate holding cells were revealed. Each contained a cultivation formation of incredible complexity: the arrays were designed not just to restrain, but to systematically break down spiritual defenses.

In the first cell, a young woman with long black hair knelt in a meditative position.

The second cell contained a man in black robes, who thrashed against his bonds as dark energy swirled around him. His eyes blazed with hatred and promised violence.

"Magnificent, aren't they?" the king mused. "Each represents a different aspect of what we need. The yin and yang of foreign spiritual energy."

He approached the second cell and studied the male prisoner with clinical interest. "Horocus, was it? Your demonic cultivation is quite impressive. The Black Heart Sect trained you well."

"When I break free," Horocus snarled, "I'll show you just how well they trained me!"

The king smiled, the expression never reaching his eyes. "Oh, you won't be breaking free. In fact, you're about to serve a much greater purpose." He turned to his advisors. "Observe carefully. This is what we've spent generations working towards."

With a series of precise hand seals, the king activated a new formation. Silver chains of pure moonlight wrapped around Horocus, who renewed his struggles with desperate energy.

"You see," the king lectured as he worked, "not all outsider souls are equal. Each cultivation path creates unique spiritual signatures. And for our ritual to succeed, we need very specific types."

The formation began to pulse and drew agonized screams from Horocus as his spiritual energy was systematically extracted. But instead of dispersing or being absorbed, the energy formed distinct patterns in the air—like roots spreading through soil.

"The demonic path," the king continued, "represents destruction and transformation. Essential components for breaking through dimensional barriers."

Behind him, a section of the chamber wall shifted and revealed what at first appeared to be an ordinary tree. But as Horocus's spiritual energy was drawn towards it, its true nature became apparent.

The trunk was covered in writhing faces, each frozen in expressions of agony. The branches reached out like grasping hands, eager to receive their offering. But it was the roots that drew the eye: they pulsed with stolen spiritual energy and were arranged in patterns that seemed to defy normal space.

"Beautiful, isn't it?" the king asked as Horocus's extracted spiritual energy was absorbed into the tree. "A living catalyst, capable of processing and storing the unique properties of outsider souls."

The female prisoner watched silently as Horocus's screams reached a crescendo. Then, suddenly, they stopped. His body slumped, empty of both life and spiritual essence.

"Beautiful," the king breathed. "Another piece of the pattern falls into place." He turned to the female prisoner. "Don't worry, my dear. Your time will come soon enough. But your soul represents a different aspect, one we're not quite ready to harvest yet."

"You're insane," she said quietly. "All of this . . . It's an abomination."

"An abomination?" The king laughed. "This is ascension! Freedom! Do you think I enjoy being trapped in this Sealed Realm? This prison that the so-called righteous sects created to contain what they feared?" He gestured at the tree. "This is our key to breaking the seal. Each soul we harvest, each pattern we complete, brings us one step closer to freedom." He then gestured to a figure standing apart from the advisors, shorter than the others and wearing a mask that covered their entire face rather than just the lower half. "My avatar," the king said. "You've spent time in the Main Realm. Made . . . connections."

The masked figure bowed deeply. "Yes, my lord."

"Good. Those connections will prove useful now. Find your fellow sect members. Lure them here."

"The friends I made there . . ." The avatar's voice held a hint of hesitation.

"Will serve a greater purpose," the king cut in smoothly. "Their sacrifices will help break the seal that has trapped our people for generations. Surely you understand the importance of that?"

The avatar bowed again, lower this time. "Of course, my lord. It will be done."

"Excellent." The king turned back to the tree and watched as Horocus's spiritual energy was fully absorbed. The patterns in its roots grew more complex, more complete. "Soon we will have enough. The ritual will succeed, and I will ascend. Then nothing will be able to stop us from claiming our rightful place in the Main Realm." He turned to his advisors. "Prepare the next phase of formations. When my avatar returns with more specimens, I want everything ready."

As his subordinates hurried to obey, the king gazed up at the demonic tree. Its branches seemed to wave in an unfelt wind as the faces in its trunk silently screamed.

"Soon," he whispered. "Soon we will have everything we need. The seal will break and our realm will finally take its proper place in the natural order."

The avatar slipped away as the others began their preparations, their masked face hiding any reaction to what they had witnessed. They had a mission now: to betray those who had once called them friend.

But it would all be worth it in the end. It had to be.

CHAPTER THIRTY-NINE

The morning sun had barely crested the horizon when a messenger arrived at the Fiery Mist Sect's gates, his robes bearing the emblem of the White Moon Sect—one of the most powerful forces in the region, second only to the Moon God Sect itself. The guard disciples immediately straightened their postures, trying to look more impressive than a typical outer sect member had any right to.

"I carry an urgent message for your sect master," the messenger announced, his bearing suggesting he was at least at the Core Formation Realm. "From Sect Master Wu of the White Moon Sect."

The guards exchanged nervous glances before one hurried off to notify their superiors. Within minutes, Finick arrived, his usually composed demeanor showing hints of strain. Running a sect, even with Zack's "guidance," was proving to be more challenging than he'd anticipated.

"Welcome, honored messenger," Finick said, bowing appropriately. "I am Finick, current leader of the Fiery Mist Sect. How may we assist the White Moon Sect?"

The messenger's expression faltered. "Apologies, but my message is for your true leader. The one called Senior Alfie."

Finick's carefully maintained expression cracked slightly. "I . . . I'm not sure what you mean. I am the—"

"Please," the messenger cut him off smoothly, "let's not waste time with pretense. Sect Master Wu specifically requested an audience with Senior Alfie.

He said, and I quote, 'Tell the one who wears the bone-white mask that I have matters of mutual interest to discuss.'"

A familiar chuckle echoed from behind Finick, causing him to jump slightly. Zack seemed to materialize from the shadows, his black robes and distinctive mask making him an imposing figure even in the early morning light.

"Now this is interesting," Zack said, tilting his head. "The White Moon Sect doesn't typically concern itself with smaller sects like ours. What could your illustrious leader want with little old me?"

The messenger bowed deeply. "Sect Master Wu requests your presence at the White Moon Sect's main compound. He says the matter is both urgent and . . . delicate."

"Does he now?" Zack's mask revealed nothing of his expression, but there was a note of curiosity in his voice. "And I suppose he's expecting me to drop everything and rush over?"

"He anticipated your hesitation," the messenger replied as he reached into his robes to withdraw a jade slip, "and asked me to give you this as a show of good faith."

Zack took the jade slip and channeled a bit of qi into it. His posture stiffened slightly as he absorbed its contents.

"Well," he said after a moment, "that is rather interesting." He turned to Finick. "Keep an eye on our . . . guests. I believe I'll accept this invitation after all."

"But, Senior Alfie," Finick protested quietly, "is it wise to—"

"Wisdom is highly overrated," Zack cut him off cheerfully. "Besides, someone who can send a message like this deserves at least the courtesy of a face-to-face meeting. Even if that face happens to be wearing a mask." He turned back to the messenger. "Lead the way. Let's see what your master has to say."

The journey to the White Moon Sect's compound took several hours, even traveling at high speed. Unlike the Fiery Mist Sect's modest mountain, their destination was an entire mountain range, with peaks that seemed to pierce the clouds themselves. Elaborate formations shimmered in the air creating barriers that would have given even Origin Realm experts pause.

"Somebody likes to show off," Zack muttered as they approached the main gates. The messenger either didn't hear or wisely chose not to respond.

They were escorted through a series of increasingly impressive courtyards, each one displaying the sort of casual wealth that only true powerhouse sects could maintain. Ancient spirit trees lined the paths, each of their fruits worth a small fortune. Formation arrays maintained perfect cultivation environments that lesser sects could only dream of.

Finally, they reached what appeared to be a private garden—though, "garden" was perhaps underselling it. It was more like a pocket dimension of natural beauty, complete with its own artificial sun and carefully maintained spiritual spring.

Sect Master Wu sat beside the spring calmly brewing tea with movements that suggested he'd refined the process into an art form. He appeared to be middle-aged, though with cultivators that meant little. His robes were surprisingly simple for a sect master, lacking the usual ornate decorations that most powerhouse leaders favored.

"Ah, Cultivator Alfie," Wu said without looking up from his tea preparation. "Thank you for accepting my invitation. Please, join me."

Zack studied the man carefully before taking a seat across from him. The messenger bowed and retreated, leaving them alone.

"I must admit," Zack said, "your message was . . . intriguing. Though, I'm curious how you knew about certain things that I've been quite careful to keep private."

Wu smiled, the expression reaching his eyes in a way that suggested genuine amusement. "Would you believe me if I said the world itself whispers secrets to those who know how to listen?"

"I would believe that you're either incredibly well-informed or delightfully insane," Zack replied. "Possibly both."

"A healthy skepticism!" Wu laughed. "Good. That will serve you well in the days to come." He poured tea into two exquisite cups and pushed one towards Zack. "But first, let us discuss the outsider you're sheltering."

Zack's posture shifted ever so slightly. "And what makes you think I'm sheltering anyone?"

"Please"—Wu waved a hand dismissively—"let's not play games. Young Master Lucious of the outsider sects is quite the interesting character. Though, I imagine he's a handful to deal with."

"If I were hypothetically sheltering such an individual," Zack said carefully, "I fail to see how it would concern the White Moon Sect."

Wu's expression grew more serious. "It concerns us because unlike our . . . zealous neighbors in the Moon God Sect, we have no quarrel with outsiders. In fact, we believe they must be protected."

"Protected?" Zack's mask tilted. "That's not a word I often hear applied to outsiders in this realm. Usually, it's more along the lines of 'hunted,' 'captured,' or 'mysteriously disappeared.'"

"Yes, the Moon God Sect's activities have been rather aggressive lately." Wu took a sip of his tea. "Tell me, Senior Alfie, have you ever wondered why they hunt outsiders with such dedication? Or what they do with those they capture?"

"I might have given it some thought," Zack admitted, thinking of his recently acquired and still unconscious prisoner.

"They believe outsiders are the key to breaking the seal between realms," Wu said bluntly. "That by harvesting their unique spiritual signatures, they can force open a path to the Main Realm."

"And you don't agree with this theory?"

"Oh, the theory is sound enough," Wu replied. "It's the application that concerns me. The Moon God King's methods are . . . unnatural. He corrupts everything he touches in his quest for power."

Zack thought of the twisted tree he'd glimpsed in his prisoner's memories. "You seem well-informed about their activities."

"I told you, the world whispers." Wu's eyes took on a distant look. "And lately, those whispers have grown more urgent. Something is coming. Something that could shatter the balance between realms if we're not careful."

"And I suppose you want my help in preventing this catastrophe?" Zack asked drily. "How wonderfully heroic of you."

Wu smiled again, but this time there was an edge to it. "Actually, Senior Alfie—or should I say outsider?—I think we can help each other."

The temperature seemed to drop several degrees. "That's quite an accusation," Zack said softly.

"Not an accusation. An observation." Wu remained perfectly calm. "Your qi signature is well hidden, I'll grant you that. But to those who know how to look, who can hear what the world is saying . . . Well, let's just say you shine quite brightly."

Zack was silent for a long moment. "And you're not concerned about having an outsider sitting across from you?"

"Should I be?" Wu raised an eyebrow. "You've shown remarkable restraint since arriving in our realm. You've built up a power base, gathered intelligence, protected others of your kind. These are not the actions of someone who means us harm."

"You seem very certain about that."

"I am." Wu's voice carried absolute conviction. "Because the world itself has shown me glimpses of possible futures. In some, the Moon God King succeeds in his plans and both realms pay the price. In others . . . Well, let's just say that your role is rather significant."

Zack leaned back, considering. "You're either a masterful manipulator or genuinely touched by something beyond normal cultivation understanding. Neither option is particularly comforting."

Wu laughed again. "Why not both? One doesn't survive as a sect master without learning to manipulate situations to their advantage. But that doesn't make the warnings any less real." He reached into his robes, withdrew a map, and spread it on the table between them. "There are others who oppose the Moon God Sect's actions. Small groups scattered throughout the realm. Some for moral reasons, others for political ones. But they lack organization, leadership."

"And you think I should provide that leadership?" Zack asked incredulously.

"I think you already are, whether you realize it or not. Your actions have attracted attention. The way you've managed to shelter outsiders while maintaining a careful balance of power . . . It's impressive. Others have noticed."

"Others like who?"

"The Wandering Sword Sect, for one. They've always opposed the Moon God Sect's methods, though they've been careful about showing it openly. The Southern Dragon Clan has also expressed interest in recent developments."

Zack studied the map thoughtfully. "That's quite the coalition you're suggesting. Though, I notice your own sect isn't marked."

"The White Moon Sect cannot move openly against the Moon God Sect," Wu admitted. "We're too close, too intertwined. But we can provide support in other ways: information, resources, sanctuary when needed."

"And what do you want in return?"

"Want? I want to prevent a catastrophe." Wu's eyes blazed with sudden intensity. "The Moon God King's actions threaten everything—not just our realm, but the Main Realm as well. The methods he's using to harvest outsider souls . . . They're creating ripples in reality itself. Surely you've sensed it?"

Zack thought of the strange tree again, of the way it had reached across mental barriers with impossible speed. "Perhaps. But why come to me? Surely there are more powerful allies you could seek out."

"Power isn't everything," Wu said softly. "Sometimes what's needed is someone who can see the bigger picture. Someone who can move in shadows while others clash in the light." He smiled. "Someone who understands both realms well enough to navigate between them."

"You're assuming a lot about my capabilities."

"Am I? The world whispers of your true nature, of the power you hide behind that mask. But more importantly, it whispers of your potential. Of what you could become if you embrace a larger role."

Zack was silent for a long moment as he considered everything he'd learned. The White Moon Sect's support could be invaluable, especially with the Moon God Sect becoming more aggressive. And if Wu was right about other groups being willing to work together . . .

"Let's say I'm interested," he said finally. "How would this alliance work?"

Wu's smile widened. "I thought you'd never ask." He began pointing to specific locations on the map. "These are safe houses we've established throughout the realm. And these marks indicate known Moon God Sect facilities. Places where they take their captives."

"Quite the intelligence network you have."

"We've been preparing for this for a long time," Wu admitted. "Gathering allies, stockpiling resources. But we needed someone who can coordinate everything without being tied to any major sect's political structure."

"Someone expendable, you mean?"

"Someone deniable," Wu corrected. "The larger sects can't move openly against the Moon God Sect without risking all-out war. But a smaller sect led by a mysterious figure of unknown origins? That provides . . . opportunities."

Zack laughed. "You're asking me to be your cat's-paw."

"I'm asking you to be exactly what you already are: a wild card that no one quite knows how to deal with." Wu's expression grew serious again. "The Moon God Sect is close to achieving their goal. Their king stands at the threshold of breaking through to the Ascendant Realm. If he succeeds . . ."

"Then having a network of allies might be rather useful," Zack finished. "Alright, you've caught my interest. But I'll need more than just vague promises of support."

"Of course." Wu reached into his robes again, this time withdrawing several jade slips. "These contain information about the Moon God Sect's activities, including the locations of several of their secret facilities. Consider it a down payment on our future cooperation."

Zack took the jade slips and quickly scanned their contents. His eyes widened slightly behind his mask. "This is . . . quite detailed."

"We've been watching them for a very long time," Wu said simply. "There's more where that came from if you're willing to work with us."

"And if I refuse?"

"Then you go back to your sect with some valuable intelligence and my sincere thanks for hearing me out." Wu shrugged. "I won't force you into anything. But I think you know as well as I do that the Moon God Sect needs to be stopped."

Zack thought of William's injuries, of Lucious's close call with the hunters, of the twisted tree and its implications. Finally, he nodded.

"Alright," he said. "I'm in. But on one condition: I maintain complete autonomy. I'll coordinate with your allies, but I won't take orders from anyone."

"I wouldn't expect anything less." Wu smiled. "Welcome to the Resistance, Senior Alfie."

"Please don't call it that," Zack groaned. "It sounds like we should be wearing matching uniforms and coming up with dramatic battle cries."

Wu laughed. "Would you prefer Coalition of Concerned Parties? Alliance Against Unnecessary Soul Harvesting? Society for the Prevention of Cruelty to Outsiders?"

"I'm already regretting this decision," Zack muttered, but there was amusement in his voice.

They spent the next few hours going over details—communication methods, resource distribution, emergency protocols. Wu had clearly been planning this for a long time, waiting for the right moment and the right person to set everything in motion.

"One last thing," Wu said as they prepared to conclude their meeting. "The Moon God Sect has spies everywhere. You'll need to be extremely careful about who you trust with this information."

"Naturally," Zack replied. "Though, I'm curious: How do I know you're not one of those spies?"

Wu smiled mysteriously. "Because the world whispers truth to those who listen. And right now, it's whispering that our paths are aligned."

"You really enjoy being cryptic, don't you?"

"It's one of the few pleasures left to old cultivators like myself," Wu admitted. "That and watching younger generations try to figure out if we're wise sages or simply senile."

"The two aren't mutually exclusive," Zack pointed out.

"Indeed not!" Wu laughed. "Now go, plan, prepare. I'll have my people contact you soon with more detailed information about our allies."

"One more thing," Zack said as he paused before stepping through his portal. "When the time comes to confront the Moon God King . . . you don't expect me to fight him alone, do you? Because I have to tell you, suicide missions aren't really my specialty."

Wu's amused expression shifted to something more serious. "Of course not. The Moon God King stands at the threshold of the Ascendant Realm. Even with your unique capabilities, facing him alone would be certain death."

"Good, because I rather like being alive," Zack replied drily. "It's become something of a habit."

"When the time comes," Wu continued, "I and the other major sect masters who oppose him will join the battle. We've been preparing for this confrontation for centuries."

Zack nodded, internally relieved. Even with the emergency supplies from the Main Body, the Origin-grade talismans and other trump cards he kept in reserve, facing a Half-Step Ascendant cultivator would be like trying to empty the ocean with a teacup. Possible in theory, perhaps, but likely to end with him very thoroughly dead.

CHAPTER FORTY

A white-robed figure stood before the final trial chamber, a sword strapped to his back. The previous trials had tested his resolve, skill, and understanding of the sword Dao—but this last challenge would determine if he was worthy of inheriting the Sword God's legacy.

The chamber stretched upwards into darkness; its walls were covered in countless sword marks. Some were precise and deliberate, creating intricate patterns. Others, deep gouges carved by techniques powerful enough to split mountains, spoke of desperate battles.

Master would find this amusing, Caelum thought, a slight smile crossing his face. *He'd probably make a joke about overcompensating sword cultivators.*

The trial activated as he stepped into the chamber. Sword qi manifested in the air and took the form of translucent blades. They hung suspended, their points aimed at his heart.

"Show me your understanding of the sword," a voice echoed through the chamber. "Not through technique, but through intent."

Caelum closed his eyes and reached for his sword—then stopped. No, this trial wasn't about displaying power or skill. The previous chambers had tested those aspects thoroughly. Instead, he sank into a meditative stance, his hands empty. The floating blades drew closer, their edges sharp enough to split hair.

"The sword is not the weapon," Caelum said quietly. "The cultivator is not the wielder." The blades pressed against his skin, drawing pinpricks of blood.

"We are one with the Dao of the sword," he continued. "Neither controlling nor controlled. Moving as naturally as breath, as inevitable as time." The pressure increased. One wrong word, one slip in his understanding, and the blades would pierce his heart. "The sword does not cut because we will it to cut. It cuts because that is its nature, as flowing is the nature of water or burning is the nature of fire." The blades began to vibrate, resonating with his words. "True mastery comes not from imposing our will upon the sword, but from aligning ourselves with its essential nature. We do not master the sword—we become one with it."

Light filled the chamber as the blades withdrew. They circled him once before dissipating into pure sword qi, which flowed into his body like a gentle stream.

Knowledge flooded his mind, understanding beyond mere technique. The Sword God's final technique revealed itself not as a series of movements or energy patterns, but as a fundamental truth about the nature of the sword Dao.

When the light faded, Caelum opened his eyes. The chamber had transformed. Where before there had been sword marks and battle scars, now the walls were perfectly smooth, as if they had never been touched by a blade.

"Well done," the voice said. "You have grasped the essence of the Formless Sword Art technique. Use it wisely."

Caelum bowed deeply. "Thank you for this gift."

As he straightened, memories of his journey through the Sealed Realm flooded back. He had arrived with the other winners of the Inter-Sect Tournament, though they'd been scattered across the realm. Their mission had seemed simple enough: gather resources and treasures to strengthen their cultivation before returning to their sects. But like most simple plans, reality had proved more complicated.

His arrival itself had been . . . memorable. The portal had spit him out in the Southern Region, right into the middle of what appeared to be someone's private meditation spot. Unfortunately, that someone happened to be a bald cultivator who had chosen that exact moment to practice his Moonlit Meditation technique. Which, as Caelum discovered, required the practitioner to strip down to their undergarments and bathe in moonlight while chanting.

"Demon!" the old cultivator had screamed as he scrambled to cover himself with his discarded robes. "How dare you interrupt the sacred Moonlit—"

"I'm so sorry," Caelum had tried to apologize, turning around to give the man some privacy. "I didn't mean to—"

"Die, foul creature!"

A blast of spiritual energy had forced Caelum to dodge while still trying not to look directly at the half-dressed cultivator. "Sir, if you could just put on some clothes—"

"Heavenly Moonlight Purification Strike!"

Master would never let me live this down if he could see this, Caelum had thought as he ducked under another attack.

The old cultivator, despite being at the Core Formation Realm, had been too flustered to fight effectively. His techniques, apparently designed to be performed while properly dressed, lost something in translation when attempted while trying to hold up falling robes.

"Could we perhaps discuss this when you're fully dressed?" Caelum had suggested while deflecting another blast.

"Silence, demon! Your eyes have witnessed the sacred—oof!" The cultivator had tripped over his own robes, but his dignity suffered far more damage than his body.

Caelum had taken the opportunity to end the fight quickly by striking a pressure point that rendered the old man unconscious. He'd then carefully arranged the cultivator's robes to preserve what remained of his dignity and left a spirit stone as an apology.

That had been his introduction to the Sealed Realm—a realm where cultivation operated under different rules, where misunderstandings could turn deadly in an instant, and where, apparently, some meditation techniques required questionable dress codes. In the months since then, he'd tried to maintain a low profile, avoiding unnecessary conflict when possible.

A sudden spike of killing intent interrupted his thoughts. Three distinct auras, all at the Nascent Soul Realm, converged on his position. Caelum stepped out of the cave just as a moonlight blade sliced through the space where his head had been.

"Impressive reflexes," a cold voice called out. Three figures in silver masks emerged from the shadows—their robes bore the emblem of the Moon God Sect. "For an outsider."

Caelum's eyes narrowed. "I was wondering when you'd make your move. Three Nascent Soul cultivators against one? The Moon God Sect must be getting desperate."

"Desperate?" The leader laughed. "No, merely thorough. Your kind has caused enough trouble in our realm."

"My kind?" Caelum's voice remained calm, but his hand drifted towards his sword. "And what kind would that be?"

"Don't play innocent," another hunter spat. "We can sense the foreign qi in your spiritual core. You're an outsider, just like the others we've hunted."

"Hunted?" Something cold settled in Caelum's chest. "So, the rumors are true. You're systematically targeting cultivators from the Main Realm."

The leader raised his hands, and moonlight gathered between his fingers. "Nothing personal. But your spiritual energy will serve a greater purpose."

Caelum sighed and drew Bloodthorn from its scabbard. The demonic sword hummed with anticipation as it pulsed with dark qi, its thorned blade drinking in the ambient light.

"A demonic weapon?" The third hunter sounded surprised. "For someone who acts so righteous to wield a weapon of darkness . . ."

"We all contain multitudes," Caelum replied. "Though, I don't expect Moon God zealots to understand such nuance."

The three hunters spread out in a triangle formation, their silver masks reflecting the morning light. They were indistinguishable except for their weapons—a straight sword, a spear, and twin sabers.

Hunter One struck first, his straight sword trailing silver light. "Lunar Arts: Moonlight Binding Chains!"

Silver chains erupted from the ground and whipped towards Caelum like hungry serpents. He moved forward and sliced Bloodthorn through the spiritual constructs even as Hunter Two's spear thrust towards his blind spot.

Their coordination is perfect, Caelum noted as he deflected the spear with a precise parry. Hunter Three's sabers carved twin arcs through the air, forcing him to leap backwards.

"Moonlight Sealing Array: Foreign Qi Suppression!" The first hunter's technique spread across the battlefield like a spider's web of silver light.

Caelum felt the pressure immediately—the array was specifically designed to weaken cultivators from the Main Realm. His movements slowed fractionally, but years of training under Slifer had taught him to adapt.

"Sunrise Slash," he whispered. His form blurred and appeared behind Hunter Two even as their spear pierced his afterimage. The spear-wielder spun and barely blocked his strike. The clash of their weapons sent sparks of competing energy into the air, darkness against moonlight.

Hunter Three attacked from behind, their twin sabers moving in perfect synchronization. "Moon Shadow Dance!"

Caelum weaved between their attacks, but the suppression array was beginning to take its toll. His reactions slowed as each movement required more spiritual energy to execute. He shouted, "Nine Lights Mirage!" and eight identical images split from his form, each moving independently.

But the hunters had fought outsiders before. Their attacks ignored the images and tracked his true spiritual signature through the moonlight array.

The spear-wielder's technique expanded and turned their weapon into a forest of silver spears that attacked from every angle. The saber-user's blades became crescents of pure moonlight that extended their reach unpredictably.

Caelum found himself being pushed back as the suppression array grew stronger with each passing moment, their moonlight techniques specifically targeting his foreign qi signature.

I could use the Thorned Lash or Crimson Vortex, he thought as he deflected another barrage of attacks. *But no . . . there has to be another way.*

"Lunar Arts: Goddess's Tears!" Hunter One launched countless moonlight arrows from above while the other two pressed their advantage.

A saber slipped through his defense, drawing blood from his arm. A spear grazed his leg. The wounds weren't deep, but they proved he was slowing down.

"Your foreign qi can't resist our techniques forever," Hunter One called out. "Submit and your end will be painless."

Caelum's response was another Sunrise Slash, but this time they were ready. All three hunters moved in perfect synchronization to form a cage of moonlight with their weapons. "Lunar Sealing Art: Heaven's Prison!"

The very air crystallized into moonlight and formed walls of pure lunar energy that began closing in. Their combined spiritual energy created a domain where moonlight itself became solid, leaving no room for escape.

I can't overcome this with conventional techniques, Caelum realized. Even his demonic arts might not be enough against their specialized anti-outsider formations.

The cage contracted further, and the pressure became overwhelming. His foreign qi fluctuated under the sustained assault, threatening to destabilize.

That's when he felt it: the deeper understanding he'd gained from the Sword God's inheritance. Not just a technique, but a fundamental truth about the nature of the sword Dao.

"Formless Sword Art," he whispered.

Reality seemed to bend around Bloodthorn. The sword moved without moving, struck without striking. The technique transcended physical form and manifested as pure sword intent, which ignored the laws of space and time.

The hunters never saw the killing blow coming. One moment they were closing in for the final strike, the next two of them had fallen, their bodies unmarked but their spiritual cores severed by an attack that had surpassed the physical.

The third hunter's eyes widened behind their mask. Their Nascent Soul burst free in desperate self-preservation and fled into the distance before Caelum could strike again. Their physical body collapsed as the moonlight techniques dissipated like mist in the morning sun.

As the echoes of battle faded, Caelum held Bloodthorn over the fallen hunters. The demonic sword trembled with anticipation. A crimson tongue emerged from the blade, eager to taste the spiritual essence left behind.

Old habits die hard, don't they? Caelum thought as Bloodthorn drank deeply, the sword's hunger a constant reminder of its true nature.

The thorns along the blade grew sharper as they drank in both blood and residual moonlight energy until nothing remained. Only then did Caelum sheath the sword, trying to ignore how satisfied it felt through their spiritual connection.

Master would want me to protect the juniors. Knowing Hughie, he's probably stirred up half the realm's sects by now. And Amelia . . . She never could resist challenging anyone who looked at her wrong.

He shook his head, a mix of fondness and exasperation crossing his face. As the senior disciple, it was his responsibility to look after his junior siblings. Even if they did seem determined to find trouble at every turn.

With one last look at the inheritance cave, Caelum set out to find his wayward junior siblings.

CHAPTER FORTY-ONE

B*OOM!*

A young man in expensive silk robes crashed through a stone wall, sending debris flying across the street. He hit the ground hard and rolled several times before coming to a stop. Blood trickled from his nose as he stared up at the figure floating in the air.

Amelia hovered above the wreckage, her long silver hair whipping in the wind. Her cold eyes fixed on the fallen noble, her lips curled in disgust.

"How dare you!" The young master wiped blood from his face. "Do you know who I am?"

"A spoiled brat who can't take no for an answer." Amelia's voice dripped with venom.

Three guards in matching uniforms landed between them, their qi radiating at the Nascent Soul Realm. The tallest one stepped forward, his hand resting on the hilt of his sword.

"Lady Cultivator, you've assaulted the young master of Sky Pearl City. This offense cannot go unpunished."

"Unpunished?" Amelia laughed. "This piece of trash tried to force himself on me using his father's name. He's lucky I only slapped him."

The young master scrambled to his feet, pointing at her. "Arrest her! I want her thrown in the dungeons!"

Amelia turned to leave. "I've wasted enough time here."

"You're not going anywhere." The guards moved to block her path, spreading out in a triangle formation. "Submit peacefully or face the consequences."

Purple energy flickered around Amelia's hands. "Get out of my way."

"Take her!"

The first guard attacked with blinding speed, his sword leaving trails of blue light. "Azure Dragon Strike!"

Amelia dodged sideways, her hand slashing through the air. "Soul Render!"

A crescent of purple energy shot towards the guard. He barely managed to block it with his sword, and the impact sent him skidding backwards.

The second guard appeared behind her, palm glowing with golden light. "Heaven's Palm!"

Amelia spun, crossing her arms to block. The impact sent her flying, but she recovered midair.

"Triple Dragon Formation!" The three guards moved in perfect sync, their weapons trailing energy as they attacked from different angles.

Purple wings manifested from Amelia's back. She shot upwards, avoiding their coordinated strike. "Soul Wings!"

"Don't let her escape!"

Energy blasts filled the air as the guards pressed their attack. Amelia weaved between them and retaliated with purple crescents of soul-cutting energy, but she was outnumbered and their coordination was flawless. A sword strike clipped her arm. A palm strike grazed her leg. Small wounds, but they were adding up.

"Submit!" The lead guard's sword became a blur of motion. "Eight Heavens Sword Dance!"

Amelia's eyes narrowed as she was forced to retreat. These weren't ordinary city guards—their techniques were too refined, their teamwork too perfect.

"Fine." Her voice changed, becoming inhuman. "You want to see what I can really do? Ghoul Transformation!"

Her beautiful features morphed into something horrific, skin turning pale as death, dark veins surfacing across her face, eyes hollowing into glowing blue sockets. The guards stepped back as her spiritual pressure doubled. She vanished, then reappeared behind one guard. Her clawed hand plunged into his back before he could react. "Soul Shatter!"

The guard screamed as purple energy tore through his spiritual core. He dropped like a stone, body convulsing.

"Brother Chen!" The remaining guards attacked with renewed fury. "You'll pay for that!"

Even with her increased power, Amelia struggled against their onslaught. They were veterans who had clearly fought together for years. Every time she focused on one, the other would strike from her blind spot. A sword slash opened a deep cut across her back. She retaliated with a Soul Render, but they had adapted to her attack pattern.

"Your demonic techniques won't save you," the lead guard snarled. "Heavenly Punishment Formation!"

Golden chains of light shot from their weapons, trying to bind her limbs. Amelia's wings carried her higher, but she was bleeding from multiple wounds now.

"Getting tired of this game," she said as she gathered power for another attack.

"Mind if I cut in?" The familiar voice made her smile as a figure appeared in the air above them, grinning widely.

"Hughie!"

"Hey, Senior Sis!" Hughie waved cheerfully. "Thought I felt a familiar qi signature. Making friends as usual, I see."

The guards shifted their stance, eyeing the newcomer warily.

"Help me kill these insects," Amelia commanded.

Hughie sighed dramatically. "Now, now, there's no need for violence. I'm sure we can work something out." He turned to the guards and bowed. "My deepest apologies for my senior sister's behavior. Perhaps we could—"

"Soul Render!"

Amelia's attack forced the guards to dodge, ending any chance of a peaceful resolution.

"Really?" Hughie shook his head. "Fine, but I want it noted that I tried to be diplomatic." He dropped into a fighting stance, grinning widely. "Let's dance!"

The lead guard pointed his sword. "Another demonic cultivator! Take them both!"

"Rude." Hughie's body blurred as he charged forward. "Black Wolf Transformation!"

His form shifted, growing larger and more bestial. Black fur sprouted from his skin as his face elongated into a wolf's muzzle.

The guards tried to reform their formation, but Hughie's wild attacks disrupted their teamwork. He fought like a berserker, all fury and instinct.

"Soul Wings!" Amelia dive-bombed from above as purple crescents sliced through the air.

Caught between Hughie's savage assault and Amelia's soul attacks, the guards began to falter. Their perfect coordination broke down as they were forced to fight separately.

"Bloodmoon Fang!" Hughie's claws raked across one guard's chest and sent him crashing into a building. "Soul Chain!" Purple energy wrapped around the lead guard's legs as he tried to dodge, leaving him open to Hughie's follow-up attack.

The battle ended quickly after that. The guards lay broken but alive, their weapons shattered.

"We should go," Hughie said, "before—"

"How dare you strike my son!"

A massive spiritual pressure descended on the street. An older man in ornate robes appeared, his qi radiating at the Origin Realm.

"Oh, come on." Hughie sighed heavily. "How do we keep managing to offend Origin Realm cultivators? And this time Master isn't here to save us . . ."

"Father!" The young master scrambled towards the city lord. "They attacked me! Kill them!"

Hughie grabbed Amelia's arm. "Time to go!"

But the city lord's spiritual pressure had already locked onto them like a mountain pressing down from above. There would be no easy escape this time.

Hughie tried to stand, his legs shaking under the pressure. "Sir, there seems to be a misunderstanding—"

"Heaven's Punishment!"

Golden light erupted from the city lord's palm, filling the entire street. Hughie barely managed to shove Amelia aside before the attack hit. The blast sent him crashing through three buildings before he stopped.

"Hughie!" Amelia's ghoul form shot forward as purple crescents of soul energy sliced through the air. The city lord didn't even bother dodging. The attacks splashed harmlessly against his spiritual barrier.

"Insects." He flicked his sleeve and sent a wave of force that slammed Amelia into the ground. "You think your pathetic cultivation can harm me?"

Hughie emerged from the rubble, spitting blood. His black wolf form had protected him from the worst of the damage, but he could tell at least three ribs were broken.

"Amelia, run! I'll hold him—"

"Divine Palm Strike!"

The attack came too fast to dodge. It caught Hughie in the chest, sending him flying again. This time when he hit the ground, he didn't get up.

Amelia screamed in rage, her ghoul form growing more twisted. "Soul Rend Storm!"

Hundreds of purple crescents filled the air, all aimed at the city lord. He raised one hand and created a golden shield that blocked every attack.

"Is this all you can do?" He sounded disappointed. "How did weaklings like you ever dare to strike my son?"

His counterattack was devastating. Golden chains of light wrapped around Amelia and slammed her repeatedly into the ground. Each impact left a crater, and her ghoul form flickered as it struggled to maintain itself.

Hughie forced himself to stand, blood dripping from multiple wounds. His wolf form had reverted—he didn't have enough energy to maintain it.

"Stop!" He coughed up more blood. "She's my responsibility. Let her go!"

"Noble, but foolish." The city lord created another golden palm. "Die together, then."

The attack never landed. A black blur shot between them—another of Hughie's transformations. His massive three-eyed toad form took the hit, its thick skin barely holding against the Origin Realm attack.

But it bought them a moment. Just enough time for Hughie to pull something from his robes.

"I was saving this." He held up an ancient-looking talisman, its surface covered in blood-red runes. "I found this in some inheritance cave. The old spirit who gave it to me said it could even kill an Ascendant cultivator."

The city lord's eyes widened. He could sense the power radiating from the talisman—it was far beyond what these young cultivators should possess.

"Impossible! How did you get—"

"I really didn't want to use this." Hughie's blood dripped onto the talisman and activated the runes. "But you're not giving me much choice!"

Red light erupted from the talisman. It spread across the street like living blood as it formed intricate patterns in the air. The city lord immediately raised his strongest defensive formation.

"Heaven's Golden Shield! Nine Layers of Divine Protection!"

Golden light surrounded him in countless layers. He poured every drop of his spiritual energy into the defense, preparing for an attack that could threaten even an Ascendant.

The red light surged forward . . . and simply formed a cage around him. No devastating attack. No world-ending power. Just a barrier that he couldn't seem to break through.

The city lord blinked in confusion. "What?"

Hughie grabbed Amelia, pulling her to her feet. "What are you waiting for? Let's run!"

"But . . ." Amelia stared at the cage. "Shouldn't we—"

"It'll only hold him for a few minutes! Move!"

They shot into the sky, flying as fast as their injured bodies could manage. Behind them, they could hear the city lord's enraged roars as he tried to break free.

"That's it?" Amelia's ghoul form had faded, leaving her looking pale and exhausted. "The super-powerful talisman just makes a cage?"

"Hey, it worked, didn't it?" Hughie winced as they flew, every movement sending pain through his broken ribs. "Besides, Master always says the best technique is the one that lets you escape alive."

They flew for nearly an hour, putting as much distance between themselves and the city as possible. Finally, exhaustion forced them to land in a small forest clearing.

"We need to find somewhere to hide." Hughie sat heavily against a tree. "The city lord will be hunting us. These old men can hold a grudge."

"And where exactly are we supposed to go?" Amelia tried to stand but her legs gave out. "We're both too injured to fly much further."

A voice spoke from the shadows of the trees. "Oh . . . It's you two."

They spun towards the voice, ready to fight despite their injuries. Hughie relaxed slightly as he recognized the qi signature, though a look of confusion crossed his face.

"Eh? What are you doing all the way out here?"

"I . . ." The voice held a hint of hesitation. "I was hiding from the locals."

Amelia leaned heavily against a tree, eyeing the shadows suspiciously. "And you just happened to find us?" she asked.

"I felt the battle." There was an awkward pause. "What did you do this time?"

Hughie coughed up a bit more blood. "Yeah, had a slight disagreement with the local city lord."

"Slight?" The voice laughed awkwardly. "I felt that Origin Realm qi from three cities away."

"His son was being inappropriate," Amelia said coldly.

"And by inappropriate, she means he's currently embedded in several walls," Hughie added.

"Some things never change." The voice sighed. "Still picking fights you can't win."

"You know how it is." Hughie shrugged, then immediately regretted the movement. "We try to be diplomatic, but somehow it always ends in property damage. Anyways, you wouldn't happen to know somewhere we could hide out? Preferably before he comes looking to finish what he started."

"Actually . . ." Another pause. "I know a place. It's . . . it's secure."

Amelia and Hughie exchanged glances.

"We're not exactly in a position to be picky," Hughie said. "Lead the way."

"Follow me. And try not to fall behind. You're leaving a trail of blood."

CHAPTER FORTY-TWO

The first thing Caelum noticed when he arrived at Sky Pearl City was the destruction. Several buildings had been reduced to rubble and spiritual energy still lingered in the air—the aftermath of a serious battle.

An Origin Realm cultivator unleashed their power here, he thought as he landed softly in the street. *And given my junior siblings' talent for offending powerful people . . .*

"Useless guards!" A young man in expensive but dust-covered robes kicked at some debris. "How could you let them escape?"

Caelum approached slowly, studying the scene. The ground bore scorch marks from powerful techniques, and he recognized the distinctive purple residue of Amelia's soul attacks.

"Excuse me," he called out. "What happened here?"

The young master spun around, face red with anger. "Another cultivator? Have you come to mock me too?"

"Not at all. I'm just trying to understand the situation." Caelum kept his voice calm and respectful. "There seems to have been quite a battle."

"Battle? Assault is more like it!" The young master's voice rose. "Some silver-haired demon woman attacked me! Me! The young master of Sky Pearl City!"

Silver hair? That would be Amelia. Caelum sighed internally. "And what prompted this . . . assault?"

"I merely offered her the honor of accompanying me for the evening," the young master said as he straightened his robes indignantly, "as befits someone of my station! But that crazy woman dared to refuse! When I insisted, she actually struck me!"

"I see." Caelum's expression didn't change, but his hand tightened on Bloodthorn's hilt. "And how exactly did you . . . insist?"

"I simply reminded her of my father's position." The young master smirked. "Any woman should be honored to—"

Caelum moved before he could finish the sentence. One precise strike to a pressure point and the young master collapsed mid-word.

"Honored to reject you? I agree." He caught the unconscious body before it hit the ground, then laid it down carefully. No need to cause more damage than necessary.

Residual qi traces still lingered in the air—Amelia's distinctive soul energy mixed with what he recognized as Hughie's wild spiritual signature. He could follow them. They'd fled east, towards the mountains.

He took to the sky, following the trail. But he'd barely left the city when a massive spiritual pressure approached from that direction.

An elderly man in ornate robes flew towards the city, his face twisted with rage. Origin Realm qi radiated from him in waves of barely controlled fury.

Their paths crossed high above the city. The old man stopped, his eyes narrowing as he sensed Caelum's power.

"Another one?" He spread his spiritual sense over the city only to find his son unconscious. "How dare you! First those demonic cultivators, and now you? Does no one respect my authority in this city?" Spiritual pressure exploded outwards as the city lord's anger peaked. "My son has been assaulted for the second time today! Two times! Where is the respect? Where is the face I am owed?"

Caelum remained calm in the face of the elder's rage. "Your son attempted to force himself on my junior sister. Where is the honor in that?"

"Honor?" The city lord laughed coldly. "What would demons know of honor? I should have killed those two when I had the chance. But no matter. Once I deal with you, I'll hunt them down and finish what I started."

The killing intent radiating from the old man was genuine. Caelum could sense the residual qi from an earlier battle—this man had seriously injured both Hughie and Amelia.

Caelum drew Bloodthorn slowly. *I can't sense their spiritual signatures anymore. What did you do to my juniors, old man?* Aloud, he said quietly, "Tell me what happened to them."

"They fled like the cowards they are." The city lord gathered power, golden light surrounding his form. "But not before I taught them the price of defying me. The girl's screams were particularly satisfying."

Something dark stirred in Caelum's chest. He looked down at Bloodthorn, feeling the sword's eager bloodthirst.

The city lord attacked without warning. "Heaven's Punishment!"

Golden light filled the sky. Caelum deflected it with Bloodthorn's blade, feeling the sword drink in the spiritual energy.

"Sunrise Slash!"

He appeared behind the city lord, sword striking with blinding speed, but the old man's defensive barrier held firm.

"Pathetic!" Another wave of golden force sent Caelum flying backwards. "Is this all the vaunted sword cultivator can do?"

Caelum steadied himself in the air, blood trickling from the corner of his mouth. The city lord's power was overwhelming—pure righteous techniques wouldn't be enough.

I'm sorry, Master. You taught me to walk the righteous path. But to protect my family . . .

"Tell me," he called out to the city lord. "Have you heard of the Bloodthorn Ascension?"

The old man's eyes narrowed. "What nonsense are you—"

Before he could finish, Caelum raised Bloodthorn and plunged it directly into his own heart.

"What?" The city lord stepped back in shock. "Have you gone mad?"

Dark energy erupted from the wound. Bloodthorn's blade began to sink further into Caelum's chest, merging with his flesh. Thorny patterns spread across his skin like twisted veins.

"Bloodthorn Ascension." Caelum's voice had changed, now deeper and overlaid with an inhuman resonance. "The ultimate union between sword and cultivator."

His skin turned pale as death. His eyes changed from brown to blood red. The thorny patterns continued spreading until they covered his entire body. His spiritual pressure skyrocketed, taking on a distinctly demonic nature.

The city lord raised his strongest defensive formation. "What demonic technique is this?"

Caelum didn't answer. He couldn't—the transformation wasn't yet complete. Bloodthorn had fully merged with his body now, and its essence was becoming one with his spiritual core. Thorny blades erupted from his forearms, and his hair turned from black to crimson.

When he finally looked up, his face had changed. Sharp thorns protruded from his cheeks and forehead, forming a crown-like pattern. His eyes glowed with the same red light that had once filled Bloodthorn's blade.

"Now, then." His voice echoed with power. "Shall we begin again?" *One minute*, he thought. *I have one minute before the transformation tears my body apart.*

The city lord attacked immediately, unleashing his full power. "Nine Heavens Golden Lightning!"

Golden bolts of spiritual energy filled the sky, each one powerful enough to level a mountain. But Caelum simply raised his hand, thorny blades extending from his palm.

"Bloodthorn Garden."

Crimson thorns erupted from thin air and intercepted every lightning bolt. Where the attacks hit, the thorns absorbed their energy, growing larger and more numerous.

Fifty seconds.

"Impossible!" The city lord backed away. "How can a mere Nascent Soul cultivator—"

Caelum vanished. When he reappeared, thousands of thorny blades surrounded the city lord in a sphere of crimson death.

"This technique lets me fight those an entire realm above me." Caelum's inhuman voice resonated through the thorny cage. "Now, what happened to my juniors?"

The city lord's face twisted with fury. "You dare threaten me? Heaven's Ultimate—"

"Wrong answer." *Forty seconds.*

The thorns contracted and shredded through the city lord's outer defensive layers. Golden light flared as the old man poured more power into his barriers.

"*Die!*" The city lord's hands blurred through seals. "Heaven's Wrath Formation!"

A massive golden fist formed in the sky, big enough to crush a small mountain. It descended towards Caelum with devastating force.

Thirty seconds. Have to end this now.

Thorny blades erupted from every part of Caelum's body. They spread outwards in a crimson wave to meet the golden fist head-on. The two techniques clashed with earth-shaking force.

Twenty seconds.

Pain shot through Caelum's body. The transformation was already starting to break down. Blood leaked from the corner of his mouth as thorny patterns began cracking across his skin.

But the golden fist shattered. The city lord's eyes widened in disbelief as crimson thorns pierced his remaining defenses.

"This is your final chance." Blood dripped from Caelum's lips as he spoke. "Where. Are. My. Juniors?"

Ten seconds.

The city lord finally broke. "They . . . they fled east! Towards the old forest! I lost them there!"

Five seconds.

Caelum retracted the thorns and left the city lord floating in the air, his robes in tatters but his life intact. An Origin Realm cultivator who'd lived this long would certainly have multiple lifesaving treasures. Trying for a killing blow now would just waste precious time as the old man activated whatever ancient protective artifacts he had hidden away.

Master always said, "Never corner an old monster unless you have dealt with all their trump cards," and I just don't have the time or desire to do that.

"If you've lied to me . . ."

Time's up.

Agony ripped through Caelum's body as the transformation began to break down. The thorny patterns shattered like glass, and Bloodthorn reformed in his hand as his appearance returned to normal.

The pain nearly made him black out. Every muscle screamed in protest, and blood flowed freely from his mouth and nose. The price of using Bloodthorn Ascension was steep—it would take days to recover. But he remained floating, sword pointed at the city lord's throat.

"Follow us, and next time I won't stop when the thorns reach your heart."

He turned east and forced his battered body to fly despite the pain. Behind him, the city lord's spiritual pressure flickered uncertainly before retreating back towards the city.

Hold on, Hughie, Amelia. I'm coming.

A trail of blood marked his path as he flew towards the old forest, praying he wasn't too late.

Blood dripped from Hughie's wounds as he flew through the night sky, each movement sending waves of agony through his body. His broken ribs screamed in protest, but he couldn't stop. Not now. Not when Amelia . . .

He choked back the rage building in his throat. *How could we have been so stupid? Walking right into a trap like that.*

The mountain peaks blurred beneath him as he pushed himself to fly faster. His qi reserves were dangerously low—he'd used most of his power as well as his talismans in the escape. The gash in his side wouldn't stop bleeding, and his left arm hung uselessly at his side.

The Moon God King. We actually ran into the Moon God King himself. And we didn't even recognize him until . . .

A wave of dizziness sent him careening into a treetop. He crashed through the branches before catching himself, gasping in pain. Blood loss was making it hard to think straight.

"Need to—" He spat out blood. "Need to find Senior Brother."

Only Caelum would be strong enough to help. He always knew what to do. But the Sealed Realm was vast, and Hughie had no idea where his senior brother might be.

Think. Think! Where would Senior Brother go?

His consciousness wavered. The temptation to activate Bloodforge Ascension pulled at him—the technique would give him the strength to keep going. But in his current state, the transformation would probably kill him.

A branch snapped in the forest below. Hughie immediately suppressed his qi and pressed himself against a tree trunk. He couldn't fight anyone right now. Not like this. Not after seeing what true power looked like.

I failed her. I'm her brother—I'm supposed to protect her. But against him . . . I couldn't do anything.

Tears of frustration mixed with the blood on his face. He'd never felt so useless. So weak. Even the talisman from the old spirit hadn't been enough in the end. Another wave of dizziness hit him. This time he couldn't fight it off. His body began to fall.

Strong arms caught him before he hit the ground. Through blurry vision, Hughie saw a familiar face looking down at him with concern.

"Senior . . . Brother . . ."

"I've got you." Caelum's voice was tight with worry as he examined Hughie's injuries.

Hughie tried to focus, fighting against the darkness closing in. He had to warn them. Had to tell them the truth. "Amelia . . . They took her . . . The Moon God King . . . He's . . ."

"Save your strength." Caelum gathered healing qi in his palm and pressed it against the worst of Hughie's wounds.

"No . . . listen." Hughie grabbed Caelum's sleeve with bloody fingers. "The king . . . his real identity . . . He's actually . . ."

His eyes rolled back as consciousness finally slipped away.

* * *

Caelum's hands froze in the middle of applying healing energy. His eyes narrowed as he processed what Hughie was trying to say—something about the king's identity . . .

"Who is the Moon God King really?" he whispered to his unconscious brother.

CHAPTER FORTY-THREE

Hughie leaned against the cold cave wall, his broken ribs protesting every breath. The Moon God hunters circled the cave entrance like predators toying with their prey. Their leader, a tall man in silver robes, stepped forward.

"Surrender, outsiders," the leader commanded. "The Moon God King demands it."

At least these ones came to us, Hughie thought, watching his senior brother's calm expression. *Saves us time having to run around finding them.*

Caelum stood between the hunters and the cave, Bloodthorn held casually at his side. The demonic sword vibrated with barely contained bloodlust.

"I'll ask one more time," Caelum said. "Where did you take my sister?"

The leader laughed. "You think you can make demands? There are six of us and only two of you. And your friend can barely stand."

"True." Caelum shifted his stance slightly. "But you're making a grave mistake."

"Oh? And what's that?"

"Assuming numbers matter."

Caelum moved. One moment he stood at the cave entrance, the next he appeared behind the leader with Bloodthorn's edge pressed against the man's throat.

"Senior Brother's gotten faster," Hughie muttered, watching the other hunters scramble to react.

Two Core Formation cultivators attacked simultaneously, their moon-blessed weapons trailing silver light. Caelum pushed the leader away and met their charge head-on.

Bloodthorn became a blur of motion. Each strike flowed seamlessly into the next, forcing the hunters back step by step. When one overextended, Caelum's counter opened a shallow cut across his chest.

"Formation!" the leader shouted. "Moonlight Binding!"

Silver chains erupted from the ground as the remaining hunters spread out in a pentagon. Spiritual energy surged as they activated their sect's signature technique.

Caelum didn't try to dodge. Instead, he planted Bloodthorn in the ground and made a single-handed seal. "Nine Lights Mirage."

Eight identical images split from his form, each one perfectly mirroring his movements. The silver chains passed harmlessly through several images before finding the real Caelum—but by then he'd already moved.

"Behind you!" one hunter shouted.

Too late. Caelum appeared in their formation's blind spot, Bloodthorn singing as it carved through the air. Two hunters went down clutching non-lethal but disabling wounds.

"Impossible!" The leader gathered moonlight in his palm. "Die! Heaven's Moonfall!"

A massive beam of silver energy shot towards Caelum. The remaining hunters added their power to the attack, turning it into a pillar of pure moonlight.

Hughie tensed, ready to help despite his injuries. But Caelum simply raised Bloodthorn and said, "Sunrise Slash."

Light bloomed from the sword as Caelum vanished. He reappeared directly above the hunters, then descended like a meteor. Bloodthorn's edge met the moonlight beam head-on.

For a moment the two forces clashed, silver against gold. Then Caelum's strike shattered their combined attack. The backlash sent the hunters sprawling.

Senior Brother's not even using his demonic techniques, Hughie noted with a mix of pride and concern. The strict adherence to righteous methods meant Caelum was fighting at reduced strength.

The leader struggled to his feet, blood dripping from several shallow cuts. "You . . . You're no ordinary sword cultivator."

"No." Caelum walked towards him slowly. "I'm a senior brother looking for his junior sister. Now, where is she?"

"The Moon God King will break you eventually." The leader spat blood. "Like he'll break her."

Something dark flickered across Caelum's face. Bloodthorn's surface rippled as if responding to its wielder's emotions.

"Wrong answer."

This time Caelum moved too fast for Hughie to track. One moment he stood several paces away, the next the leader was pinned against a tree with Bloodthorn's edge drawing a thin line of blood from his throat.

"I'll ask again." Caelum's voice grew softer, more dangerous. "Where. Is. My. Sister?"

The leader laughed despite his position. "You can kill me. It won't matter. The king's will is absolute."

"Who said anything about killing you?" Thorny patterns began spreading across Bloodthorn's surface. "There are worse things than death."

Hughie pushed himself off the wall. "Senior Brother, wait—"

A presence appeared behind Caelum—a figure in black robes wearing a white bone mask. Caelum spun instantly, Bloodthorn blurring with killing intent.

"Formless Sword Art!"

The strike, transcending physical space, manifested as pure sword intent, but the masked figure stood still as it passed through them harmlessly.

"My, my," the figure murmured. "You've improved since last time."

Caelum's eyes narrowed as he put himself between the newcomer and Hughie. "Who are you?"

The figure laughed. "I heard an interesting rumor. A Nascent Soul sword cultivator defeated an Origin Realm city lord down here in the south. I thought, 'Who could that be?' But the only name that came to mind was yours."

"That doesn't answer my question." Caelum gathered qi for another strike.

"Always so serious." The figure raised his hands in a placating gesture. "Relax. It's me."

Hughie frowned. Something about the voice seemed familiar . . .

The figure reached up and removed the bone-white mask.

"Zack?" Hughie whispered in disbelief.

But Caelum didn't lower Bloodthorn. If anything, his grip tightened on the sword's hilt. Hughie pushed himself away from the wall, his broken ribs forgotten as spiritual energy gathered in his palm.

Zack's grin faltered. "Hey, now, what's with the hostile reception? It's me— your junior brother from the Black Rose Sect!"

"Our junior brother?" Hughie's voice turned uncharacteristically cold. "Like Nomed was our brother?"

The temperature seemed to drop several degrees. Zack's normally cheerful demeanor shifted slightly. "Nomed? What does he have to do with this?"

"He betrayed us." Caelum's words cut like ice. "Led Amelia right into a trap."

"That's . . ." Zack went very still. "That's not possible. He wouldn't . . ."

"He would." Hughie spat blood, his injuries making his voice rough. "Because Nomed isn't who we thought he was. He's an avatar."

"An avatar?" Zack's mask revealed nothing, but something in his voice changed. "Whose?"

"The Moon God King's."

The words hung in the air like a death sentence. Zack's eyes narrowed to slits. *The System should have identified any avatars near me. Unless . . .*

Two possibilities presented themselves, the second more troubling than the first. Either Nomed possessed some technique or treasure that could fool even the System's detection abilities, or the System had deliberately remained silent.

Which means either the Moon God King has access to power beyond what should be possible in this realm, or the System wanted this to happen. Neither option is comforting.

"Let me help," Zack said finally. "I can extract information from these hunters. Find out where they're keeping her."

"Using what method?" Caelum's sword hadn't wavered.

"A soul-searching technique. It's . . . effective."

"How can we trust you?" Caelum eyes narrowed at the mention of such a vile demonic technique.

"Senior Brother," Hughie said as he pushed himself off the wall, "we don't have many options. And Junior Brother Zack . . . He's always been straightforward with us, at least."

"Your trusting nature is going to get you killed one day," Caelum muttered.

"Probably," Hughie agreed. "But right now it might help us save Amelia."

Several tense moments passed. Finally, Caelum lowered his sword, though he kept it unsheathed.

"One hunter," he said. "And if I sense any deception—"

"You'll try to kill me," Zack finished cheerfully. "Wouldn't expect anything less from the responsible senior brother."

He approached the nearest unconscious hunter and placed his palm on the man's forehead. "This won't be pleasant. For him, I mean. You might want to step back."

Dark energy gathered around Zack's hand as he activated Soul Search. The hunter's eyes snapped open as screams tore from his throat.

Memory fragments flashed through Zack's mind.

A hidden valley in the Central Region, shrouded in mist . . . Massive formation arrays maintaining a barrier that bent light itself . . . Underground chambers filled with cultivation resources beyond counting . . . And deeper still, cells where captured outsiders waited to be processed . . .

The hunter's screams reached a fever pitch as Zack pushed deeper into his memories.

A throne room carved from living stone, where the Moon God King holds court . . . The twisted tree he'd previously seen in the other Moon God Sect member's memories, but larger now, its branches reaching towards distant realms . . . Amelia being dragged through white corridors, her struggles growing weaker as special formations suppressed her power . . . Nomed walking beside the Moon God King, their features blurring and shifting as if neither form was quite real . . .

Zack released his hold. The hunter slumped unconscious, blood trickling from his nose and ears. His spiritual core had been damaged by the forceful extraction—he wouldn't cultivate above Core Formation again.

Caelum's face showed clear disapproval, but he asked, "Well, where is she?"

"The Central Region. They have a hidden base under the mountain range—bigger than anything we imagined. But"—Zack turned to face them—"we can't do this alone. Not against what's waiting there."

"What exactly did you see?" Hughie asked.

"Something worse than we thought." Zack's voice grew serious. "The Moon God King isn't just collecting outsiders for power. He's building something. Something that could tear both realms apart."

"Then we need to move quickly," Caelum said.

"We need backup," Zack countered. "I might know some people who can help. But first"—he looked at Hughie's injuries—"we need to get you healed."

Caelum's hand tightened on Bloodthorn again. "And why should we trust you?"

"Because right now," Zack said quietly, "I'm the only chance you have of seeing Amelia alive again."

The silence stretched between them, broken only by the soft whimpers of the soul-searched hunter. Finally, Hughie spoke.

"He's right, Senior Brother. We need help."

Caelum closed his eyes for a moment. When he opened them, his expression was hard. "Fine. But the moment you show any sign of betrayal . . ."

"You'll kill me," Zack finished. "I understand. Now, shall we go save our sister?"

CHAPTER FORTY-FOUR

Slifer sat in his newly constructed quarters, frowning at the System message floating before him.

> *Ding!*
> Alert: Critical Condition detected
> Disciple Designation: Amelia
> Status: Fatally Wounded
> Task: Save Amelia
> Caution: Death of a disciple incurs severe consequences.
> For specifics:
> Hidden
> Hidden
> Hidden

Great, another crisis. Can't I enjoy my new furniture for five minutes? He glanced at his barely used bed with its expensive silk sheets. *I haven't even broken in that meditation cushion yet.*

The message pulsed insistently, refusing to be ignored. Slifer had sent Zack to track down Amelia after receiving the first warning signs. His avatar had located Caelum and Hughie, but Amelia remained in enemy hands.

The Moon God King. Slifer's frown deepened. *Something never sat right about that weird kid Nomed.*

His mind drifted back to the Disciple Selection Ceremony. The System had practically forced him to pick Nomed.

Should have known something was wrong when the System was so specific. Slifer shook his head. *It's about as trustworthy as a cultivation-manual salesman offering a two-for-one special.*

A knock interrupted his brooding. "Enter."

Morvran stepped inside, his expression grim. "Master, we have a situation."

"When don't we?"

"There's a woman standing outside the sect gates."

"And this requires my attention because . . . ?"

"She's been there for hours, staring. The guards asked her to leave. She ignored them. When they tried to remove her . . ." Morvran paused.

"Let me guess: it went poorly?"

"She killed them with a look."

Oh, perfect. Death-stare lady. Because we didn't have enough problems.

"There's more," Morvran continued. "The plants around her wither and die. Birds fall from the sky when they fly too close. And she's wearing a black dress with red trim."

"Evil fashion sense—always a bad sign." Slifer stood up. *This has "major antagonist" written all over it. Dramatic entrance? Check. Ominous powers? Check. Color-coordinated outfit? Definite check.*

"Master Hong's new formations didn't stop her?"

"She walked through them like they weren't there. Even the reality-warping barriers had no effect."

Of course not. That would be too easy. Slifer sighed. Being sect master meant dealing with threats like this personally. *Better stock up.*

No convenient protagonist power-ups at the last second for him. He purchased ten Critical Block Cards and five Reflection Barrier Cards.

Most cost-efficient options. No point wasting credits on fancy cards when these do the job. Speaking of wasting credits . . . Slifer glanced at another recent transaction.

Previous Purchase:
Energy Beam Talisman (Origin Realm): 20,000 Karmic Credits
Spatial Ring with Emergency Supplies: 20,000 Karmic Credits

Maintaining a clone is like having an expensive girlfriend, minus any benefits. He sighed. *At least girlfriends don't need monthly treasure allowances.*

"Have the remaining guards cleared the area?" Slifer asked Morvran.

"Yes, Master. Though, several are requesting transfers to less . . . eventful posts."

"Can't blame them." Slifer checked his equipment one last time. *Cards ready, emergency talismans charged, escape routes planned. Time to see what flavor of doom is knocking at our door.*

They walked through the sect's corridors, passing nervous disciples who pressed themselves against walls to avoid contact. Word of the death-stare visitor had spread fast.

"Any theories on who she might be?" Slifer asked.

"The elders are divided. Some think she's an assassin from a rival sect. Others suggest a demon cultivator seeking revenge. Elder Wushuang insists she's his ex-wife, but he says that about every female cultivator who threatens the sect."

"Lovely." They reached the main gates. *Here's hoping she's not actually Elder Wushuang's ex. Those are scarier than demon cultivators.*

The woman stood motionless outside the Black Rose Sect gates, her black dress rippling in a wind only she seemed to feel. Dead leaves swirled around her feet and crumbled to ash where they touched her shadow. The bodies of the guards who'd tried to remove her lay scattered in a perfect circle, their faces frozen in expressions of absolute terror.

Perfect. Just what we needed: a homicidal fashionista with death powers, Slifer thought as he observed her from above the sect's barriers.

Disciples peered fearfully from windows and doorways, whispering among themselves about the mysterious woman who'd walked through Master Hong's supposedly impenetrable formations like they were paper screens. Even the formation master himself had gone unusually quiet as he watched from a safe distance with an expression that suggested he was already planning upgrades to his defenses.

The woman paid no attention to any of them. Her gaze remained fixed on some point deep within the sect grounds, her lips moving in a constant murmur.

"This is where my beloved lived . . ." Her voice carried clearly despite its softness. "This is where my beloved was killed . . ."

Great, she's talking to herself. Because unstable cultivators are exactly what this sect needs more of.

A slight shift in the air announced Slifer's presence as he emerged fully from behind the sect's barriers. The woman's head snapped up, and her eyes locked onto him with unsettling intensity.

"Are you the one?" she asked, her smile sharp as broken glass. "The one who killed my beloved?"

"That depends," Slifer replied carefully. "Who was your beloved?"

"Darius."

The name hit like a physical blow. Slifer's mind flashed back to the letter he'd found on the elder's body—flowery declarations of eternal love written in elegant calligraphy. He knew whoever wrote that would pose a problem, he just didn't expect it to be so soon.

Of course. Of course his girlfriend would be some overpowered psycho. Because nothing in my life can ever be simple.

The System helpfully provided an assessment.

Name: Unknown

Realm: Immortal Realm, Rank Unknown

Known Techniques: N/A

Known Affiliations: Black Rose Sect

Disposition: Crazy Lover Archetype

Note: Target's cultivation has been suppressed by the realm to Half-Step Immortal Realm.

Even with realm suppression, she's still way above my weight class.

"Elder Darius," Slifer said carefully. "An unfortunate situation."

Her smile vanished. "I know it was a 'Slifer' who killed him. Are you Slifer?"

Before he could manufacture a convenient absence, Morvran appeared beside him.

"Indeed, he is!" his right-hand man declared proudly. "Our sect master defeated that bully Darius with a single move after enduring his persecution!"

Thanks, Morvran. Really. Fantastic timing there. Slifer fought the urge to facepalm. *I know you think I'm an Immortal, but maybe check if the scary death lady is friendly first?*

The woman's scream shattered the air. It wasn't a physical sound—it bypassed the ears entirely to claw directly at the mind. Disciples collapsed clutching their heads as visions of horror overwhelmed them.

Slifer remained floating calmly, though internally he was anything but calm.

Can't cover my ears like I want to. Got to maintain that Immortal image. Even if my brain feels like it's being put through a mental blender.

It was then that the world tilted sideways as reality fragmented like broken glass. Slifer found himself standing in a dimly lit hospital corridor, fluorescent lights flickering overhead. The linoleum floor stretched endlessly in both directions, spattered with dark stains that looked uncomfortably like blood.

Where . . . What is this place?

A wheelchair creaked somewhere in the darkness. The sound of metal wheels scraping against tile sent chills down his spine. The air smelled of antiseptic and something else—something rotting.

A child's laughter echoed from somewhere behind him. He spun around, but the corridor was empty. The laughter came again, closer now, accompanied by the soft padding of bare feet on tile.

"Hello?" His voice sounded wrong, muffled, like he was speaking underwater.

The lights went out one by one, and darkness crept towards him. In that darkness, something moved. Something big.

The wheelchair rounded the corner. Empty yet moving on its own. Behind it, dragging themselves along the floor, came twisted figures that might once have been human. Their joints bent at impossible angles, heads lolling on broken necks.

This isn't real. This isn't real. This isn't—

A hand grabbed his ankle. He looked down to see a nurse's face split into a grotesque grin, her jaw unhinged like a snake's. "Time for your treatment, dear," she croaked.

The ceiling began to drip. Not water—something thick and black that burned where it touched his skin. The walls pulsed like living flesh, and faces pushed outwards as if trying to break free.

The child's laughter turned to screaming. Not just one child—hundreds. The sound built to a crescendo that threatened to shatter his sanity.

System . . . cultivation . . . None of that existed here. There was only the hospital, the darkness, the—

Pain shot through his arm. He looked down to see medical tubing burrowing into his flesh like worms, pushing deeper, carrying that black fluid towards his heart.

"No . . ." The word came out as a whimper.

The nurse's grip tightened and bones cracked. More hands emerged from the floor, grabbing, pulling. The twisted figures drew closer, their broken bodies moving in jerky stop-motion.

This is wrong. This feels too real but it's wrong! Something in his mind rebelled against the horror. *I'm not in a hospital. I'm outside the Black Rose Sect. This is a technique. Just a technique.*

The horror scene fractured. For a moment he saw double: the nightmare hospital overlaid with reality. The nurse's face melted into the woman in black, and her grip became ethereal.

"Get. Out. Of. My. *Head!*"

His Void Being Aura flared and shattered the remaining vestiges of the illusion. Reality snapped back into place with almost physical force. He was in the sky again, facing the woman who'd tried to trap him in that nightmare.

Thank whatever cosmic entity gave me that Void Being Aura perk. Without that fifty percent mind attack resistance, I'd be rolling around seeing my worst nightmares right now, unable to ever escape.

"Impossible," she whispered. "No one breaks that technique."

"Lady," Slifer said, his voice steadier than he felt, "you really need better hobbies."

He looked around and noticed that disciples were bleeding from their eyes and ears. Master Hong had curled into a fetal position and was whimpering about rainbow formations turning black.

Time to take this elsewhere before she kills everyone.

Slifer shot skyward, pulling away from the sect. The woman's attack had already killed several of the surrounding trees, their leaves withered and falling as black ash. He didn't want to find out what prolonged exposure would do to his disciples.

"Your problem is with me," he called down. "Leave them out of it."

The woman rose to meet him, her dress billowing dramatically.

Why do all the powerful cultivators get cool special effects? My robes barely flutter unless I'm paying attention.

"You killed him," she said, her voice thick with emotion. "You killed my Darius."

"He tried to kill me first," Slifer pointed out reasonably. "Multiple times."

"He was going to propose!" Black energy crackled around her hands. "We were going to rule the Immortal Realm together!"

Oh good, she's not just powerful—she's powerful and crazy. My favorite combination.

"Look," Slifer said, "I'm sure we can discuss this like reasonable—"

A blast of pure darkness erupted from her palm, moving faster than anything he'd seen before. A Critical Block Card saved him from being erased from existence.

Crazy cultivators never want reasonable discussions.

CHAPTER FORTY-FIVE

The withered plants around Darius's lover twisted and writhed as black energy seeped from her body into the dead vegetation. Slifer watched as the corrupted life force spread through the roots and caused the plants to rise up like twisted serpents. Where once beautiful flowers had bloomed, now thorny vines bearing pitch-black roses emerged.

Great, she's not just killing plants, she's making evil garden decorations, Slifer thought as he assessed the situation. He had five Reflection Barrier Cards and around thirty Critical Block Cards left. Not great odds against an Immortal, but he'd worked with worse.

The corrupted plants continued to spread, creating a circle of twisted vegetation around her. Trees bent at unnatural angles, their bark turning black as obsidian. Flowers mutated into grotesque shapes, their petals sharp as razors and dripping with dark fluid.

At least she has a consistent aesthetic, Slifer mused. *Though, the whole "corruption" theme is a bit on the nose.*

He sighed, realizing how ridiculous his situation was. Here he stood, facing an Immortal Realm cultivator, and his battle strategy consisted of . . . standing still. No dramatic sword techniques, no special martial arts, no secret trump cards. Just cards and patience.

Most protagonists get cool battle scenes with fancy techniques. I get to practice my statue impression.

Still, he couldn't complain too much. The alternative would be trying to fight with his actual Core Formation cultivation, which would end about as well as bringing a butter knife to a nuclear war.

The woman stared at him with growing confusion. She'd clearly expected him to attack by now, to give her an excuse to unleash her full power. Her fingers twitched with barely contained rage as more plants twisted and corrupted around her.

Time to put on a show, Slifer decided. If she was unstable, maybe he could provoke her into using her strongest technique right away, then reflect it back and end this quickly.

He straightened his robes and adopted his best "young master" expression: nose slightly upturned, eyes half-lidded with disdain.

"How boring," he drawled, examining his nails. "I expected someone of actual importance, not some lovesick girl throwing a tantrum."

Her eyes narrowed dangerously. The corrupted plants writhed faster.

"You dare—"

"Dare?" Slifer interrupted with an exaggerated yawn. "My dear, I wouldn't dare waste my energy on someone so beneath my notice. Why soil my hands when you're barely worth acknowledging?" He gestured dismissively. "Run along, now. I'm sure there are plenty of other men who might tolerate your . . . enthusiasm. Though, I can't blame Darius for choosing death over your company."

The corrupted vines struck like vipers, thorns gleaming with deadly poison. Slifer didn't move. The attack wasn't strong enough to waste a Reflection Barrier on. A Critical Block Card flared and the vines dissipated harmlessly against its protection.

"Was that supposed to hurt?" Slifer examined an imaginary speck of dust on his sleeve. "How embarrassing. Even my disciples hit harder during morning exercises." He adopted a mock thoughtful expression. "Though, I suppose I shouldn't expect much from someone who couldn't even keep a man's interest. Tell me, did Darius die to escape your clutches, or did he simply fake his death for a more graceful exit?"

The woman's scream of rage shook the very air. Dark energy pulsed from her body as she launched a mental attack far stronger than before. This time Slifer activated a Reflection Barrier Card.

The woman stumbled back and clutched at her head as her own nightmare turned against her. "No . . . Darius, please," she whimpered. "Don't leave me . . . I can change . . . I'll be better . . ."

Wow, some serious baggage there, Slifer thought. His hand twitched towards a Void Piercer strike, but he stopped himself. Against a normal cultivator, the technique might work. But against an Immortal Realm body? He'd have better luck trying to pierce a mountain with a toothpick.

"How dare you!" she snarled, recovering from the reflected nightmare. "*How dare you!*"

Power exploded from her body. The corruption spread faster, plants withering and transforming in seconds. The very air seemed to crack as space itself began to splinter under the weight of her qi.

Well, that's probably not good.

Slifer looked up as golden light began gathering in the sky. Unlike any tribulation he'd seen before, this one shone with divine radiance. As the woman's aura pushed beyond Half-Step Immortal, the very world started rejecting her presence.

The heavens themselves want her gone, Slifer realized. *If she doesn't stop, that tribulation will strike her down. Maybe not kill her, but definitely ruin her day enough to make her leave.*

"Is that all?" he called out, spreading his arms wide. "Please, continue powering up. I'll wait right here until you're ready to actually try hurting me."

More cracks spread through space as her power continued to rise. The golden tribulation clouds grew thicker as divine lightning flickered within.

"I'll kill you!" she screamed. "I'll tear your soul apart!"

The corrupted plants formed a writhing wall around her, thorny vines weaving together into horrific patterns. Black roses bloomed and immediately withered, only to bloom again in endless cycles of death and twisted rebirth.

Come on, just a little more, Slifer thought. *Push yourself past that realm boundary. Let the heavens do my work for me.*

"Your beloved Darius couldn't kill me," he taunted. "What makes you think you'll do any better? I suppose failing to measure up was a common theme in your relationship."

The golden tribulation clouds began spinning, forming a massive vortex directly above them. Divine pressure pressed down as heaven itself prepared to strike.

"You want to know how Darius died?" Slifer called out. "He died pathetically, whimpering about his precious 'flower.' Though, given your gardening skills, I can see why he was disappointed."

"*Silence!*" Space shattered completely around her as her power erupted. The corrupted plants merged together to create a massive creature of thorns and twisted vegetation. Its form kept shifting—one moment a dragon, the next a phoenix, then something altogether alien.

The golden tribulation responded instantly. Divine light pierced through the clouds as massive bolts of heaven-blessed lightning prepared to strike.

Finally, Slifer thought. *Now she just needs to—*

The woman's eyes suddenly widened. In a flash, her power pulled back, drawing just beneath the realm boundary. The golden tribulation clouds dispersed and the divine lightning faded away.

Oh, come on! Slifer wanted to scream in frustration. *She has to be smart* now?

"Clever," she said, her voice unnaturally calm. "Trying to bait me into drawing heaven's wrath. But I've lived too long to fall for such obvious tricks."

The corrupted plant creature dissolved, and its components spread out in a wide circle around them. Every piece of vegetation within sight had been transformed into her weapons.

"You want to play games?" A cruel smile spread across her face. "Let's play."

The entire field of corrupted plants attacked at once, approaching from every angle. Slifer's Critical Block Card flared, but the assault didn't stop. Wave after wave of twisted vegetation struck his defenses.

She's trying to wear down my defenses, he realized. *And it's working.*

Another Critical Block shattered under the relentless assault. Then another. The woman's smile grew wider as she watched his protections fall one by one.

"What's wrong?" she asked sweetly. "No more clever taunts? No more brave words?"

Slifer remained silent, conserving his remaining cards. He still had a few Reflection Barriers, but timing would be crucial. If he wasted them on weak attacks, he'd have nothing left when she used her real techniques.

The corrupted plants formed into various weapons—spears of thorns, swords of twisted wood, axes of hardened vine. They struck his barriers in coordinated patterns, testing for weaknesses.

She's not just powerful, Slifer noted, *she's experienced. She's fought other cultivators who use defensive treasures.*

"Your barrier treasures are impressive," she said, confirming his thoughts. "But they'll break eventually. And then . . ." The plant weapons pulled back and reformed into a giant hand of corrupted vegetation. It reached for him almost gently. "I'll peel away your defenses layer by layer," she continued. "Then I'll do the same to your body. Maybe I'll keep you alive long enough to watch as I corrupt every disciple in your sect and turn them into my garden decorations."

Lady, your evil monologue needs work, Slifer thought. *Though, I guess after centuries of practice, they all start sounding the same.*

The hand of plants struck. Another Critical Block shattered. Slifer had less than half his defensive cards left now.

"Still nothing to say?" She pouted mockingly. "How disappointing. I thought we were having such a nice chat."

The corrupted vegetation rippled and formed into a crude replica of Darius's face. "Would you prefer to talk to him instead? I can make it very realistic. Give you a chance to apologize before you die."

Okay, that's actually kind of creepy, Slifer admitted to himself. *Points for creativity in the psychological warfare department.*

The plant-Darius lunged forward, its mouth opening to reveal rows of thorny teeth. Another Critical Block Card was sacrificed.

"Or perhaps . . ." The plants shifted again and formed into smaller figures. Slifer recognized the shapes of his disciples. "Would you rather watch as I practice on them first?"

The corrupted plant copies of his disciples began moving in disturbing ways, their forms twisting and breaking as the woman demonstrated exactly what she planned to do.

That's new, Slifer thought. *Most cultivators just threaten to kill disciples. She's going full horror movie with it.*

But he kept his expression neutral, refusing to give her the satisfaction of a response. His remaining cards were precious—he needed to make them count.

The woman's eye twitched at his continued silence. The plant constructs collapsed, then reformed into a sea of writhing thorns that surrounded them completely.

"Fine," she snarled. "No more games."

The entire mass of corrupted vegetation rushed in at once. Slifer's remaining Critical Block Cards flared desperately, but the assault was too massive. The last of his defensive cards shattered under the onslaught.

Here it comes, he thought as he readied a Reflection Barrier. *Her real attack.*

Dark energy began to flow towards the woman's mouth, where it condensed into a sphere of destructive qi. Slifer watched with mild interest as the orb grew larger, reminding him distinctly of certain animated shows he'd seen in his previous life.

Just like those tailed beasts, he thought. *Though, I doubt she's going for the same aesthetic. Still . . . the similarity is uncanny.*

"Is that all?" he called out. "I've seen bigger light shows at cultivation tournaments. Perhaps you need more practice?"

The woman's eyes blazed with fury as she poured more power into the technique. The sphere of energy expanded rapidly, its dark surface shot through with crimson lightning. The corrupted plants around her withered further as their essence was drawn into the growing attack.

Perfect. The more power she puts into it, the harder it'll hit when I send it back.

"You know," Slifer continued, "Darius could probably have managed something more impressive. Then again, he always was overcompensating."

The woman screeched, her voice distorted by the energy gathering in her mouth. The sound sent ripples through reality itself, creating visible distortions in the air. Several nearby mountains developed cracks from the sonic pressure alone.

The sphere, now large enough to dwarf most buildings, had reached its critical point. Its surface roiled with barely contained power, promising absolute destruction to anything in its path. Slifer could feel the weight of the gathered energy pressing against his skin, trying to crush him through sheer presence alone.

"*Die!*" The woman's voice emerged garbled but comprehensible as she unleashed her attack.

The beam of condensed qi erupted from her mouth, carving a path through reality itself. Everything it touched simply ceased to exist—not destroyed, not disintegrated, but erased from existence entirely. The ground beneath the beam vanished, leaving a perfectly smooth trench that stretched beyond sight. The air itself seemed to scream as it was torn apart.

Slifer stood perfectly still and watched the apocalyptic attack approach with the calm of someone checking the weather. At the last possible moment, he activated a Reflection Barrier Card.

The barrier shimmered into visibility for a brief instant as it caught the devastating beam. There was a moment of absolute stillness as the attack hung suspended, its power straining against the barrier's reflection properties.

Then, like a mirror showing its subject, the beam reversed course.

The woman's eyes widened as her own technique rushed back towards her. Her mouth opened in what might have been another screech, but the sound was lost as the reflected beam struck her squarely in the chest.

The impact created a shockwave that flattened everything within several miles. Trees uprooted, buildings collapsed, and clouds were blown away, leaving a perfect circle of devastation. The woman's body disappeared into the explosion of power as it was launched backwards like a meteor.

Slifer watched her trajectory until she vanished into a pile of rubble in the distance. He shook his head, genuinely confused by her surprise.

"Seriously?" he muttered. "I've been blocking attacks this whole time. I literally reflected one of her techniques earlier. How is this shocking?"

He began casually dusting off his robes, satisfied that the fight was over. A few gentle pats removed the worst of the debris, but he suspected his laundry bill this month would be astronomical.

I should probably invest in self-cleaning robes. There has to be a formation for that. The ground trembled.

Slifer looked up slowly, already dreading what he'd find. His expectations were somehow simultaneously met and exceeded.

Rising from the rubble was a massive figure that defied easy description. It appeared to be a fusion of woman and tree, though calling it either would be like calling a hurricane a light breeze. The figure towered over the landscape, its body a twisted amalgamation of corrupted plant matter and divine flesh. Its right arm had transformed into a colossal swordlike appendage composed of hardened wood and thorns.

"You've got to be kidding me." Slifer sighed. "The giant monster transformation? Really? Are we checking off every villain cliché today?"

The hybrid creature roared, its voice shaking the heavens. The sword-arm swung down with devastating force, aiming to cleave Slifer in half.

"And now the obvious attack," he commented dryly as he activated another Reflection Barrier Card.

The barrier caught the massive blade, and for a brief moment, reality seemed to fold in on itself. Space twisted as the reflected attack sought its new target and finally emerged behind the transformed woman.

The sword-arm, now turned against its owner, plunged directly into the creature's head.

A scream of agony and rage echoed across the battlefield as the transformation began to unravel. The massive form started breaking apart, corrupted plant matter falling away in massive chunks. The divine power holding the fusion together destabilized, creating a cascade of failures throughout the hybrid form.

As the transformation collapsed, a naked woman emerged from the dissolving mass. Her face contorted with fury and disbelief as she fell to the ground.

"Impossible!" she shrieked. "Your control over space . . . How? *How?*"

"Trade secret," Slifer replied blandly, though internally he was counting his remaining cards. Three Reflection Barriers left. If she had a few more power-ups up her sleeve, things could get awkward.

The woman's eyes blazed with hatred as she struggled to her feet. "This isn't over," she snarled. "I'll return stronger than ever. I'll find a way to counter your spatial abilities. And when I do—"

"Let me guess," Slifer interrupted. "Revenge, destruction, eternal suffering, etcetera, etcetera. Could you be more specific about the timeline? I need to know whether to keep my schedule clear."

"Mock me all you want," she spat. "But remember this day. Remember the name Lady Chi. Because next time . . ." She began sinking into the ground, her body merging with the corrupted earth beneath her feet. "Next time, I won't underestimate your spatial abilities. Next time, I'll tear apart the very foundations of your power. Next time—"

"Next time, bring better threats," Slifer suggested helpfully. "These are getting repetitive."

With a final snarl of rage, Lady Chi vanished completely into the earth, leaving only withered vegetation and destruction as evidence of her presence.

Slifer waited several minutes to make sure she was truly gone before allowing his shoulders to slump slightly.

"Well," he muttered, "that could have gone better."

He noticed the devastation around him. The landscape was completely destroyed. What was once a lush forest was now reduced to a barren wasteland. Massive trenches carved by the qi beam stretched to the horizon, and the ground was littered with withered, corrupted plant matter.

The entire area looked like the aftermath of a natural disaster.

At least I managed to draw her far enough from the sect, he thought, glancing back at the distant Black Rose Sect's walls barely visible on the horizon. *Though, the cleanup is still going to be a nightmare.*

"Morvran!" he called out.

His right-hand man appeared instantly, looking somewhat singed but otherwise intact. Behind him, a group of braver disciples had gathered at a safe distance, whispering among themselves as they surveyed the battlefield.

"Did you see that beam?" one young disciple whispered excitedly. "It erased everything it touched!"

"Forget the beam," another replied. "Did you see how the sect master just stood there? Not even moving! Like it was nothing!"

"And when that giant tree woman appeared—"

"Quiet!" an elder disciple hissed. "Show some respect!"

"Yes, Master?" Morvran asked, ignoring the chattering disciples.

"Add 'homicidal ex-girlfriend of former elder' to our threat assessment lists. And see about getting some anti-plant formations installed."

"Right away, Master." Morvran paused, then added with a slight smile, "Though, I must say, the way you handled her attacks was most impressive. The younger disciples are already composing songs about 'The Immovable Master Slifer.'"

"Please tell me you're joking."

"I believe the current version mentions something about 'standing firm as mountains crumble.'"

Slifer pinched the bridge of his nose as he heard excited whispers about "space-controlling powers" and "divine reflection techniques" from the gathering crowd of disciples.

As more cultivators emerged from the sect to assess the damage, Slifer's mind wandered back to the System message he had gotten before needing to take care of this mess.

Amelia is still in danger, and now we have an Immortal with a grudge. Perfect. Because my life wasn't complicated enough already.

"Master," a young female disciple called out hesitantly, "some of us recorded the battle with recording talismans. Would you like us to share the footage with other sects? It would surely increase our reputation . . ."

"Absolutely not," Slifer replied firmly.

The last thing I need is more attention from powerful cultivators. Especially when half my tricks rely on them not knowing what to expect.

CHAPTER FORTY-SIX

Deep beneath the earth, back in the secret chamber, the Moon God King stood before a twisted monstrosity of nature. The demonic tree loomed behind him, its branches reaching towards the ceiling like grasping hands eager for their next victims.

Four Origin Realm elders knelt before him. Their faces remained impassive as their king spoke, though their eyes betrayed a hint of anticipation.

"My faithful servants," the Moon God King said, his voice carrying through the chamber. "The moment we've waited for has arrived." His lip curled in disgust. "The *Sealed* Realm has contained us long enough."

Contained us like animals, he thought, remembering the tales passed down through generations. *Trapped here by those who deemed themselves our betters.*

Aloud, he continued, "For eons, our ancestors endured this prison." He gestured at the dark stone walls around them. "While those in the Main Realm prospered, we scraped by on the scraps of spiritual energy they left us. But today"—a cold smile spread across his face—"we prove what makes us stronger."

Behind him, the demonic tree released a low growl that echoed through the chamber. The Moon God King turned and placed his hand against its twisted bark. The faces beneath his palm screamed silently.

"Soon," he whispered to the tree. "Soon you'll have what you need."

He motioned to his elders, who rose and moved towards the far wall. Four cages materialized from the shadows, each containing a figure from the Main Realm.

In the first cage, Celestia sat cross-legged, her golden hair catching what little light reached the chamber. Her expression remained serene despite her circumstances, as if she'd accepted whatever fate awaited her.

Beside her, Larissa threw herself against her cage's bars. The muscular woman's snow-white hair whipped around as she struggled, but the formations carved into the metal held firm. Each impact echoed through the chamber accompanied by curses in the Ice Phoenix Sect's ancient tongue.

The third cage held Amelia. Her silver hair was matted with blood, and she lay unconscious, her chest rising and falling with shallow breaths.

In the final cage, Raphael knelt despite his injuries. Blood stained his silver hair and once pristine robes, but his eyes burned with defiance.

"You primitive savages," he spat, his voice dripping with contempt. "You'll regret laying hands on a disciple of the Heavenly Light Sect. When I escape— and I will escape—I'll show you the difference between our realms. Your pathetic cultivation methods can't compare to—"

Celestia watched Raphael's tirade with growing unease apparent on her face. His usual mask of careful control had shattered, revealing a hidden ugliness.

The Moon God King's fingers twitched. Raphael's eyes widened as invisible threads pierced his lips, then sewed them shut with spiritual energy. His muffled screams filled the chamber as blood trickled down his chin.

"Much better." The Moon God King smiled. "Now we can begin."

The four Origin Realm elders moved in perfect synchronization to position the cages before the demonic tree. Its branches swayed despite the still air, reaching towards the prisoners with anticipation.

Roots burst from the ground and wrapped around each captive. Another root, thicker than the others, emerged behind the Moon God King and plunged into his back. He didn't flinch as it connected, linking him to the tree's power.

The process began slowly. The roots pulsed with sickly light as they drew out the prisoners' souls. Each extraction strengthened the aura surrounding the Moon God King and pushed him closer to the Ascendant Realm breakthrough he craved.

On the tree's trunk, a massive closed eye began to stir.

Raphael's soul proved the weakest. His countless battles had left scars not just on his body, but on his spirit. The tree drank deeply of his essence, causing the eye to crack open slightly.

Celestia and Amelia fought back. Their souls burned bright against the tree's hunger, slowing the extraction. Even unconscious, Amelia's spirit resisted, her innate stubbornness evident in death as in life.

The eye opened wider with each passing moment. Raphael's struggles grew weaker as his soul began to separate from his body. The Moon God King's power swelled, cracking the stone beneath his feet.

BOOM!

An explosion rocked the chamber.

Debris rained from the ceiling as a massive hole appeared above them. Through the dust and chaos, four figures descended. They landed in formation, their robes billowing dramatically despite the lack of wind.

The four leaders of the local sects stood ready for battle.

Sect Master Wu of the White Moon Sect took point. To his right, Sect Master Bu of the Black Moon Sect adjusted his dark robes. On the left, the younger Sect Masters Fu and Lu of the Red and Blue Moon Sects moved in perfect synchronization.

The demonic tree's roots retracted from its victims, drawing back to protect its core. Only the root connecting it to the Moon God King remained, pumping power into his body.

"This ends now," Sect Master Wu declared. "The heavens themselves reject this abomination. The Sealed Realm may seem like a prison, but what you're attempting goes against the natural order."

"The Moon God Sect has gone too far," Sect Master Fu added. "We won't stand idle while you corrupt our realm's future."

Sect Master Lu nodded. "Your ambition will destroy us all. The barrier between realms exists for a reason."

"Your hatred has blinded you." Sect Master Bu's deep voice resonated through the chamber. "We may resent our circumstances, but this path leads only to destruction."

The Moon God King stepped forward, and his aura exploded outwards. It pulverized nearby stones and sent cracks spiderwebbing across the walls. The root in his back pulsed faster as it fed him more power.

"Traitors," he snarled. "You've grown comfortable in your chains, too afraid to reach for true power." His white robes began to stain black as corruption spread from where the root connected to his spine. "I'll remind you why the Moon God Sect rules these lands."

Spiritual pressure filled the chamber as nine Origin Realm cultivators prepared for battle. The demonic tree's eye twitched as though it was eager to witness the carnage that was about to unfold.

High above the underground chamber, three figures watched the battle unfold. Zack, Caelum, and Hughie, his broken ribs now healed, crouched at the edge of the massive hole, their eyes tracking the chaos below.

The four sect masters moved in perfect harmony against the Moon God King. Their coordinated attacks forced the white-robed figure back step by step, though his smile never wavered.

"They're actually pushing him back," Hughie whispered.

More cultivators poured into the chamber from hidden passages. Origin Realm elders from the four sects engaged the Moon God Sect's own elders in fierce combat. Light and shadow danced across the walls as techniques clashed.

These Early Origin Realm fights won't matter, Zack thought. *The only battle worth watching is between the sect masters and the king. The others are a sideshow.*

A flicker of movement caught Zack's attention. The demonic tree's roots had snaked back towards the prisoners and wrapped around them once more.

"We need to help them!" Hughie shouted as he pushed himself up, but Zack's hand shot out and grabbed his arm.

"Don't," Zack said. "Going down there is suicide."

"But—"

"Zack's right," Caelum cut in. "The power they're throwing around would tear us apart."

Hughie slumped back with a sigh. "So we watch them die?"

Zack stared at the twisted tree, frustration building. *If I had access to the System like the Main Body, I could analyze that monstrosity. But no, my only cheat is getting overpowered treasures from him.*

A scream pierced the air. Raphael thrashed in his bonds as silvery strands of light poured from his body into the tree. His soul, torn from its mortal shell, vanished into the writhing trunk.

Power exploded from the Moon God King. The sect masters' attacks bounced off his barrier as dark energy pulsed through the root connecting him to the tree.

"We could have saved him," Hughie muttered.

Zack shook his head. "The remnants of their battle would kill you in an instant."

"We need a way past the battlefield," Caelum said. "If we can reach the tree—"

"No," Zack cut him off. "You two stay here. I'll go."

Hughie frowned. "But you said the remnants would kill us."

"Would kill *you*." Zack smiled. "Not me."

Caelum's eyes narrowed. "The phasing ability."

Zack nodded. "Ten seconds of intangibility. Long enough to cross the field, but"—he glanced at the tree—"surviving on the other side will be interesting."

"Good luck," Caelum said.

Smoky gray armor materialized around Zack's form. The aura of a Nascent

Soul cultivator radiated from him as his body turned translucent. He took a deep breath and jumped.

Energy blasts and stray techniques passed through his ghostly form as he sprinted across the battlefield. Origin Realm cultivators clashed around him—their attacks were harmless while his ability held.

He materialized on the far side, directly before the demonic tree. Its eye focused on him as it tossed aside Larissa's empty shell, her soul consumed.

The Moon God King's power surged. Space itself trembled as he drew closer to the Ascendant Realm breakthrough. The very fabric of the Sealed Realm groaned under the pressure of power it was never meant to contain.

Zack's body solidified—the Nascent Soul armor was still protecting him.

Stellar Nova Strike!

Golden light blazed as he attacked the root holding Amelia. The technique carved deep into the twisted wood, but the root maintained its grip. An inhuman scream filled his mind.

Paralysis locked Zack's muscles as the mental assault crashed over him. The tree's wordless cry resonated through his consciousness, trying to shatter his will.

"Die!" The Moon God King's roar shook the chamber as he turned to face Zack. But before he could strike, Sect Master Wu's palm strike caught him in the chest and sent him flying back into a stone pillar.

Wisps of dark energy pulsed from Zack as his Void Being Aura dispelled the paralysis. Roots burst from the ground, trying to ensnare him. He danced between them, each dodge bringing him closer to disaster.

The tree's only at the Origin Realm. Strong, but not the transcendent being it appears to be.

Amelia remained limp in the root's grasp. "Sorry about this," Zack muttered. Then he took a deep breath and flames erupted from his mouth, washing over the trunk in waves of supernatural heat.

The demonic tree screamed, its bark blackening under the assault. But instead of releasing Amelia, the root constricted tighter, threatening to crush her.

No choice, then. Void Piercer Strike!

Space itself split as his attack connected. The root holding Amelia separated cleanly, dark sap spraying from the wound. He spun towards Celestia, but the tree had learned: its remaining roots retracted with supernatural speed, pulling back to the safety of the trunk.

Amelia's body hung suspended in the air, caught in that moment between falling and flight. Her eyes snapped open, blazing purple. Her right hand shot out, impossibly fast, and caught one of the retreating roots. Dark energy exploded from her grip as she began to drain the tree's power.

The demonic tree thrashed, trying to break free, but Amelia held firm. Her aura began to change, growing denser, darker. Waves of pressure rolled off her form as spiritual energy flooded her meridians.

Mid-Nascent Soul breakthrough, Zack realized. *She's a soul cultivator, so she's using the tree's own soul force to power up.*

The root in her grip withered and blackened as she drained every drop of power it contained. Veins of purple light spread across her skin like lightning, marking the paths where demonic energy flowed through her body.

She landed in a crouch, the stone cratering beneath her feet. The aura of Mid-Nascent Soul exploded outwards and shattered nearby formations, sending debris flying in all directions. But something else happened: her body began to change.

Purple veins spread across her skin like a spider web as demonic energy reshaped her form. Her fingers lengthened into razor-sharp claws, black as night. Each strand of her silver hair swirled around as though it had a life of its own. Her teeth sharpened into fangs, gleaming in the little light that was able to enter the chamber. Bone spurs erupted from her shoulders and spine, piercing through her torn robes. Her ears elongated to points while her skin turned ash-gray. Most striking were her eyes: they blazed with purple fire, twin infernos of raw power that promised violence.

The transformation was complete in seconds, leaving her looking more demon than human. Spiritual pressure continued to pour from her altered form, each pulse maybe not as impressive as the Moon God King but still strong enough to crack the chamber's stone walls.

Lesser cultivators would have fled at the sight, but Zack stood his ground. He'd seen her transformation multiple times, even though this was one was, admittedly, scarier . . .

A grin spread across her face, revealing rows of needle-sharp teeth. "My turn." Her voice carried inhuman harmonics, as if multiple beings spoke through her at once.

"Yo," a familiar voice called from behind them.

Zack spun around to see Hughie strolling towards them looking completely unharmed despite the apocalyptic battle raging overhead. Caelum followed close behind, sporting a few injuries but nothing too serious.

"How did you . . ." Zack stared at them. "How are you not dead?"

Hughie shrugged. "I figured we'd die up there watching anyways, so might as well run through the battlefield and hope for the best."

Of course. Classic Hughie protagonist luck. The guy could probably walk through rain without getting wet.

The demonic tree loomed before them. Somewhere in its twisted trunk, Celestia's soul hung between life and death. The golden-haired cultivator remained suspended in the root's grip, her life force draining away with each passing moment.

"We save her," Amelia's multi-toned voice growled, "or the Moon God King breaks through."

Zack nodded, watching the battle rage above them. The four sect masters still pressed their attack, but the king's power grew with each soul the tree devoured.

"If he reaches Ascendant," Zack said, "this entire realm dies."

Purple flames danced around Amelia's claws as she prepared for battle. "Then we better not mess this up."

The demonic tree's eye focused on them, its pupil dilating. More roots burst from the ground, writhing with hungry purpose. The trunk pulsed as it prepared to defend its final prize.

Four disciples of the Black Rose Sect stood before an ancient evil, while Origin Realm cultivators clashed overhead and reality itself trembled on the edge of collapse. They had one chance to save Celestia. One chance to stop the Moon God King's plans.

If they failed . . .

"Ready?" Zack asked.

Hughie cracked his knuckles. "Born ready."

"This should be interesting," Caelum added as Bloodthorn growled with anticipation.

Amelia's fanged grin widened. "Always."

The final battle for the Sealed Realm was about to begin.

CHAPTER FORTY-SEVEN

I will end this quickly!"

Caelum raised Bloodthorn, its surface already beginning to ripple with dark energy. The twisted veins beneath his skin pulsed as he prepared to plunge the sword into his heart.

A hand landed on his shoulder. He turned to find Zack watching him with an uncharacteristically serious expression.

"Save it," Zack said quietly as his eyes tracked the chaos above them, where the Origin Realm cultivators clashed. "This might seem like the final battle, but we don't know what's coming next."

"If I don't use it now—"

"Then we'll find another way." Zack's grip tightened. "Trust me. You'll need that trump card later."

Caelum hesitated. The demonic sword's bloodthirst pulsed through their connection, urging him to embrace its power. But Zack had a point. Once he used Bloodthorn Ascension, he'd be useless for the rest of the battle.

He lowered the sword with a sharp nod. "We do this the hard way, then."

Hughie cracked his neck. "Hard way's more fun anyways."

A howl split the air as his form blurred and shifted. Black fur erupted from his skin as his body contorted and lengthened into a massive black wolf. His eyes blazed with a red light as he launched himself at the tree.

Razor-sharp fangs tore into the nearest root, shredding through twisted wood. Dark sap sprayed as Hughie's claws ripped deep furrows in the trunk. The tree's eye narrowed, focusing on this new threat.

Roots exploded from the ground and whipped through the air like striking serpents. Hughie dodged the first wave, his wolf form darting between the attacks with supernatural speed. But there were too many. A root caught him mid-leap and slammed him into the chamber wall hard enough to crack stone.

"Hughie!" Amelia snarled, purple flames dancing around her claws.

She thrust out her hand and unleashed a wave of soul force. "Soul Render!"

The purple energy slashed across the tree's trunk. Unlike physical attacks, this one cut deep. An inhuman screech filled their minds as the tree thrashed in genuine pain.

"Of course," Zack muttered. "It's more soul than plant." He raised his voice. "The tree's vulnerable to soul attacks!"

Hughie spat out a mouthful of dark sap. "So, we create openings for Amelia?"

"Keep it distracted. When it's focused on defense, we can get Celestia out."

Caelum vanished in a flash of light, shouting, "Sunrise Slash!" He reappeared behind the tree, and Bloodthorn sang as it severed one of the larger roots. Before the tree could retaliate, he'd already teleported away.

Zack watched the battle unfold, mentally cataloging his remaining treasures. The Main Body had supplied him well: three offensive artifacts and five defensive ones. The question was which ones to use?

The Soul-Shattering Needle could work—it's an Origin Realm attack designed for exactly this kind of target. And the Nine Yin Frost Bomb, though only a Nascent Soul treasure, might slow it down. But the Void Shattering Arrow . . . He touched the space-rending arrow hidden in his storage ring. *Better save that one. If something worse shows up, we'll need the firepower.* The Phoenix Feather of Rebirth pressed against his chest. *Death-activated revival sounds great until you consider all the ways it could go wrong. What if it malfunctions? What if my soul gets eaten before it triggers?*

A bestial roar shook the chamber. Hughie had transformed again, this time into a massive three-eyed toad. His tongue shot out and wrapped around one of the tree's thrashing roots.

"Now!" he shouted, his voice distorted by his transformation.

Amelia didn't hesitate. She threw back her head and *screamed*.

The sound transcended physical noise and became a wave of pure soul force that hammered into the tree. Its eye rolled wildly as the assault battered its consciousness. Roots whipped through the air in a frenzy of pain and rage.

Caelum saw his chance. "Thorned Lash!"

Bloodthorn elongated impossibly as its edge sought the root that held Celestia. But the tree's chaotic movements made targeting nearly impossible. The strike carved a deep groove in the trunk but missed its primary target.

"We need to pin it down!" he shouted. "It's moving too much!"

Red qi erupted from the demonic tree's twisted trunk, pulsing like blood through veins. The dark wood began to shift and crack, and plates of bark peeled back to reveal pulsing flesh beneath. Its branches writhed and split as it sprouted thorny protrusions dripping with crimson sap.

Why do ancient evil things always transform into worse versions of themselves? Zack sighed internally as the tree underwent its metamorphosis. *At least wait until we're done fighting you.*

The massive eye on the trunk snapped open fully, its iris blazing with crimson light. Energy gathered in its pupil, focused directly on Zack.

Oh, come on. I haven't even done anything since the others showed up.

He activated his phasing ability just in time. The energy blast passed harmlessly through his intangible form and obliterated the stone wall behind him.

"Void Piercer!" Zack struck back immediately, his sword trailing distorted space. But before the technique could connect, the tree released another mental scream. The psychic assault hit like a hammer to the skull. Zack stumbled backwards, shaking his head to clear it. "That's getting really annoying."

Roots erupted from the ground without warning. Hughie tried to dodge but wasn't fast enough—the wooden tendrils wrapped around his transformed toad body, pinning his limbs.

"Little help here?" Hughie called out as he struggled against the bonds.

Caelum and Amelia managed to avoid the initial wave of roots, but the tree wasn't done. A blast of corrupted soul energy caught Amelia mid-dodge and sent her flying across the chamber. She crashed through several stone pillars before hitting the far wall with bone-crushing force.

Caelum's eyes narrowed as he watched his junior sister fall. "Formless Sword Art!"

The technique struck true and carved deeply into the tree's enhanced bark. But the attack drew unwanted attention from above.

The Moon God King turned his head, one hand raised. Raw power beyond the Half-Step Ascendant Realm gathered in his palm. Caelum's eyes widened as the attack launched towards him. He had no techniques that could defend against power of that magnitude.

A figure appeared in front of him, and golden light erupted as Zack activated the Golden Body Protection Talisman, the barrier extending to shield them both.

Zack turned his head sideways. "You okay back there?"

"Yes." Caelum nodded. "Thanks."

"Hey!" Zack shouted up at the sect masters still battling the Moon God King. "Maybe try keeping him busy?"

"We're doing our best!" Sect Master Wu called back as he deflected another of the king's attacks. "His power keeps growing!"

From the corner of his eye, Zack spotted Amelia climbing out of the crater her impact had created. Purple flames still danced around her claws as she shook off the effects of the tree's attack.

Perfect timing.

"Caelum! Hit it with Formless Sword Art! I'll create an opening for Amelia!"

Caelum nodded and raised Bloodthorn. The sword's surface rippled as he gathered spiritual energy. "Formless Sword Art!"

The strike manifested as pure sword intent and sliced through the tree's enhanced defenses, carving a deep wound in its twisted flesh. Dark sap sprayed from the gash as the tree released another psychic scream.

Zack's hand closed around the Nine Yin Frost Bomb in his storage ring. *Hope this works as advertised.* He hurled the artifact towards the tree's bleeding trunk.

The bomb detonated in a blast of supernatural cold. Ice crystals spread rapidly across the tree's surface, freezing its movements. Frost crept along its branches and roots and temporarily locked them in place.

"Now!" Zack shouted.

Amelia launched herself forward, claws trailing purple flames. Her demonic features twisted into a snarl of concentration as she gathered soul force for her strongest attack.

"Soul Extinction!"

The wave of purple energy dwarfed her previous techniques. It slammed into the frozen tree with devastating force, tearing through its defenses and striking at its very essence. The tree's eye rolled wildly as the assault battered its consciousness.

Cracks spread through the ice as the tree thrashed in agony. Its psychic screams reached a new pitch of desperation. But the root holding Celestia remained hidden close to its center, protected by layers of twisted flesh.

Not enough. Zack's fingers closed around the Soul-Shattering Needle. *Time to see what an Origin Realm soul attack can really do.* The needle was barely visible, engineered specifically to bypass physical and spiritual defenses. He took careful aim at the tree's massive eye. *This better work.*

He threw. The needle streaked through the air, leaving a trail of distorted space in its wake. It struck the eye dead center and shattered.

The mental scream that followed drove them all to their knees. Blood leaked from their ears as the tree's soul energy went haywire. Roots thrashed wildly, pulverizing stone as the entire chamber shook.

"Incoming!" Hughie shouted.

A wave of corrupted soul energy exploded outwards. Zack's hand flew to the Golden Body Protection Talisman. Golden light surrounded them just as the wave hit.

The barrier held—barely. When it faded, they saw the tree had partially collapsed in on itself. The eye was a ruined mess, and dark sap poured from dozens of wounds.

But it still held Celestia.

"Caelum! Now!"

Caelum didn't hesitate. "Sunrise Slash!"

He vanished in a flash of light and reappeared once more behind the stunned tree. Bloodthorn sang out anew as this time it severed the root holding Celestia. She fell limply, but Caelum caught her before she hit the ground.

"Stay back," he said as her eyes fluttered open. "You're in no condition to fight."

Celestia tried to stand but stumbled. The tree's soul-draining effects had left her severely weakened. "The king . . . he's . . ."

A howl of rage echoed through the chamber. The Moon God King stared down at them, and his face twisted with fury as he realized his plan had failed.

"You insects!" His voice shook the walls. "Do you understand what you've done? What you've prevented?"

The four sect masters pressed their attack, but he barely seemed to notice their techniques anymore. His white robes had turned completely black, and corruption spread across his skin like ink in water.

"For generations we've been trapped in this prison realm!" he ranted. "Sealed away by those who feared our potential! They called us demons, monsters—but we were the ones who dared to seek true power!"

"Here we go," Zack muttered. "The villain monologue."

The Moon God King's eyes blazed with madness. "I found a way! A way to break free! To ascend beyond the barriers they placed on us!" He gestured at the wounded tree. "This divine parasite feeds on outsider souls, growing stronger with each one it devours. And through it, I would have achieved what none have done before!"

"He's lost it," Hughie said quietly.

"The Moon God Sect was meant to rule!" Spittle flew from the king's mouth as he screamed. "We were meant to be gods! And you . . . you *dare* . . ."

Without warning, he shot towards the tree's bleeding trunk. The sect masters' attacks bounced harmlessly off his barrier as dark energy gathered around his form.

"If I can't have the power"—his face split in an insane grin—"then I'll take it by force!"

He plunged into the tree's wounded flesh. The twisted wood seemed to welcome him as it parted to accept his body. Dark energy exploded outwards as he merged with the ancient evil.

The chamber shook as reality itself protested the unnatural fusion. Cracks spread across the walls and ceiling as the very fabric of the Sealed Realm groaned under the pressure.

The tree's flesh writhed and stretched, taking on a vaguely humanoid shape. Branches twisted into arms ending in razor-sharp claws. The trunk split and reformed into legs thick as ancient oaks. Where the massive eye had been, the Moon God King's face emerged from the wood, his features distorted and inhuman.

Power radiated from the hybrid being—power beyond the Half-Step Ascendant Realm. The Moon God King had achieved his breakthrough, but at a terrible cost. His consciousness had merged completely with the tree's hunger, creating something that should never have existed.

The sect masters backed away, their faces pale. Even their combined might wouldn't be enough against an Ascendant Realm monster.

Zack stood with the other disciples, watching the abomination tower over them. The chamber continued to crack and split as reality strained under the pressure of power it could not hope to contain.

Now this is the final battle, he thought. *I hope . . .*

The hybrid monster towered over them, wood and flesh fused in an unholy union. Branch-like limbs creaked as it raised its arms and began gathering power that made the air itself shudder.

Across the chamber, Celestia rested against the eastern wall, away from the main battle.

"Celestia!" Caelum shouted. "You have to move!"

But she couldn't. The tree's soul draining had left her too weak to even stand. She tried pushing herself up, but her arms trembled and gave out.

The final pulse of transformation energy erupted from the hybrid. This wave was different—darker, more violent. A wall of corrupted debris blocked their path to Celestia as the power approached her.

"No!" Hughie tried to climb over, but Zack held him back.

"We'll die too if we try to reach her now!"

Celestia looked across the chamber at them and managed a small smile despite everything. "Thank you for trying," she whispered.

The wave struck. Where normal qi would have simply thrown her back, this corrupted power did something far worse. It broke down the very essence of her being. Her body dissolved into motes of golden light, which scattered and were consumed by the darkness.

They could only watch in helpless horror as their friend vanished, leaving nothing behind but a lingering warmth in the air where she had been.

"BEHOLD!" The hybrid's voice boomed through the chamber. "THIS IS TRUE POWER! THE POWER YOU DENIED US!"

But why do these things always get worse before they get better?

CHAPTER FORTY-EIGHT

Sect Master Wu stepped forward, his white robes billowing. "Everyone, formation! We must contain this abomination!"

The other three sect masters moved into position. Bu took the rear point while Fu and Lu flanked the sides.

"Four Moons Suppression Formation!"

Silvery chains of pure spiritual energy shot from their hands and wrapped around the hybrid's twisted form. The monster's movements slowed as the technique tried to bind its power.

"INSECTS!" the hybrid roared. Its branch-arms flexed and shattered several chains. "YOUR PATHETIC TECHNIQUES CANNOT HOLD ME!"

Dark energy pulsed from its body. The remaining chains strained and snapped as corrupted spiritual pressure filled the chamber. Cracks spread across the ceiling as reality groaned under the weight of its power.

"Watch out!" Sect Master Bu shouted as the hybrid attacked.

A massive branch-arm swept through the air. Fu and Lu barely managed to dodge, but the attack still caught Bu's shoulder. The impact sent him crashing into the far wall.

"Moon Binding Light!" Fu and Lu attacked in perfect sync.

Silver crescents of energy sliced through the air. They struck the hybrid's wooden flesh, carving deep gouges . . . which immediately began to heal.

"USELESS!" The hybrid laughed. Smaller branches erupted from its wounds and whipped through the air like tentacles. "I HAVE TRANSCENDED YOUR LIMITED POWERS!"

The branch-tentacles caught both Fu and Lu, lifting them into the air. Before they could break free, the hybrid slammed them together with bone-crushing force.

"Sister Fu! Brother Lu!" Wu's face twisted with rage. "Heaven's Punishment!"

Golden light filled the chamber as Wu unleashed his strongest attack. The beam struck the hybrid directly in the chest, burning through layers of corrupted wood.

But the monster's laughter only grew louder. "IS THAT ALL? LET ME SHOW YOU REAL POWER!"

Soul qi gathered in the hybrid's mouth. When it spoke again, its voice carried waves of corrupted spiritual force. "SOUL CONSUMING ROAR!"

The sonic attack hit like a physical blow. Wu's defensive barrier shattered as he was thrown backwards. Blood leaked from his ears as the soul-destroying sound battered his spiritual core.

"We have to help!" Hughie said as he started forward, but Zack grabbed his arm.

"You'll die in seconds," Zack said. "That thing's way beyond—"

A branch-tentacle shot towards them without warning. Zack's eyes widened as he realized it was aimed at Amelia. He moved without thinking and appeared in front of her as his hand closed around the Golden Body Protection Talisman.

Golden light surrounded them just as the attack hit. The barrier held—barely—but Zack felt the talisman crack from the strain.

"Thanks," Amelia muttered.

"Don't mention it." Zack watched the hybrid carefully. "But you should get back. This is way beyond our pay grade."

"MORE INSECTS TO CRUSH?" The hybrid turned its twisted face towards them. "GOOD! I SHALL DEVOUR YOUR SOULS AS WELL!"

"Sunrise Slash!"

Caelum appeared behind the monster and sank Bloodthorn into the wooden flesh. But the hybrid barely seemed to notice. A casual swipe of its arm sent Caelum flying.

"Senior Brother!" Hughie shouted.

Caelum landed in a crouch, blood trickling from his mouth. His eyes narrowed as he studied their opponent.

"No choice, then." He raised Bloodthorn, its surface already beginning to ripple with dark energy.

Zack recognized what was coming. "Caelum, wait—"

But it was too late. Caelum plunged the sword directly into his heart. Dark energy erupted from the wound as Bloodthorn's blade began to merge with his flesh.

The transformation happened faster this time. Thorny patterns spread across his skin like twisted veins while his hair turned from black to crimson. Sharp thorns erupted from his face in a crown-like pattern as his eyes blazed blood red.

When the change finished, his voice carried that same inhuman resonance as he said, "Now, then. Shall we begin again?"

The hybrid actually paused, studying this new development. "INTERESTING. YOU WOULD EMBRACE CORRUPTION TO FIGHT ME?" Its twisted face split in a grin. "PERHAPS THERE IS HOPE FOR THIS REALM AFTER ALL!"

"Shut up and fight." Caelum vanished and reappeared above the monster. "Bloodthorn Garden!"

Crimson thorns erupted from thin air and surrounded the hybrid in a sphere of deadly spikes. They struck from all angles, piercing wood and corrupted flesh.

For the first time, the hybrid actually screamed in pain. Dark sap sprayed from dozens of wounds as Caelum's attack found purchase.

"Now!" Wu shouted. "While it's distracted! Heaven's Final Judgment!"

Golden light filled the chamber once more as Wu poured everything he had into the technique. The hybrid's wooden flesh began to crack and splinter under the combined assault.

"ENOUGH!" Dark energy exploded outwards as the monster's power surged. "I WILL NOT BE DENIED!"

Branch-tentacles shot out in every direction. Wu managed to dodge most of them, but one caught his leg. Before he could break free, the hybrid slammed him into the ground with earth-shattering force.

"We can't beat this. We should retreat," Bu shouted as he tried to dodge the branches, but the hybrid's attack caught him mid-leap.

The corrupted branches coiled around his body like serpents. Bu's eyes widened in horror as the branches constricted. There was a sickening crack as Bu's body was crushed, and dark sap and blood mixed as they dripped to the chamber floor.

"Sect Master Bu!" Fu cried. She tried to help, but a massive branch-arm swept through the air and caught her directly in the chest. The impact didn't just throw her back—it punched straight through her torso.

Fu hung there for a moment, impaled on the twisted wood, before the hybrid casually flicked its arm. Fu's broken body flew across the chamber and crashed through a stone pillar before crumpling to the ground.

Lu lasted the longest, his legendary speed letting him dance between the hybrid's attacks. He wove through the storm of branches and got close enough to land several powerful strikes. But even Lu couldn't dodge forever.

As he spun away from one attack, a smaller branch-tentacle erupted from the ground beneath his feet. It pierced straight through his leg and anchored him in place. Before he could break free, dozens more branches burst from the chamber floor. They skewered Lu from every angle and lifted his body into the air. Lu didn't even have time to scream as the corrupted power dissolved his body from the inside out, leaving nothing but empty robes drifting to the ground.

Only Caelum was still fighting; his borrowed Origin Realm power barely let him survive. Thorny blades erupted from his arms as he carved through wooden flesh again and again.

But the monster's regeneration proved relentless. Every wound sealed almost instantly—the corrupted wood grew faster than Caelum could cut it away.

"DIE!" The hybrid's branch-arm caught Caelum in the chest. The impact sent him flying into the ceiling hard enough to crack stone.

"DISAPPOINTED!" The monster laughed. "IS THIS ALL THE VAUNTED SWORD CULTIVATOR FROM THE MAIN REALM CAN DO?"

"Bloodthorn Garden!" Crimson thorns filled the air once more, but the hybrid simply laughed them off.

"TOO WEAK! TOO—"

A blast of purple soul force caught it in the face. Amelia stood with her claws raised as purple flames danced around her transformed body.

"YOU STILL LIVE?" The hybrid turned towards her. "ALLOW ME TO FIX THAT!"

A wave of corrupted energy shot from its mouth. Zack appeared in front of Amelia again and activated another charge of the Golden Body Protection Talisman. The barrier held, but he felt the second charge shatter.

One left, he thought. *Where's Hughie's protagonist luck when we need it?*

He glanced at his friend, wondering why the usual plot armor hadn't kicked in yet. By all rights, Hughie should have found some convenient ancient treasure in the rubble. Or maybe discovered he had some special bloodline that made him immune to the hybrid's attacks. Hell, even having some powerful expert show up to save them would work.

But no. The one time we actually need main character bullshit to save us . . .

Another blast of corrupted energy filled the air. Zack activated his phasing ability and let the attack pass harmlessly through his ghostly form.

But Hughie wasn't so lucky. The wave caught him directly and sent him crashing to the ground. It was clear he wouldn't be getting back up for a while.

"Hughie!" Amelia started towards him but another branch-tentacle forced her back.

Above them, Caelum's transformation reached its time limit. The thorny patterns shattered like glass as his appearance returned to normal. Blood poured from his mouth as he fell from the ceiling, his body racked with agony.

"PATHETIC!" The hybrid's twisted face showed only contempt. "IS THIS ALL THAT STANDS AGAINST ME? CHILDREN PLAYING AT POWER?"

Branch-tentacles filled the air as it prepared to finish them off. Zack's hand closed around his final defense: the last charge of the Golden Body Protection Talisman.

Not good. Really not good at all.

The chamber shook as the hybrid gathered power for its final attack. And this time, there would be no convenient power-ups or last-minute saves to bail them out.

Sometimes the hero's luck just wasn't enough.

The hybrid raised its twisted arms as dark energy crackled between its branch-fingers. "NOW, INSECTS! WITNESS TRUE POWER!"

Wu pushed himself up from the ground, blood streaming from countless wounds. His white robes had turned crimson, and several bones jutted through his skin at odd angles. But his eyes burned with an unyielding will as he watched the hybrid preparing its final attack.

"So, this is how it ends." Wu spat out a mouthful of blood. "Very well. I had hoped to never need to use this technique."

His hands blurred through a complex series of seals. Spiritual energy began to gather around his broken body as he activated a forbidden technique.

"What's he doing?" Amelia whispered.

"Three Moons Sacrifice!" Wu's voice echoed through the chamber as golden light erupted from his body. "With my life as the price, grant me the power of the heavens!"

The hybrid paused its attack, its twisted face showing the first hint of concern. "WHAT IS THIS?"

Wu's spiritual pressure skyrocketed. His aura tripled in strength as golden energy poured from his body. But blood now flowed freely from his eyes and mouth as the technique began consuming his life force.

"Better to die standing than live on my knees!" Wu shot towards the hybrid, moving faster than ever before. "Moon God Binding Chains!"

Golden chains erupted from his hands, but these were different from before. They blazed with power bought with Wu's very life.

The chains wrapped around the hybrid's twisted form before it could dodge. This time when the monster tried to break free, the bindings held firm.

"WHAT IS THIS?" The hybrid thrashed against the chains. "WHAT HAVE YOU DONE?"

"My life"—Wu coughed up more blood—"for your imprisonment. A fair trade, wouldn't you say?"

Dark qi crackled as the hybrid struggled, but Wu's chains grew tighter with each movement. The forbidden technique was literally burning away Wu's life force to fuel its power.

"Now!" Wu screamed at Zack. "While it's bound! End this!"

Zack's hand closed around the Void Shattering Arrow, and he took aim at the hybrid's twisted core.

One shot. Make it count.

The arrow left his hand and trailed distorted space as it streaked towards its target. But the hybrid wasn't finished. Even bound by Wu's chains, it managed to gather power for one final attack.

"DIE WITH ME, THEN!" Dark energy gathered in its mouth. "SOUL EXTINCTION WAVE!"

The corrupted blast shot towards Zack with unstoppable force. His phase ability was still on cooldown from the last dodge, and he'd used the final charge of his protection talisman earlier.

Well . . . shit.

Time seemed to slow as both attacks raced towards their targets. The Soul Extinction Wave roared towards Zack, reality warping around its edges.

For a brief moment, their eyes met across the battlefield. Then both attacks struck home.

The Void Shattering Arrow found its mark first and buried itself deeply into the hybrid's twisted flesh as it headed straight for the hybrid's core. Space itself cracked around the point of impact as the weapon's power was released.

"IMPOSSIBLE!" the hybrid screamed as its body began to break apart. "I AM A GOD! I CANNOT—"

The explosion of spiritual energy that followed defied description. The hybrid's form literally tore itself apart as corrupted power burst from every pore. Wood and flesh separated violently as the unnatural fusion began to collapse.

But Zack didn't see any of it. The Soul Extinction Wave struck him directly in the chest, and his world dissolved into agony. The attack didn't just destroy his body—it erased him from existence itself.

His last thought before oblivion claimed him was oddly mundane.

I really should have saved one of those talismans.

Then he was gone. No body remained, no spiritual remnants lingered. The attack had completely erased him from reality.

Wu's body crumpled to the ground, a peaceful smile on his face as the last spark of life left his eyes.

The golden chains he'd created with his sacrifice continued to bind the hybrid, growing even tighter as its form began to break apart.

The monster's twisted flesh bubbled and warped as conflicting energies tore through its body. Chunks of wood peeled away from corrupted skin while dark sap sprayed from widening cracks. Its branch-arms spasmed wildly, shattering stone pillars with each uncontrolled movement.

"NO . . . NO . . . NOOOOO!" The hybrid's screams grew more distorted as its face began to melt. "THE POWER . . . CAN'T . . . CONTAIN—"

Spiritual pressure exploded outwards in waves. The first pulse shattered every formation array in the chamber. The second crushed the remaining pillars to dust. By the third, reality itself began to crack like glass.

The Moon God King's face emerged briefly from the writhing mass of wood and flesh, his features twisted in agony as his body rejected the unnatural fusion.

A sound like reality being torn in half filled the chamber as the hybrid's spiritual core finally ruptured. Multicolored qi erupted from its body in geysers of raw power. Each blast carried enough force to level a mountain, but Wu's chains kept the destruction contained in a sphere of golden light.

The hybrid's form continued to break down. First its branch-arms dissolved into pure energy. Then its twisted legs collapsed into clouds of spiritual essence. Finally, its torso began to disintegrate as the competing powers within tore it apart atom by atom.

One last pulse of power, greater than all the others combined, lit the chamber brighter than the sun. When it faded, nothing remained of the hybrid except scattered piles of ash and twisted wood.

Wu's chains hung in the air for a moment longer before they, too, dissolved into nothingness.

CHAPTER FORTY-NINE

Through the settling dust, three figures limped towards the spot where Zack had stood. Hughie supported Amelia with one arm while Caelum dragged himself forward using Bloodthorn as a crutch.

"He's gone," Hughie said, voice cracking. "He's really gone."

Caelum stared at the empty space, his grip tightening on Bloodthorn's hilt. "I should have trusted him sooner. All this time, doubting his intentions . . ."

Even Amelia's usual cold demeanor had cracked. Her demonic features had receded, leaving her looking small and lost. "Junior Brother . . ."

"I never got to thank him," Hughie whispered, "for all the times he saved us. For being there when we needed him."

Caelum closed his eyes. "He died protecting us. Like a true brother should."

Suddenly, flames erupted from the ground where Zack had stood. The fire twisted and writhed, taking on a vaguely humanoid shape. As they watched in shock, Zack's body materialized within the flames.

His eyes snapped open as the fire faded. He patted himself down, checking that everything was in place. "Well . . . it worked. Though, I really wish I hadn't needed to find out."

"*Zack?*" Hughie's jaw dropped. "But . . . how?"

"You were erased from existence," Amelia said, her eyes narrowed. "We saw it happen."

Caelum studied him carefully. "Another talisman?"

"Phoenix Feather of Rebirth." Zack pulled out the burned remnants of a red feather. "Activates on death, brings you back once."

"Where do you keep getting these talismans from?" Hughie asked. "You never seem to run out of them."

Zack hesitated for a moment. *Can't tell them that the Main Body supplies them. They'd start wondering about favoritism.* "Remember that inheritance trial in the southern mountains? Found a cache of artifacts there."

"That . . . makes sense, actually." Caelum nodded. Ancient inheritance sites often contained powerful treasures.

Before they could discuss it further, pain shot through their heads. The world around them began to blur and distort.

"What's happening?" Amelia grabbed her temples. "Some kind of technique?"

Zack tried to activate his phase ability, but nothing happened. His spiritual energy refused to respond.

The blurring intensified until everything faded to white. When their vision cleared, they found themselves floating in an endless white void.

"Where are we?" Hughie spun in a circle but saw only emptiness in every direction.

Zack attempted to break whatever technique had trapped them, cycling through every counter he knew. But nothing worked. *This is bad. Really bad.*

A strange sphere of energy materialized before them. It pulsed with colors they'd never seen before as it spoke in broken, distorted words.

"GREETINGS . . . SURVIVORS. I . . . AM . . . WILL OF REALM."

"The Will of the realm?" Caelum's eyes widened. "The Sealed Realm is conscious?"

"NOT . . . CONSCIOUS. AM . . . PROGRAM. CREATED BY . . . THOSE WHO MADE . . . PRISON."

Zack went very still. *A program? Like the System?*

The glowing sphere pulsed gently before them. "THANK . . . YOU . . . FOR SAVING . . . REALM."

"You're welcome!" Hughie grinned despite their strange situation. "Though, about that . . . Any chance of a reward for our hard work?"

"Yeah!" Zack perked up. "We did just save everyone."

Caelum sighed at their behavior but remained silent. After what they'd been through, perhaps they'd earned the right to ask.

The sphere flickered for several moments, as if considering. "WILL . . . GRANT . . . REALM'S BLESSING."

"Just a blessing?" Hughie crossed his arms. "We want something that makes us stronger! We almost died like fifty times today."

"THE BLESSING . . . IS BLOODLINE . . . SUITABLE TO . . . EACH."

Zack's eyes lit up. "Can we pick which one?"

"NO. WILL CHOOSE . . . MOST SUITABLE."

"Better than nothing." Hughie shrugged. "I'll go first!"

Light surrounded Hughie's body as the blessing took effect. Knowledge flooded his mind as the power settled into his spiritual core.

"Heaven-Devouring Serpent Bloodline," Hughie whispered in awe. "This is . . . this is way better than my old transformation technique! Instead of just changing shape, I can actually absorb the powers of things I defeat!"

"That actually sounds useful," Caelum admitted.

The sphere turned towards Caelum. "NEXT?"

As the light enveloped him, something unexpected happened. Bloodthorn began to change in his grip. The demonic sword's dark energy transformed into pure starlight. When the process finished, it gleamed like a blade forged from the heavens themselves.

"Starforged Sword Bloodline," Caelum said softly. "The power to create swords from starlight . . ."

Hughie whistled. "Looks like you won't need those demonic techniques anymore."

"A righteous bloodline for a righteous cultivator." Caelum smiled, feeling the cosmic power flow through his veins.

"My turn!" Amelia practically bounced forward.

The light wrapped around her, and her face went through a series of expressions—excitement, confusion, and finally . . . horror?

"Spectral Lotus Bloodline?" She looked disgusted. "Healing? Purifying? What is this flowery nonsense? I wanted something vicious and dark!"

"BLOODLINE CHOSEN . . . IS MOST SUITABLE."

Makes you wonder, Zack thought. *Is our sadistic sister actually a soft-hearted healer deep down?*

"Hey, maybe you're actually a nice person underneath all that—" Hughie didn't finish the sentence before Amelia's fist sent him flying across the white void.

"Alright, my turn." Zack stepped forward, wondering what the realm had in store for him.

The light felt cold as it entered his body. Dark power settled into his spiritual core as knowledge of his new abilities filled his mind.

"Shadowfiend Bloodline." He frowned.

Why does this feel like I'm being set up as some kind of stealth assassin for the Main Body?

"PORTALS WILL OPEN . . . IN SEVEN DAYS," the sphere announced. "CAN RETURN . . . TO MAIN REALM . . . OR STAY."

"Quick question," Zack said as he raised his hand. "If people can just use portals to leave, why did the Moon God King go through all this trouble?"

"ONLY THOSE FROM . . . MAIN REALM . . . CAN PASS THROUGH."

"Ah. That explains a lot."

"FAREWELL . . . CHOSEN ONES." The sphere began to fade. "USE POWER . . . WISELY."

The white void disappeared. They found themselves back in what remained of the underground base—though, "underground" wasn't quite accurate anymore. The ceiling had completely collapsed, which left them standing in a massive crater under the open sky.

"So . . ." Hughie looked around at the destruction. "What do we do now?"

Zack pulled out his bone mask and put it on with dramatic flair. "Well, since the sect masters have all unfortunately passed away, someone needs to take charge around here." He spread his arms wide. "Might as well be me while I'm still around."

"You're going to run the sects?" Caelum's eyebrows rose.

"Why not? I've got seven days to make some changes." Zack's mask hid his grin. "Let's see how much chaos—I mean, *improvement* we can cause in a week."

Amelia groaned. "This is going to be a disaster."

"That's the spirit!" Zack clapped his hands together. "Now, who wants to help me redecorate the sects? I'm thinking less 'doom and gloom' and more 'party palace.'"

And so began the strangest week in the Sealed Realm's history.

EPILOGUE

7 Days Later . . .

Portals shimmered into existence across the Sealed Realm like tears in reality. The ethereal doorways were the only way to return back to the Main Realm.

In the Northern Region, Zack removed his bone mask as he stood before one such portal. Behind him, Hughie bounced on his toes with barely contained excitement while Amelia examined her nails with feigned disinterest. Caelum stood quietly with his new starlight sword gleaming on his back—he had renamed it Starforge.

"Seven days of running the sects." Hughie grinned. "I still can't believe you made the White Moon Sect's uniform hot pink."

"They needed some color in their lives." Zack shrugged. "Ready to go home?"

"Finally." Amelia stretched her arms. "If I have to attend one more sect meeting about proper cultivation etiquette . . ."

"You did good here," Caelum said quietly. "The changes you implemented might actually help unite the sects."

"We'll see how long that lasts," Zack said, shaking his head.

Without further discussion, they stepped through. The portal's light engulfed them, and for a brief moment they felt reality twist and bend around their bodies.

Miles away in the Central Region, Ziven approached another portal alone. His green eyes narrowed as he studied the doorway.

"I won't let those demonic scum be the winners of the Sealed Realm," he murmured. Then he adjusted his white robes before stepping through.

But it was in the Southern Region where something truly disturbing occurred. A robed figure glided towards the final portal. Where their skin showed beneath the hood, it seemed to shift and ripple as the flesh became bark before returning to skin again.

Their footsteps left small shoots growing from the ground, only for them to wither moments later. When they reached the portal, a twisted smile crossed their face—though, whether it was carved in wood or flesh was impossible to tell.

Back in the Main Realm, three figures sat in the highest chamber of the Heavenly Light Sect's main peak. Through the massive windows, clouds drifted by at eye level, occasionally obscuring the other mountain peaks that housed the sect's vast territory.

Ace, the Sect Master of the Heavenly Light Sect, sat at the head of the table, his white knuckles gripping the armrests. His usually pristine white hair was disheveled, and his golden eyes flickered occasionally with hints of red. Every few moments, his jaw would clench and a tremor would run through his powerful frame.

To his right sat Ming Yue, Sect Master of the Pure Soul Sect. Her pretty features bore the signs of recent worry: dark circles under her eyes and a slight furrow in her brow hadn't been there months ago. She wore simple white robes with silver trim, and her black hair was tied in a practical bun.

Completing the triangle was Feng Lei, the massive Sect Master of the White Tiger Sect. His muscular frame seemed almost too large for the chair, and scars crisscrossed every visible inch of skin. A thick white beard covered his lower face, but his eyes remained sharp as steel.

Ming Yue broke the silence. "Ziven's report is . . . disturbing. A hybrid abomination devouring souls? The death of the Sealed Realm's sect masters?"

"And worse," Feng Lei's deep voice rumbled. "According to the boy, the Black Rose Sect's disciples not only survived but emerged stronger. While our own—"

"Were sacrificed." Ace's fingers drummed a slow rhythm on the table. "Convenient, wouldn't you say?"

Ziven knelt before them, his usual arrogant smirk replaced by carefully crafted concern. "The Black Rose disciples . . . they protected themselves while our people died. One of them even had treasures that could resurrect the dead."

"Legendary Origin Realm artifacts." Feng Lei's massive hands clenched. "Where would a young disciple get such things?"

"Either he found it in an inheritance realm," Ming Yue said, her eyes narrowing, "or he got it from that master of theirs."

"Slifer." Ace stood, walking to the window. "Someone who was of no importance two years ago, yet now controls all three demonic sects."

"Their disciples survive while ours die." Feng Lei pushed himself up, his chair creaking in protest. "Seems very . . . convenient."

"Celestia—" Ming Yue's voice caught. "She was the kindest soul. The most talented healer in a generation. They claim she was killed by the remnants of the battle."

"And Larissa," Feng Lei growled, "my sect's most promising disciple in two hundred years. Her potential guaranteed she would enter the Ascendant Realm."

"Raphael as well." Ace's golden eyes hardened. "All lost while the Black Rose Sect's pawns survived and grew stronger."

Ziven bowed his head, hiding his satisfied smile. "If I may speak boldly, Masters . . . The Black Rose Sect has grown too powerful. Their supreme elder gathers strength through methods that defy natural law. How long before they turn those methods against us?"

"The boy speaks truth." Feng Lei's eyes flashed red. "We can't let this continue!"

"My sect has three Ascendant Realm cultivators," Ace said quietly as he turned rigidly from the window. "The Pure Soul Sect has two and the White Tiger Sect one. Together we command the strongest righteous force in the mortal realm."

"War?" Ming Yue's brow furrowed. "The cost would be catastrophic. Our disciples aren't ready for—" She stopped mid-sentence and her face contorted as if she was fighting an invisible force. Her eyes flashed red for a brief moment before returning to normal. "You're right," she murmured mechanically. "We must strike first."

"No." Feng Lei's eyes returned to their natural green as he slammed his massive fist on the table. "My sect follows the way of the warrior, but even I see that open war could tear the realm apart. We should—" His whole body tensed, muscles straining as he gripped the table's edge. Red light flickered in his eyes before he slumped slightly. "The Black Rose Sect must be destroyed," he said in a flat tone. "There is no other way."

Ace stood by the window, struggling with his own thoughts. "Something isn't right. This bloodlust, this drive for war . . . it feels foreign. Like something is—" His golden eyes flared red as he fought against the compulsion. Sweat beaded on his forehead as he resisted longer than the others. But eventually, his shoulders sagged in defeat. "War it is, then," he whispered.

The chamber doors swung open. Lady Chi glided in, her ethereal form solidifying with each step. Her beauty was terrifying—too perfect, too inhuman. Her black robes seemed to absorb the light around her.

"War is the only path forward," she said softly. "You know this in your hearts."

The three sect masters turned towards her voice. Their eyes flashed red once more as they dropped to their knees.

"Yes, Lady Chi," they said in unison.

"The Black Rose Sect threatens everything we've built." She walked among them, running her fingers through the air above their heads. Red qi flickered between her hand and their bodies. "Slifer's emergence has forced our hand. Wouldn't you agree?"

"We agree," they responded, their voices hollow.

"Then let the Second Great War begin." Lady Chi smiled, and there was nothing human in that expression. "Rise, my puppets. You have preparations to make."

The sect masters stood mechanically. As they left to gather their forces, Lady Chi's form began to fade.

Soon, she thought, *I will bring your killer to justice, my beloved.*

ABOUT THE AUTHOR

Kalzara is the author of the Demonic Sect Elder series, originally released on Royal Road. He is an avid reader of LitRPG and cultivation novels so it was only a matter of time before he decided to write one of his own.